SHADOW LANDS OMEGA

BEASTS OF GATAMORA

ELIZABETH
STEPHENS

Cover Design by Regina Wamba (reginawamba.com)
Cover and Character Illustrations by Lu Tenorio (@lhunatica)
Maps of Gatamora by Lu Tenorio (@lhunatica)
Edited by Happy Ever Author (www.happyeverauthor.com)

THE BEASTS OF GATAMORA
Dark City Omega
Shadowlands Omega
Fallen Omega
Gang Mountain Omega
Glass Flats Omega

www.booksbyelizabeth.com

To Velia…
△
I wish you were here for this.

KIANDAH
ORIAS VILLAGE

"OMEGAS SAY BOOM! HAAAAAA! HA-HA-HA! HA-HA boom!" The words whip through the air, my older sister Zelie and youngest sister Audet leading the chant. It's old school and everybody in the kitchens picks it up by the second line. "Alphas say grrrrr! *Oooooh!* Ah-ah-ah! Ah-ah grrrrr." Half the kitchens erupt in laughter as we do our best to imitate an Alpha growl.

I take the fresh spices Zelie hands me, separate half, and hand her back the rest. There's a reason *I'm* the one who seasons the food. "Betas say blisssssss. So ah-ha. So ah-ha. Blisssss!"

The soup bubbles in front of me and I stir it absently, confident in the consistency and the fact that the okra won't stick to the bottom of the pot. Meanwhile, I concentrate as most folks in the kitchens glance my way, waiting for me to solo this next part. My voice lifts and I grin as the words spill out of me, swirling through the room, adding a certain serenity to the chaos.

"Sing the song of shadows, quick before he comes…" While my voice carries louder than the others, we turn towards one another, setting aside the pots we're drying, the soups we're stirring, the breads we're baking, as we beat a steady tempo against the ground with our heels.

We get lower and lower to the ground and, in the shadow of my words, the others repeat, "Quick before they come…"

"The Beast will steal your heart, taste your fear, lick your bones…"

"The Beast will lick your bones…"

"Beware his battle axe and lay down your swords…"

Mercy, my mama, steps into the open doorway leading out to the herb gardens, Owenna, my oldest sister, behind her. My dad would have definitely rolled his eyes and slapped a palm over his face and said something like, *I don't pay you to sing all day! Get back to work!* even though he doesn't pay us at all and loves our singing, besides. We'd have laughed and he'd have been caught by Mama bobbing his head along to the beat and murmuring the lines under his breath, and when I finished singing solo, he'd be looking at me with pride and love…but he isn't here now. And Mama? She's got the pot in her hand turned upside down and is beating on it like a drum.

"Lay down your swords…"

"Your only chance is to run and sing the shadow song."

"Sing the shadow song…"

Then everyone, in a hushed tone, chants, "Omegas say boom! Alphas say grrr! Betas say bliss! Be lucky if you don't ascend and cheat his deadly kiss. Boom! Grr! Bliss! Boom! Boom! Bliss! Grr! Grr…" And soon the words are overlapping. I'm off of my stool, my hands up like I've got claws as I prowl around and paw at my friends and my family. My brother and I clash and he pretends to chomp at me with his teeth. He lunges fast and I can't help the giggle-scream that I release.

Soon, everyone is laughing, pounding on the floor with their feet, stumbling around. The sounds of our overlapping chants get louder and louder and louder until the tension threatens to devolve completely, and only when it almost does — when the giggles are too violent to contain — does Zelie release us.

She cups her hands around her mouth, her loose and fluffy twists flying around her face as she spins, and shouts, "Betas say what?"

"BLISS!" Everyone screams and, even though we're twins — and grown-ass adults — I lunge to tickle my brother. I'm tall for a woman, but he's taller and has always been muscular where my limbs are more willowy, so it's no surprise when he easily takes me down. His fingers are wiggling under my armpits and I'm screaming with laughter, and grateful when Mama rushes up behind him and tickles him in the sides. He arches back on a howl and I roll to avoid getting trampled by Justine and Farro locked in a tickle frenzy, but accidentally get kicked by Owenna who's not even participating in this.

Owenna rolls her eyes — looking so much like our father in that moment even though she has the same dark brown irises as our mama — reaches down and easily picks me up and sets me on my feet. "Your soup." She points with the jar of vinegar in her hand and I squeal when I see my soup burping angrily at the edges, thick globs of the spicy tan-nam threatening to spill out and over.

I have to push my way through the crowded room, laughing as I do, in order to return to my spot at the stove. From there, I turn down the heat and stir. I'm still chuckling to myself as the room quiets back to its normal level of chaos.

"No matter how many times," Zelie says, stepping up to my side, Audet moving into place beside her. She shakes her head.

I nod, knowing exactly what she means. "She's always going to give us that look — you know how much she hates it here in the kitchens... Can you hand me that bottle of red wine?"

"What's to like?" Audet hisses, staring at her fingernails instead of handing Zelie the bottle in question.

"Are you going to chop that onion?" Zelie says as she reaches for the red wine.

"I did." Audet waves her hand at the massive chunks. I snort, but Zelie says, "Try again."

In retribution, Audet pinches Zelie's side and she slips, letting go of the bottle. I try to catch it, but my sisters move at the same time I do and all three of us end up knocking our heads together. The bottle crashes to the ground, glass pieces spraying across the black tiled floor — and I fall right after it.

I scream as I go down, prepared for the painful sting, but a hand catches the back of my dress — a wrap dress, which means she nearly pulls it off of me — and I squeal as I'm quickly yanked upright. Owenna's glaring at me now. "You three, get it together and clean up this mess before somebody gets hurt." Her skirt swishes as she collects another few items in the woven basket hanging off of her arm and follows Mama out the back door into the garden.

Through the flashes of open door I see in between so many jostling bodies, I spy pink and purple light streaking across the sky. It's a magnificent sunset. Thoughts of it plague me for the next half an hour as I mindlessly stir until my soup simmers a perfect, rich brown and tastes absolutely divine. A slight variation on kandia soup, with some added spices that come all the way from the northernmost cities on the North Island, I set this perfect pot off to the side for our Lord and then move on to make the second. The second one doesn't have to be so perfect since it's just for us staff, so I take Audet's chunks of unevenly chopped onion and okra and toss them in.

Yaron's pot needs to be *just* right.

I fantasize about what it might be like to one day deliver the meal. It's not my duty, but Audet's, though I don't know how she drew that lucky straw. She says it's because she's prettiest and puts on the best face for our Lord, but I don't see what her being the prettiest has to do with food. One day, I'll protest and take her place. One day, when I muster the courage.

I bite my lip and chuckle a little to myself. I don't know when I'll ever have courage enough for that. The ancestors only know how much I'd like to see him up close in person, to feed him, to unfasten his cloak, *to command him to his knees…*

I jerk upright, feeling overly warm all of a sudden, and tell Zelie to keep stirring. Outside, the chaos of the kitchens… continues. I grin at the wild, wide world around me. The castle lies south of here and I can just see the keep's crest over the sprawling village. Short houses made of wood and stone line wide, winding streets, drawn in no particular order I can make sense of. If you walk far enough east, you'll get to Undoline, the next closest village to Orias and where lots of our extended family live. To the north, you'll get to the ports and the Sea of Zaoul — but only after crossing the clashing forests of Paradise Hole and the Heart Forest, first. And, if you've survived the crossing, then and only then will you finally arrive at the southern border of the North Island.

You'd arrive in Mirage City, first.

You'd come to Mirage City, first, and I frown. I've heard the rumors. Rumors of dead Alphas waking and walking, of the powerful Omegas known as the Fates and whispers of an impending war between them and the Berserkers of the existing cities — but then I snort. Omegas? Against Lord Yaron? Preposterous.

Yet…

The rumors suggest that the Fated Omegas and their dead army are strong enough to kill not just Berserkers, but everyone. The only ones strong enough to fight them are the Fallen Omegas, their counterparts, and so far, only one has been discovered. The Fallen Earth Omega who has extraordinary powers over plants and dirt, over water, too if the rumors are to be believed. It is said that her magic is helping restore the diseased and rotting woods of Paradise Hole where only death lives and where nothing new grows. The Fallen Earth Omega called Echo lives in Dark City. I can't imagine I'll ever get a chance to meet her, or even see her in person, but I'd like to. Maybe, if the attacks on the outer villagers — Alpha farmers and other rural-residing

Alpha residents of the Shadowlands — continue, she'll have to come help us.

I shudder. It's an alarming thought, but I suppose not one that concerns me much. I'm a Beta, too old to ascend as anything else — not that I'd want to — poor as the dirt the Fallen Earth Omega has so much dominion over and, as Audet likes to remind me as often as she can, not pretty enough to tempt any Alpha. I smile, not bothered by that in the least. I love my family. I love my friends. I love my station and I love the kitchens. I love my life.

Things are pretty good.

"Kiandah? Kiandah! Kiand — oh, there you are!" Having wandered into the gardens now, I turn to the open back door to see Justine's frazzled expression. Her freckled white skin is drawn in a grimace, lines pronounced around her eyes. "I can't find anybody. Your mama and papa and Owenna and Zelie are all missing and we're ready to take dinner up to the keep. Audet says if no one shows up in the next two minutes, she's going to do it herself."

"Do not let that woman leave alone with Lord Yaron's meal! She will get us all fired if she tries to seduce him!" I'm already running around to the side of the low building as I shout over my shoulder. "Let me check the basement!"

"Hurry!"

I skid to a stop in front of the open cellar door. Sounds echo from below, Mama's voice and Papa's, too. I take the stairs down. They're damp under my heels and I nearly slip as I get to the bottom and come face-to-face with a female I'm sure I've never seen before and who I know for a fact does not belong in this building.

"Who-who are you? You're not from here."

She snorts gruffly and one side of her mouth lifts. She's a white woman with a mop of blonde hair shooting up in all directions. Her cheeks are so wind-chapped they look like they hurt. Instinct has me reaching for aloe to give to her, but the aloe plant is upstairs in the kitchens and none of that matters anyways because slung across the strips of her black patchwork clothing, she carries the biggest — the only — gun I've ever seen in my life.

The length of my whole arm, maybe longer, it's all shiny and chrome. She drums her fingers across it and lifts an eyebrow condescendingly, her smile looking more threatening than it did a moment ago. I reach for the railing to the stairs, but I'm nowhere near it and fall into a stack of pots. They clang, the stack teeters, then it topples. I mentally curse and reach for the pots, but Mama's voice fills my ears.

"Kiandah! What are you doing down here?" My mama's dark brown eyes are filled with panic. She dusts off her apron and comes towards me and I get the sense that she's trying to block the sight of the room behind her.

I gasp, "What…"

"No questions now, little Kandia," she says, using my family's pet name for me. It's the word for *okra* in the language of our ancestors. Her voice is gentle, but her hand is harsh around my upper arm as she drags me away from the pots and away from the blonde woman and back up the stairs.

When I reach the soft soil of the gardens, slipping once more for good measure as I ascend that last stair in my soft leather slippers, my mama calls out to our ancestors in a curse. She never curses. "Who left the cellar door open? It must have been your father…"

"Papa's down there?" I hadn't seen him. I hadn't seen anything past…

…*the bodies.*

White people, a middle-aged man and a young woman, maybe others, because there had been another couple tables shielded by my mother's body. They were still wearing clothes though their faces were sunken in, cheeks hollow, eyes black. The young woman's eyes…they'd been open and grey, clouded and lifeless. I'd stared into them, and lifelessly, they'd stared right back.

"Kandia, you'll forget everything you saw down there, okay? That stuff's just for us grownups, me and your father, Owenna and Zelie."

I frown. "I'm thirty-four years old," I say dumbly. "I'm of age in every possible way. So is Cyprus. Even Audet is twenty-six."

My mother stutters, her mouth opening and closing several times until she finally settles on, "Just…be off with you! We'll be up in a moment." She hesitates, then turns back to me and brushes her hand over the kerchief tying down her wild curls — curls that I share. My Afro is my best feature and I'm proud of it. I get compliments every day I wear it loose, though when I'm in the kitchens, I keep it braided or twisted, which means I keep it back most days. "I love you, Kia."

I smile, but it feels shaky. I glance down at the open cellar door and I don't like the way my mama flinches towards it. "Love you, too, Mama. Whatever you're doing down there… um…be careful."

"Don't you worry about that."

But I do worry. I don't move.

She doesn't either. Her strong brown hands fist her apron. Covered in scars and scrapes from a lifetime of working hard for every penny. I have always admired her hands. Like my father's, they aren't the hands of someone who was given anything for free. As a result, my hands aren't quite so scarred.

"I trust you, Mama," I tell her, looking meaningfully into her eyes.

She lowers her gaze in a way I don't like. I frown. "I…I want more for you than this humble life," she says, and I don't fully understand.

"I like our humble life."

She shakes her head ever so slightly, then offers me a smile I've never seen her wear before. It's a smile that speaks of uncertainty, which is bizarre coming from a strong Orias woman whose belief in the ancestors having her back means she's only ever been sure. "I know you do, Kandia. Now go on, and tell no one of this."

I do as I'm told, moving back to the kitchens as if caught in a dream. I don't notice that I've passed the threshold until Justine's voice snaps me back to the present. "So? Where are they?"

I blink and see Justine standing directly in front of me, the kitchens a strange chaos they normally aren't because only those of us who cook are left while everyone responsible for deliveries is downstairs tending to dead bodies. Farro and Audet flank her, looking stressed.

I glance around and quickly make decisions because I'm the only one left who can. "Audet, you and Cyprus will make the delivery."

"We can't do it alone," Audet squeals, her loose curls springing around her cheeks. She's the pretty sister — whether it's a title she's earned or given herself, I've never been sure and never cared, really. Twelve years younger than I am, she's always been the baby, doted upon and spoiled as rotten as a poor family of mostly girls can spoil one of its own. She believes one day on one of these deliveries Lord Yaron will see her and be so moved, he'll take her for a wife instantly, even though the Shadow Lords wed only their city. They don't take mates, no matter how young or how pretty.

The thought of her hassling Lord Yaron and embarrassing my entire family is the main reason I say what I do next because only my ancestors will truly know how little desire I have to be up close and personal with our Lord. I mean…I do…but I don't…because I don't want him to look at me like I know he will.

Like he doesn't see me at all. A poor, not particularly attractive female Beta cook — how could he do anything but dismiss me? But for my family, I'll have to put my pride aside.

I swallow hard, sweat already beading between my breasts, thoughts of dead bodies in basements already long forgotten. "I'll…I'll make the delivery with you and talk to Radmilla." Hopefully Lord Yaron won't even be present for any part of this exchange. "We'll need Cyprus's help unloading the wagon, though. Where is he? Because if Cyprus is busy, then Farro and Justine, you'll have to come, too."

"Farro is already loading the cart with Tor. But, umm…" Justine nods and looks down at her clothes. We're all covered in dirty smocks and filthy aprons, except for Audet who's wearing a dress without a smudge on it. "Okay?"

I pretend I'm not having the same internal panic at the thought of crossing Lord Yaron and say, "It's fine. We won't see any of the Crimson Riders or Lord Yaron himself. We're just taking trays to Radmilla."

"Out front!" Farro says, appearing around the side of the house. "Come on. The food is loaded! Cyprus is here!"

We follow him around the kitchens en masse to find Cyprus sitting on top of a horse cart laden with way too many things. Our fat horses are going to struggle under this weight. I'll make sure to give them extra carrots and sugar cubes tonight, I think as I scramble up into the back of the wagon, leaving the place next to Cyprus for Audet. Then again, maybe too many sugar cubes is the problem.

The cart starts a slow, staggering climb away from the kitchens out to the road. Justine and Farro wave us off with stressed faces, like we're green soldiers headed off to our first battle. Halfway up the hill, Cyprus says, "What's going on?"

I'm so deep into my own thoughts and fears that I answer absently, "Ask Mama."

"What? What would she know of this?"

"What?"

"Kia, are you even paying attention to me? I'm talking about the village. Orias is dead."

The word makes me shiver as it tumbles from his lips, landing with a splat on the ground before the cart rolls over it. I glance up and down the Orias highway line and see that he's right. People who were milling about only minutes ago are suddenly gone. The doors and windows of all the residences and shops are shut and shuttered. The lights inside are on, but the kerosine lanterns that run up and down the street hang unlit, even though the darkness is encroaching and nearly upon us now.

"We're late," I say.

Cyprus guffaws. "Late? How can you worry about being late at a time like this? Everyone is home, but they're boarded up, like they're expecting an attack." He sits up straight and stares over his shoulder at me, his hazel eyes lancing into mine. I know what he's saying without him having to speak. *The undead.* "Maybe we should return."

"You think the undead would attack here?" I hiss.

"The undead? Don't be daft. We probably just missed a notice. A red moon festival, maybe." Audet makes a gruff, frustrated sound. "Mama and Papa never are in the know. We miss all the fun parties."

"It's not a party, Audie," Cyprus says, sounding annoyed himself. My twin brother is never annoyed.

I point up at the thick clouds veiling the sky and say, "There is no red moon tonight, Audie."

"You two are just trying to scare me…"

"We're not…"

"Stop, both of you," I say loudly. They hush instantly. I never raise my voice, but right now, over the sound of our fat horses breathing, I can just make out a distant rumble. "Do you hear that?"

I look up at Cyprus to see his head cocked at a funny angle. Then all at once, he gasps, "Run… Run!"

He launches himself off of the edge of the cart and Audet is slow to follow. I start, jerk, jump off the end of the wagon…only for my slipper to get tangled in a jagged piece of worn wood. I windmill my arms and flail wildly, but neither action saves me from hitting the packed dirt and cobblestone road. I groan, my chest blazes, I'm out of breath. But I don't have time to categorize my injuries. Cyprus's hand is on my upper arm and he's yanking me onto my feet, and together we run back towards the kitchens.

"Cyprus, what the fuck are you on about?" Audet shouts, panting as she appears at his side. I didn't realize until now that I'm being carried. My own legs are jelly, hardly helping Cyprus at all. "We're going to be late with dinner and now poor Kandia is going to need to go to the doctor!" See? She does love me. I smile. She's rare to show it. "You know she's not a runner and about as elegant as a horse in high heels." Whatever. It's still love. I'm taking it.

"There are horses coming!" Cyprus shouts, sounding out of breath himself and he's always been fit. We reach the kitchens in record time and Cyprus tosses me in the garden bed amid a pile of carrot tops so that he can alert everyone inside the main kitchens. I scrabble up to my feet and run around to the back of the kitchens, our home. I bang on the rough, wooden exteriors of the now locked cellar doors. "Mama! Papa! We've got trouble!"

The doors explode open and I canter back, losing my footing and falling ass first into the squash patch. The blonde woman and a whole host of Betas I don't recognize emerge, all of them wearing the same dreary rags she is. All of them wearing guns. The blonde one who appears to be their leader swivels her weapon around then, and seeing me, drops her goggles from her forehead to cover her eyes.

"Lou," she barks, then quickly rattles off a couple other names. Her eyes settle on mine. "What the fuck did you do?" She turns her gun on me and I raise my hands, voice caught in my throat as I prepare a weak defense. Because I don't know what I did. I don't have a fucking clue what's happening.

My parents emerge from the cellar and my dad, seeing the female with her hand on the trigger, hisses, "Merlin, lower your weapon. She's done nothing. She knows nothing."

"Then why the *fuck* do I hear horses on the wind?" They're louder now. I can hear them too, the clop of many hooves sounding like thunder on the breeze. Against the silence of the village, that sound is deafening.

Threatening.

A beat passes. I can see the female called Merlin debate whether or not to kill me. Several other Betas emerge around her and one of them says something in her ear in tones too low for me to catch. Finally, at his words, she calls out, "Juliette, Oscar, Angel — with me and Lou. Rendezvous point L. The rest of you head to Q with the cargo."

Betas emerge from the cellar carrying dead bodies between them. The older male I saw before, the younger female, another female, two more males. One of the dead is a brown-skinned man that I do recognize from the Undoline markets. He was an Alpha who used to sell precious metals for jewelry smelting. What is he doing here? How did he die? I can't see any indications of what would have killed him. There are bruises around his neck and violent autopsy stitching across his abdomen and chest, which appears in grim clarity every time the rough woven cloth wrapped around him flaps up. He's not well wrapped. Not at all. Nothing about the wound or the bruises or the stitching or the way he's wrapped suggest he's been handled at all with care.

My lower lip trembles. I feel heat prick the backs of my eyes. Who did this to him? Why? And where are they taking him now? The Betas have turned towards the woods and are moving at speed, hauling the bodies between them. My father stands at Merlin's arm. He doesn't touch her, but he stands close. He speaks quietly, words directed to me though he never takes his eyes off of her.

"Come on now, Kandia. Let's get to the church," my father holds out his hand. I slowly, carefully reach for it.

"Merlin!" A voice shouts from the hill. They're headed north, yes, but not towards the highway line. No, these Betas look like they *want* to reach Paradise Hole's creepy, encroaching woods.

The woman in front of me rips her gun up away from me and I feel like a foot's just been lifted from my chest. I gasp in a breath. She winks down at me. "You look familiar," she says. "And I have a feeling we might be seeing each other again." She turns and flees.

My father grabs me by the shoulder of my dress. "Come quickly now, Kia!" He wipes the back of his hand across his forehead, smearing blood there too, and glances around. "Where's Audet?"

I just shake my head.

"Fuck." He curses. I've never heard him curse. And suddenly he's grabbing my arms, hauling me forward and we're hurrying around the kitchens to the road out front.

There are suddenly so many of us running together, at least forty of us, everyone from the kitchens and many who don't work in the kitchens full time or ever. Some are people I saw with my parents in that basement, their clothes dotted in blood and what looks like black ink, all of them Betas. Half of the sprinters are screaming and panicking, the other half of us don't have any idea what's going on. All I know is that if my father's hand hadn't been on my arm, I'd have been trampled. Not just by my own family, either, but by the horses whose hooves are eating up the ground between us. They're gaining on us.

"Everyone, seek sanctuary in the church!" It's my auntie Mae who shouts that. She's up ahead with my mama, who's somehow leading the pack, running despite her heft. She has a thick build that's prized in the Shadowlands, sure, but especially in our village. It's a build I don't share, not that that helps me run any better.

I go flying as soon as we hit the church's short steps, my feet snagging on themselves, maybe on the worn, wooden floorboards. I'm missing a slipper, I realize with dismay and distress. I have the urge to go back for it, but I can't because I'm falling. The force of the fall propels me out of my papa's grip. The legs of a dozen people crowd my vision as they veer around me. Owenna's among the last to make it into the church at my back. She's shouting my name, shouting at me to move, but I can't even begin to obey her. Not when the entirety of my concentration has been subsumed by the vision that exists past her, on the highway line. At that vision, all other sounds become muted, distant thumps like the screams of a prisoner trapped behind thick glass, their fists banging for release.

He's here…

Orias Village sits in the valley of a hill. The kitchens sit at its farthest edge, closest to the crossing of the highway lines and closest to Paradise Hole. But south, on the other side of the hill's next crest is Shadow Keep. That is where Lord Yaron lives and administers justice. That is where he trains his Crimson Riders, the death dealers of the Shadowlands, the feared and the revered. I've seen them in passing many times, their dark, deep crimson cloaks flapping in the wind, and as a child I always held them in awe. But I've never seen them gathered en masse, out for blood and war.

And right now, they're headed straight for us like an arrowhead, and at its tip, Lord Yaron. *The* Lord Yaron. His black cloak sails out from his back, the blade and handle of his axe visible because he grips it, pointing it at us with violence. I've never seen him battle ready before. I'd love to draw it. I will later. Because right now, he's out for blood. Ours.

"He's here," I whisper.

"Kia, get up!" Hands are on me, no longer my father's but my brother's again. He drags me deeper into the church and the scent of rich cherrywood overwhelms me. I've smelled this church a few times before — in my childhood the scent's familiarity always brought comfort but over the years, I started coming to church less and less. I didn't expect my first visit in years to be under these circumstances.

Back at the door, my father and Tor lift the Shadowlands sigil from its flag post near the pulpit and slide it between the door handles. Standing on a raised pulpit in the apse, Owenna shouts orders to secure the windows. I don't move, though. I can't. I'm stuck in between two pews, looking up towards the rafters at the painted faces of the many Orias ancestors that we worship.

And then Justine screams and Farro shouts across the chaos, "They have oil! I can smell it!"

"They mean to burn us inside!" my mama screams. "Everybody out!"

Screams rise up and I look around at all these people, my boisterous and wonderful family, in a daze. Tor and my brother are trying to remove the barricade they just erected and throw the front doors open. An arrow, as thick as I've ever seen, greets them and I blink and have the most horrible thought that's ever come to me. I pray that it hits Tor and not Cyprus. Anybody but my twin.

The arrow, as thick as a thumb, pierces Tor's chest, right in the center. It drives deep, hitting him with force enough to throw him off of his feet. He canters back, the people between us unable to catch him. He stumbles directly into me. I open my arms, but I'm too weak to do anything but collapse uselessly underneath his weight.

Hands drag me out from underneath him. People are racing around, trying the other windows and exits, but for every door opened, another arrow greets the one to make the attempt. I can hear their screams. "Farro!" The shriek wrenches out of Justine. Only a few feet away from me, Zelie is trying to staunch the wound in the center of Tor's chest, but I know already that Tor's not going to make it.

"Kia, help me!" she shouts. Automatically, I roll onto my knees, crawling until I reach his body. I press my palms over Zelie's to increase the pressure around the arrow's thick shaft. We try to hold back the bleeding while Tor sputters up mouthfuls of blood. It slashes across his pale skin and his eyes roll back.

"Should we try to remove it?" someone says.

I shake my head, but it's Zelie who vocalizes it. "No!" she shouts. I'm still shaking my head and staring into Tor's lifeless blue eyes as huge gales of thick grey smoke bleed around the edges of the front door.

Everyone is crying. My heart is a battle axe in my chest, *just like the one that he bore*, cleaving away everything that matters. Everything that counts.

I picture his face, the little I saw of it, as he came up the road. Wreathed in darkness, just as his skin had been cloaked by it. I'd sensed more than seen his justice, his firm hand, his desire for retribution. I know it has something to do with my parents and my sisters and the Betas and the dead bodies in the cellar. I know it does.

I love my family more than life itself, but right now I can't help but wonder why they did what they did? Why did they feel they had to? My mama said she wanted more for us. More. More more more. More will be what kills us. And I find a sentient rage simmering in my chest along with that all too potent grief, too. *I was fine with less.*

A window shatters and I look up in time to see the flash of glass sailing through the air, something alight sticking out of it. "Someone catch it!" a voice says. But no one catches it. It shatters against a row of empty pews near the altar and they blaze instantly.

The church was built to burn, its body nothing but a crucible. *My body was built to burn. I am nothing but a crucible.*

The heat is immediately sweltering. My eyes start to water. Several more of my people try for the broken windows and I see in cold clarity as Justine takes an arrow to the stomach. Justine. She'd been my friend for as long as I can remember. I went to all of her birthday parties. We snuck out once together and took our punishments together, too.

She went with me to the Heart Forest once — that was back before Paradise Hole had grown over that section of it. Just on the southernmost edge healing berries used to grow. We even managed to sell some of them in our village market before Owenna and Justine's older brother, Victor, caught us. They sentenced us to take over the latrine duty in the castle. We'd had to do it for a week and, though they thought it was punishment, it had been one of the most memorable weeks of my life. It'd been my first time inside of the castle and I'd been cleaning a latrine on the first floor when I saw him for the very first time up close.

He'd been talking to one of his Crimson Riders in the long, breezy corridor. He hadn't seen me, of that I'm sure. I'd been twelve. He'd been twenty. The energy cascading up and down the entire hall had shifted with his presence — it was what drew me out there in the first place. It's the same energy I feel in the air now. Subtle vibrations. They're terrifying, unwelcome. *Unwelcome, but still magical.*

Fire licks up the walls. Bodies fall over one another in desperation. Someone is screaming my sister's name and I see that Owenna has thrown herself over my father, who is…he has an arrow sticking out of his back. What… How…

"Cyprus!" Zelie screams. The room fills with smoke. I can't see. Everything stings — my eyelids, my nostrils, my lungs, with every inhale. I glance to my right to see Sandra and Nikolai shrieking as they hide beneath the pews. Engaged, their wedding is set for next month. They asked me to bake the cake. It's not the first time I've baked a wedding cake, but I was honored.

A burning fills my chest. I release Tor and clutch at my apron with bloody hands. *Bloody, like my father and mother's aprons had been in the cellar.* Zelie screams my name next. I try to look up and find her, but I can't see… And then Cyprus's voice chimes, "Move, Kia, *move!*"

But he's too late. A huge weight slams into my back.

The fire. Something's on fire. It's on fire on top of me, pinning me to the ground and I can't move. I open my eyes and see Cyprus crawling towards me on his belly, but I want to tell him to stop, it's no use. I'm dying.

"Kiandah, no!" Cyprus roars and he's suddenly up on his knees, touching at whatever's got me pinned, moving it off of me. Lifting it like it weighs nothing.

"Cyprus," I whisper, amazed. He's almost got the beam completely off of me now, but before he can fully dislodge it, a massive, splintering sound shakes the foundation of the church. Cyprus says my name again and I look up at him over my shoulder as he burns both of his hands, just to help me. Save me. But I notice that his hands aren't the same hands they've always been. They're *bigger*. His chest swells. His eyes flare as they connect with mine. All at once, he emits a powerful scent marker, like he's wearing cologne, and while it doesn't appeal to me — he's my brother — I still gasp as I watch him ascend.

"Cyprus," I say again, shocked. It's...not possible. No one ascends this old. No one in the Shadowlands has *ever* ascended over the age of twenty. Most ascend by the time they're thirteen, if not younger. He shouldn't be ascending. It's a miracle from the ancestors. I want to laugh, because it's terrible that he may be Gatamora's greatest miracle and that he won't survive to prove it, and I won't survive to tell the tale. No one will.

"Cyprus..." I inhale and his eyes widen to orbs.

"Kia..." he starts to say, but his voice is taken over by a massive cracking sound. In the next moment, Cyprus is gone, his lower half fallen beneath flaming floorboards while his torso tries to crawl back over the floorboards that remain to get to me. But the fire is too hot, the flames too high. They burn right against the skin of my arm. They dance over my dress, eat at my hair, my eyelashes...but who gives a shit about any of that because Cyprus... I can feel in my bones that I'm losing him and I have to do something.

I open my mouth. Pain hits me again as the fire climbs inside of my mouth, but as I swallow it whole, it *moves* through me, changing...transforming...becoming something beautiful. My eyes roll back as a horrible, wonderful bliss chars my entire body.

Cyprus is moaning, still alive, but not for long. I exhale and inhale that desire to save, that belief that I can, and then...I feel warm. Fire comes to me, like a distant friend, like a lost lover, like the warm embrace of every charred and fallen ancestor.

Cyprus is pinned underneath a fallen rafter, just like I am, but he's not on fire anymore. The fire seems to have dispersed to smoke around him and he coughs these terrible, hacking coughs as he breathes it in.

Cyprus, you ascended, you can't die now, I would've shouted at him, had I the voice. My left cheek is pressed to the floor. I manage to move my arms, get my palms beneath me. I push, knowing that the beam that has me pinned is too heavy to move, but that's okay, because I'm not trying to move it.

Fire flicks at my vision, brilliant and blue. I look past it, wondering how it's possible that I can see through it. Maybe I'm already dead. But I can't believe it. I don't think death would hurt like this. Pain rattles all over me in too many places to process at once. Sweat slicks my skin and I close my eyes longer than the standard blink, and when I open them, I see everything through a filter of blue and what I see astonishes me.

The bright orange fire? The red flames licking at the walls? They're creeping towards me. The fire is crawling, shimmying, dancing gleefully over the rafters and the thatch roof above it — what's left of it — down the walls, over the pews towards me. The fire leaves black scorch marks everywhere it touches, but it avoids the people. It bypasses them, disappearing when their bodies lie across the journey it wishes to take and resuming right after or simply carving broad paths around their outlines.

It doesn't even touch Tor even though he's right in front of me. It doesn't touch Cyprus even though he's right beside me, but skips across the beam pinning him in the floor. The flames converge against me, becoming me, joining with the blue fire that coats my body like oil until the pews become blackened ash. The windows and walls are pocked with holes that look like mouths with shards of glass for teeth, but they are no longer burning. Now, the only thing burning is me.

I hear people coughing. I hear shrill shrieks. They may be in pain but they're alive. Thank the ancestors. *Thank me.* Tears prick my eyes. I did it. I don't…I don't understand…

"Kiandah," my brother whispers. I jerk and the blue fire recedes from my vision. It sits in my core, in my stomach, which is still pressed to the hard floor beneath me — a floor that didn't disintegrate despite my entire body being engulfed in flame. I don't unders… "You did it," Cyprus says, his torso collapsed on the remaining floor. He meets my gaze with a smile that's entirely inappropriate for the situation we're in. "You ascended, Kia…you're an Omega…"

I open my mouth to reply, but his smile falls abruptly. "Kia!" he roars, fingers scrabbling over floorboards to try to pull himself up and out and to me. He can't. He's pinned. I am, too. "Get away from my sister!" he shouts at something past me — *someone* past me.

The sound of wood planks snapping grips my vision as a sudden wonderful relief grips my chest. The beam at my back releases and I can suddenly take in full breaths. I gulp in air deeply, but most of what I get is smoke. It carries pain, but I'm not scared of pain. No, I'm scared of the fingers on my arm turning me over. They're heavy and thick, even meatier than my newly ascended brother's are. They're also tipped in jagged shards, like claws. *Because they are claws.*

They roll me onto my back where I land heavily. I feel a cough rise up in my lungs that I suppress. It would be rude, after all, to cough in the face of the Shadow Lord, wouldn't it?

"Omega," he sneers and despite his disdain at the sight of me, I don't feel an ounce of equal disdain to see him. Oh no. What I feel instead is far, far worse and hits me in the gut like a fist — *lust.*

"Yaron," I say and abruptly stop. *What have I done? Speaking to our Lord in such a way? With such familiarity?*

His obvious displeasure has no effect on me. My lust only swells like a wave at the sight of his broad shoulders, body heavy with muscle that I should find threatening. His thick, black eyebrows draw down over his sharp nose as he watches my gaze peruse him, like I'm eyeing various spices at the Orias town market — spices imported from far away, that I know I could never afford.

His full, red lips twist bitterly at the corners. His white cheeks, dusted with a faint tan and stubble, hold color. Not like he's embarrassed — though I'd pay good money to see him shy or embarrassed or coy, just once — but like I've done something to royally piss him off. His black hair hangs down towards me, streaked with grey at the temples.

"That is *my Lord* to you, murderer." And then he crouches down on his haunches at my side and leans in very close, so close I can smell his haunting pheromones, so much sharper than that of an Alpha's, than my brother's new scent. It slaps me like I would slap him, if he'd let me. If we were lovers.

But that's a thought for the afterlife. He may be older than me by nearly a decade, but if I am a good girl in this lifetime, then when I join my ancestors on the Shallow Plains, I'll spend the rest of eternity holding his chain in between my fingertips and training him to be my very good boy. The very best boy.

He wraps a massive, furry and clawed hand around my neck. "I should leave you here, Omega," he sneers.

I nod. "Cyprus," I mouth, more than speak. There's something in my mouth that makes talking an impossible feat, but I still try. "Save him... Innocent..." My eyes flick to where he lies pinned but I don't know if Lord Yaron sees it.

His meaty, furry fingers squeeze, crushing my windpipe. I lose the ability to breathe. "You may be an Omega, but that will not spare you or your family's punishment. For your crimes, you are sentenced to life imprisonment and I will take great pleasure in inflicting every torture onto you and your kin that you inflicted onto those Alpha families." His fingers hold me tighter. "You will suffer." My core contracts. My lower lips feel swollen and pulse with maddening pressure like he's spouting beautiful soliloquies, not threats of death. "You will rot."

Pleasure slices through me like itty bitty shards of glass, but when he slides his hand from the front of my neck to my nape and lifts me off of the ground, pain finally manages to club its way through. A terrible pressure claws across my spine, likely from where the beam collapsed on me, but I don't cry out.

Lord Yaron's just confessed his plans to torture me, so I don't suppose my screams will sway him now, and if he gets off on them, I don't want to give him that satisfaction. I stiffen my legs as I try to make sense of the upending and unending sensations of pleasure clashing with the cutting pain in my back, in my arms, in the back of my head, in my left ankle and in my lungs, which still feel charred, like there's a heavy weight sitting on them. I focus on the brutal way his dark grey eyes slice into mine and his expression narrows, becoming increasingly severe.

He hates me. I just met Lord Yaron for the first time, and this is the impression I've given him. Hatred. Disgust. I cough blood all over his chest and clothing as he carries me out of the church and tosses me into a wagon where, despite his words, a Beta male with skin the same dark brown color as mine starts to administer to me with a care that borders on tenderness.

I don't manage to pass out until the concerned doctor shows me a needle and inserts it into my throat. And I know that after the horrors and humiliation of today, the bliss of unconsciousness is likely the last mercy I'll ever receive from the Shadow Lord.

YARON
ORIAS VILLAGE

MARA GIVES ME ONE LAST QUESTIONING LOOK.
"There are no children inside, my Lord?"

"None." If there were, my beast would scent them. Inside are thirty-three Betas. Twenty-two female, eleven male. All mature enough to scent strongly. All destined for a death I am eager to administer for crimes as heinous as these were. "Burn it down."

Mara does not question me again. She tosses the torch and the rest of my Crimson Riders immediately get to work setting the church ablaze. I watch for the minutes it takes for the age-battered wooden structure to disintegrate. It feels therapeutic. It feels like justice. Justice for the fallen family. Justice for all of the Alphas whose lives have been taken by Trash City scum and the Mirage City Fates who employ them and deploy them for nefarious purpose and malignant gain.

The Fates intend to swallow Gatamora whole by ridding it of one Alpha at a time, killing them only to bring them back as mindless venom-soaked pawns in their growing army. I didn't believe it, at first, did not believe the stories of my villagers of strange attacks by even stranger aggressors. But now, after venturing to the darkest corners of the North Island, where once lush and green forests have entirely been overrun by the rot now known as Paradise Hole...I believe.

I have seen the *zombie* army. A perversion of Omega magic. My predecessors should have challenged Mirage City centuries ago — the moment Paradise Hole began to spread up the river. The moment it was carried south by Mirage City ships onto our shores. We cannot prove it was thus that Paradise Hole crept across the South Island. No one can prove definitively the provenance of the infection that has killed so much life across all of Gatamora...but we could *feel* it.

When I met Berserker Maengor — the male I *thought* he was — as a child at my very first Red Moon Festival, I *felt* the disease of his presence. It was also borne by the Fated Omegas who never left his side. I'd felt it then just as loudly as I'd felt it at the Dark City Omega's Ball that took place so recently — the last time I'd met Lord Maengor before I knew who he really was. Shortly thereafter, I allied myself with Dark City to share in the common goal of rooting out the rot borne by Mirage City, its Fates and its imposter Berserker. I intend to raze them all from the shores of Gatamora and inflict brutal punishment on any who ally themselves with the city and its spreading sickness.

Starting with these Betas here. My very own people.

Cooks, they call themselves. Chefs. Their food might please me, but right now, their howling cries please me more. Were they pleased at the cries of the children they murdered?

Young Gwyneth? She was only sixteen when they broke into her home, slit her neck and stole her corpse.

I know Trash City is behind the attacks on my villages. I know it's Merlin who leads them, as well. She was clever coming here, to the home of the one who burned her garbage world to ruin. Too clever. I have never known a Beta to be so clever. Few Alphas and Omegas have been so clever, either. Too few. That she was able to convince these spawn to hunt for her, hurt for her, kill and enslave for her is equally mesmerizing. What promises did she make them? What luxuries did their greedy hearts burn with? What kindling did she set fire to and with what spark?

In what way did I fail them? Have I not given them my life? My vows of protection? I am their servant. Have I not given enough —

The door flies open as two men attempt an escape. My bow hangs off of my saddle. I swing it up, notch an arrow and fire before any of my Alphas can claim the kill for their own. One Beta man sails backwards through the air amidst a chorus of shrieks and screams.

Mara looks to me and I nod once. She issues the order and my Crimson Riders circle the church, notching and loosing arrows, ensuring that no Beta escapes alive. It takes some time for the church to burn, for their screams to tarnish the wind, for the blaze to scar the sky. I wonder if the contingent of Crimson Riders who I sent into Paradise Hole have found any who might have escaped. My hunters deduced that some ran. I do not doubt Merlin would have. She is not one to cower and hide. She was not in Trash City when I burned that to the ground, either.

I growl. And then —

"My Lord," Dorsten says, his horse rearing wildly beneath him. All of the horses are agitated, Brega beneath me included. Brega is rarely ever swayed, but now he neighs and shakes his mane. "Should we…"

"Silence," I hiss as the first punch of energy hits me, followed almost immediately by the second. It feels like a fist to the gut then an uppercut to the chin. My head swivels, my cock swells. "No…"

Rage simmers beneath my skin. Anger. Violence. And worst of all, *desire*. My desire engages in ways that are entirely unwanted and though I attempt to ignore the most potent of my emotions at present, ignoring them doesn't change the fact that I'm so hungry. *So fucking starving.* My beast rears beneath my breast, my Berserker form surging forward and my head changing form for an instant — growing a snout and fangs and thick black and grey fur — before returning to my Alpha state.

The pressure of the first wave of energy has faded, though I recognize the marker as one that's strange. It draws a reaction out of me and incites my beast to *challenge* every other Alpha here. I urge Brega forward, but he stamps his feet in protest, his hesitation reminding me that, no matter the scents I smell or the sensations they stir, a murderer is still just that. It is my duty as Lord here to leave whatever Betas — *or* Alphas *or* Omegas — that are within the church to burn.

"My Lord…"

"Lord Yaron!"

"What in the saints…"

My Crimson Riders' voices reach me from the depths of my strain. Sipho, atop his horse, trots up to my side and points to the thatch roof that had been a great big ball of red-hot fire a moment ago. "The flames are receding. As if drawn into the church by magic."

He's right. The fire seems to be migrating to the lowest point of the roof, where it disappears inside, like a mouse crawling through a small hole. The thatch roof may have all been eaten by the flames, but the bones of the church still remain, blackened and ruined. A tingling in the air seeps into my skin, affecting not just me, this time, but the other Alphas among my guard. One of them, Dorsten, perhaps, says, "Omega magic." The others whisper like schoolchildren.

"Silence," I order, though my erection is straining my trousers and my beast is claiming my hands for his claws. "Brega," I growl, but even Brega is no match for my beast's wants and as he surges, Brega lowers his neck in submission, forcing me to either control my beast or slide off.

My beast is in a feral state as I swing my leg over Brega's mane and kick off of the traitor's back, landing hard on the cobblestones below. I stow my crossbow and drop my axe. Anyone alive inside will be no match for me, but I am not immune to flame. I will fight my way inside of the collapsing structure, retrieve the Omega who, regardless of their sudden ascension, will still die by my hand, and finish razing the traitors from the island.

"My Lord, the foundations are weak," Malik shouts.

I don't care, the suddenness of my desire to be inside and to find the Omega making the rest of me weak. I punch through the flimsy pieces of the door, which flake to my feet in chunks and ash, and make my way across perilously charred floorboards. I don't have to travel far to find the ascended pair.

The newly ascended Alpha is male and shouts up at me, warning me away from the female in a way that makes my beast want to tear his head off until I register his words. *Sister.* Yet I know she must be more than that to him. *Twins.* That is the only thing that would explain twin ascensions.

I dismiss the Alpha male. He's caught beneath a heavy sheet of wood. His hands are burned, but strangely. Almost as if they were burned a long time ago and have already begun to heal over. The female beneath me should be a mess of gooey, molten flesh, but isn't. I lift the piling off of her back and roll her over, wondering how she could possibly be alive. Her dress is all but disintegrated and even her hair has caught fire in most places and is burned all the way down to the follicle. But her skin is unblemished by flame. *Her skin is rich and smooth and dark brown and fucking beautiful.*

My hand on her shoulder becomes beastly when I meet her gaze head on. She's awake and watching me as if she'd been merely lying here among the ruins awaiting my arrival. Her eyes are huge and round. "Omega," I say.

"Yaron," she answers.

Yaron. No one calls me Yaron. My erection presses at my leathers, a tickle forming in my knot, a tickle of *need.* She's staring right at me, meeting my gaze in a way few are apt to, and in a way no villager ever does. The only ones who meet my gaze directly are Radmilla and a select few Crimson Riders, and of course the other Berserkers.

Dragnovic's Omega looked me in the eye, and so did the witch of the woods. Now, this Omega looks at me like they did. Like we're equals.

She speaks to me like we're lovers. Like we've met each other already in every one of our lifetimes that came before.

But then I remember her crimes and know that it is my duty to imprison, torture and kill her.

"That is *my Lord* to you, murderer." I grab her by the neck, fighting the urge to kill her here and now, just end this. *End this.* My beast takes over and stays my hand. *I cannot. Why the fuck can't I kill her?* "I should leave you here, Omega."

She makes no move to defend herself or beg for her life. Instead, her gaze pans to the right. She says, "Cyprus. Save him. Innocent." Four words that seem to take every ounce of strength she has left. Her eyelids flutter. The lashes have burned off. She has ash on her cheek and cuts on her face. I wonder what she looks like, truly. It's difficult to see through the carnage.

It doesn't fucking matter. My beast and I war and rage together in my chest. He is me and I am he — we have been since I was four years old, among the earliest Alphas ever to ascend — and we have never been at odds like this before.

Claws form on my hands. I will them back, but they remain. "You may be an Omega, but that will not spare you or your family's punishment. For your crimes, you are sentenced to life imprisonment and I will take great pleasure in inflicting every torture onto you and your kin that you inflicted onto those Alpha families. You will suffer. You will rot."

She coughs up blood. I pick her up, knowing that the floor won't hold for long and even now strains beneath my weight. Other Beta bodies have already fallen through. I can hear them screaming near the pulpit at the rear of the church. My awareness is tickled by the fact that the fire has dissipated and I can feel the room swollen with Omega magic. *She did this.* She ruined my chances for revenge. She denied the slain Alpha family their due. And now I must kill her myself. But to do that, I must first ensure that she lives.

I am careful where I place my feet as I dance between patches of flooring that are more stable than the rest until I arrive at the exit and move down the steps. I place her on the wagon with Okayo and Horace — the medics responsible for caring for my Crimson Riders, brought along in case the well-armed Trash City had wanted to battle. Now, I use Okayo for this. It feels wrong.

"Care for her," I grunt at him before issuing orders I despise to the rest of my guard to retrieve the Betas from the church and take them to the keep. I want them all tossed into the dungeons and interrogated until we determine exactly which ones of them were responsible for aiding Trash City and killing the Orias Village Alphas.

I turn to Brega, prepared to mount my horse once more… however, her words echo in my skull and I can't shake them. I *hate* them. I hate them more than I've ever hated anything before.

Cyprus…innocent…

Before I return to Shadow Keep, I trudge back into the church and retrieve the brother myself. I carry his inert body out to the medical cart to lay him down beside the sister who fought for him with her fading breaths. Why, here and now and in the face of my wrath, should an Omega appear to torment me like this? I cast my beast's most primal desires aside, return to Brega, and do not look at her again.

KIANDAH
SHADOW KEEP

THIS IS NOT MY MATTRESS. MINE MAY BE LUMPY AND shared with Zelie, but it's mine and it smells like lavender shea butter and old, old cotton and family. My family.

I feel a tugging in my chest, right over my sternum, like a needle pushed through a stiff piece of leather. Every direction I move, it tugs and pulls. "Cy...Cyprus?" I fight against lethargy, against whatever invisible bonds hold me back. I fight into the world of wakefulness and sit up straight.

My head spins. "Mom?" I wince as a dull, throbbing ache picks up in my back. I'm in a fog. My mouth feels like cotton and so does my throat. My head feels like it's been stuffed full of cotton, too. I can't see quite straight, but I still manage to find the edge of the bed and pull myself off of it and onto the floor. By some miracle, my legs hold.

I make it to the door and from the door, out into a hallway where I choose the breezy left corridor on instinct. I'm out of breath. I stumble and crash into stone. It's a wall and cool to the touch. Beneath my feet that same stone feels icy.

The world around me swirls in dark greys. There are no carpets here, no hallway runners, no torchlight. Only windows barely bigger than archers' slits high in the walls. It must be night, though, because there is only the palest grey light shimmering through them. Only enough for me to see my hand in front of me. I keep it outstretched as I stumble along, the tugging in my chest becoming stronger and more insistent.

I feel like I've walked for hours, taking turn after turn, wandering mindlessly. Maybe I'm already dead. Maybe I'm lost in the Shallow Plains, the nowhere land that exists between the mortal plane and those where our ancestors walk for eternity. I should be with them, or I should be with my family. But I shouldn't be alone. I'm never alone and I'm frightened.

I open my mouth to speak my sisters' names, but nothing comes out. My throat feels raw and I'm too scared to talk even if I could've. Because there are sounds coming from up ahead...sounds of pain and terror. I round the next corner and see orange light emanating from an opening in the wall. In front of it, an iron gate hangs open.

Someone screams and I start to shake. I don't like this. The tugging in my chest is telling me to go forward to the one place I never imagined because I refused to imagine it. Because this place...I've heard the stories...and it's not for me.

Yaron may be a good boy, but I'm also a good girl. I've always been a good girl. I cook, I don't take more than my fair share of the meal like Papa does, I don't sneak sweets like Mama and I certainly don't sneak around with boys like

Zelie. I don't spend hours in front of the mirror like Audet and I don't ever ask for the expensive fabrics for my dresses or shoes like she does, either. I don't lie...like Owenna sometimes does. I don't cheat like Cyprus does at cards...or like he did on his ex-girlfriend once. I don't want for more than I get. *I shouldn't be here.*

But even as the thoughts come over me in waves, they don't alter my reality. I am here, standing just a few feet from the dungeons, whose wide-open iron doors seem to be beckoning to me, calling me to them. They don't know that I'm a good girl, or that I don't belong here. Or maybe they don't care because they know as well as I do, it doesn't make any difference. I have to go forward.

Cold cuts through the soles of my feet and wraps its hands around my calves, tugging me back, the force strong but not strong enough to stop me from crouching down and moving to the very edge of the opening. I peek around the stone quickly, but the wide stone hallway ends in an opening that leads off to the left. I can't see around it and the short hallway itself is empty except for a small table covered in blankets, two chairs shoved beneath it. A jug and two cups sit atop it — it must be a guards' station. I wonder...if the guards are gone...maybe I can just sneak in...

I start to crawl down the hall when a sharp scream arrests me instantly. The scream is one I recognize. *Audet.* And then my father's voice, "Hush now, Audie. Stay strong. It's going to be alright."

"It isn't." Yaron. His voice is unmistakable and my brain scatters at the sound, the deep tenor striking at me in ways that are devastating, because he isn't speaking to me at all, but in threatening tones to the people I love most. I cower against the stone ground, but at the sound of my father's voice, I crawl forward towards it.

"They're just girls," my father croaks, sounding like he's in so much pain. My eyes water. "They're innocent, my Lord. Believe me…"

The rattle of chains, the whack of something hard against something softer. A grunt of pain… "Just like the sixteen-year-old Alpha girl you murdered."

Murdered? No. Yaron's wrong. He must be…

But my father says nothing. I can't…understand. Can't… believe…

I keep crawling further down the hallway until I can't go any farther without being seen. I hover at the opening, wondering if I should risk trying to reach the guards' table, then realizing I'll have to. There are footsteps coming from the corridor behind me. I have to move.

I glance around the corner once so rapidly all I see is the black smear of Yaron's cloak and my family gathered around his feet. *He's alone. There aren't any other Crimson Riders present.* Facing away from me as he is, he can't see me. *I can make it.* I see the guards' table and hone every ounce of my adrenaline to keep my shaking limbs moving soundlessly over the floor as I crawl for it.

"My girls had no part in it," Papa says abruptly, loudly. "I swear!" I glance up and though he isn't looking towards me, I see several of my other family members are. He must know I'm here.

"You lie."

My left calf is shaking, the muscle inside jerking with tiny tremors that I don't seem to be able to do anything about. Just as little as I can control the ragged breath tearing in and out of my lungs. It tastes of smoke. *It tastes of shame. Yaron is known to be a good lord. He wouldn't make this up. He must be mistaken. Why doesn't my father say anything?*

"My Lord, you know I do not. I admitted freely to being the sole one responsible…"

"We are still interrogating the other Betas in your community…"

"It was us, no one else."

"And now you say us. A moment ago, you said it wasn't your children…"

My mother, frazzled in ways she never is, screams, "It was me, Reginald and Owenna, but Owenna was acting under our orders, doing what we asked because we asked out of love and she loves us. Don't use our love against us, my Lord, I beg of you!" She sobs and her sobs shake me, but I hold firm as I lift a corner of blanket and slide beneath it under the table.

The darkness surrounds me, stinky but welcoming. I feel the breath shake in and out of my chest. I'm sure I'm making noise and quickly cover my mouth. I press my palm against my lips so tightly I'm going to bruise them, but I don't relent. Instead, I duck my head, crouched on my knees in a ball so small, I hope it makes me invisible, and I peek between the legs of the chair in front of me.

I see Yaron's cloak swish as he turns towards my mother, chained against the wall. My whole family is in chains, their arms splayed out to the sides. My brother is the only one standing, his chest bare. There are bright red abrasions against his brown skin. My father has blood all over his him, whether it's new or from when he was pierced by an arrow, I'm not sure. My mother's scarf is untied around her shoulders and the tips of her short curls are badly singed.

"We cannot beg for forgiveness for ourselves, my Lord. But for our eldest, we must beg. She is innocent…"

"And what of your other offspring? You truly seek to claim their innocence when you were moving bodies beneath their feet for weeks? They may be your children, murderess, but they are not children. They are not blind and deaf and I do not assume them to be so stupid that such an aggression would go unnoticed for as long as it did."

"We were careful," Owenna says, clearing her throat so that she might speak louder on her second try. "My Lord, my sister Kiandah is a loud supporter of yours. She would not have let us continue had she come across our operation. She would have told someone, tried to stop us. She is too honorable…so, we knew that we needed to be discreet…"

"Where is she?" my mother shrieks. "Where is my baby?" She must not have seen me crawl here.

Lord Yaron advances on her and I freeze, fighting every instinct in my body to go to her, throw my arms over her and beg Lord Yaron for her life.

It'll do no good. So I'm going to have to *be* no good, I realize. Lord Yaron won't be reasoned with. I'm going to have to do something more drastic if I want to save any of their lives.

"Do not make the mistake of thinking that because you are fools, I am equally foolish. The girl had her throat slit, the mother had been gutted and the father had been poisoned. Alphas. In their homes. *Neighbors* to you, separated by three streets' distance. They were merchants. You traded with them. You knew them and still, you disgraced and defiled them." Yaron's voice rises to a deadly crescendo, made more terrifying by the fact that he doesn't yell. He *booms*.

"We swear we didn't know," my father says, "The bodies were brought to us already dead. We simply were paid to wrap the bodies and prepare them for transport."

"Prepare how?"

My father speaks after a short silence. "Embalmed. They wanted them preserved so they wouldn't degrade when they were transported."

"Transported to where?"

"We don't know…we weren't told that much. We were told very little…"

"And you did not think to ask more questions." Lord Yaron's voice is filled with disgust. "You simply did what you were told…and for what?"

Another pause, longer this time, until Cyprus interrupts, "Papa, say something!" Cyprus's voice is hoarse. His neck is chained to the wall as well as his hands. "Tell him the truth — that you didn't know…that you're sorry…"

"Go on. Say the words. We both know that they are meaningless."

"You…" My father sucks in a shaky, broken breath. "You're right, my Lord. We…*I*… When the bodies were brought to us, we were told that they died of natural causes, but we…I saw the marks. The girl's throat had been slashed and I…didn't ask any questions. What Trash City offered was too good to refuse. I deserve this. I do. But don't punish my family for my crimes, Lord. I beg of you. I know that the Shadow Lord does not take a mate, does not have offspring… but if you did, if you had…you would know that to have your children take your licks is the ultimate humiliation, the ultimate torture. I beg of you to spare me this, my Lord."

"Daddy…" Zelie whimpers. I can tell she's crying even though she's twisted away from me, facing our parents.

"I really didn't know about any of this," Audet sniffles.

"She's telling the truth. Spare her, my Lord," my father says. "To spare our children is all that my wife and I can ask of you."

There's a hush, disrupted only by my family's loud breathing. I've still got my mouth covered, but I wouldn't be surprised if Lord Yaron could hear my heart, how loud it pounds. The tension in the quiet hall feels stifling, the air cold as a crypt's.

Finally his boots scrape over the floor. He takes a step back, away from them and towards me. "I will check on the interrogations of your other co-conspirators and return with my verdict on your family's guilt in due time. Should days pass and you perish from your injuries in the meantime, so be it. I will hang your bodies from the keep's gates as a warning to any others who dare align themselves with Trash City. That is how killers are treated in the Shadowlands, regardless of whether you are an Alpha, Beta or an Omega. Your daughter lives for now, but if I find out she had any dealings with Trash City or ever so much as touched the mutilated body of a dead Alpha, she will hang just like the rest of you."

His heels slam against stone as he comes to the table and sets something roughly upon it. Panic comes on so strong, I sway. And then *whoosh* goes his cloak as he turns into the next corridor. *Clash* goes the gate as he closes it behind him and *clang* goes the lock in the chamber as he traps us all inside. Then, the lightest flutter as he leaves us behind.

I wait until his footsteps have finally faded away entirely, and then a little longer than that, before I inch forward on bruised knees and push the chair out from under the table. I slide out after it, emerge and stagger upright only to realize that I'm entirely naked when my family's heads turn my way and their eyes go wide.

"Kiandah!" my brother and Zelie say at the same time while I quickly grab a filthy blanket from atop the guards' table and wrap it around my body.

"Are you…okay?" I say, my throat so dry as I stagger forward, tripping over the edge of the blanket every third step as I move further into the dungeon and realize that the conditions Lord Yaron has kept them in are worse than they initially appeared. They also haven't been housed here alone.

My family sits in a small room with stone walls, a stone floor and a stone ceiling. Every surface is covered in what appears to be either shit or dirt or blood. There are several cells branching out of this room. In one sit six or seven rag-covered people. In another, Merlin hangs from the ceiling by her heels. In the shadowy darkness of her private cell, I can't tell if she's conscious or not.

"We're okay, but Kiandah! Ancestors be, you look awful. Are you okay?" Zelie yells.

I swivel my head left and see her seated closest to me, chains shackling her arms over her head. She's not fully seated, her butt just barely grazing the ground. Her legs are chained to a ring on the floor out in front of her so she *can't* sit and she also can't crouch. It must be placing incredible strain on her shoulders. That they haven't dislocated yet is a miracle.

Meanwhile, next to her, Owenna has her arms and legs both shackled behind her back, forcing her into a kneeling position. Audet has her hands chained to her feet. Mama's got her hands chained to her neck. Cyprus is chained against the wall, standing, but so high that his toes barely touch the ground. He's choking already and he's going to suffocate if I don't do something fast. My father is the only one whose chains are bearable and I assume that's only because the arrow sticking out of his shoulder hasn't been removed. He's going to bleed to death.

"I'm going...to get you all out of here..." I say, voice funny, chest heaving. It's hard to breathe. I don't feel well and am struggling.

I go to my brother first. His fingers are clenching uselessly and he's got spit on his lips as he tries to talk. "Kia, are you..."

"I'm fine. Fine, just...just...tell me what to do." I rattle the thick metal ring around his neck and hands, but it's bolted into the wall.

He grits his teeth, but I don't let my gaze linger over his face. I don't assess the carnage. He's covered in filth and soot. I can't tell if he's burned or bloodied. His eye is swollen and he's got an abrasion in the distinct shape of a rod or leather strap across his chest. He looks like he's dying. But he's fighting.

"You aren't strong enough to pull out the bolts. They're loose, though…can you…with your magic…I think if you can get the bolts hot enough where they go into the rock, I can break them or…or pull them out."

"Hot enough?"

His gaze pans to mine. He looks at me with such confidence, he gives me no choice but to feel it. "You took the fire away, I figure you can create it."

"Create *fire*? Me?"

He smiles at me and his teeth are so white against the blood on his lips. "You can do it. I know you can."

My lower lip curls down. His confidence in me makes my heart hurt. I try to fight it but the tears are coming… He shakes his head — tries to. "Don't do that, Kandia," he says, smiling — trembling out of the exertion it costs him to not choke to death, but still smiling. "Chin up. Don't cry. Just try. Try for me?"

I nod, lip still curved all the way down to my chin as I fight valiantly against the sobs rattling through my chest. I secure my blanket and press my palms flat to the metal ring on either side of his hands. That's where the bolts are. Nothing happens at first. I glance into my brother's eyes, worrying my lower lip between my teeth. I can't help him, but I can't tell him that — not with him looking at me like I can do anything.

And then he screams. "Fuck!" My brother jerks abruptly forward, ramming straight into me as the bolts explode free of the wall. The bracket clatters to the stone and we land beside it, him on his back and me on my butt.

My family is all talking at once, but I focus on Cyprus as he pushes up into a sitting position. He kicks the bracket across the floor, closer to me. I flinch from it and Cyprus chuckles, "You did it, Kia. Fuck, I knew you could do it."

"You really are an Omega," Audet whispers.

"I can't believe it. My baby…" My mama's grinning at me with half of her mouth. The other half is sagging a bit, her upper lip busted. She's missing a front tooth she wasn't before the night started. Luckily, she doesn't look like she's been struck. Right now, she just looks proud of me.

"Alright. Alright, let's uh…let's do the others," Cyprus says, standing to his full height. He limps once, then seems to walk a little more easily as he takes a few more steps around the dungeon. He rolls out his neck as he crosses the room and stops before Zelie. "Help me, Kia?"

I nod, so confused, but I use his surety for my own and join him at Zelie's side. He grabs the chain attaching her ankles to the ring on the floor. "Can you heat up the ring? Where it attaches to the floor?"

No. "Yeah."

"On the count of three," he starts, and the ring grows bright, bright orange by the time he finishes counting us off. He pulls and, together, we break Zelie free. We do the same for the rest of my family and by the time we've finished unchaining our father, Zelie, Owenna, Audet and my mom are already gathered in the middle of the floor.

"Here!" Audet says, "come help us with this."

I stagger over and see that they've gathered around a trap door. One that's latched and barred shut but that's made of wood, not metal. I nod and stretch my hands forward, pressing them to the wood. The wood starts to char, burn and then flake away. My brother catches me by the shoulder, keeping me from falling into the abyss that opens up beneath. I sway, feeling drained and depleted, too drained even to recognize my magic for what it is. *Incredible.*

"It...it should be enough for us to squeeze through," Owenna says.

"It'll have to be," my father says. He leans further down, but lurches back up just as quickly. His large hand covers his mouth and nose. "Zelie, take this." He takes off his shirt and starts tearing it into strips. "Tie it around your faces."

I understand what he's doing the moment I take my next breath — my first breath in minutes. "No." I lurch up, bile rising in my throat, and vomit. I throw up all over the wall where Cyprus once laid.

"Zelie, go on."

"You want me to go down there?" she squeaks, staring down into the void. "I think I see dead bodies." *That's what it smells like, for sure. Bodies* long *dead.*

"There aren't bodies floating there. There wouldn't be. The water is rushing. It'll take us out of the castle," Owenna says, shimmying past her into the cubicle of darkness, a wrapped cloth around her nose and mouth. "We have to go now."

Cyprus grabs her shoulder. "You don't know where it leads."

"If water is moving it has to lead out, and out is our only chance for survival. He won't let us live and if he does, it'll be *here*. He's going to skin us along with them." Her chin jerks towards the two remaining cells. I feel my chest clam up as I notice that Trash City is still in their cells. They watch us with apathy, but don't ask for help. They look resigned to whatever Yaron has told them he has in store. Or…maybe not so resigned. Perhaps, bored? As if, they're waiting for something…

Owenna moves again towards the dark hole in the floor. I whisper, "He's really going to flay them?"

"And worse. He's preparing the poles for them to hang from outside of the gates. And her, he's going to do even worse to." She gestures to Merlin with her chin, her short Afro matted and charred and tilted askew. "He'll keep her down here for some time before he hangs her with the rest of them. He has plans for her." She shivers — shivers — and that's what does it for me.

"Cyprus, help me."

"Help you? Help you with what?"

I run to the first of the steel gates trapping the six Trash City members that Yaron has planned to flay and hang. "I can heat up the lock." I can. Because my hands are miracles. They can *save*. "We have to bring them with us."

"They're criminals," he scoffs.

"So are we," I shout. I stare at him and he stares at me. Our standoff lasts until Mama says, "Please. He'll be back soon. We need to hurry."

Cyprus curses and rushes to my side. He places his hands on the bars near the lock while I use my palms to completely surround the place where the lock secures into the stone wall. "Count us down, Kia."

Cyprus looks at me and I meet his gaze, and together, we break Trash City free. They stand together, smiling at us as they pass by. "Thank you," a younger woman says to me. "I'm Angel," she offers me her hand, then hesitates. "You're not going to burn me, are you?"

I smile back and shake my head. "No. But you should hurry." I don't shake her hand, a little unsure of myself.

She's not half so sure, and makes her way straight to the opening. Without hesitation, she jumps in, plummeting into the below where light cannot touch her. By the time the rest of Trash City has jumped into the abyss — all but one man who waits for their leader — Cyprus and I have freed her.

She's in bad shape, badly beaten, slashed and sliced with what look like a Berserker beast's claws, but she offers me a tip of her head and a smile to Owenna as she passes her. A wink, too, that I can't quite make sense of.

"You're a good kid," she tells me as she turns to face me and slides her goggles, which she miraculously still has, from inside a pocket within her raggedy clothes and back onto her face. Her hair is entirely red with blood. "I'll tell them to take it easy on ya." She laughs, like she's somewhere out in the light, not at all trapped in the darkest place in the world. "Not that they listen to me, though. Come on, Lou."

"After you, Merlin."

"Rendezvous point Z," Merlin says, and the strangest thing about this entire miserable situation is that she's looking at Owenna as she speaks.

Merlin disappears, followed closely by Lou. There's a moment of silence, and then a splash, and then Owenna's voice, "Let's go."

"Owenna, what was she…" Zelie starts, voice muffled from the bit of Dad's shirt she's got tied around her mouth. Mama hands me one and I'm slow to lift it as I watch and wait for Owenna's response.

She doesn't give it. Instead, she merely urges Zelie towards the opening and all but pushes her in. "Zelie, go!"

Zelie splashes into the darkness with a short screech, followed by Audet and Mama next. Cyprus helps Papa toward the opening and carefully lowers him into a seat on the opening's lip.

"Come on, Kiandah. You next," Owenna says. I go towards the hole in the ground, but I still hesitate.

"I…" think I should stay. My body wants me to stay. I can't feel anything clearly, but I can hear the word in my head replaying on a loop, over and over and over again. *Stay stay staystaystaystaystay.*

And then another word, many of them, spoken out loud, in a voice that I've dreamed of, but that I now have no desire to hear for the rest of my existence. At least not in person. "What is the meaning of this?"

"Kia, come on!" Owenna yells.

But it's too late.

It's too late for *all of us*. But it's not too late for them. Owenna tries to grab me but I dodge her hand and spin out of her grip, turning to face Yaron as he crosses the short, blood-spattered space between us in just two long steps. His gaze is pinned to Owenna and Cyprus at my back — until I start to run. I move towards him as fast as I can with both hands outstretched, and I feel it…a huge swell of sensation in both of my arms…

And then I trip. My feet stumble over the metal shackle on the floor that once caged one of my family members and I fall so hard that my feet momentarily leave the ground. I feel like I'm flying…directly at Lord Yaron.

His surprise is the only thing I register before our bodies collide. And in that final moment as his hand wraps around my upper arm, almost as if he's trying to catch me and not kill me, the energy within me releases in a burst of blue fire and he goes flying into the stone behind him, taking out the entire contingent of his Crimson Riders.

They all fall, crimson coats catching fire. I fall, hitting the stone beneath me hard. It hurts. Everything hurts. My blanket's gone. My dad and brother are calling my name but with every ounce of everything left in me, I look back at them and fling my hand out, sending one last cascading flare of energy in a burst of orange light towards them, knocking them both back into Owenna, who falls into the hole in the floor first, followed by the other two. I hear the splash some moments later and, moments after that, I look up into Yaron's furious grey eyes.

"What have you done?" He's kneeling right in front of me. *Right.* In front of me.

"Yaron," I whisper, the word so wrong, so informal, yet so automatic.

His eyes flash, and so does his hand. He strikes my cheek and I land hard against stone, rattling that fallen, forgotten shackle, unable to decide what, of my many ailments, hurts worst of all. *All of them. Everything hurts worst of all.*

I blink, look up and see him flexing his hand over and over. He's staring down, tone icy and startling as he says, "Omega." His nostrils flare, nose morphing seamlessly into that of an enormous beast before quickly shifting back. The whole thing lasts less than a second and momentarily makes me think I'm losing my mind. He reaches for me, probably to hurt me again.

"No," I say.

He hesitates, hands flexing into claws, before he closes the distance and grabs me by the shin. He yanks me beneath his body and with his free hand cups the back of my head and lifts my torso off of the ground. His nose drags down my cheek, sometimes hard and angled, other times soft and wet. It's still wet and cold and massive as it presses directly beneath my ear, stimulating senses I didn't know I had. My toes curl. Desire and pain split me in two, but I have another thought that eclipses both.

"You have no idea what you've done," he growls. "You will pay for this. You will suffer. But first, you will track down the murderers you have freed."

I don't care what he's talking about. All I care is that he's this close to me. "You really are a good boy, aren't you, Yaron?"

He rears up and back and meets my gaze before letting it rake down my naked chest. His mouth opens, his fangs flash, he dips his head. "You call me Yaron again, I'll tear out your tongue…" His palm slides up over my stomach to rest right between my breasts. I tense. "And rip your heart out of your chest."

I may *know* that he's a good boy, but I still don't dare speak again.

YARON
PARADISE HOLE

THIS OMEGA ISN'T WELL. NOT ONLY IS SHE STRUGGLING along, in clear agony, but somehow still upright — but she's addressed me by my given name now. And she's done it *twice*. She called me a good boy. I feel my trousers tighten, hardly able to believe that I heard what I did. I must have hallucinated it. I've met Omegas many times before in my life and none have dared speak to me as she did. Even the Fallen Earth Omega, for as feral as she was, seemed to know her place. The Fallen Beast Omega avoided speaking to me altogether, disgusted by Alphas in general.

I watch the Omega in my care now, lagging as she attempts to keep up with the Alphas and Betas in crimson. She has dark brown skin covered in scrapes and scratches, unwashed since I pulled her from the rubble. She wears a plain shift. I'm not certain where Radmilla procured it, because it looks like a potato sack with holes for a head and arms. She looks impossibly tiny inside of it, even though for a female, she is tall. Above it, her face shines with brutality, especially now that she has no hair to cover it. Without hair, she looks smaller. Okayo must have shaved away the burned sections when he administered to her. He cut it all the way down to her scalp. And now, the mark left behind from when I hit her shines in violent clarity. She's a murderer, at the very least complicit in murder…but it still didn't feel good to hit her, to strike her face…

Her face…the resemblance…

The Fated Omegas and their Fallen counterparts appear as doppelgangers with some small, subtle differences. The Fated and Fallen Earth Omegas share the same hair and skin color. The Fated and Fallen Beast Omegas share the exact same face. This Omega looks eerily like Odette, the Fated Fire Omega, but without hair, it's not entirely effortless to connect them. *She can't be.* It would be too coincidental and I do not believe in coincidence. Besides, this Omega is nothing like the other two I met in the woods. The sturdy and robust Earth Omega or the Beast Omega fully in control of her gifts. This…this Fire Omega is…not *weak*, no, certainly not that… but she feels nearly waifish…threadbare, just as thin as the smoke that she creates.

And my every sense is keenly attuned to her.

I am not the only one, either. The Alphas among my Crimson Riders have strayed from formation. The Omega trips, again, this time over a thick mangrove root. Malik lunges out of his way to catch her arm.

"Thank you," she whispers to the Alpha. The Alpha bites his lower lip, nods and does not release her even as she regains her footing. My hand forms claws.

"Malik," I grit. The Omega and Malik both turn to me, their hands locked like lovers. "If she can kill on her own, she can walk on her own." I bare my teeth and allow my beast to reveal his fangs. They extend past my lower lip.

"Yes, Lord Yaron." Malik nods and steps back into formation. I stand at the front of one cluster, which fans out behind me in a V while Sipho leads the other. Malik and Dorsten flank the Omega, who walks in the center of the formation I lead.

I turn my attention away from the group, allowing my beast's senses to prowl and pull me forward — though it takes effort, much more than it should. "West," I announce some time later. My Crimson Riders take their next steps in that direction in near perfect unison.

The Omega is a distraction that I abhor. She falls twice more, and the sounds her body makes crashing through the foliage resonate like explosions. It's grating. I catch the scent of something on the wind, but my beast's ears seem finely tuned to her shallow breaths and the fact that her parched throat needs water. *What is that scent?* I turn towards it. *The Omega needs water.* I turn back.

"My Lord, do you smell that? Sickly sweet," Sipho says, stopping abruptly. "North." His face twists away from me, his gaze cast in the direction of the ports. He's right. I should have identified the scent long before.

It's distinct, too memorable to ever be forgotten. My hackles rise instantly. Fur sprouts down my spine and stiffens. My toes curl and the claws tipping them threaten to tear through my boots. I lift my nose to the wind and my face forms a snout. With my beast's senses, I can taste something foul and rotten on the wind, but I can also smell Trash City so precisely, I know the moment that their clan changed direction, veering from north to west, and I can pinpoint the exact place that the murderous Betas lost Trash City's trail and chose a different path. The wrong one if their intention was to escape me, though I don't suppose they ever really had that chance.

"Trash City continued west, but the killer's family changed direction. They've gone east, towards Undoline." The fools.

I have my guard patrolling the village border. It is the nearest village to Orias and I expected them to seek out their familiars there. From the information I gathered of the killer's family, they are well liked among the traders in Undoline and may very well have extended family in that area or in the next villages even further east.

"Trash City, meanwhile, ventured deeper into Paradise Hole. They're headed west."

"There is nowhere for them to go west," Sipho says. "Unless they intend to spare us a great effort and throw themselves off of the cliffs."

I nod. "It is only a matter of time before we root them out, wherever they're hiding. We will continue west for now through the woods of Paradise Hole, leaving the killer's family to our guard positioned outside of Undoline."

Paradise Hole is the name given to the rotten woods that spread and spread and spread. No one knows their provenance, but the rot that once only plagued the North Island has come here and, while Trash City was able to successfully hide itself in the woods of Paradise Hole on the North Island. On the South Island, they will not be so lucky. I guarantee it. I take a step west to lead the charge, but am arrested by Sipho's voice.

"And the northern scent, my Lord?"

"We will return to investigate after we have apprehended Trash City," I say. Sipho nods. "Remember, Riders, I want Trash City taken alive."

"Hau!" my Riders chime in unison, the hard clash of so many voices startling the Omega, who jolts. She looks to me immediately after she settles as if...seeking comfort or reassurance.

No.

I take another step further away from her, and then another...but...I cannot divorce myself from the sight of her swollen eyelid — *and I did that* — or the sound of her ragged breathing. *She suffers.* She should. And Dorsten is offering her his water skin. *No.*

"Killer, come to me."

The Omega jerks again, dropping her gaze from Dorsten's extended hand without touching the skin he holds, though she looks at it longingly. She bites her bottom lip. It's full and the prettiest colorscape, pinker towards the center and ringed in a light brown. I frown, not liking that I am noticing the small details. I have seen Omegas before and not been so distracted by them. Omegas are distractions. This is why Shadow Lords since long past do not take them. I must remain steadfast. I must remember my duty to my people.

The Omega picks her way across the dense forest floor then stops, still not close enough to touch. "I will not waste time and you cannot afford to waste time, given the state of your many injuries. We know that your family intends to seek refuge in Undoline with your extended kin. Do they intend to reconvene there with Trash City?"

She drops her gaze to her feet and shakes her head. She touches her ear and then flinches and I wonder if it's pain that causes her to react like that to the touch of her own flesh. *Her fingers are long and elegant, nails trimmed short. Palms likely callused if she makes food for a living and dismembers Alphas for sport.*

"I don't know, my Lord," she says.

Anger makes me stiffen. "Do not lie to me, Omega."

She shakes her head, gaze only flashing to meet mine infrequently. I *hate* the way it feels when our eyes meet. Like a clashing of swords. Sparks rain over me. "I'm not, my Lord. I don't know where my family's gone and Trash City only mentioned different rendezvous points. Point L, Z and…and I think there was one other. I just…I can't remember. I swear. I'm sorry."

"And you have no idea what those letters may mean?"

"I told you, Yaron," she says, expression flashing with frustration as her gaze strays once again to me. "I've never met those people before today and I had no idea my family was working with them. I don't know anything."

I am already advancing on her. She is already stumbling back. All of my Crimson Riders are watching us, watching me as I grip her neck roughly. My other hand is on the small of her back, fisting her hideous shift. "You seem to think you know me well enough to call me Yaron."

"I…" She blinks, her eyes so fucking beautiful. But they're both brown. The Fire Fate has one blue eye. Perhaps their resemblance is only coincidental. I am momentarily distracted and don't hear what she says when she answers.

"What, Omega?" I hiss.

She swallows. I can feel her throat work beneath my palm. "I said that I was sorry. I don't know why I keep calling you… that. It just feels right…my Lord."

My beast whimpers. *Whimpers.* "You…" I start. There's a cracking in the woods that draws my beast's attention. His ears are already visible — massive flaps on the side of my face — and they twitch in the direction of the crackling. It's picking up now and it's not coming from the east or from the west, but the north.

"My Lord?" the Omega whispers, voice softer than ash.

I look back into her eyes, and then at her body, bent slightly backwards over my arm. Her feet are sunk into the mud up to the ankle. We are off of any known path. Yet she walks without complaint, without shoes on because I have given her no other choice.

She looks over her shoulder. "Is…"

"Can you hear it?"

She shakes her head, eyebrows furrowing over slightly swollen eyelids from where I struck her so monstrously. "I don't hear anything, my…Lord. But I can feel…something." Her fingers fan over her stomach.

My beast releases a short, flared roar in response to the pain that warps her expression. My hands instinctively pull her against my chest, my gaze sweeping the woods to the north. I open my mouth, but before I can speak, a rolling thunder comes crashing through the woods. Distant, at first, it quickly becomes louder. Louder and louder.

My beast is sniffing at the wind, suddenly capable of disentangling itself — *me* — from the scent of *her.* And the scent I pick up? It's foul and familiar, a scent one who crosses it never forgets. If they survive the encounter.

"My Lord?" Sipho calls. "The heart trees are migrating..."

The heart trees are agitated, few that there are this deep into Paradise Hole. Though the rains have not yet begun, their roots have begun to move, disentangling from the soft soil as they carry themselves away to safer ground. I am reminded fleetingly of the horses' unease at the church when I intended to burn the Omega and her family. The natural world senses something immense approaching. Like the coming of the dawn. Or the end of it.

"They're coming," I shout, clutching the Omega close. "Riders, defensive formation!"

My beast surges, my hand forming a paw with claws before returning to a hand, though my claws remain. "Omega," I hiss in a tone I've never used before, because though I try to remain severe, it's difficult to infuse hatred and rage into my tone when she looks up at me like that, eyes wide, hands cupped beneath her chin as if she's nothing more than a battered orphan seeking shelter. *Shelter her.* "Remain by my side, no matter what comes through those trees."

"What's coming, Yaron?"

Yaron. Her disobedience will need to be punished. *Or praised.*

"I believe we are about to be beset by..."

But before I can say more, before I can take a step in any direction, before I can soothe her with the purr that's threatening to bang its way free of my chest, before I can unhook my battle axe, the ground explodes open beneath our feet. I'm thrown off of mine, the Omega thrown away from me in the opposite direction. Several of my Riders take flight with us, several more fall to the ground. One of my Riders releases a pained shout, yet not even that is enough to grab my attention like the disembodied torso of an Alpha dragging its way out of the ground.

Surging up onto my feet, I reach into the waterlogged soil, grab the undead Alpha by the forearms and tear them free of the body they belong to. The Alpha might have once been a white male, but he's been beneath the soil for so long, his skin has turned blue and is crusted in a sheen of dirt. He is not swollen — why would he be? He's already dead and not taking on water. But I can still tell that this Alpha has been buried for a while.

No, not this Alpha. *These.*

Alphas fight their way out of the soil all around us, begging the question of whether they were planted here and only here and we were drawn into a trap, or if there are Alphas out here planted everywhere. *Everywhere.* Lurking just beneath the soil of the entire Shadowlands, the entire South Island, all of Gatamora.

No.

"Destroy the brain stem! Dismember the bodies!" I roar, trying to see past three undead Alphas surging towards me to find the Omega. I can't see her. "Omega!"

"Yaron! I'm here," she says, voice breathy and soft. I glance towards the sound of her voice and see that she's standing between two trees, her hands touching both. She looks panicked and afraid, but I find it curious that she hasn't thought to run. She could use this opportunity to try to escape. I might have even believed she planted the corpses here, is working in cahoots with Trash City and the Fates, and lured me here on purpose.

Except she's still here looking so panicked and nervous.

She isn't a killer, is she? *No.* She hasn't lied to me yet, has she? *Not once.* She's a good girl, little Kiandah, and I'm still going to kill her because she's just standing there and right now, I actually do want her to run.

There are only two dozen Crimson Riders with me here, the full breadth of my army dispersed across the island to continue the hunt. I thought two dozen excessive hours ago, and now I regret our nominal numbers. The Omega is entirely exposed. An undead Alpha female has noticed her and is turning in her direction. The Omega slinks back between the trees, looking like she might run, *finally*, but she looks at me first.

Yaron, she mouths and I can't fucking stand it because she speaks my name like she knows me, knows something I don't, like I belong to her and she needs me and she knows she can count on my protection, and the response in my chest is all but catastrophic because I want to be that for her. I don't want to let her down.

I unhook my axe and sweep the heads of the two undead Alphas in front of me before launching my axe through the trees, over the tops of the now headless bodies and into the back of the undead Alpha zeroing in on the Omega. The Alpha slams into the tree to her left, its body severed in half vertically.

Kiandah jumps, bones leaving her skin, before her gaze flashes back to me. She meets my stare, her one eye swollen, filling me with a renewed revulsion because she looks at me like she *trusts* me. And I was the one to give her that mark.

"Kiandah, run!" I say and the surprise in her face confuses me for a moment that lasts just a few heartbeats too long. *This is the first time I've said her name aloud.*

Nails gouge into my calf, sinking in deep enough to cause my left leg to buckle. *Claws — the dead Alpha has claws.* I roar and kick the creature free, but it just keeps coming. I slam my heel through its skull while another two undead launch themselves at me. I fight them off with fangs and claws as they cling to my arms with fangs and claws of their own.

"Omega!" I roar, concern blistering my throat.

"Yaron?" Her tone is shaky, so afraid. And still fucking here.

"Omega, get out of here now! Avoid their fangs!" I shout to my Riders as I see Guy to my right take a bite to the shoulder. He roars in pain. I lunge toward him and shred the undead Alpha clinging to him, removing its head. "Close in! Malik! Dorsten! Fall back to the Omega!" Why isn't she leaving? Why hasn't she left?

I watch Dorsten and Malik attempt to charge towards the Omega and I try to follow them, but more undead Alphas lunge into their paths, five on two. I take a moment to expand the depth of my hearing to try to calculate just how many we're up against here, but the thrashing of those in the foreground is too great. Plus, there's something else in the woods, just out of reach of my senses. A great presence that my beast raises his hackles to, that I know to destroy because it's also something to fear. But it's too far away.

I draw my awareness back around me, momentary panic surging at the realization that the Omega is entirely unprotected and my Alphas are nearly overrun. The undead Alphas number in the thirties, forties, perhaps. They swipe with their claws, catching cloaks and tearing through flesh. My Riders are not wearing their full battle armor and I hesitate to draw my beast forward fully because he presents such a large target and one single bite from one of these foul creatures wreaks havoc.

I have not forgotten the pain and the devastation to my body, having been bitten at least three times in my last battle against these creatures. My reflexes were slowed for weeks, I was groggy, couldn't easily draw my beast forward, not to mention the pain. It was nothing I'd experienced before and it affected not just the site of the bite, but rampaged throughout my entire body like a poison — like venom, but with the intention to maim and not to bond or to heal.

A creature lunges for me now, and I take my claws to his throat, decapitating him cleanly. I kick through the next undead blocking me from reaching the Omega as Malik and Guy successfully battle another cluster of undead back. I finally reach my axe, still impaled in the back of the undead Alpha female and remove it, letting the ball collapse onto the ground, each of its two separated halves still writing until I remove the head.

I turn to the three undead Alphas now chasing my Omega deeper into the woods and take off at a run. I leap, landing between them and Kiandah just as she falls in the mud. I swing my axe. My stroke takes out two at the neck and the top half of the third's head. I swing my battle axe over my head and when I bring it down into the third undead's back, I split it apart along the seam of its spine.

"Riders," I roar. "Give them no ground!" We fight on, me with the Omega pressed against me, her body bouncing awkwardly against my back. She holds herself up and just as my concern mounts and we are swarmed by half a dozen undead at once, I feel it, the first droplet plummeting from the sky, heavy and threatening. I curse.

My Riders can struggle to fight through the sludge of Paradise Hole. We can cede stable ground and fight on the turf of the undead. But we cannot fight against the rain. "The rains are coming! Fall back to Orias!"

I slash my way through the head of another monster and turn, only to come face to face with three more leaping for us. Kiandah clutches my clothing and doesn't move out of my way when I try to thrust my body between hers and the incoming attackers.

"Fuck," I curse. I'm stuck and going to have to suffer a bite. I lift my left forearm but as the creature nearest to me jumps, he hits a wall of shimmering blue fire. Her hands are up, outstretched and shaking, but powerful enough to produce a translucent wall of blue that ripples and shimmers just beyond her fingertips. The creature incinerates against it and just as quickly as it arrived, it disappears. The Omega slumps against my body, spent, and I curse again. The rain droplets are spattering more rapidly now against my hair and shoulders and the top of her head. I need to get her out of here.

"Riders," I roar, hoping to high hells they can hear me over the chaos. "Disperse! Back to Orias now!"

That is what I tell them, but that is not where I head. My legs grow beastly, morphing to their more lycanthropic shape. My claws dig into the ground and my hind legs explode the seams of my pant legs. I gather the Omega in my arms, clutching her close, and launch myself off of the ground with every ounce of my strength. I feel claws catching at my lower limbs and when I land, I crush an undead beneath me. I want them fucking off of me and so I leap and sprint again. I hold the Omega tight against my chest, trying to shield her as I fight my way free of the last of the undead at the same time that I run straight against a wall of water.

The rainy season is brutal and exposure like this won't lead to anything but death for the Omega and I both if we don't find cover. Her need is more urgent than mine. I would have no trouble making it to Orias with my Riders, but my Omega is already injured, breathing erratically, pulse weak, skin on fire. Already, we're both soaking wet, my hair plastered to the sides of my face, water sluicing from it down my back beneath my cloak.

The rain beats with far too much force against the Omega's bare arms and the result is that my concern for her beats far too loudly in my ears. It makes it far, far too easy to ignore the sound of the fighting continuing at my back. The zombie horde are still thrashing away, sure to be conquered by the rains soon if my Riders don't get to them first. The undead will survive the rains, sure, but likely in pieces. We will recover and destroy the pieces when the rains relent, but that won't be for some time. Time that my Omega does not have. She needs cover. I survey the trees before me, waiting for the right tree, waiting for the right time.

Heart trees are famous. They grow only here in the northeastern-most region of the South Island. They once covered the Shadowlands' entire northern shore, but that was before my time. Before Paradise Hole. Even as a boy, I remember my first visit to the Heart Forest as a newly ascended Berserker. The infection of Paradise Hole had already begun to spread, but the Heart Forest was bigger then, still teeming with life. Now, despite my restoration team's best efforts, anything that once was green has turned grey. The heart trees are all that remain. But, we will not lose the heart trees. Not while I remain Shadow Lord. Just as I will not lose this Omega.

My jaw clenches with renewed determination as I find what I'm looking for, as if the heart trees themselves have heard my vow and accepted my offering. Similarly to mangroves, heart trees have roots that bury deep into the waterlogged ground, however the roots are as thick as my biceps and their trunks are swollen at the bases, tapering up towards crooked branches. The roots keep the trunks and sparsely decorated boughs up off of the ground and, when the rains begin, the trees *dance* in abject delight. Trunks as wide as ten, twenty feet in diameter, like the one I stand before now, *move*, their roots physically carrying them great distances. Heart trees are known to migrate as far as twenty miles in a heavy storm as they seek out new pastures.

"Omega, brace yourself for the darkness." She doesn't reply and I don't let myself be distracted with her wellbeing. I wait for the heart tree to take its first breath.

The trunk splits, revealing the darkened interior. I hear the sound of the Omega gasping in between the much louder sound of her teeth chattering. Yes, it is a beautiful sight. The heart tree lifts, its roots pushing deep into the swampy earth, and the Omega in my grip jumps, clinging to my cloak and shoulders as it rises up. It is a spectacular thing to behold, the Heart Forest coming alive.

Trees begin to slowly move, walking in all directions. The one before us takes its next breath, opening at the whorl on its front — its heart — and I use the opening now, which is just wide enough, to lift the Omega up and toss her inside. The rains are *punishing* as I track the tree another dozen steps, waiting for it to breathe again so that I may join the Omega inside of it. My paws are sucked into the swollen soil on each step, making motion difficult. I snarl up at the skies, my chest tightening at the thought of her alone inside of the tree for all this time.

The tree inhales, the opening finally large enough for me. I launch myself inside, my legs twisting to those of my Alpha from those of my beast. I crash onto the ground, hands and feet scrambling over the smooth wood, trying to gain purchase. I worry I'll crush her, and then I worry some more when my hands don't find her at all.

"Omega," I snarl.

She gasps and my hand meets skin. "Yaron..." she whimpers. *Whimpers.*

"Omega, come to me." I haul her against my body, switching my sight to that of my beast so I can see her more clearly. She's soaked and so am I, my heavy cloak and leather armor weighing me down. I unhook the clasp at my neck, liberating myself. My cloak squishes on the floor. I shove it behind me, remove my wet shirt and toss it into the pile. My boots and trousers were shredded throughout the course of my many transformations. I tear their remains away from my skin now.

I sink into the bowl-shaped hollow with my knees spread and my back against the heart tree's interior wall. I grab the Omega's thin shoulder and lift her up into a seat. I grab the material at the back of her neck and use one of my claws to carve a path through the wet cloth, following the line of her spine.

She shivers violently, her teeth chattering together. She tries to clutch the rag to her chest, or maybe, she's so cold her arms have locked — in either case, I have to pull her between my thighs and wrestle the garment away from her. I toss it against the far wall, wrap both arms around her naked body and wrench her against my bare chest.

"Omega, calm yourself," I order, but the longer I hold her against me like this, the harder her breathing becomes. Harder and more erratic, punctuated by involuntary whimpers and whispered moans, she's shaking badly now. I hold her tighter. "Omega, I will not harm you," I say, and the shock of what I've just told her hits me a delayed moment thereafter.

She is my prisoner. It is my duty to harm her. Have I... lied? No. No... I am the Shadow Lord. I do not lie. Perhaps, what I meant to say was that I will not harm her *now*. Not until after Trash City has been found. Then she will be punished for her treachery.

Cold air slams inside of the heart tree on each of the tree's deep inhalations. The Omega shakes violently each time. Rainwater has begun to fill up the basin of the tree — a reserve for the heart tree to draw on later, but right now it simply soaks us through to the bone. Outside, I see nothing but a dark grey wall of rain, no matter if I use my beast's sight or my Alpha's.

"Omega. Breathe. Follow my breath." I take exaggerated inhales that she promptly ignores in favor of jerky breaths that make it sound like she's drowning. The sensation burns into my chest, lancing me like a brand, every time. I worry that, in the dead of night, months from now, I will still feel the pain of that sound.

I feel *unsettled*. Scrambling now, I tell her, "The heart tree travels east towards Undoline but far before that, we will reach a hunter's hole. It is dry. There is food. That is where we will ride out the storm." Another violent tremor rocks her. My gut clenches. I need my beast to warm her better, but within this heart tree there is not space enough for that. "Omega, nod if you understand me."

She nods and the slightest relief causes me to tighten my arms around her. "Good girl."

She shivers even more exaggeratedly, but I merely fix my grip, fastening it around her unflinchingly. She does not relax, but shivers more wildly. My abdomen is clenching in panic. I feel fear — genuine fear — for the first time in as long as I can remember. I feel helpless to do anything to end her suffering, to save her life, if that is what is on the line here because she seems like she is falling to pieces. I have not felt helpless *ever* before now. And I cannot stomach it. *I will not forget this sensation. It will torture me months from now. Years.*

"Omega, do not show your weakness now. You, who threw flames from your fingertips to defend your family…" To defend me. "We are nearly there." I peer out into the world on the tree's next exhale and as the rain cuts down hard, I can only locate approximately where we are. "The tree will move us within walking distance on the next exhale, maybe two." What I don't tell her is that walking outside now, through the thick sheets of icy, pelting rain, will be brutal.

She nods so pitifully and yet it shoots heat all the way down my legs to the heels of my feet. She's here. She's hearing me. And yet, she's so weak. My Berserker howls and bitches and moans, but I refuse to give him my voice. I say nothing, until, "Brace yourself, Kiandah." Because on the heart tree's next exhale, I jump down out of the heart tree and I carry Kiandah into the storm.

YARON
HEART FOREST

THE JOURNEY TO THE HUNTER'S HOLE WAS SWIFT, BUT that does not save us. We still arrive beaten and abused. The storm wails ferociously as I force open the swollen, waterlogged door. The hunter's hole is built into the side of a low hill, the spartan cabin set on the hunter's line, a path now utterly indistinguishable from the swamplands surrounding it. It will be an undertaking to have it reestablished. It always is, and it needs to be maintained more often with how violently and frequently the rains come. The world is changing. Gatamora is getting darker. Something is coming.

I manage to find the latch and force our bodies across the threshold, the wind lashing our backs, water nipping at our heels, trying to drag us back. The majority of the structure is wood, but it's largely reinforced by the earthen walls that form two of the four walls that make up the small space. I turn towards the rain whipping through the doorway and roar as the storm tries to force its way inside. I manage to place the bar across the door with the Omega in one arm, but I cannot batten the windows properly with her in my grip.

With the door closed, holding some of the rains at bay, I round on the cabin and quickly cross the short distance to the hearth. I find a pile of neatly folded blankets beside it and shake the first out, lay it before the hearth and then grab the second. I go to wrap it around the Omega, but my beast rears his head. The blanket smells of the hunters that came before. Three distinct scents, all male. I'll lay this over her over my dead body...

Or hers.

Or hers. Fuck. I grunt and wrap the Omega up. I lay her down on the floor, hating the way her head thunks against the floorboards, even through the blankets. I quickly flip open the small metal box located beside the blankets, locate the firestarters and set flint to steel. I have a fire simmering — flickering — in the smooth stone hearth within a few moments. It takes me longer than it should. Even though the cabin is dry, the moisture in the air is enough to dampen the kindling, making it harder to catch.

Stacking a few of the smaller sticks in a pyramid shape above the flame, and inserting the smallest among them directly into the fire, I leave the small pile to burn and finish battening down the windows. Once finished and satisfied, I add a few of the larger logs to the hearth. The fire is not too smoky and seems to be brightening quickly. Quicker than it should. I turn and glance over my shoulder, wondering if it isn't the Omega's doing. She's awfully quiet.

The hunter's hole is a single-room cabin, a narrow bed against the earthen wall with dry wood chopped and stacked beneath it. Against the wooden wall across from it is the small kitchen, complete with a basin, but no running water, a gas stove, single pot, wooden spoon and nothing else. The fireplace sits against the other earthen wall, its chimney tunneling through the hillside. It's a testament to how well it was constructed that the winds and rains don't pour in from the mountain, allowing golden flames to flicker more peacefully now in the stone hearth. Before it lies the cowering killer, the Omega, wrapped in blankets that smell of a foreign male. I frown, not liking the direction of my thoughts, and frown harder when the Omega shivers again. Muscles tighten across my chest. My lungs strain.

In a voice I hardly recognize, I say, "I will go fetch water. Don't move." Don't move? I feel like a fool, but my tongue is surprisingly thick in my mouth. I can't find the right words to correct myself.

Out in the rains again, they come down so hard, I know that the killer and I won't be going anywhere anytime soon. Fine. I've dealt with worse. The kitchen is stocked with a supply lasting at least seven days and she is so slight as to hardly be visible. I round the cabin and find the troughs in the back. Three are set up side by side and all of them are near full with water already. There is an additional metal cistern also set up to collect rainwater. I remove the lid and allow rainwater to collect. After this storm, there will be plenty for us and the next hunter and the next and then some.

I grab two wooden pails of water, filling them to their brims before returning inside. "Omega…" I start, but I don't know what order I would have given her next. I drop my pails, shut and latch the door behind me, task promptly forgotten as I inhale and then inhale again more deeply. I was not surprised before, but I am surprised now.

"You are not in pain." That's not what I meant. That's not even close to what I meant to say.

She shakes her head, though, as if she knows what I'm truly asking. Because this trembling does not come from pain, though she can surely feel pain, too, after all that she's been through. No, this trembling comes from something far more dreadful.

"You will remain like this," I command her.

She nods, her lips pressing together into a thin line, or at least, as thin a line as is possible. *She has such full, pretty lips.* Fuck.

"You *cannot* be entering your heat now," I say, willing it to be so.

To this, she does not respond except to writhe on the floor, her forehead pressed against it, her knees shoved under her body as she tries to curl into a ball of nothingness, but she can't do that. Because I'd sense the explosion of her from any forgotten corner of Gatamora. The heat rushing out of her is *powerful.*

"Depriving you is no less punishment than you deserve," I say, merely for the cruelty of it, even as my Berserker's legs take hold of mine and the claws on my feet bore four holes in the wood. He presses a whimper between my bared teeth. "No," I snap, the warning meant for him, but the killer glances up, looking at me for the first time.

And just like her killing spirit, her glare is lethal, too.

Fuck.

Her pupils are blown, her left eyelid still slightly swollen. So are her lips and left cheek. The light from the hearth seems to wick off of her skin, like it's afraid of her. As am I. It's like she's made of gold, a fire's light within her that puts this puny flame to shame. It's stunning. She's stunning. She looks so fucking young that I'm reminded, if she ascended so recently, she's likely barely of age and off fucking limits.

I recoil, backpedaling, but nothing that should be a consideration is doing anything but making my beast salivate. Her swollen cheek. Her swollen lips that tremble. Her head, perfectly shaped and free of hair, that makes it impossible to look anywhere but at her face. Her beauty is understated and calls to me like a fucking siren song. She looks absolutely ravaged, devastatingly so. My beast wants nothing more than to add to that devastation and then *bond* her, so that she'll be reborn.

Sinking my fangs into the side of that delicate, breakable throat... *No.*

My cock is swelling and my nakedness hits me acutely then. I reach down and have two choices — to grab my dick or try to cover it. One would be admitting defeat to her heat, because if I so much as brush my fingers over the swelling shaft, my knot already thickening at its base, I will have no choice but to mount her. The other would be to stand before her like a little boy covering his manhood and would fill me with embarrassment and shame.

"Omega, cover up. I will not bond you." Bond her. I meant to say *rut.*

She has one of the blankets draped over her shoulders, but when she passes her dark brown eyes — which, in this light, are the color of melted tar and just as sticky — over my face and then *lower* to my body, she shivers. Her blanket slips further. Her shoulder comes into view, shining like the goddamn sun, and I come unhinged.

A wave of heat flushes my body. Venom drips into my mouth. I shake my head once, definitively, but my resolve feels like sand, gritty and incapable of standing up against such exposed, lethal flame. I bark, "Omega, I will not be tempted by you. I would not bond an underage female for all the secrets of Gatamora. I will toss you out into the rain first. Do. Not. Test. Me."

Her lips press together so tightly it looks like it hurts. She makes the smallest, most tantalizing mewling sound before her elbows buckle and her body bows over itself. She clutches her stomach as she tries to lift her blanket and my Berserker does not like this, he *loves* it. The arousal I feel watching her ache, knowing that I am the only Alpha for miles that can soothe her hurt, take away her pain and replace it with limitless pleasure, has my erection pulsing to its own heartbeat. It stands stiff, out from my body like a goddamn third leg. It's heavy. Its weight unbearable. I try to will it down, but anytime my thoughts move to it, my legs push me forward another half step.

"Calm yourself, Omega. Breathe deeply. Know that I will not touch you. You are underage and there is *nothing* on this island or in this world that would tempt me to touch an underage female."

She balks and her lips curve up in a smile just wide enough I catch the flash of her teeth, pearly white. I cannot believe it. She's smiling at me. I…did not think I would receive the honor and now that I've had it and it has faded, I wonder if I hallucinated it because it was striking, her smile. Not because it was sweet and shy as I suspected it would be from all I know of this Omega's weak, flowery countenance, but because it cut like a knife.

"Yaron," she says, so informally and out of turn, but she shows no remorse. Her hands are curved protectively around her head. She's constantly in motion, unable to stop. "I am thirty-four years old. I haven't been underage…" A knot of pain must strike her severely enough to rob her of whatever words she'd been poised to say next. She gasps and collapses forward onto her hands and it takes me a moment to realize what's so odd about this position. *She's presenting…she's presenting for me.*

"You…aren't…" I say, voice threadbare, a frightened whisper.

"I am. I am thirty-four years old."

And I remember that it is not impossible. The Fallen Earth Omega I so recently met also ascended older than the others usually do. Looking at her face, any doubt I had that she is not the Fallen Fire Omega, the Fire Fate's counter, is erased. That is, if what she is saying is true…

"What year were you born?"

"Under the evening light of our four hundredth blood moon." My beast howls and my other foot drives forward though I mean to keep it rooted. It, too, has claws. So do both of my hands. My fangs are fully protracted and my face is half snout as my beast and I war for control.

In my mind, I canter backwards, wondering if I should not rather brave the rain, but it's too late for that. With her words, I am undone. "Omega," I say and my tone is different now.

She must hear it, too. Her eyes flash open. She looks at me and straightens her arms beneath her so that she's on all fours, the blanket slipping...just waiting for her... "Beast."

My stomach clenches. My thoughts dissolve. My clawed fist flies to capture my cock, the rough pads of my hand doing nothing for me at all. I want her. I *want* her. "I am Lord of the Shadowlands. You are a killer…"

"You are," she whimpers, eyelids fluttering. My gaze rakes down her body. She is thin, but not overly so. She carries weight in her hips and thighs, which are pocked slightly and calling for me to take a bite out of them. Her breasts are heavy and weighted and peaked in nipples that look inky and black in this light. I want to suckle one. I want to bite one. I want to bond her there, and then everywhere else. But I can't. "But I'm not."

"Remove the blanket." The blanket that smells of another male. The thought of another male here, now, in the presence of her heat and perfection, makes my vision dim, tinting red first, then black. *Rip the throat out of the Alpha who would challenge you, then fuck her in his blood.*

She flings it off without hesitation and rolls onto her back, then spreads her legs. She's fully naked and completely bared for my gaze. There's nothing touching her. Not one single thing. She has a dusting of short black curls between her legs and that's all. The brown petals of her core peek out between the soft mounds of her labia and I want to part them with my claws carefully, so very carefully, and have her trust that I will not harm her. *I have already harmed her.* I glance at her face and I forget for only one instant that she's a killer, and I pretend for only one instant that I could have the dream I've only ever hoped to dream…

This Omega is mine, and we are in love, and this is not our first heat we've been through together but one of many, and she will carry my kits one day and we will touch each other gently with fondness, for we are bound and we are best friends and we share everything with one another, our hearts most of all.

My lungs are robbed of breath and I can't speak as the reality of this world comes crashing back on her next full-body shiver. I take a step. "You are…" So unabashed. So uninhibited. So unafraid. So fucking lovely.

I swallow hard, willing steel into my tone as the floorboards bend beneath my flexing claws. "This changes nothing between us. I will not seek to claim you at the Festival of the Red Moon, but give you up to whichever Alpha or pack wins you, and I will not lessen my punishment against you or your family because of this. I will only ease your need and my own because we are trapped here. I will only sate your heat at my own personal expense."

Ha. My beast laughs at me. As if I do not want this. It will be easier to let her think that. And safer for me. She is a peasant. I am her Lord. I want no ideas of grandeur coming into her mind that I would break tradition hundreds of years old. Shadow Lords are mated to their lands. There is no beauty set to tempt them. They are above such mortal things like want and affection.

"When your heat ends, we will not speak of this again."

Several emotions flash across her face, but I'm uncertain whether they are on account of my words or on account of her heat pangs. The scent that blooms from her core is intoxicating, rapidly ballooning to fill up the small cabin. The sound of the rain battering the outside of this little shack is nothing but white noise, lulling me further into the trance of her cutting scent and her soft beauty and her fiery gaze.

"Do you understand?" I say.

"Yes," she says, voice twisted on a moan. Her knees tip further apart, spread so far that her inner thighs are quivering. She rolls her head on her neck for a moment, as if in ecstasy, before looking back up and meeting my gaze fiercely, as if she's heard everything I've had to say and not only doesn't care, but finds it boring. The look in her eyes is condescending and murderous and so fucking powerful — I stagger at its force and my hand on my cock squeezes hard enough that my balls jerk and precum spills from the tip, robbing me of thought.

"Are you finished?" she says flatly.

My head whips back, as if struck. I'm shocked. "Your impertinence knows no bounds, Omega. Though I should not be surprised to hear such a lack of propriety displayed by a criminal. I am your Lord and you will show me respect." I speak through clenched teeth, my words hardly intelligible. My mouth is full of fangs.

The Omega's hips buck and her scent…gods, her fucking scent…it could bring me to my knees. My legs are shaking now. She moans and it's a whispery, needy little thing. "You are my Lord outside of this cabin, but in here, you're just *mine*. Now, stop talking, Yaron, and fuck me."

What the fuck? Heat unfurls in my gut while something larger than that shifts in my chest. I…am at a total loss. And with no thoughts in my mind other than a mild confusion mixed with a far greater lust, I take a terrifying step towards her.

She gasps as if I've slapped her clit even though several feet still separate us. She bites her bottom lip. Her eyes flare and she lifts her hips, tilting them up and using her hands to reach down her body and spread herself wider for me. *My gods.*

"Gods…" I choke.

She smiles and it's a horrifying expression because I can feel my…control…slip… She's giving me a vision of what it will be like when I'm deep inside of her, sunken into her heat up to the knot. I palm my knot now, the ring around the base of my erection covered in the same silky skin as that of my penis, only twice as thick, about an inch wide — for now. When it inflates, it'll be three, four times thicker and two inches wide, fitting snugly into her opening and holding her in place for me while I…

I release a prayer to the old gods for strength not to bond her because right now that's all I can think about, filling me with an even greater longing than knotting and fucking her sweet, breakable body and her perfect, dripping cunt.

I feel savage as I take a step towards her, only for her gaze to snap to mine, an awareness there that hadn't been before as she battled her heat and her desire. Now, she seems in control and my beast hesitates. I hesitate. She shakes her head, *no.*

"No?" Gods no… Don't let her tell me no now. Not at this precipice.

"No, *my Lord*," she sneers, as if the title is not mine at all. "If you want to claim me, you'll come to me on your knees. Crawl to me, Yaron."

That heat in my groin rolls through me and claims my entire body. I can't…believe…what she's said to me. I can't respond. "You…dare…" I choke, but the words are rotten in my mouth and I can only just barely spit them out.

And then Kiandah does the damnable. She laughs. Her face is black and blue and she laughs with her brown pussy lips spread until I can see the pink at their core. "Fine. I'll just do it myself…" She leans back and starts to rub her clit, rolling that tight little nub between her fingers…

"Kiandah…" I bark, not having intended to use her name.

Her neck snaps up. She looks at me and the soft vulnerability that crosses her face and pulls her eyebrows together is the last piece she needed to ruin me. She has already studded my chest with arrows launched from her quiver but that vulnerability clamps around my heart like an iron maiden. Her lips work. Her bottom lip trembles and she winces, as if in pain.

"Crawl, Yaron," she says, she begs, and I have no choice.

She's issued an edict, a challenge, and while I cannot believe the insanity of what I'm about to do — me, Lord of the Shadowlands — I can see no other choice. There is no other choice.

I fall to the ground on my knees like a worshipper at the altar.

KIANDAH
HEART FOREST

"CRAWL, YARON," I SAY TO THE LORD OF THE
Shadowlands, my idol, my personal, untouchable god, the
male of my dreams, the beast of my nightmares, the one who
my entire sketchbook is filled with likenesses of.

I watch the surprise and the rage flare behind his eyes and
the moment hangs suspended in time. I'm so aware of
everything. And nothing. I can't explain it. It's unlike anything
I've ever felt and it's nauseating and sickening and I never
want to stop feeling it.

My feet throb painfully and I flex my toes while the arches
lock. My face screams, so do my nipples, so does my swollen
core. Everything feels wrong, and beautiful. So swollen and
aggravated and needy, the brush of my fingers causes
immeasurable pain, but I know that the brush of his fingers
would not.

The mud that slicks my skin doesn't matter. Neither does
the rain threatening to bring down the roof of this small
house. I'm cold, yes, my nipples hard enough to cut glass even

without my heat and Lord Yaron's presence, but it's his presence that makes it possible to overcome the pain. It's his presence and the sight of his naked flesh, broad and massive and shattered and unsure, that makes it impossible for me to remember that he's the bad guy hunting for my family through the wind and the rain. I can't focus on any of it beneath his slate-grey stare. Because for the first time since I saw him — met him up close, I mean — he's not looking at me like a stern, all-knowing Lord. He's looking at me like he no longer knows anything.

And then, Lord Yaron falls.

The sound of his knees hitting the ground jolts my whole body. A moan rushes out of my mouth and I stroke my clit faster. His fist is around his cock, blocking the sight of his knot from my view. From what I've heard, every Alpha has a slightly differently shaped knot, and I've never seen a knot before in my life, not in person. I want to see Yaron's, memorize it so I can draw it again later. If this haze ever clears. But right now, he's still covering it with one hand as he collapses onto the floor, his other hand holding him upright as his legs lose their thick black fur and morph back into those of a man.

He groans deeply within his chest, his eyes slashing all over my body as if he doesn't know where to look — my clit, my fingers spreading myself wide for his perusal, my stomach and the padding of flesh beneath my belly button, my thighs and their cellulite, my breasts and chest and throat and face. It's the fact that his gaze lingers on my face the longest of anything that paints my insides in warmth. Not heat, but warmth.

"Ki…andah," he says, voice a whisper as he claws his way forward. I inhale and dip my fingers inside my body. A look of fury crosses his face which forms a snout full of angry, dagger-like teeth before reverting. "That's *mine*," he hisses.

I gasp as a horrible pain twists in my lower abdomen. He says my name again, forcing my attention to his face. His full lips are bright red, brighter than before, as he flips his face up to look at me. He releases his erection and it swings down, heavy and weighted and so deliriously thick. It pulses red and blue-green veins stand out all over it, reminding me of his strong, thick and veined forearms as he prowls closer and closer and closer…

That streak of grey hair at the front of his hairline hangs down now, wet, into his eyes. He bares his teeth at me, looking more animal than man — I think he *is* more animal than man — but I'm not afraid. Not here, injured and naked with my legs spread, in the most vulnerable position one could think of, where my hidden confidence shines.

Closer and closer he comes. The rains beat against the side of the cabin harder and harder, thrashing like their intent is to tear this place down around us. Let them. I don't care about anything except for the twisted pleasure-pain coursing through me, and the wild and manic look in his perfect sword-colored eyes.

His scent envelops me as he reaches the edge of the blanket. His right hand snakes out to grab my ankle, but I snatch my foot away and place it firmly on his shoulder, holding him at bay but only because he lets me. Most men lack the self-confidence to let themselves be dominated like this. But I knew Yaron wouldn't. I've always known. Maybe that's why half the pictures I've drawn of him have been images of him at my feet just like this. Every fantasy I've ever had since I first discovered my own sexuality comes to life, rising around me like a swell of clouds that carry me up into the sky.

"Ah ah," I say, voice not like my own. This is the voice of a vengeful angel, not a peasant born on the edge of Paradise Hole.

His rage flares again, but he stills. I can see the violent tremors happening underneath his skin, in his heavy, beautiful muscles. He's built like a statue. He's built like a god, a private god, one created just for me.

"Would you like to taste me, Yaron?" My words wrench a sound from him that can only be described as an animal's whimper.

Lord Yaron clenches his teeth and grunts through them, "Yes."

"Then you'll need to ask...*nicely*." Pain flowers through me, greedy and demanding but quieter than before, almost as if my body senses it's about to get what it wants and is happy to wait seconds. Not more.

His eyelashes reach for his heavy brows and he chokes out words I know he never thought he'd say. "Let me taste you, Omega." He surges forward. I press my foot harder into his shoulder and he flashes me his fangs. The canines are coated in silver, like he's just finished sucking the blood of some mythical creature.

"That's not what I asked for, Yaron..."

"Stop this. Let me fucking taste..."

My big toe strokes the side of his neck and then slides up the column of his throat to the underside of his jaw. I tip his head up a little further, past the point of comfort. All because he lets me. Because he's such a good fucking boy. "You're being a bad, bad boy, Berserker. If you want a taste now, you'll need to *beg*."

"Fuck you…" He roars, his eyes rolling back as he reaches down and grabs his length. He collapses onto his other forearm and roughly tugs at his hair before wrenching back up and grabbing my ankle. He bites the arch of my foot before letting it fall back to his shoulder. He looks up at me. His eyes are glowing, like starlight. "Let me taste you, Omega…*please*. Kiandah, please…" *Kiandah…* It comes as a shock, hearing my name in his voice. I didn't…even know he knew it.

"Such a good boy." My heart is pounding. Can he hear it? "Come, collect your treat."

He launches himself forward, the bands holding him back snapping all at once. His jaw unhinges as he slaps my hands violently away from my thighs and latches himself to my core, as if his intent is to swallow all of me, all at once.

Pleasure stabs me in the chest, in the stomach, in the brain, and I collapse back onto the dirty, scratchy blanket underneath me as his tongue strokes me from the inside, hot and strong. It swirls and tugs, way, way longer than the tongue of a normal man, while his soft human lips suck and pull. His fingers dig into the outside of my hips and I distantly register pain as he punctures me with just the tips of his claws. I don't care, anyway. He can shred me to pieces so long as he doesn't stop.

"Yaron," I howl, reaching between my legs and grabbing him by the hair. I tug him where I want him and he responds to every stroke, moving down from my entrance to my ass and eating that, too, before moving back up to my clit. It takes no time at all for me to climb to that first peak. His hot mouth is all over me, tasting everything with the ravenousness of a starving man, a dying man, a wild thing, utterly lost.

I'm writhing across the floor, my body bending and contorting in unnatural positions. He's pushing me harder and higher with a punishing violence that I try to escape by jerking my hips, but he wraps his biceps underneath my thighs and holds me so that I can't move anywhere.

"You're such...such a good...Berserker...such a good... boy..." My voice spirals into an almost embarrassingly high-pitched scream as the first orgasm attacks me like no other ever has. The pain twists first like a knife in my gut before the pleasure rides over it like a horse trampling grass.

My mind spirals out, my thoughts short. Lightning crashes somewhere nearby and I feel a swell of heat at my back. The fireplace. It erupts. Lord Yaron's arms tighten on my thighs and I feel his body jolt and his tongue pause in its next stroke, but I'm not afraid. I battle my emotions back as easily as I batter the fire. He should know that I'd never let fire hurt him.

"I won't let it hurt you," I think that I say, but maybe I don't. I can't catch my breath and am still struggling to determine if I'm alive or if I've already passed through to the Shallow Plains. If I have, then my time has come early, but to have gotten the chance to experience this, it would have been enough.

I stare up at the ceiling, my heartrate exploding through me blisteringly as satisfaction snowballs into something else. *Need.* *"Kiandah,"* comes the strangled whisper as his tongue finally slides out of my body.

I moan wildly, but I manage to struggle up onto my elbows. I look down the length of my body to see Lord Yaron staring at me with an expression that causes my insides to do something dangerous. Something I'm not sure they'll ever come back from. Because I know I won't.

He...the Shadow Lord...the man I never thought I'd ever be alone in a room with, let alone...like *this*...is looking at me after having satisfied me even though I've done nothing to reciprocate... He's watching me with pure adoration and desire while he nuzzles the inside of my thigh with his human nose.

He's looking at me like I imagine someone would look at another when they are in *love.*

"Yaron, please..." Fuck. Now it's my turn to beg. I hadn't planned on that. I'd planned to kick him in the shoulder, force him onto his back, sit on his face and take his cock in my mouth. But now... His eyes flare. I choke out, "Come take me."

He growls, sounding appreciative, grateful even, and I haven't even done anything yet. I drop down onto the scratchy blanket beneath me while Lord Yaron prowls over my body. A momentary spike of panic grips me as I register how completely huge he is — in every possible sense — his presence, his penis, his muscular build, his thick neck. He plants one forearm beside my head and his other hand flits over my body from my neck to my breast, tickling my nipple before skating over my rib and stomach and hip to my thigh. Never lingering, teasing mercilessly, while the pressure of my heat builds, ready for him to sate me a second time.

He hooks his hand beneath my knee and spreads me open wide while I pet his hair and his neck and his jaw. I try to pull him down to me, but he resists, eyes flaring. "I won't kiss you, Omega," he says to me, killing the fantasy…which is foolish, really, if I think about it…

I should have known better than to fantasize.

Through my momentary dismay, I just smile. "Yes, you will, Yaron." I'm not even sure if I care that much if he kisses me, but this is what I like. The power I don't have and can't exert in my daily life comes out here in full bloom. He does not love me, and if I used my whole head, I'd remember that I wouldn't want him to. He's my enemy. He holds my life in his hands and, more importantly than that, he collared and chained my family. But right now? I don't need his love. I need him to be a good fucking boy or take his licks.

"You will submit," he says to me, but his voice is pitched in question.

I can't help but laugh. "No, Yaron. This time, like every time, *you* will submit to *me*. Now fuck me, before I decide you've been too naughty to touch me anymore. But kiss me first."

Yaron sucks in a sharp breath, as if truly compelled by that threat, and rocks his hips forward without another word of protest. His pubic bone rests heavy on mine, trapping me against the floor in a way that makes me want to die just so I can stay here forever. The bloated head of his erection slides between my lips, hitting my clit as he pushes forward, sliding his cock through my slick. I try to stay confident, try not to let my eyes roll back, or to release the crazed wail building in my throat.

Yaron moans first, filling me with vindication. His head flops forward like it's no longer tethered to its anchoring string. His stubbled cheek brushes my swollen one and he whispers in my ear, "What are you doing to me?"

I whisper back, "Nothing you don't deserve."

He lifts up ever so slightly, just enough to tenderly, oh so gently, kiss me. It's a closed mouth kiss. One might call it chaste if they ignored everything else about our position. But it's good. *So* good. Sweet, almost, if anything about him could be called that. To reward him, my hips lift up and roll, massaging his cock and feeling the bulge of his knot at its base. My gods, it's going to feel so good inside of me… I can't wait.

I slide my arms around his shoulders and Yaron releases a strangled sound. He pulls back, his giant hand cradling the back of my head. He tilts my face up and kisses my upper lip, tasting it with his tongue and trying to deepen the kiss, but I pull back. Kissing is…very intimate. And he's good at it. And if he doesn't really want to be here, I need to protect myself against getting attached.

"You can fuck me now, Yaron," I say, panting.

But he hesitates. He is still hovering above me, his hand around my face. He's watching my mouth with his eyebrows drawn together, like I'm speaking in tongues.

"What are you waiting for, Lord?"

"For this feeling…to go away…" he chokes out while one of his great big hands reaches between our bodies. He lines himself up with my entrance, the smooth, rounded head of his erection pushing at my opening. He pushes any harder, he's going to fall inside of me. I'm slicker than I've ever been.

"What feeling?" I ask, though I don't care. He's torturing me and I refuse to allow him to unravel me before I can do the same. "Come on, Yaron…"

"You feel like fire."

Something patters in my chest out of tune with my heart's beat. "You…"

"And I cannot douse you." He jacks his hips forward, the movement sharp enough to splinter my concentration on whatever he might have been about to say next. He sheaths himself inside of me and I almost die of a heart attack when I realize he's only halfway in.

"Yaron, you're huge," I whisper.

"And you're clenching me like you're trying to ruin any other female for me…" He barks out, "Or snap my dick clean off."

I can't help but laugh. My claws rake down his back, scoring him, hopefully. He hisses and pulls up enough to be able to lean back down and kiss me again. This time, he shoves his tongue past the barrier of my lips and drags it over the roof of my mouth. He surges forward just a little further, filling me up so right, so tight. It's like nothing I've felt before. He's the biggest I've ever taken, sure, but this heat is magnifying that pressure. I'm so swollen down there, everything hurts. So tender.

He jerks forward one final time, enough that his not yet inflated knot slams into me, still thicker around than the rest of his penis. Pain strikes at me with its claws and I tense.

Yaron wrenches his lips away from me, brows furrowed. My eyelids flutter and I'm aware only enough to know that he's searching my face with his eyes while smoothing his hand from my forehead back over my bald scalp.

He frowns and manages to sound strangely sober even with red blotching his cheeks and his pupils fully blown. "Are you in...pain?" he clenches out.

I nod feverishly. "I need to come, baby. Please. Don't you dare stop."

He thrusts a little further and I seize up. Maybe, I was wrong. Maybe, this isn't going to work. I thought he was finished, fully seated inside of me. I didn't think he could be this large. A little of my other self — Kiandah the cook — crawls into my confidence and stirs the pot. I feel restless and struggle suddenly to meet his gaze as water wells in mine. My nose feels puffy and suddenly my swollen eye and puffy red lips and bald head feel scarily unattractive. Holy hell. I completely forgot what I looked like until now. I shouldn't be here. I can't take him...

"Kiandah," he whispers, his fingertips trailing over my cheek successfully snapping me back into the present. "Do not deny me now..."

"I can't..."

"Must I beg, again? Because I will." His hips start moving in tiny circles, pumping slowly in and out of me. "Please, Kiandah, please...I am utterly and entirely at your mercy. Please...have me..."

I gasp and lightning comes alive inside of me. The fire crackles viciously and I open my mouth and my back arches involuntarily. A spasm slaps my clit and when his pubic hair roughly rubs against it, I almost detonate. I almost come right there, just from hearing my name in his voice. From hearing him beg, using words so beautiful, I'm never, ever going to forget them.

"Holy fuck," I gasp.

"Fuck," Yaron roars at the exact same moment. He grabs my shoulder and, when that doesn't work, he places his entire forearm across my chest, holding me down. He drops his head and pants, like he's in a full-out sprint. "Are you going to incinerate me while I'm inside of you, Kiandah?"

"No," I reply, eyelids fluttering, fingers scratching his back, seeking purchase in his flesh anywhere that I can. My hesitation is gone, that other Kiandah is dead. I can't find her within me anywhere now. "I'm going to bring you to heel."

He moans and before I know what's happened, he's withdrawn and pushed himself all the way inside of me again. His knot stuffs me full, tickling the most delicious spot at the base of my entrance. I have a sensitive spot there, in addition to one just inside, and my clit, and somehow, with all his unholy parts, he's hitting all three at once.

Pleasure and panic war within my channel, everything stretching, too big and too swollen and too sensitive. Nerve endings I didn't know existed alight all the way up to my cervix. It hurts. It feels magical. I can feel tears pressing from my squeezed eyelids like diamonds squeezed from between rocks. I'm taut, tension lacing my body…

"Are you okay, Kiandah? Does it feel good? Tell me. If it doesn't, command me and I'll do something else — whatever you want — I'll stop…" And then his lips touch my lips, just a whisper, just a brush of them, and everything comes apart.

I return his kiss with every ounce of me, my untethered leg hooking around his back while he keeps my other propped open to the side with his knee. The fingers of his left hand are buried in my ass cheek again while his right hand holds the front of my throat, angling my head so he can better devour me while he thrusts. He's worked back up into a steady rhythm now — fast and hard, not too hard but just enough of both. He's making animalistic sounds and I'm fucking screaming.

"Yes, Yaron, just like that…don't stop…" and every time I tell him how well he's doing, he thrusts harder, changes position, rubs my clit, applies more friction. His hands are scrabbling over me and mine are clinging to him like we're both trying to climb the same mountain and it's a competition that we both want to win.

I grab the hair at the back of his neck in both of my fists and wrench his head back, exposing his neck to me. I bite down hard along his jugular, wanting him to feel pain as I work my way up in bites and licks, soothing the places I've bitten him, wanting to draw blood.

To mark.

To claim.

To bond. No…

"Omega," he tries, but he's gasping for air.

I give his head a rough shake, bordering on cruel, and the behemoth of a male above me shudders. His legs grow taut. "I'm going to come…"

"No," I practically scream, "Not until I do. You'll wait or I'll have to punish you."

"Gods, fuck you, Kiandah. You're…already punishing me." He fucks me harder, pounding into me with powerful thrusts that aren't *safe*. He's much bigger than I am and I'm aware that he's *too* big and I'm injured already and haven't had food or water or rest in what feels like days. But still I say, "Yes, Yaron! Harder." I order and he obeys.

My breaths start to come shorter and my muscles start to burn with a familiar tingle that feels like it usually does, only a hundred million thousand times more potent. He snakes his massive arm around my backside and slides a finger into my ass. His pubic bone grinds hard against my clit and he bellows out a moan as he breaks first.

"Fuck…sorry…Kiandah…I can't…hold…" I open my eyes and it's seeing Yaron's face twisted into something unrecognizable, losing himself to the feel of me, that catapults me off of that cliff's unforgiving edge.

I wrench his dark red lips to mine and force my tongue inside to sample the taste that is his, entirely unique, while I fling out into oblivion. Everything vanishes. I fall into the void. I know that the fire has exploded and I can feel a gush of cold air and icy water trying to douse me, but it's still warm. Everything's still warm. My legs…the places where they should be…are all raw tingles. My heartbeat is erratic, my clit is a single kernel of intensity, and my inner walls are thunder, but I am aware of a greater pressure expanding inside of me.

He roars, a guttural and raspy sound, and even though my mind is dancing far, far away from me, I can still hear that. I can feel fur under my fingertips and I hold onto it, trying to cage both man and beast. My eyes flutter open and I see him staring at me. His gaze drops and I follow it down and see that he's fully seated. His knot is inside me and I smile, even as I feel it ballooning threateningly. Everything is right. Almost everything. Just one thing is missing.

I glance at his teeth. His fangs are out, long and shaped like arrowheads and dripping silver venom onto me. It feels warm and pleasurable as it bursts onto my face, my cheeks and forehead and chin. If this were any other heat, he would bond me now. But that can never be and even if it could, neither one of us *wants* that — to bond a peasant and a criminal, to bond the Lord whose captured her family.

Without the bond, the pain of the knot is cutting through my high. My orgasm has crested and I feel like it might have been able to continue if he'd given me an antidote for the pain. But he won't and I couldn't accept even if he had.

His voice hitches as he looks into my eyes and I can sense that he's on another plane still as his knot swells and he continues to release inside of me. *No condom.* Fuck. I can't think about that now.

The swelling hasn't stopped. I try to pull away, but the sting is acute. Oh no. I want off this train. *Now.* I whimper and Yaron's eyes flare with panic. He moves just slightly to reposition himself, but it's uncomfortable enough that I cry out.

"No," Yaron grits. He clenches his teeth. More venom spills and a sudden fervor comes over him. He milks his incisors for venom and then reaches between us and uses his venom-coated fingers to stroke my clit. At the same time, his lips alight on my neck. He kisses me everywhere, again and again.

"I can feel your slick," he says against my earlobe. He sucks on it lovingly, laving it with his tongue while his hands worship my clit and breasts. He toys with my nipples and while I've never been exceptionally sensitive there, the dual sensations war and I feel pleasure once again start to take over. "Yes, that's a good girl. Take my knot. You know you can take it."

Good girl, he says to me. No one's ever said that to me before.

I gasp and mewl, whimpering emphatically and encouragingly. I want him so badly I feel my arms fly out and grasp at anything they can. We're suddenly kissing harder and he's working me up, building me, taking me higher and higher again.

"Yes," I whisper.

"Tell me what you feel," he says.

"I feel you, Yaron. I feel you everywhere... You're such a good Berserker, taking care of your Omega like this."

"Yes..." His hips twitch and I feel a prick of pain — and then pleasure. It's a beautiful thing. I lose control, and accept everything he's offering.

I come for him, and though it's not as powerful as it was the first time, it's enough to keep me sated and to fight off the momentary pain of his knot for now, and hopefully, for good. He's kissing me as I come down from my orgasm, still touching me in my places that are all too sensitive and yet still wanting. I've come three times but I still crave him. This isn't over.

"You're such a sweet Omega. You feel incredible. Like nothing I've felt before. Thank you. My knot will last a while… I'll let you know when it's okay to release… But I warn you now, Kiandah. Your heat isn't over. When I release you, I'm going to want more…"

"No," I whisper as my consciousness starts to fade and I drift into a strained sleep in the cage of his arms. "You're going to beg for it."

YARON
HEART FOREST

I BEG FOR IT. "PLEASE, OMEGA, PLEASE... KIANDAH, take my cock, please. Will you please taste me? Will you please drink my cum?" If I beg her, I learn quickly, she'll do whatever I want.

Dear gods help me.

Help us.

I'm vaguely aware that there's blood somewhere, that I should be concerned. It's also touched my awareness that the fireplace is no longer where it was when the evening began and that earth from the hillside now pours into half the cabin. The shutters on the windows and door are blown open. Rain has spilled all over the floor. There were rations of food, but they're ruined now. There is only the Omega and her sweet slick and her body that calls to me and her voice that works me like an instrument to play whatever notes she likes and do whatever she commands.

My Omega mewls while I nuzzle her neck with my nose, seeking comfort, seeking affection. I am not who I was when I entered this shack. I am no Shadow Lord. I am Lord of Desperation.

"You're such a good Berserker," she whispers and I bellow out a roar that shakes the foundation of the cottage. No, the few floorboards that are left. Cold air whooshes across my back, but the fire is still strong. There is no hearth, but a scattering of stones. The fire emanates from them in soft waves, beating in time with her pulse. It pays no mind to the rain.

The moment my knot deflates enough for me to be able to move, I start to pump in and out of her. I don't know how many times I've knotted her — at least six — and I cannot stop now. Lying on our sides, limbs intertwined, I inhale against her throat, wishing, wanting to bond her... Maybe I just should.

"No biting, Berserker," she says, voice all but a whisper.

I snarl and tip her chin up so I can better access her mouth. "Why not?"

"You haven't been a good enough Berserker for that." Her voice is breathy, but severe. I don't understand the combination. I don't understand this woman at all. All I know is the need I feel for her, not just to have her body, but to prove her wrong.

I kiss her slowly, as if we are safely in my chambers in the castle, warm and dry and well-fed with all the time in the world. I match her thrusts to the rhythm of my tongue and she moans, swallowing as my venom drips against her tongue. If she won't let me bond her yet, then this will have to be enough.

Bond...her... I never meant...

"Berserker, you're doing so well…"

So easily she matches the pace that I set. My eyes roll back. *She was made for me.* I feel my seed building again, ready and eager to breed her even though her body is full of my cum already. It coats her thighs, a sticky paste that fills me with dark male pride. I shudder out a groan when she tugs on my hair and slowly rakes her fingers down my back, scoring my skin with her nails. Never has there been a more tortured or languid descent into madness, I'm sure of it.

"Please come for me, Omega," I plead. "Please come for your Berserker."

As if I've pressed a button, the Omega comes on my command. I thrust frantically, hoping to chase her into a second release before the first fades. She wails my name. My *name.* "Yes, yes! Oh gods! Yaron…" She screams and I try to hold, wanting this to last even as her body squeezes mine in every possible way. Her channel tightens and spasms around my length and my hips stutter.

"I'm going to come, Kiandah. Do I…have your… permission?"

I pause, waiting, wanting the permission she gives so discriminately. Wanting to know how she'll change the game, or up the stakes. She doesn't disappoint. The moment she comes down from her high, she lifts her tired, swollen eyelids and spears me with a gaze belonging to a goddess.

"You did such a good job, Berserker, I think you deserve a reward. Don't you?" She whispers in my ear and I stiffen, mouth drying. I nod frantically, wanting it, craving it with a passion and zeal that borders on insanity.

"Yes, Omega," I choke.

She smiles devilishly and her loose limbs start to disentangle themselves from my body, robbing me of her warmth. I feel cold, chilled to the bone and I don't like it. I reach for her but she holds up one finger and I still, desperation changing me irrevocably.

Her sweat-and-cum-slicked body glimmers. She's so perfect. Pure. Hellish. I want to own her. *What?* The thought strikes and it's all wrong, but it's there and unshakable, just like the desire to bond her. There's some part of me that knows how wrong it is, but the other part — the entirety of my soul — doesn't care. She's mine. She has carved her name inside of my eyelids with the embers she wields.

The fire explodes just a little hotter and the Omega turns her back to me, presenting me a vision of her tight asshole and sloppy, swollen sex. Oh my gods, please tell me to lick her clean… I want that badly. I jerk forward, wanting to take her with my tongue, but before I can, she arches her back and walks her palms out in front of her until her left cheek touches the ground and her hips remain propped up over her knees.

She slips her left arm beneath her body and spreads her lower lips wide. Semen drips out of her and I release a burst of precum. It shoots out of me with such force, it paints the back of her right thigh. I curse and she laughs softly. "Your Omega is presenting for you, Berserker. Come take me like a beast."

My human legs turn into the massive hind legs of a lupine creature as they bear into wet soil. There are no floorboards, not anymore. My entire body slams into her, taking her to the floor directly before her sentient flames, and it's here that I continue to rut her savagely and on her command. It is here that I lose my mind.

Inside, my beast preens.

It's a beautiful thing. Mad, savage destruction. Not of the hunter's hole, not of her body or mine, but of my soul.

YARON
HEART FOREST

THE SKY CRACKLES WITH THUNDER AND, AGAINST MY bare back, I feel the soft woosh of an icy wind. Where is she?

My eyes open on a pounding panic, frantic and worried for my Omega. Where is she? But the moment I move my arms — my limbs, for they are completely covered in fur, as is the rest of me — I hear a soft sigh. I look down and, past my snout, can just see the top of the Omega's head. Her limbs are curled against my beast's torso, tangled in silver fur, and I exhale.

She's warm. She's dry. My beast did well. I did not, rutting her out here in the woods like a savage. I hit her, harmed her, while my beast provided shelter. It is…not much of a shelter — better than nothing, but certainly not sufficient enough for her to stay here, no matter how peacefully she may be sleeping at the moment.

Gathering the reserves of my strength from deep, I rise with the Omega cradled against my chest. I hold her in one of my arms, which forces me to walk uncomfortably on three legs. It is a great distance to the keep, but I have no other choice. I've torn the hunter's hole to pieces. There is nothing left but a few posts still miraculously standing. The fire that she lit is gone. The rains have stopped, but the air is still heavy with their memory. It is my favorite weather, but I wish for something else now. I wish for sun. I need it for her, because her skin is cool even though she smells of a bonfire roaring in the daylight.

She sleeps the entire way back to the keep. I would be proud of my gracefulness that I made it possible for her to sleep so well and so continuously, but I wasn't graceful and still, she sleeps. The swelling in her face has not gone down and her body temperature seems too low for her having been pressed against me for all this time. Her heartrate is persistent, but slow. It feels like...like her body is shutting down.

I've never experienced panic like this before. True fear. A harrowing horror. My body is consumed and physical pain shoots through my heels as I pick up speed, eventually reaching the far edge of the Heart Forest, which gives way to the darker terrain of Paradise Hole, which ends at the highway line that leads to Undoline. But I don't take the roads. I sprint across the farming villages, across the sodden ground, through cornfields and flat farmlands until finally, I see the keep on the horizon.

I kick up clods of soil the size of boulders as I race until the gates cast a shadow long enough for me to fall beneath. The gates are black and imposing, studded with spikes that usually boast the heads of my enemies — and will boast the head of the Trash City female soon enough — but right now the spikes are all vacant. The guards, spying me, immediately issue orders to open up.

I advance into the courtyard of the keep and become aware of the Alphas that number among my staff. I don't like their presence, don't like them here. On a snarl, I race inside with her, the towering stones of the keep swallowing us whole. My beast is still here. My other form is nowhere to be found.

My staff all stare and duck out of my path as I charge down the open corridors into the main vestibule. The keep is structured poorly, despite it being new. Four outer walls contain a courtyard which surrounds a massive castle, but the castle has been expanded and then expanded again. An entire partition has been built out down the southern hill and the western wall curves clumsily to meet it. A lower floor half submerged in earth holds the upper dungeons, where the Omega's family was held, and below that there is a lower dungeon for the more insidiously aligned prisoners who will never see light again.

Inside the vestibule with its vaulted ceilings, airy walkways branch out in every direction. A double helix staircase wraps around itself before me and ascends all five floors of the castle. I take it, my claws scratching at the carpet and the stone beneath it, up to the second floor. I go east, down to the farthest point of the longest hallway, and then through the double doors up the grand staircase that leads to the east wing and my private quarters. I take her to my private quarters without thinking. Thought does not matter, anyway. It's where I would have taken her had I thought about this decision for a year.

My beast form is too large to fit through the doorway to my chambers so, reluctantly, I reach deep within the recesses of my sanity to find my bipedal legs and furless limbs and draw them forward. Still cradling Kiandah, I throw open the door and barrel inside, but it's here that I hesitate. Standing just inside of my private chambers, surely looking like a wild man with skin covered in dirt and mud and hair in tangles, I'm uneasy. Whispers echo up the stairs from below and are followed by the sound of footsteps, trudging up here to my private quarters. How *dare* they.

"Back," I hiss, edging further into my room, prepared to defend it as if it were a castle and she the treasure in my arms they intend to plunder. *Over my corpse.* The trespassers have reached the door, which still hangs open. Shielding Kiandah from view, I look over my shoulder, my face half monster, half man. My gaze narrows on Radmilla — one of only four individuals ever allowed into my private quarters and only with permission, a permission she does not now have. The other two with her are not on the guest list and Horace… Horace is an Alpha. If I were not carrying the Omega with such delicacy, I'd cross the threshold and tear him down where he stands.

He must sense how close he is to danger because he speaks first, despite being the most junior member of the cluster, and stops dead in his tracks. *He's going to be dead in his tracks.* "My Lord, I mean no harm. I am only here to support Okayo in assessing your injuries and tending to the Omega, if that's what you wish…"

"That is not what I wish. Get out!" I release a roar so loud it causes Radmilla to trip.

Okayo catches her upper arm, but he is fearless. He continues a casual advance through the doorway to my quarters. Casual, all but the swallowing. He swallows many times. *Perhaps, not so casual.* "My Lord, we heard alarming reports from the Crimson Riders in the Heart Forest. It seems that you defied standard protocol and bred the Omega over the course of two days." Two days. "A little more." A little more. "I'm assuming she went into heat." He continues speaking, but I am too stunned to hear him. I am astounded. Both that we were gone for so much time and that we were gone for so little. A two-day heat is short for an Omega. The standing record for an Omega heat is twelve days.

"...in the hunter's lodge you'd have found provisions, yet she may still be undernourished." Undernourished. Provisions. I fed her nothing. I gave her no water. "Most Omegas tend to suffer from poor nutrition after a heat, especially when serviced by a single Alpha and not a pack. Dehydration, as well." Dehydration.

He's a dozen steps away from me now and reaches up to scratch his throat. But he dares to meet my eyes. "Were you able to feed her at all or did the rains interfere? I'm assuming you were able to give her water, given the abundance." He tries a smile, which illuminates his youthful face, but I've begun to panic. I stop where I am and lay the Omega down on the thick black fur at my feet. My beastly claws scratch at my chest, morphing back into nails. My beast is retreating on whimpers I can hear in my skull, but that do not rise in my throat. My two legs feel suddenly inadequate. I'm shaking. My heart beats erratically.

"I offered her neither food nor water. Her heat came on strong and I was lost to it."

Radmilla, somewhere nearby, gasps. I want to claw out her esophagus to keep her from making such a sound again. It fills me with so great a shame I have not the emotional depth to process it. She has been more of a mother to me than my own mother ever was. To hear her disappointment now would have crushed me, if I were not already crushed by the sight of the Omega in my grasp.

"You…" Okayo starts, sounding flabbergasted for a moment before he straightens and points with authority. "Get her on the bed unless you'd like to bond her here."

I would like to bond her here and it is not a sense of duty that stops me from it, but a memory of a story that was told to me once by the Berserker of Dark City. My heart is hammering. Venom drips into my mouth from fangs that have yet to fully retract. I look at Okayo, mud and sticks whipping off of my hair and splattering his skin as he crouches beside her and looks down at her body with worry and anger.

"What if it does not work?"

His neck snaps up. The three beings in the room besides the Omega and me go so still it feels as if they've been frozen by time. Then a cool breeze filters up from the stairwell below and through the open door. "I…" Okayo begins. His mouth opens and closes several times.

Radmilla comes to his rescue, shuffling further into the room, pink high in her otherwise pale cheeks. She looks at Okayo, speaking to him directly and subsequently ignoring me. It is a foreign sensation. "What medical equipment do you need?"

That snaps him out of his trance. "Horace, you know what we need. Fetch it now. Bring Finn to help. Radmilla, we'll need hot water, potable water, and food prepared for when the Omega wakes. Something soft and easy to chew for now."

"Of course. In the meantime, Lord Yaron, I suggest you bathe. I'll be in shortly with sustenance for you as well…"

"No." I'm still seething, panic riding me hard, making me clench so violently I'm concerned I'll splinter all of my teeth. "I'm not leaving her."

The world goes still again, but for a shorter beat. Okayo is in motion. Horace is racing backward down the stairs and I'm carrying the Omega to the only place I can think to bring her — my bed. And as my feet trip over one another, struggling to maintain human toes as I continue to fight with my beast, I make him assurances to regain control… assurances that I am not sure how I will keep. Because all my beast wants in this moment is a guarantee that my bed will be the only place she ever sleeps.

YARON
SHADOW KEEP

I AM NOT THE MALE I WAS BEFORE THE RAINS. BEFORE the hunter's hole. Before she asked me to do something damning — to drop to my knees and crawl. My entire world has been thrown off of its axis and I do not know who I am anymore.

I am shame.

I am need.

It's been hours and the Omega's vitals are scarcely improving, even though Okayo and fucking *Horace* and Finn, a medic and a male Beta, have been working tirelessly to keep her pulse steady, her lungs pumping and her temperature up. Yet, for all of their efforts, the only visible displays of their progress are the doctored wounds on her feet and hands, the smaller cuts on her lip and cheek. She's still slipping away, a small, contented smile on her face, like she's at peace. Like she's perfectly fine to leave this plane of existence and that's not going to fucking work for me. It cannot.

The males look to me. Radmilla hovers in the room, standing awkwardly some feet away from the foot of the bed. She's uncomfortable in here, but there are places she could have chosen in the center of the wide-open space to sit. No, she's worried. She wants to see what's happening to the Omega, too. To *me. I don't know. I don't know anything.*

Radmilla's fingers fumble over her lips uselessly as she prays to the old gods. Many worship the old gods, some the new, some revere animal gods, while others worship their ancestors. Like the Ubutus. I wonder if Kiandah's ancestors are here with her now or if they abandoned her in the heart tree or even, before that — the moment that they brought the dead into their kitchens for purposes only the damned can guess at. I glance at Radmilla, hoping that for the Omega's sake, she calls to them, too. Because if any moment calls for prayer, it is this one. We've exhausted other options.

"Lord Yaron, what'll it be?" Okayo says to me.

I open my mouth to reply, but all I can think about is a memory that isn't even mine, but that belongs to Berserker Dragnovic. He failed his Omega when he attempted to force his bond.

"My Lord, we don't have much time. What do you decide?" Finn says, out of turn and out of line. He is the lowest ranked person in this room, but I do not reprimand him for it. Not now. I look up at the room full of worried stares with one single looming worry of my own. They think I have a choice to make, but they're wrong. I have already chosen. But I am not certain that *she* has.

"It is understandable for you to decline to bond this Omega," Horace says softly. Fucking Horace is the last person I'd like to hear from now, especially when it comes to the topic of cutting this Omega free for another Alpha pack to ravage her and worship her and breed and bond her and take her away from me. I release a low snarl, which Horace promptly misinterprets or ignores. "No Shadow Lord has bonded an Omega in six hundred years. It is a heavy choice to make simply to spare this one, especially knowing that she and her family are criminals…"

"Is there a way to test its efficacy?" I say, ignoring Horace entirely and focusing on Okayo so that I don't do something drastic. Like bite Horace's head clean off.

Okayo blinks at me from over the Omega's sleeping body, looking strained, looking stunned. He has beads of sweat coalescing along his hairline. His hair is short, a shock of tight black curls and coils. His nostrils, wideset already, flare further. "You aren't hesitating because she's a criminal or because of tradition, are you?"

A dawning comprehension changes his face entirely, its shape rounds. He softens. He looks like he's aged in reverse a decade or more, and he already looked young before. Now, he looks at me with all the green novelty of a boy discovering a fictitious deity was real all along. And then the smile he wears falls as he turns over my words. His brows knot. He whispers, "You don't think it will work."

He's right. And one more drop of blood lost could be what kills her. "I wish to be certain before I tear open her throat." *As Berserker Dragnovic did once.* My voice sounds far more ragged than I intended.

A look of grim determination replaces the surprise Okayo wore before. He reaches across the Omega's body and pulls her wrist out from beneath the black blanket. "We'll try to be direct. See if we can't ensure that you inject your venom into her vein as directly as possible. The puncture wound you create will have to be precise and small."

I nod, understanding what he means and hating it. This is not how I dreamt of bonding my Omega. Though of course, as Lord of the Shadowlands, I'd never, ever have dreamed or hoped or longed for this. Never.

After securing a band around her upper arm, he guides her wrist to my mouth and instructs me to open. He uses his own goddamn hand to position my fang and I hate it. Hate it. Having to rely on another to bond my Omega properly. My Omega. *Mine.* I meet Okayo's gaze and it's as if we share the same thought at the same time because we both look down at Kiandah's face.

"She'll be your Omega, Lady of the Shadowlands, if this works, Lord Yaron — and a criminal besides. The fallout will be…"

"I know."

Okayo nods. "Then, are you ready?"

"You don't have to do this," Horace insists and it's that insistence that does it for me.

I bite down *softly*. I can feel the moment her blood meets my fang because the venom within my glands surges, feeling cool on the inside of my fang and hot on the outside in a rare combination that's painful and only soothed when the fang is fully submerged in the flesh of its target, which mine is not.

"That's enough," Okayo says, guiding me away. "Let's see how she handles it."

I pull back, unspent venom filling my mouth and forcing me to swallow the slightly bitter taste. I don't like it. I don't like any part of this. I especially don't like Okayo administering to my Omega when that responsibility should now be mine, and I truly loathe the way Horace is looking down at her with his head slightly cocked as if he remembers her from somewhere he can't quite place.

"What is it?" I bark, startling the three medics.

Okayo rounds the bed and pushes me out of the way, leaving Horace to take his place. Okayo is staring down at her wrist while occasionally looking up at Horace, a silent conversation that I hate passing between them.

"Your Lord asked you a question," Radmilla tuts, having come closer to the foot of the bed. She takes a seat upon it and reaches out to touch the Omega's foot through the blankets. Like a mom. A good mom, though she never had any of her own children and it's too late now. Her husband died young, in a battle with Hjiel that took place before I was born and whose casualties caused our two cities to finally sign the Treaty of the South Island. Though there are still lingering tensions and skirmishes among tribes and villagers at the borders, there haven't been battles between our cities since.

Radmilla's gaze is soft — and it is never soft — as she stares down at Kiandah, wearing a frown. Her grey hair is unbound down her back. It was once raven-black, though few traces of that remain. Her skin, which holds a pale, peachy hue, is now flushed. She looks like there is much she'd like to say but she manages to hold her tongue, for once. For the most part.

"Is our Lady well?" Lady. Our Lady.

Gods. The warm pride that surges through my chest is wholly unexpected. It pulls and strains, like stitching pulled taut over a wound. My tongue feels bloated in my mouth and my stomach fills with *butterflies*. Butterflies. I look down at the female and stroke the back of my hand over her still-dirty cheek. Her face, which had been impassive, eerily so, twitches and turns towards me. *She's mine. Of course she would react to...*

Okayo makes a clicking sound. "It's unclear."

"Unclear?" Radmilla says, brows furrowing.

The three medics nod. Finn, having pulled a desk over, closer to the bed, seems to be painting small dabs of the Omega's blood over strips of fabric. He shakes his head. "Her blood is coagulating properly, her temperature has come up and her lungs sound clear — they weren't before."

My heart beats harder. Slower, but more forcefully. Does that mean...

"Her heart arrhythmia has also faded. Her pulse is steady and stable," Okayo says, listening once again to the scope he has placed on her chest. "She'll make a full recovery."

"But..." Horace. Fucking Horace. "She doesn't scent of you, m'Lord." He turns his gaze to meet mine, but doesn't hold it for long. I'm distracted from wondering whether Kiandah would find Horace good-looking with his thin build, slick black hair, naturally tanned skin, round face, wide set nose and narrow eyes that I don't immediately understand what he's said. *Would he be her good boy?* "My Lord." He has spent so many years among high born classes, yet his accent still slips.

"What." My tone is flat, not a question at all.

"Her external wounds also aren't closing." Okayo shakes his head and, beneath his breath, mutters curses. "Her body is using your venom for some things, but not others. And you say she doesn't have a deterring scent marker?" he asks Horace, though that infuriates me. He could ask me. I don't smell it, either.

Horace glances at me again with black eyes and rosy cheeks. "No. In fact, she still kind of smells like she's in heat."

I growl and feel my shoulders rise. Okayo speaks over my restrained threat. "That's normal. Her heat cycle only just ended, the scent will clear in a day or two, in which time she'll be sequestered here anyway, healing. Hopefully Lord Yaron's venom has healed her most significant wounds. As for the rest, we'll continue to administer to them. Lord Yaron, you should be relieved to know that it seems you haven't successfully bonded the Omega, you've…sort of bonded her. And at least, the worst of the damage seems to be healing, albeit slowly. Really slowly."

Relieved?

I hear his words, but they filter to me slowly. So slowly. The trickle of rain droplets over a smooth stone. The warmth in my chest dies, though the butterflies in my stomach don't.

"It would seem that this Omega has the same problem the Fallen Earth Omega did when Berserker Dragnovic attempted to bond her. It looks like she's the one calling the shots." Yes, she does, I think to myself, though I don't have any clue what Okayo is referring to. "It looks like it isn't just about whether you've chosen to give her your bond. This Omega will need to choose the Alpha she'll be bonded to."

Choose. Choice. Desire. The words feel flimsy and foreign to me, and yet, I can feel that warmth kindling in my chest once more, fanned by the urgency to make her mine.

In my reluctance to speak and voice these thoughts aloud, Radmilla steps up to my left shoulder and lowers her voice to a near whisper. "My Lord, you should also know that while you were gone, the Crimson Riders were able to recapture the Omega's family. They have been returned to the dungeons."

Choose — she will never choose the Lord who keeps her family in chains.

Choice — there is none when it comes down to me against allegiance to her kin.

Desire — is moot. Hers will never be again. Mine? Mine will fade as I arm myself with the knowledge that I can never have her. This Shadow Lord will remain like all the rest. Unmated. Alone. History will not be rewritten on this day and it is for the best. "It is for the best."

"My Lord?" Radmilla says. The medics are no longer looking at me but conferring amongst themselves.

"Okayo is right. It is for the best that the Omega and I were not able to complete a true bond. I will see her to good health and she will be mated with an Alpha or pack beneath the next red moon." *Over my dead* — "Meanwhile, I will handle her family." As I say the words aloud, I batter my beast down, forcing him to heel. Him. He feels like an outsider for the first time since my ascension thirty-eight years previous.

He howls and spits and bays. I ignore him. I douse the glow in my chest. I take all of the tattered pieces of that boyish desire I've never dared hope to hold and gather them up, lock them in a chest, and toss that chest to the bottom of the ocean. Because I did have such hopes. *A* hope, singularly.

The hope of having one thing that belongs, not to all of my people, but just to me. The hope of having her, Kiandah, look down at me with fire in her eyes and flames at her back and bring all my yearning to the fore. The hope of serving the Lady Kiandah as a good Lord should serve the Omega that belongs to him and only him. That is his and only his. The good Lord who is only hers.

Mine. What would it be like to call her mine in longing and in life? No. That moment is over. My beast howls. I tuck my grief away. It has no business with me now. I am the Shadow Lord.

"Let me go now and deal with the traitors." I nod once to Radmilla and struggle to my feet. The greater struggle is leaving the room, leaving the Omega behind, and leaving that one singular hope behind forever. Where I go now and what I intend to do, she will never forgive and I do not need her to.

I remember who I am.

I am Lord of the Shadowlands and she is not my Omega.

KIANDAH
SHADOW KEEP

I DON'T FEEL WELL. I DON'T FEEL WELL AT ALL. I FEEL
sick and hurt and just downright *strange*. I've felt this way since
I woke up three days ago. And the presence of the Shadow
Lord makes it worse. He's here now. He's been here a lot and
I don't understand why. At first I thought they'd taken me to
the infirmary, but I'm alone here and the room is large and
lavish. So then, I was left to assume that I've been placed in a
guest annex of the castle — which is confusing in itself. I'm
no longer on the brink of death and I'm a prisoner, besides
— why would they care if I died? Why I'm not in the
dungeons with my family is vexing.

Yaron hasn't spoken to me much. *Your family has been
recaptured and returned to the dungeons.* That was the second thing
he said to me right after, *Are you well?*

Other than that, he's only come in and out and looked
around the room for items that he's either not found or taken.
The moments last a long time, though. He should be able to
find whatever he's looking for faster than this. He's across the

room around a corner now. I don't know what's behind the bend, only that bookcases and drapes show on the other wall. Perhaps, a small library or reading nook? I wouldn't know. I'm unwell, but still well enough to walk — not that I do. I'm terrified to get up. Too terrified to move. And that makes me feel like a coward. *I need to escape, to find my family...to beg Lord Yaron to tell me what he plans to do with them...*

My lips part...but the words don't come.

"You can relax," Finn says, placing a hand on my shoulder and giving me a tight, reassuring squeeze. He's counting my pulse, his brow furrowed. He's done this a few times over the last days. He's been mostly the one to monitor me, kind of annoyingly — ah, em, continuously — though Okayo stops by twice a day to check on me. I like Okayo, and not just because he looks like one of my cousins, though that helps. He's funny and has managed to make me smile, despite the circumstances.

"Finn." Yaron snaps from across the room. I jolt, but the Shadow Lord isn't looking at me. He's glaring daggers at Finn. More specifically, at the contact of Finn's hand on my bare shoulder. I've been naked for the three days that I've been here, wherever I am. I haven't bathed either, and I'd like to, but only after I find my kin.

I shrink away from Finn, who slowly removes his hand from my skin. I keep my eyes pointed to the sheets, clench my knees together and just wait and wish for the Shadow Lord to go away. "Kiandah."

I flinch and reach up to stroke my hair...but it isn't there. I swallow and open my mouth...but my voice isn't there, either.

"Are you well?" He's closer — still over twenty paces away, but the distance doesn't seem to matter. I feel the tops of my thighs begin to tingle. It's an unwanted sensation. I zipper them shut.

I don't know how to answer the question. I just feel frustrated. He asks me this question multiple times a day, and every time, we have the same exchange. *Fine.* Then he leaves. But my frustration and this sick feeling in the pit of my stomach are playing tug of war with my heart.

I blurt out, "Where is my family, Yaron?"

Even though Finn is no longer touching me, I still feel the tension he radiates.

My eyes don't manage to make it up to Yaron's face, so I can't gauge his expression as he says coldly, "Finn, leave us."

"No, don't." Panic subsumes me. I reach up and out and lock onto Finn's retreating hand. I meet his gaze. "Please."

And then comes something I've never felt before. A hot, invisible wave full of *rage.* Pure anger radiates across the room. It's of Lord Yaron's own making, yes, but that rage...I inhale...it *belongs* to me. My eyes start to roll back, but I rebel against the sudden pleasantness that threatens to relax me. Gripping Finn's arm tighter helps me refocus. I don't know why I feel this way. I must still have a fever. Okayo pronounced my fever broken, but it must have come back.

"Leave us, Finn, if you'd like to keep your arm."

Finn doesn't hesitate, but untangles his fingers from mine, shoves away from the bed and moves promptly and directly to the door. He's still holding his hearing scope, the one he'd been using to check my pulse. I'm sure the concern on his face had to do with the fact that my pulse was beating fast enough for him to believe I was having a heart attack.

My hand hangs suspended, reaching for where Finn was. I watch the door shut behind him. A black, carved piece of wood. It's beautiful and austere, severe and cold. Everything that is Lord Yaron. *But in the icy rain, he was so warm…*

Yaron wants me to look at him. I can feel it like I can feel the grime on my skin. I look at the sheets instead until the force of his rage pulses so hot, I have to close my eyes against it. I clench everything together. My sanity, my fear, my fists. He comes to the edge of the bed.

Silence hangs between us like a noose. With his next words, he loops the killing end around my neck. "You do not seem well."

Rage surges between us, but it's mine this time. I inhale deeply, feeling the painful tinglings of aches and healing wounds all over. "I'm not well. I don't know where my family is."

He shifts his weight between his feet. Another wall of silence and animosity builds between us. "You know where they are."

"And that's why I'm not well."

"Be that as it may, you know I am referring to your healing process. Physically, you also seem unwell."

"Why does…" I choke. I mean to sound strong, but I'm really scared, angry, and uncomfortable. I turn my face away from him and stare at the curtains. The thick, black outer curtains are partly pulled back to reveal a gauzy, translucent curtain that lets in light but prevents me from seeing anything of the outside world. "I'm a prisoner, *my Lord*. I don't see why you'd care about my physical state."

He makes a sound in the back of his throat and I know it's because he didn't like the way I called him what I called him and I know that it was boorish, but I can't help it. I'm scared and I'm pissed off and I know it doesn't matter. He's going to return me to the dungeons at some point. What...happened between us in the woods...that was just once. That was just to sate my heat. I'm nothing to him, clearly, less than nothing — not even a no-name peasant, but an accomplished criminal and a bloodthirsty killer. *Right*.

"You are also an Omega." *Riiiight*. That, too. "It is the duty of an Alpha Lord to ensure the safety and security of the Omegas in his charge." He recites the words as if he read them somewhere once and has them memorized.

I snort even though I don't mean to. He growls low, but I don't react to it except to tense further, knotting my arms across the blanket I have pulled up to my chest. "I am safe and secure, so you don't need to worry yourself. You can leave me to rot in this prison, knowing you've upheld your duty as Shadow Lord."

I'm speaking to Lord Yaron petulantly. It makes me want to bite off my own tongue. I'd never disgrace myself in this way. Never. My family would be horrified. But there's a good chance they're already dead, tortured, brutalized...and even if they aren't, it doesn't seem like Yaron has any intent to reunite us, so they'll never know anyways. I don't cry. I won't cry. I refuse to cry in front of him.

He takes another step. It's loud. Leather-soled boots, I'd imagine. They're huge. He has enormous feet and hands, and that's without the claws. Everything about him is larger than life. And yet…this male, imposing in any form…*I've seen him kneel before.*

"Does this look like a prison to you?"

"I think…" I swallow and when I answer, my voice is soft, a direct response to the sudden flash of vulnerability I thought I heard in his tone. "It feels like a prison. It could look like anything."

Quiet falls like an axe this time, the one he carries. He shuffles again and I spare a single glance up to see him roughly running his hand over his face before carding his fingers through his hair. He glances around and I look down quickly, scared to get caught in his steel-eyed snare. "Is there some…temporary adjustment that could be made to increase your comfort?"

"You know what I require to be comfortable," I mumble, though what I really want to say is, why do you care? He's told me already that I mean nothing more to him than the obligation any other ruling Alpha would have to an unclaimed Omega in their territory. His asking me now… borders on cruelty. I didn't think he'd be cruel, our Lord. I thought he'd be severe, sure, and fair, but not cruel. But it's been cruel, his questions, and his visits, keeping me constantly on edge and yet depriving me of information, of assurances…

…of clothing and a bath…

…of sunlight.

I glance to the window, but he steps between it and me, scattering the little light that there is and casting a shadow that covers me completely. Another cruelty, this one slight. "You know I can't do that."

I fist the sheets over my thighs. "You *can* do that, but you choose not to, Lord."

"You are not a simpleton. You understand why."

"I must be a simpleton, then, because I don't understand." And this is the part that I've been trying to avoid. The one coming on for days now. The part where I start to cry. I bite my bottom lip hard enough to hurt so that I don't choke. "You believe us killers, fine, but we are a family of killers. A family. I should be at their side."

"You'd rather be with them in the dungeons than here…" He scoffs and looks away. I glance up again. His cheeks are ruddy, likely with anger. It makes me nervous. I don't like it. I'm afraid of it, of him, of this.

"Yes. I'd rather to be anywhere with them than anywhere else with anyone else."

"In lieu of my locking you in the dungeons, is there something else?"

"Just to see them would be enough."

"I'm not taking you to the dungeons and my word is final." He raises his voice and I jump. My lower lip quivers. I stroke my hair again — my head — and shiver. "Something else. Anything else. Please."

Please. He said please.

I shudder violently now and cover my face with both hands. I press the heels of my palms to my eyes and try to remember that my family committed crimes, heinous crimes, and that justice needs to be doled out. He is their Lord. How he deals justice is his prerogative and if he chooses not to include me in this…part — or if this is my penance — then I will have to bear it. *And he said please.* I truly am a simpleton if I'm swayed by that.

"The windows," I whimper, doing nothing to keep the tears from my tone, just as my palms do nothing to keep the tears from my eyes. I cry. Tightly and terribly, I cry.

"The windows," he says, voice stilted. "You'd like the windows…to…" It takes him a while to figure it out, but I don't help him. "You'd like the window curtains opened?"

I nod.

He balks. "You've been here three days. After the first, your injuries were more than healed enough for you to walk this short distance to open them yourself. Why have you…" Another realization changes the accusatory nature of his inflection. I don't know what to make of it when he says, "Have you left the bed for any reason? Other than to use the washroom?"

I shake my head.

"Have you even washed?"

I shake my head.

"And you'd like now…to look out of the window."

He doesn't seem to be asking a question, but I still nod.

Rage pulses out of him again, this time like a cold wind against the Cliffs of Oblivion, carrying hints of frost. "Don't do this to me," he says, voice all but a whisper. I have no idea what he's talking about. He comes right to the edge of the bed, thighs pressed against its elevated platform. He reaches for me, as if to touch my shoulder, but I wince.

He snarls and pulls back, whirls around on his hard-soled heel, advances to the window like it's a traitor he's been itching to strike down his entire reign, rips the curtains all the way open and then leaves. He doesn't look back as he storms out of the room, slamming the door shut behind him.

I turn to face the window fully and notice how huge it really is. Nearly twenty feet tall, it stretches two thirds of the way up the outer wall and it looks out over the entire courtyard of the keep, down the rolling hill — I can even see Orias Village in the distance. Smoke rises from chimneys. The village square is bustling, people whisking their wares to and fro. I can even see horse carts disappearing over the rise of the hill, climbing the Orias highway line towards the ports.

My mouth drops open as I realize where I'm sitting, relative to the castle. My vantage is from a position that I know well. That everyone knows. I'm currently positioned in the east tower of the castle that stands slightly taller and slightly apart from all the rest, in the tower that everyone knows no one is allowed to enter. Because this is Lord Yaron's private wing and I'm in it — not in his guest quarters, but in *his* quarters, in his private area, in his bed…

I'm his prisoner, but I'm sitting where his queen should be.

YARON
SHADOW DUNGEONS

I CROUCH IN THE CENTRAL CORRIDOR WEARING THE legs of my beast, at least the lower half. My trousers torn open at the knees and around the upper thighs. Her family was moved to a lower rung of the dungeons after they were found where daylight does not exist. It was not an order I gave, but I would have given it. Only a fool would return them to the dungeons they escaped from the first time. I am impressed that they are all still alive.

Their escape attempt was riddled with difficulties — a hard fall, a long swim, a sharp climb, and that's all before they began running for their lives across the farmlands and fields, then through Paradise Hole. Then, the rains got to them and forced them to stop and seek shelter. They made it to shelter, or so I'm told. They hid for a full day in the abandoned ruins of the former Shadow Keep's church — not the one I burned, but one found within Paradise Hole that was abandoned generations ago, a fact I found rather...*sad* for reasons I have chosen not to explore further.

Though they were in poor shape when I last saw them, they were alive, but they seem to be deteriorating now. Out of the elements, out of danger's direct path, in the dry cells in which they have been placed. Each one occupies a different cell and each cell is four walls, no windows and a heavy wooden door. The only truly salient difference between their first arrest and now is that they were together then. They have been separated now.

Fed and watered, offered paltry linens to sleep beneath and rushes to sleep upon, yet it is now that they fall apart. I can hear their sobs, their cries for each other through the thick walls. No, my beast can hear them. The walls down here are well insulated. There is no chance they'd be able to hear anything other than distant sounds of sorrow.

I rub my face roughly, feeling uncharacteristically uncertain, and sit there a moment more. Then I rise on two human legs and walk up the way I descended, back up the narrow, jagged stair. And as I eventually emerge into the light of a torch-lit castle, I carry with me a dangerous thought: *mercy*.

YARON
SHADOW KEEP

"I UNDERSTAND YOUR ANGER…"

"You don't understand anything, m'Lord!" the boy shouts at me. His father tries to hold him back, but I lift my right hand, signaling that he should let the boy rage. It is his right in the face of the wrongs I've committed.

Robert advances on the throne, his face splotchy with anger, yes, but also an even more powerful grief. He comes within ten paces of where I sit, only elevated by two simple stone steps on my throne seat, yet still lording over him in a way I ordinarily find useful. I do not find it useful now.

I stand and he freezes in his advance, wavering where he stands as if uncertain whether or not to move forward. Pride begs him to do so, but self-preservation keeps him from it. He is a young Alpha, yes, strong and large for his age, but he is also not stupid. His father and mother are both present, both looking fearful as I descend the two short steps from the throne. I advance on their son and his mother winces, turning her face into her husband's shoulder, seeking comfort. His father curls his arm around his wife's shoulder, hugging her close, and I feel...pain lance across my chest at the picture they make.

Not pain, *longing.*

"You need not fear," I tell them, voice strangely hoarse, as I place my hand on the boy's shoulder and give it a squeeze most gentle. "And you are right to rage," I tell him privately. His gaze is downcast, though he tries to hold mine. It will be difficult. He is only sixteen and he loved the Alpha daughter very much. With his whole heart, a heart so unblemished as to have space for such a thing. To love something wholly. After this, after what happened and what the Omega's family took part in and even perhaps caused, he will no longer have such an ability. After this, his heart will be missing a piece. It will eventually scar over, but it will always be lost.

"You will have your revenge. My Crimson Riders will not stop hunting for the culprits responsible for the killing of your mate — and so many other Alphas within the Shadowlands. Trash City will be found."

"But you have the killers and you've let them *go...*"

"I have done no such thing. The Ubutu family will remain confined to my castle until the end of their days unless their innocence can be proven or their penance can be paid by other means. They will serve in the kitchens as their family has always done for generations..."

"They should be in the dungeons! Tortured! They killed Gwyn!"

He has interrupted me and though I attempt to show him leniency here, I am not used to tolerating such flagrant disrespect. *Unless the words are ripped from the lips of an unruly*

Omega. My mind flashes. I feel my testosterone surge. I clear my throat and calm myself. "I do not believe they did."

He winces when my claws dig into his shoulder and gives me a harried look. "What…"

I did not wish to voice this truth out loud. Not now. Not ever. It is not the position of the Shadow Lord to make conjectures based on instinct — Fact. Reason. Law. Justice are what must prevail. And yet it was none of those things that affected my decision to pull the Ubutu family from their cells and throw them into the lower east wing of the castle, into an unused room that used to serve as grain storage until a more sophisticated system external to the castle was developed. It is in the room adjacent the castle kitchens, I tell myself. It is dank and unwelcoming, I tell myself, little better than the upper dungeons. It is a punishment fitting of their crimes, I tell myself. But the truth is much more difficult.

"They are not innocents. They worked with Trash City — criminals I chased from the North Island and who had the audacity to come to my own territory to use for their hunting grounds. However, what the Ubutu family is known to have done was work with the corpses. It cannot be said that they laid the killing blow to any Alphas within the Shadowlands."

"It cannot be said that they didn't."

"And for that, they will remain in captivity forever. Never to see the sunlight beyond the castle walls again."

He blinks and rubs his watery eyes, the fight leaving him slowly. "And what if you do find out they killed Gwyn? What then?"

I clench my teeth. He is a clever boy, for I had not wanted him to ask that. "If they are guilty of murdering the Alphas with their own bloody hands, then you shall choose the manner of their torture, for they shall not be allowed to live."

After a terse back and forth between the family and me, they leave, leaving me with a sour taste in the back of my throat. I look at my throne as the doors to the throne room slam shut on their departure, but I have no desire to mount those short steps. The massive black chair draped in shimmering grey and black fabrics that fall down the steps and spill onto the floor looks too large for me in this moment. I feel doubt.

"Report from the border scouts," I command of Dorsten and Sipho, who hover nearby.

The mood in the small stone throne room shifts, as do the dozen Crimson Riders present. They move to action, bringing forward a large, heavy table covered in maps marked by moveable pieces shaped like soldiers, some painted black for the undead that have been spotted.

"They had to have had help," I say as my throne room dissolves into a war council chamber, the mood harsher and more severe. The scent of too many Alphas gathered together fills my nostrils when I breathe. Ordinarily, I respond to it with dominance, but now all I can think is that I'd like another scent to cut it. One that smells of gunpowder and unholy things.

"There are sinister rumblings at the ports, my Lord," Sipho says, his short black hair shimmering like it's been freshly cut and oiled. He hasn't seemed to care so much for his appearance before today. In fact, as I look up, I see that all of my Alpha Riders seem to be presenting much more elegantly than usual. I do not like it.

"What is the news?"

"It seems that an unmarked trading vessel was allowed to dock last week. We have yet to determine by whom and how it was allowed to go unnoticed for so long, and we are also unable to ascertain what it carried…"

"We know what it carried," Hector interrupts in a way most unbecoming. Though he and Sipho are members of rival packs, it is rare that displays of dominance are put on between them, and never so boldly, so publicly, before their Berserker Lord.

Most of my Alpha Riders are members of a pack and only Mara's pack already has an Omega — a slight female with jet-black hair and an affinity for animals but little in the way of true magic. Two other Alpha packs overlap among my Crimson Riders. Sipho and Dorsten are members of a pack of three with another wealthy Alpha merchant, Renard, while Hector, Malik, and Guy form another.

Though Hector, Malik and Guy's pack has been known to play with Beta females, they have yet to lay claim to one. They've been waiting for an Omega, wanting one. That is known. However, Sipho and Dorsten and Renard have made no moves to claim an Omega and did not show interest in the female with the black hair at all when she was presented before the red moon all those years ago. It could not be…that they are presenting in such a way as a response to the Omega in my chambers… No, it could not. *She's mine.*

My beast snarls sharply in a way that causes heads to turn. Hector flushes. "Apologies for the interruption, my Lord."

I nod at him once, though I feel the muscle beneath my left eye twitch as I look over these Alpha packs gathered before me with new consternation. After I give the Omega away during the next Red Moon Festival, it is very likely that one of these two packs will have her.

I glance at Sipho and he mistakes my desire to raze his flesh as permission to continue speaking. He clears his throat. "Hector is implying that this is the vessel that the undead assailants who attacked us in the woods arrived on. There is nowhere else on the shores they might have docked a fishing vessel as large as this one, however, none of our fishermen, ferrymen or traders report having seen hundreds of undead Alphas parading through port city streets."

I glare at him, only half concentrating, but disliking the irritation I hear in his tone nonetheless. *They are getting riled.* So be it. *I will devour them.* No. *Yes.* No. *Yes.* Yes... "You will contain your tempers unless you'd like to see mine." I slam my knuckles down on the table, knocking several undead figures over. "I will visit the docks myself," I say, though as I speak the words aloud I instantly regret them.

Visiting the docks will pull me away from the keep. But perhaps...some space will be good for me. I haven't been able to keep my distance at all to now, finding the most threadbare of excuses to return to my chambers and check on her multiple times daily. Yes, some distance will be good. *No.* Yes.

"Tomorrow at sunrise," I choke. "Guy, you will have a contingent of eight Riders ready to accompany me to the docks. I will inspect the ship myself and the rest of you will interrogate the dock workers once more and question the business owners and stall operators that were not questioned before. Ensure you question anyone who might have been awake during the night — at the brothels and taverns, the shopkeepers at the Night Market.

"If they came by ship, Sipho is correct — there is nowhere else a ship this large could have docked and smaller ships would not have made it across the Strait of Zaoul. They *had* to have gone through the ports and someone *had* to have seen them. Sipho, you will ensure order in Shadow Keep during my absence." So he can stay close to the Omega? The thought grates.

Though there is nodding all around, I keep my gaze trained on Sipho. "No one is to approach the Omega while I am gone. No one." I will give Radmilla specific orders that he is not to go near my chambers. She will be the only one allowed in or out to check on Kiandah.

"I…um… As you command, my Lord. However, I was under the impression that this Omega would be presented at the coming red moon. If so, would it not be appropriate for the Alphas who wish to vie for her to call on her?"

My teeth clench so hard I feel the pain of it in my forehead. I stare at Sipho. I stare at him and say nothing. I will swallow his heart if he says another word, but he doesn't, and I don't trust myself to respond.

I force my gaze away from him to Malik and exhale roughly through my nose. "Malik, you will join us at the docks and take the opportunity to send correspondence to Dark City. They were quick to answer our summons and offer aid, yet it must be made clear as quickly as possible that they are not to travel to us and leave Dark City exposed. They are our only trusted ally on the North Island. The city cannot fall and the departure of the Fallen Earth Omega from their territory in such a critical time could be what propels Mirage City to attack them."

"You truly believe Mirage City would go after another city?"

"I believe they will go after any city they believe to be harboring a Fallen Omega." Ours included, once word spreads of her powers, the shape of her face, the resemblance that she bears to the Fire Fate. "Dark City must protect itself."

Malik is taking notes on parchment and looks up as he finishes. "Would you like them to take any action at all, my Lord?"

"Yes. Our alliance is tenuous, separated as we are by land and sea. We need to secure another port, one out of the control of Mirage City. I would encourage them to review the plans I previously proposed for an eastern port city."

"That would be in violation of our trade agreement..."

"Should Mirage City have issue with our trade agreement, I encourage them to send their Berserker to confront me at *his* earliest convenience," I spit, showing fangs as I know the rumors to be true. The Mirage City Berserker is dead. The Death Fate who is responsible for creating the undead army has reanimated the Berserker's corpse, too, and has been *wearing* him for years like a fucking suit.

Uneasy glances are passed between my Riders, but I ignore them. "While they begin construction on a new port city, I would like to extend an invitation to Berserker N'Dogo to visit us here in the Shadowlands. While we are not enemies, neither are we allies. We need to strike up and formalize our alliance with Ruby City to ensure that our current and only viable trade route to the North Island remains open to us. They have been good to us and trade has been consistent, however, I need not tell you all how dire the situation for the South Island will become should they close their ports to us. Dark City is still a young city with a young, green Berserker at its helm. Should Ruby City ally with Mirage City and close their ports, and should Dark City fall, Mirage City will have won and we will not be able to defend against the North Island if every Alpha within it has been turned."

More scribbling. Then Malik says, "My Lord, might I suggest… We could invite Berserker N'dogo as your honored guest to the upcoming Red Moon Festival. She could sit at your right hand while the Alphas and packs compete for the Omega."

It is a good suggestion. A great honor. A meeting, well timed. I cannot say no, and yet, it is the only answer that echoes in my mind. And it pounds with a force that is deafening. "Yes," I grit, my jaw hurting with the force it took to press the word through my lips. "That is a good suggestion, Malik."

My Riders exchange quick glances they know they should not. They spell doubt and confusion. But I am not to be doubted and there is no confusion in my mind.

Only chaos.

We conclude the business of fortifying the trading alliance with Ruby City and working out more detailed plans for a highway line from Dark City to their proposed location for a new North Island port, as well as our plans to meet with the Berserker of Hjiel as soon as possible to discuss any undead sightings further south. It takes the better part of the day.

My Riders exit and as their cloaks flash, I see Radmilla standing just beyond the doors to my throne room. She is dabbing a kerchief to her face. Rage roars within me and I turn from my throne and advance on the door, ripping it open as the final Rider's cloak disappears around the far corner.

"What has happened? What is the news?" Something bleak must have occurred to affect Radmilla like this. She raised me, a mother figure of sorts — if mothers are thorny creatures with spines of steel and an affection that oscillates between abundant and severe — but I have only seen her shed actual tears once. I caught her observing a group of small babies playing together. I did not know then, but later discovered that she had had a miscarriage some months before her husband's passing. She never told me she'd wanted children of her own and she'd never had them. I'd been young then, but I still had the panic in my chest that I feel now. I'd gone up to her and hugged her, buried my face in her stomach for I'd been small and she'd been so much taller than I was. She'd laughed and hugged me back and it had felt *warm*. But now, I am Lord of the Shadowlands. I don't hug. My hand twitches to reach for her shoulder, but I don't let it land.

"Who harmed you? My dungeons have places for many bodies these days." Since I moved the Ubutu family, is what I don't say.

Radmilla barks out a wet laugh and waves her clean pressed kerchief at me. She shakes her head. "These are not unhappy tears, my Lord. They are nothing for you to concern yourself with. I was waiting for your Crimson Riders to leave so that we might have a chance to discuss preparations for the upcoming festival." She sucks in a breath, tears gone as if they never were. "Now that my kitchen staff has been returned to me, I believe it possible to prepare a festival worth attending by the next blood moon. What say you?"

"I say fine. Whatever you want, you shall have. But first, you will tell me why you were...tearful just now."

She laughs and looks up at me with a peculiar expression glimmering in her light green eyes. "Oh my. Is that all it takes to get my way? I should cry around you more often, young Lord."

I frown as she evades the question once more. "That I ask you again, Radmilla, is the only courtesy I will afford you."

She sighs, some of the warmth leaving her eyes and filling me with a chill, rather than neutrality. I dislike the sensation. "Per your request, I finished settling the Ubutu family into their new quarters." It took three days to get them settled. Three days that I have attempted to avoid the Omega...and failed. I find threadbare excuses to see her all the time.

"Per your request, now that their furnishings are fit for habitation and they have been cleaned up and tended to, I took the Omega to see them. It was..." Her eyes become glossy again and I brace myself for whatever her reaction will be...but she inhales deeply and wipes her eyes, tucks away her kerchief with a certain finality. She folds her hands across the full skirt of her dress. My aide, once more, not my family. Family... I don't...suppose...I truly understand the concept. "It was a special thing to behold. Kiandah is an emotional, fiery creature. I did not expect it, having spent the last few days in her presence."

"I did not expect it either," I admit before I mean to.

Radmilla's dusted-on eyebrows rise, just a peppering of grey across her skin. "It is a special thing, to see how members of that family care for one another. If only there were one fiery creature to care for you thus…"

"Radmilla," I growl, emotion surging through me like a storm. I hear the thunder, feel the rain pelting my back as I arch over Kiandah and suck kisses from her lips like I could survive on her life force alone.

I blink and do not know how I moved, but I am now standing with one forearm braced against the open doorway, one knee cocked as if I struggle to stand. I glance down the wide corridor to the double helix staircase at its far end. My feet twitch in my boots to go to her. And yet…I conjure an image of poor Robert's face. I have wronged him by rewarding her. He was not deserving of my sin, as she is not deserving of such grace.

"Come in. We will review your list of requirements for the festival and then you will see Talbot about paying for them. Come to me with your final proposal tomorrow."

Radmilla snorts and the tension between us dies. "Your master of coin is no friend to me."

To which I restrain a smirk. "He is no friend to anyone and that is why he has his position."

"He will be even less friendly with me when I ask him for additional budget to refurbish the castle kitchens. They are in need of upkeep now that the castle cooks have been returned to where they belong in Shadow Keep." Where they belong. Rightful places. Things Radmilla has no right to say to me.

But I do not correct her.

We review her plans and she is dismissed once I find them satisfactory. I meet with several other members of my staff and Felix, a Crimson Rider responsible for managing the Riders that patrol my southern border — who would have ever expected my border to Hjiel to be the lesser of my border problems?

I meet with the Orias town blacksmith, a big man called Olac, and with grain master Ghoran, who has concerns about this year's wheat production. I eat when food is brought to me, though I frown at the taste of the pie and at the lack of offering. *They did not cook this.* She *did not cook this.* I scarf the tasteless food down and bury myself in work. I take meetings in my throne room until the sun sets over the horizon and I know I should retire to my chambers, where the Omega will sleep tonight as she will sleep every night until the Red Moon Festival *and every night thereafter.*

Desire compels me to see her, to see how grateful she is for what I have done for her, but guilt keeps me from her. I freed her family for that gratitude, for the promise of what it might bring me, for selfish reasons. For that, I must suffer my own damnation, and sit in a prison of my own making. So though I remain stiff and aching at the thought of the greedy, grateful Omega…of *Kiandah*, and I yearn to turn down the corridor that will lead me to her, I don't.

I close myself in the small personal chamber behind the locked door in the throne room, and I do what I was always meant to do. Work for the people of the Shadowlands. And I do not fantasize about foreign concepts like desire, or having her for my own.

KIANDAH
ON A MISSION

I'M NERVOUS AS I CLUTCH THE LIST OF SUPPLIES IN my pocket in a trembling fist and sneak through the bustling castle halls. No, I'm not nervous. I'm downright terrified. I can't believe I let Audet, of all people, talk me into this.

Since my family was moved from the dungeons to the kitchens twelve days ago, things have strangely returned to normal. Well, our new normal. In addition to the location having changed, our stuff being gone — all of our belongings and trinkets, my sketches and a paltry few possessions handed down from the ancestors that came before — there's a sort of...undercurrent of tension that exists between us that makes things...not so easy. And things have always been easy. The easiest, really, between my family members and me. Now, there are things unspoken that make me want to rant and rage at them — at Owenna and my parents — but I have never dared talk back to the three of them, so I just don't say anything at all.

My father and mother seem meeker than they did, a little cowed, which also keeps me biting my tongue. I can feel their guilt. It's like a new cousin that's moved in with us that nobody really likes, but we can't turn out into the cold.

They haven't spoken about why they did what they did, only uttered meek apologies for "us being in this mess" and saying they "wish we could have done better for you" but these words feel so hollow. Owenna's response has been worse. She's shown almost no contrition at all. I overheard Cyprus ask her what was wrong with her in a harsh tone I've only heard him use a couple times before, and her response shocked me. She said, "You think we're the only ones helping them? We're just the only ones who got caught. I'm trying to figure out how that happened..."

Cyprus had been shocked. He and I had shared a look. We'd always been able to communicate without words. Owenna hadn't just shocked us, either. It felt as if even my parents were on edge around her.

It was *painful* to watch. These golden beings who I viewed with reverence and love, brought down to this mortal plane. They were human, it seemed, after all. It wasn't a pleasant realization.

Not like realizing Lord Yaron was only human. The discoveries I've made of him have been...incredible.

So things continued on. We resumed our duties in the kitchens, working with the limited supplies and stock we have. Because the other thing that's changed? Our supply lines have been cut. Our suppliers for so many of the foods, spices and tools that we rely on to do our jobs won't come near us. The farmers who bring us fresh vegetables and meat have been ordered to resume operations, but they won't. Neither will our normal wine merchant or the handyman we need to repair the oven. Something's wrong with the chimney and it fills the kitchen with smoke anytime we light it. We've had to get creative with our meals, but our creativity is meeting its end. If we want to keep the castle fed, we need to convince Orias's villagers and merchants to resume trade. And they hate us. Many of them are Alphas or are friends with Alphas or married into Alpha families. They received the order from Radmilla to work with us, sure, but so far most things that have been sent to us have been the dredges of the stock, or even worse — spoiled and rotten. The butcher sent us a pig's head with maggots in the eyes. The wine we got from the merchant was vinegar caked with sludge. The fruit had worms. The vegetables were slimy. The last shipment made Audet vomit.

That's why she suggested I leave the castle to go to the market to try to make repair.

My family told her she was insane, told me not to listen, but the moment the words left her lips, I couldn't unhear them. "He ordered *us* bound to the castle, but you he lets galivant about, traipsing through his keep as if you're his Lady," she scoffed. "If you weren't an Omega, I'd think he even likes you. But since you are, it's clear that his oath to protect Omegas must be stronger than his swift hand of justice. He won't touch you. So you have to go to the market and convince them to send us good food. Otherwise, we won't be able to cook and if we can't even do that, then we're doomed. Lord Yaron will truly have no more need of us, and even if he freed us tomorrow, no one would work with us for any amount of coil. We're just a trio of murderers and their accomplices."

My sister Zelie had pushed her. She'd been pissed. My brother had broken up the tussle. Owenna had seethed, lashing Audet with her tongue. My parents had sulked, offering nothing in the way of guidance, and it had been their lack of fight that gave me mine.

List clutched in my fist, I cross the quad. Here, in the open courtyard in front of the castle, between the castle doors and the keep gates, Riders train in small groups, swords clash, dogs bark, nobles and Lords converse as they make their way across the cobblestones with purpose, some flashing me curious glances. Vendors bring their carts and wares in and out of the gates where they are stopped by various castle staff and directed on where to go.

I approach the open gates of the keep just as a small contingent of Crimson Riders make their way through it. They stop talking when they see me and though they continue walking, they watch me over their shoulders in silence as I pass them. I'm wearing a cloak I found in Yaron's closet and tug down on the hood to help hide my face. It's black and heavier than sin. I bustled the hem it so that it won't drag on the ground when I walk, but there was nothing I could do for its width short of cutting it — which I wouldn't dare. It envelops me.

Beneath it, I'm wearing one of Yaron's tunics tucked into a pair of his trousers. Everything is huge on me, but I did my best. The only thing I couldn't find were shoes, so I had to borrow Owenna's. She's barefoot now in the kitchens, which are still a mess. It's clear the staff haven't been keeping the kitchens up to date given that the old keep's kitchens were in operation.

Radmilla's been kind, giving us time to get ourselves and the kitchen in order while staff make do with a very threadbare kitchen outside of the great hall and some prepared food that had been stockpiled for emergencies and in case of war to supplement what we've been able to provide. I worry that the stockpiles will run out before we can resume full operations, but there isn't much more we can do without workers willing to help us. We're also down a dozen staff.

I think of Justine, then of Farro. Our friends who made it and survived the burning of the church. We haven't seen them since, but I know that they are alive and that, after a brief interrogation, they were released from the dungeons. They probably hate us for the terror we brought unto them. *Tor...* I blink and can feel the way his hot blood had soaked into my palms... *How will they ever forgive us? My parents and Owenna cost us everything because they cost us everyone...and all for coin.*

Squeezing my eyes shut tight and clutching the list to my chest, I step through the gates. They tower over me, two imposing doors that swivel open on hinges in their centers. Against the black wood are carvings that I'm too scared to examine in great detail now. But I catch a flash of monsters with fangs and beasts with wings and scales in scenes of war and I shiver. Spikes jut out from the doors at even intervals. Lord Yaron is known to behead his enemies and slam the backs of their skulls onto the spikes, like sick polka-dots. I shudder, hoping to the ancestors watching over me that my head doesn't become one of them when Lord Yaron discovers I've left.

The gates behind me now, I'm surprised with every step that no one stops me. The guards clearly saw me — so many people clearly saw me — but maybe, Audet was right? Maybe, Lord Yaron really is giving me run of the castle just because of my Omega nature, the signature of my pheromones that marks me different from the rest of them.

I don't exhale fully until I'm all the way at the base of the knoll, taking the highway line north, towards Orias, even though further north, past Orias and past Paradise Hole all the way to the docks and the infamous Night Market is where I yearn to go. That's where the richest spices and the most exotic produce and the fanciest syrups and the most decadent butters are sold. Silks and fabrics, too, would be useful. My family's clothing is in a state. They haven't been given new clothes or material to repair what they wore out in the storm. We look, together… Well, we look like prisoners.

Sadness blisters my chest, making something swell inside of it. I know Yaron doesn't like me. I know that. He all but told me before he rutted me to the brink of death that he didn't like me then and never would like me. But there's a small part of me, so small as to be almost invisible, that sees that he released my family, though he didn't need to, that he put me in his chambers, though he didn't need to, that he… checks up on me — with decreasing frequency, yes, but that he checks on me at all is surprising — that wonders if he doesn't like me just the tiniest bit. Or at least, he gives me some leniency and honors me in small ways because I am an

Omega. I am not sure, but I wish…I wish…for things I have no right to wish for.

It's not a long walk to town, and a short distance through town to get to the marketplace set up in the central town square. Narrow roads full of smiling faces that fall when they see me are what I'm greeted with upon my arrival. I tug my hood lower and hasten my pace, taking a left near the spice stalls to go see Marnie first. She tosses a fistful of cayenne in my eyes the moment I pull my hood back. Trying not to scream bloody murder, I sprint to where I know the horse troughs to be near the stables. I shove my face into the water and scrub my eyes furiously until the stinging abates.

Well. That went about as expected. I glance down at the list in my hand, the charcoal now all smudged and bleeding, and laugh bitterly as I right myself and pat my damp skin dry with an edge of Yaron's cloak. I vowed not to get it dirty, but I realize now that was a fool's hope. He hasn't checked on me in a couple days, though, so I'm not too worried. I'll have time to clean and dry it before he can see what I've done to it. What I will do. Because I don't doubt that having hot pepper thrown in my eyes is the least that the Alphas of Orias will do to me. And I'm not wrong.

The vegetable farmer charges me with his rake. I trip and fall on the cobblestone, bruising the heels of my hands and cutting a bloody streak across my right palm. The weaver throws her shed rod at me so hard it breaks skin where it connects with my forehead. Blood leaks into my eye. The pig farmer is the kindest — the one who sent the maggot-infested pig skull. He only throws dung. I use Yaron's cloak to block most of it, but he's persistent and he's got a big shovel. If I still had hair, this would have been a catastrophe. As it stands now, I can wipe most of the shit off of my head with the backs of my wrists.

I'm sure I can find some way to clean myself up when I get back to Yaron's room. I haven't had the courage to ask yet for the staff to draw me a bath, but I've been wanting one. Sponge baths are all my family has, though, so even though I've been in the Lord's private chambers, I still find solidarity with them in this. It's one way that I can.

A group of Beta children whisper as I walk by. A pack of Alpha boys heckle me lasciviously in a way I don't like. I make it to the fountain in the center of the marketplace, a stone statue of a Berserker beast lunging out of its center, water spraying from its massive maw. Children play here during the warmer months, but even though it's a warm day and the fountain is running, there aren't any children out today. I cup the water in my hands and splash some on my face to try to clear the blood and — I'm going to go with *dirt* — hanging from my eyelashes. I'm still staring up at the stone Berserker when I hear a loud blast. I freeze and jerk back, eyes wide, searching for an explosion.

Instead, my gaze snags on the blacksmith shop, a stone structure built right on the square. Its wooden door hangs open, looking like it'll fall right off of its hinges as the blacksmith barrels through it. He charges straight at me and the distance between us disappears so quickly, it feels like time leapt forward, leaving me behind. Maybe it's just the shock of it. Because even for as hated as I am right now by the town, I never expected Olac to put his hands on me.

He grabs me by the neck with both hands and lifts me off of the ground. He shakes me, spewing hate as he whips my body around. I'm distantly aware that I have Omega gifts now and that I could save my own life right now if I wanted to, but maybe it's the wanting that's the problem. I don't want to die, that's for sure, but I also don't think he's wrong for wanting to hurt me. He knew the family. *I deserve this.* No, I don't. But I still don't stop it.

The sound of whooshing in my ears is all I can hear, until the sounds of shouting override them. There's a push and a pull and my body is flung from the grip of the blacksmith. I hit the fountain, my body slamming into cold, hard stone at the waist. It knocks the breath out of me and though I try to clutch the fountain to keep upright, I'm shaken and drop to my knees. For a second, I panic. I can't breathe. Then air slowly returns to me. It burns like fire, but it returns. I thank the ancestors and inhale again, feeling grateful and ashamed. On my next inhale comes a greater whooshing, which finally makes way for the sounds of a vengeful world.

"...shows her leniency just because she's an Omega... Where was leniency for Gwyn? For Yonel? For Gretchen? Gwyn was just a kid! They were a happy family. I hammered the wedding bands for Yonel when he got down on one knee and proposed to Gretchen when they were just wee children themselves! I was there when Gwyn was born. I was Gwyn's godfather!" His rage dwindles from there and when I open my eyes, I see a man in a red cloak holding Olac by the wrist. His body is jolting forward, but when his gaze meets mine, I can see no real fight in him. Only grief.

"I'm sorry, Olac," I mean to shout, but my voice comes out raspy and weak. "My family didn't…"

"They may not have lifted the axe, but they did not need to. Your bloody, conniving parents — your sister worse than the lot of 'em — ruined lives all the same."

He's right and I know it. His leathery brown skin is worn with lines that are always smiling. But not today. "I'll make it right, Olac."

My response only enrages him further. He surges against the grip of the Crimson Rider, who looks back over his shoulder at me with disdain. "Leave, Omega. Lord Yaron may have released you temporarily from your punishment, but if you don't hurry back, I'll have your ass here over the edge of this fountain."

Olac's fury momentarily shifts from me to the Rider. He shoves the man off and says angrily, "This quarrel has nothin' to do with you."

The man's face twists, expression becoming more hawkish as he stares the other Alpha down. "No? Then perhaps our Lord would like to know who bruised his precious Omega."

"I'll be sure to tell him who offered to rape his Omega in the town square, too. We'll see which he finds the greater offense."

The Crimson Rider stands as tall as he can, but the tips of his spiky black hair don't even come up to Olac's meaty jawline. He's a slender male besides, where Olac is pure muscle. "Fine. I'll drag her back myself."

The Crimson Rider is on me. He fists the front of my tunic and drags me down the road. My feet kick up loose stones as I fight to stay on my feet. I still have my gaze trained on Olac and a fiery sense of misguided righteousness fills me up when I say words I want to mean, but can't possibly. "I'll find Trash City. I'll make sure Lord Yaron holds the guilty party responsible."

Olac just laughs spitefully, his shoulders jolting up by his long earlobes, the wrinkles in his face flattening in defeat. "Who are you to hunt killers? You're just a killer yourself. And come the Red Moon Festival, you'll be even less than that. Enjoy your freedom while it lasts, Omega."

He turns away from me, and the crowd that I hadn't even noticed gathering parts around him. Warm hands of villagers that I used to call friends coalesce on his back, offering him encouragement and comfort. Tears well in my eyes as it hits me then — the true magnitude of what my family has done. They've made us among the most hated people in all of Gatamora. We're *ruined*. Not just our reputation, our chances to ever find partners and husbands and wives and have kids — our chance at happiness. To have what that Alpha family had before Trash City took their lives from them. And my family helped.

The ancestors won't help me now, will they? We've ruined their entire line and tarnished their legacies. *There are no ancestors for me, now.*

I'm sick to my stomach as the Crimson Rider escorts me out of the village. He's handsy and it hurts where he gouges his nails into my stomach and ribs. He whispers nasty things into my ear the whole time. It takes too long for the last of the buildings fall away and the highway line to open up before us, leading up to the next cresting hill before it descends and crests again at the keep. But the strange thing is…traffic here between the edge of the village and the next crest has thinned. The sky is dimming and the highway line is empty. The trellises of the castle loom too far away, peeking up over the crest of the following hillside. We're alone and the rage he radiates causes a short, sharp panic to spike within me.

"I can walk…" I tell him, but he abruptly pushes me away from his body and as I turn to face him, he *slaps* me.

I fall, hitting the ground hard enough to choke on my next breath. As my vision comes to, I still struggle to make sense of what's happening… I'm on my back, my legs splayed. The Rider is looking down at me with disgust, but it doesn't seem to have done anything for his erection, which pokes out of the slit in his trousers, angry and veined and red.

I turn and try to run, but he catches my cloak easily, the pin I found to clasp it cutting against my windpipe. He releases me with a kick to the backside and I collapse into a muddy depression on the side of the road. Pain lances through my back and through my wrists, which buckle under my weight. "That's right," he says, no humor in his tone at all. Only menace. "Present for me, like a good little whore."

I look over my shoulder and I don't feel as afraid or angry as I should. I don't even know what's going on. My brain is firing slowly, my thoughts struggling to understand as the Rider flings his cloak back and tugs his trousers down further. "Lord Yaron may be bound by his oaths to protect Omegas, but I'm not."

Ancestors help me, I'm going to have to *fight*. I'm not…not prepared. I gulp, tasting mud on my bottom lip. Yaron's cloak is heavy, weighing me down. My fingers are slick as I try to unclasp it so I can better crawl away, turn around, and fight

him. But even if I could right myself and turn to face him…
there's no magic here. I can't feel it anywhere.

I can feel the jerking at the front of my already bruised
throat as the Rider grabs the bottom of the cloak and tosses it
to the side, exposing my backside. I yelp as his hand finds my
trousers. He pulls my tunic free of my pants and the breeze
that touches my lower back gives me the chills. I feel a strange
and distant yearning to present in the presence of an Alpha,
but even my Omega nature knows that this is not the Alpha it
wants. It wants Yaron. *I want Yaron.*

I open my mouth to say something — anything I can think
that might stop this — but a crisp, calm voice cuts between us
just as he touches my bare hip. "Ugaros."

A full-body chill runs through me. I keep my gaze pointed
to the ground and I blink slowly, several times. I don't dare
look over my shoulder at the owner of the voice, because it is
unmistakably Yaron. The Shadow Lord will punish me for
this. So I stare down at the mud between my fists. As still as I
am, I can see my reflection in the small pools that have
formed in the divots. My eyes are wide and round and white
around the edges. My ordinarily round face looks slimmer
than usual, gaunt. I'm not well, comes the distant thought.

"M-m-m-my Lord." The Rider, with all his confidence,
now stutters like a boy caught torturing animals behind the
school yard. Evil little cretin. Evil little coward. "You…you're
here." I can hear the sound of fabric rustling, of his trousers
being retied. The latch of a buckle.

"I am." Lord Yaron doesn't say more.

"I didn't hear you come. You're without horse."

"I am," he says again.

"You-you-you're alone."

"Yes."

"D-do you have business in the village, my Lord?"

"My business, ordinarily, would be none of your concern. However, as you presently seem prepared to rape the business that I am here for, I shall enlighten you. I am here for the Omega."

The Rider says nothing.

Lord Yaron asks, "Do you deny that you intended to rape the Omega?"

"No, my Lord." He answers so quickly, with such honesty, it catches me off guard.

"And you were aware that the Omega was not to be touched, as per my edict?"

"I…" he starts, then seems to think better of it. "Yes, my Lord."

"Very well. For your honesty, you will be offered a choice."

"Thank you, my Lord."

A choice? He was going to let him…

"Agony, or a swift death. Should you choose agony, you will survive it."

He takes a moment to decide. I don't even breathe. I don't understand what's happening. Lord Yaron is so *casual*, it's as if he's asking the Rider to choose between a slice of pie or cake. "Agony."

"Good. Then present for me. Like a good little whore."

"Wh-what?"

Heavy fabric shifts, and I hear the sound of a latch released. I know that sound. Lord Yaron freeing his axe from where it rests beneath his cloak, across his spine. "Present for me. I will not ask you again."

"I-wh-how-you…" He stammers again and again. I can hear the sound of his feet shuffling. I wonder if he's going to try to run. I wonder if *I* should try to run, but the thought is immediately cut short by my overpowering will to live and the understanding that, if I run, the Shadow Lord will cut me down.

Don't run, I long to shout at the menacing Rider, my feeble attempt to spare us all from the violence to come, but the words don't make it past the gate of my teeth. Shuffling steps are punctuated by much louder footfalls. Thud…thud… thud…

"You will present for me like a good little whore, and I will impale you with this blade, just as you would have impaled my Omega."

I'm going to piss myself as emotions clash over and through my body. A bitter, icy cold is what makes sense upon hearing what Lord Yaron has in store for the Alpha, but what's strange is the heat that washes over me right after. *My* Omega.

"N-no."

"No?"

"No."

Thud.

Lord Yaron comes to a stop. He's close to me now. There's another sound, this one more daring. A slicing sound. The Alpha, he wouldn't, would he… He wouldn't have drawn his sword, would he?

There's a horrible *thwack* very close to me and I dare a swift glance to the right and see Lord Yaron's axe embedded in the dirt. It's half sunk into the road, like it's demarcating the boundary line between life and death. Beyond it, the Alpha holds a sword aloft while Lord Yaron now stands weaponless. I kneel, prostrated at the inflection point, waiting for my sentence.

"Is this your choice? To fight?"

Hesitation. So much of it. Finally followed by a warbled, "Yes."

"Very well. Kiandah." *Kiandah.* It does things to me when he says my name. Makes me want to dole out praise and issue commands that I know he'll want to obey.

"My Lord." I'm surprised that my voice comes out whole, rather than in tattered pieces.

"Can you stand?"

Choked with fear and emotion, I don't dare bet I'll have the same luck speaking as I did before. So I nod rapidly.

"Rise."

I stand up. I have to fight my way there, but after an eternity, I make it onto my feet. I don't want him to see how ragged I look. I know he will, but maybe it's that I just don't want to *see him* see it. I keep my gaze trained on the axe in the road.

He doesn't say anything for a prolonged moment. "Can you walk?"

I nod.

"Come stand behind me. I want you to face the keep and continue to face it. Don't turn around, no matter what you hear."

I take a step, but his cloak is soaked through with mud and weighs a bloody ton. My left knee gives out on my second step and I collapse onto the bank of the road, my feet still in mud, but my hands finding dry, packed earth. I lurch forward, determined, but when I find my feet — on the road this time — one of them is bare. I lost Owenna's shoe, but I'm not going back for it. I keep my chin tucked, my gaze down, my hands fisted, my arms tucked tight against my sides. I lurch up the hill, where he told me to go, but before I can take another step, a shadow falls over me. I know it's the Lord of them. He looms larger than he ever has before.

I flinch back and continue to tremble as his massive hands reach for the pin at my throat that chokes me. "I'm sorry... for your cloak. I'll...repair..." I whisper.

"Shh." His voice is sharp and he presses his thumb against my lips. His fingers slip under my chin and he tips my face up. I close my eyes so as to avoid his gaze. Not that it helps. I can feel the soft burst of his rage. It puffs out of him like a cloud and envelops me completely, even as his other hand drops to the cloak and, ignoring the pin entirely, rips it free. It hits the ground with a thwunk and I feel a thousand pounds lighter. But I don't stand up any taller. If he'd let me, I'd hide beneath the cloak he let fall. Instead, his hand on my chin doesn't relent. He tips my face back, then to the left and the right. He inspects me all over. I can feel the cold sweep of his gaze.

"Which of these injuries did this Rider here cause?"

I gasp, "None." But my hands move to my stomach. *Why did I do that? It came so involuntarily.*

Lord Yaron rumbles deep in his chest. He closes the distance between us by half and we were already standing so close. His huge hand caresses the outside of my tunic — his tunic. He presses his full palm against my stomach. I inhale and can't stop my eyelids from fluttering open. I look up, meeting his gaze directly, drawn there by something unearthly. He's looking right at me, too. His expression is terrifying. So cold. So emotionless. I cannot see rage there, but I can feel it. He cannot conceal that. It pulses in waves that come thicker and thicker. Too thick to breathe through.

"You do not lie to me," he says.

I wither. "I'm sorry."

"Where did he hurt you?"

Tears well in my eyes. Not because I'm scared, even though I am that, too. So many people hurt me today. I didn't expect it. I should have, but I'm naive and an idiot. I didn't do anything wrong. And these are *my* people. My fellow villagers. My neighbors and friends. Why can't they see that? I am not my family. *I am not my family?* The thought stutters and stops short and I'm not given time to inspect it further when Lord Yaron prompts, "Kiandah, speak to me."

His storm cloud eyes are so deliriously spellbinding. And not just because of their color, their shape, the inky black lashes that frame them. Because they look at me like he sees me and the shape of my soul, all the colors of my heart. Beneath my fingertips, I feel the pull of a distant magic beat like a pulse.

"Just my stomach," I whisper, voice barely there. "He grabbed me too hard when he was carrying me from the village…" I rub my hand over the back of his. His hand on my stomach tightens. I can feel it tense beneath my touch. "And here…" I lift my hand to my cheek. "He slapped me."

Yaron's nostrils flare. His gaze is pure brutality, there's no other way to describe it. But I don't wilt this time when that shadowy grey gaze slams into me. I want to, but the warm pressure of his hand on my stomach grounds me. "And your other injuries?"

"Other people in town… I thought I could talk to them, but they're too angry." I lick my lips. They feel swollen and taste like blood and dirt. I look like hell and I'm embarrassed. I want to reach up and touch my hair, wipe the shit off of my scalp, but my hands are shaking too badly and I know anyways that it wouldn't help.

"It's not their fault." I move my hand back over Yaron's. His fingers flex and tense. His body looms closer. We are inches apart. Close enough that our noses would press together if we were the same height.

Yaron drops his tone and speaks loud enough only for me to hear. "And Ugaros? Was the fault his?"

I know what he's asking and it's not fair. "I'm no justice dealer, Yaron."

His eyes widen, his pupils flare. "Answer me, Kiandah."

"Don't make me hurt anyone. Ask anything of me, my Lord, but not that. Please, not that."

He releases a harsh roar and pulls away from me so quickly, I sway into his vanishing warmth. "Then I will draw my own conclusions and make his suffering a thousand times worse than what you feel he deserves."

I wince, hating him a little bit for his words, which are at odds with the way my Omega preens inside. She loves his violence. She has no embarrassment. She wants him and doesn't care that she's covered in shit and blood and has no clothes and no hair and is at his complete mercy.

"Walk twenty paces up the road. Keep your gaze towards the castle and cover your ears." He withdraws from me entirely, taking back his shadows and his warmth. He looks back over his shoulder at me. "I want you to hear nothing. Hum to yourself, if you must. I'll return to you quickly." He turns again, but seems to hesitate. His hands are forming fists, clenching and unclenching. Fur is popping up on the sides of his face, his ears shifting to that of his beast, his hands forming claws before resettling.

His uncertainty makes me hesitate. I glance down at the road. "Yaron, you…you forgot your axe." I feel silly pointing to it, but when I turn, I see that the Rider is still standing there, looking prepared, looking determined that he might actually be able to take down Yaron. It makes me uncertain.

Yaron is staring at me with a bewildered expression.

"I…" I start, but as I speak, the Rider uses the advantage to edge towards Yaron on light feet. He wouldn't be so dishonorable as to attack while Yaron's back was to him though, would he? *Yes, a coward would do that.* I shout, "Yaron, your axe! Be careful!"

But Yaron doesn't move. He just stands there staring at me like I'm an alien thing while the Rider advances with the tip of his sword aimed to kill. Yaron's eyebrows are knitted together so neatly they nearly make a complete line, his gaze moving across my face like I've got the secrets of the universe tattooed across it and he'd know them, if only he could read the language. I wipe the blood dripping in my eye away with the back of my hand. A muscle below his left eye twitches and I don't miss the clenching of his hands.

I point at the approaching Rider, now only five long paces away and looking prepared to lunge… "Yaron!"

The Rider attacks, but Yaron bats the blade away with a paw, sending the Rider spinning to the side and shocking the hell out of me. His eyes never leave my face. He says softly, "I don't need my axe for this."

My lips fall open. Warmth cascades through me. Little bubbles that burn every place they pop.

"Wait for me, Kiandah." His expression softens, his brow smoothing as the Rider behind him struggles back upright. He's clenching his teeth, spittle flying out between them. Yaron doesn't look bothered at all. "Please."

Please. I start to move without intending to, but before I'm out of earshot and he turns away from me completely, I manage to squeak out a quick, "Be careful." It sounds trite, saying something so glib to *him*, the Berserker Lord of the Shadowlands, and I fully expect him to ignore me. He doesn't.

Instead, he stiffens. His expression twists in and out of that furrowed, soft look he seems to be wrestling with before finally settling on something so severe it looks painful. That same muscle high on his cheek ticks. "Move, Kiandah," he barks, his voice harsher.

I jolt, wondering what I did wrong, and — determined not to do anything else to displease him today — I place my hands over my ears and limp up the hill. I sing the Beta song quietly under my breath to drown out anything I might hear. It doesn't really help. "Alphas say grrr…Betas say bliss…

Omegas say….Omegas say boom." The lyrics are punctuated by the muffled sounds of a struggle behind me. Thud, thud, thwack, slice.

The battle doesn't feel like it lasts that long, but it doesn't help me any. I feel overexposed, my dewy skin blistering in the wind that I don't think is really that cold, but it feels it to me. My face is hot. My throat burns. And I can still feel every place that Rider touched me. My bare, mud-encased toes curl into the dry road as I think of what could have been if Yaron hadn't found me.

Screams fight through the barrier of my palms and my song and my scratchy voice fades when I see a small contingent of Crimson Riders cresting the hill. I don't know if that's good or bad. I don't know if he's noticed them and my scratchy voice rises, "Yaron?"

I shrink, my shoulders curling inward as they advance and so many sets of eyes sweep my body. The male in the front, a white man with reddish hair, looks stunned at the sight of me. And then an axe flies over my shoulder towards him.

I nearly jump out of my goddamn skin as the axe sinks deep into the highway line, right where the red-haired Rider's horse had been about to take its next step. His horse rears up and the Rider hisses as he struggles to get his horse back under control. Behind him, the other Riders' horses roughly scatter.

I turn, worried that something's happened — worried that I should be worried about the approaching Riders. Like the one he called Ugaros, do these others mean me harm? I open my mouth, but I don't manage any words.

Lord Yaron is standing there, the breadth of his shoulders covered in dark, torn fabric. Black strands of his hair slash across his face and hang past his cheeks. His arms are held slightly out to the sides and his sleeves are torn, missing too, which means I have no problem at all seeing that his hands are covered in blood up to the biceps.

He's staring straight into my eyes, even as he points at the approaching Riders and roars, "Do not cross that line." To me, he lowers his tone and speaks so gently. "I'm nearly finished. I'm sorry to make you wait, but please turn back around and wait for me another moment more. You've been such a good girl."

I could faint. I'm nodding absently and as I turn back around, I pretend that my gaze doesn't stray to the sight of the bloody mess of a person on the ground behind him. My stomach churns. My throat is too ruined to sing anymore so I hum loud. As loud as I possibly can. *Yaron...he.... Did he dismember the man?*

The Riders that had been approaching are all stopped on the road, fourteen of them in two lines of seven spaced well away from Yaron's axe in the road. The first two Riders of each line are male, both Alphas, and both watching *me* fixatedly despite the carnage that's taking place past me down the road.

It's the man with skin a slightly darker shade of brown than my own who says, "Are you alright?"

I meet his gaze briefly and shake my head. "No."

The second the word leaves my lips, I feel the temperature of the air change. It heats with Yaron's rage and I notice the horses and the Alphas that ride them stirring. But I don't. I feel my shoulder blades sag down my back, strangely soothed by it.

I feel him before I see him. I feel him through the sole of my bare foot. His feet thud so loudly on the ground, I can feel the vibrations. And then he swivels around my body, appearing like a gathering storm against a backdrop that seems suddenly too bright. I hold fast as my gaze tracks the blood droplets pouring down his face. It looks like he bathed in the other man's blood. The carnage is spectacular and like nothing I've seen before. And it's for *me*, in my name and in my honor even though I'm his prisoner and he's supposed to hate me. At least…that's what I thought. I waver, but somehow catch myself on the bruised heel of my foot. I don't breathe, but I don't fall.

His gaze is locked on the ground and when he follows it, dropping suddenly to one knee at my feet, I jolt. In the absence of my humming, the world is starkly quiet when he reaches forward, his thick, rough fingers caressing the back of my left calf. He gives my foot a tug and I look down to see that he's holding Owenna's shoe. It's not clean by any stretch of the imagination, but he handles the slipper as if it's made of the finest crystal.

"May I?" he says without meeting my gaze.

I don't speak, breathe, move. But I do let him pull my left foot out from under me, and I place my full weight on my right. He slides my shoe on my foot and I thank him. Well, I try. My voice comes out as puffs of air with no coloring. Yaron's gaze snaps up and locks on my lips momentarily before traveling lower.

He rises to stand and his fingers reach forward and trap my face tenderly. His blood-soaked fingers are so warm. So warm and violently careful as he tilts my head side to side. He's already inspected my wounds thoroughly though, so I don't know what he's looking for. Especially not when his expression changes — not to rage or worry, but to something harder to interpret. He makes a choking sound in the back of his throat, his nostrils flare and then he swallows stiffly.

"Come, Kiandah. Let me take you home."

KIANDAH
SHADOW KEEP

"You can open your eyes." Yaron's whisper is delicate, fragile, and uncharacteristic.

It causes me to jolt and pull away from where my face was buried in his chest. I could have fallen asleep there, in the safety of his shadows, if I hadn't been freezing. Though he wrapped me in his dry cloak, the wetness from the mud on my clothes sank into my bones and I couldn't stop shivering as he carried me in a cradle hold all the way back to the keep, his upper body Alpha while loping along on the legs of his beast.

I peel back from his body, peel my eyes open and look around just as the heavy sound of a door shutting registers. I recognize that sound and know where we are even before the haze clears from my eyes.

We're back in his private chambers. His legs are human again and I hover at a slightly higher than normal human height off of the ground. Shyness and shame roll over me as the scent of pig shit clashes violently with the fresh scents of his room. Spicy incense, rich leather, sandalwood, and something distinctly Yaron. It's too much.

I stutter out a torn whisper, "Thank you. You can put me down."

"Yes, I can," he replies, but he doesn't.

Instead, he walks us back to the bathroom, which is separated from the rest of his open-air chambers by a large arched door. It's colored slate, etched in so many beautiful and terrible depictions of beasts on the hunt and beasts coupling with one another, ravaging and rutting. I've tried not to overinterpret the symbols every time I had to go to the bathroom, but it's been hard. I don't know if the overall message is of devotion or destruction.

He pushes the door open with his foot and carries me into the bathroom. The cavernous space feels teeny tiny with him in it as he closes the door behind us, then moves to the far wall where he sets me down on the wide stone edge of the bathtub.

He keeps his hand on my thigh, just above my knee, as he reaches past me to turn on the spout. I can feel the heat from the water and shiver for the thousandth time as longing to be fully submerged fills me up just as water fills up the basin. I don't comment on the modern water pump technology. Most homes in the Shadowlands use water pumps imported from the North Island, among other illegal technological necessities. To see the Shadow Lord with his fancy water in his rough-hewn stone tub is a contradiction that has made me smirk in the past. Not now, though. Now, I'm grateful for the chance to wash myself completely free of that foul Rider's touch. *His hands on my body, the feeling of him tugging my tunic loose…* I shudder.

"Let me check your wounds first."

He grabs a very, very small stool from beneath the vanity and drags it over. The stool looks far too small for him and he teeters in it in a way that makes the corner of my mouth twitch. He sees it and narrows his eyes. "Something on your mind?"

Only the manner of my torture. I shake my head.

He gives me a lingering look before changing the subject. "I can smell blood on your hands. May I see them?"

I show him my palms without protest.

"Stay still, please." Please.

"S-sorry," I croak.

His eyes narrow further as he plucks my right wrist off of my lap and hunches over it. "Now, I'll ask you again and do not lie to me twice, Kiandah. I do not tolerate liars. I have told you this before and do not intend to repeat myself again. Ever. So, tell me now what thoughts are causing you to look at me thus."

His gaze is focused on my palms as he picks little rocks out of them with the tips of his very sharp claws. My gaze is focused on his shirt — it's almost uniformly red. As if it's been soaked in dye. "My thoughts are…at odds with each other."

"In what manner?"

"I…" I swallow hard and when he glances up at my face, he must see my focus on his shirt. He looks down at his torn and bloodied clothing, releases my hand for a moment, then tears his shirt free of his chest with a hard yank. He tosses the bloodied rags against the wall by the bathtub, in a corner I can't see, then returns to my hands without another word. I can feel him waiting for me, expectantly.

"I um…I was thinking how funny you look sitting on that tiny stool." He jerks up, then looks down at his stool, his eyebrows high on his forehead. Then I say, voice much softer, "And then I was looking at your bloody clothes and wondering how you planned to punish me."

He glances over me once more, an unknown expression on his face. He inspects me from the top of my shit-smeared head down to the bottom of my mud-crusted shoes. "Do I look like I intend to punish you?"

I shake my head. "But I feel like you should."

"Why?"

I bite my bottom lip. It stings and I wince. I struggle to meet his gaze, but force myself to. "I shouldn't have left the keep."

"Clearly. But did I command you to stay?"

I shake my head.

"Then you did not disobey. It was my mistake to assume you would remain put. It was my mistake not to have guards on you at all times. I saw how little you were willing to move around my own chambers. It did not so much as occur to me that you would attempt to leave — not just my chambers, but the castle completely. What were you doing in the village, Kiandah?"

"I…um…I left to help my…family…"

"Family," he exhales the word with me and looks a little annoyed. "Is there nothing you would not do for them? Jump headlong into fire?"

"It wasn't just for them." I flex my hands, trying to retract them, but his hand on my wrist pinches slightly and I'm easily bound. "It was for you, too."

He balks. "Do not lie."

"I'm not. It's…I wanted to make you dinner."

What is *wrong* with me? I feel heat flash in my face and linger, then roll down my neck when his beast pushes at the underside of his chest. I can *see* it in the patches of fur that crop up all over him and fade just as quickly again. He blinks at me with huge, round eyes and I can't breathe. The steam from the bath has started to thicken, creeping between Yaron and me, acting as a buffer, a veil, making the world feel too small, too close, too intimate.

"You wanted to make me dinner?" he says, as if practicing the words in a language not native to him.

I nod.

He shakes his head, clearly flabbergasted. "Explain."

I speak fast. "I…my family and I are still cooking for you and the Crimson Riders. But we haven't been able to get the supplies we need because the farmers and butchers and other vendors in the Orias marketplace hate us. They give us only spoiled and rotten things."

His brows furrow. His jaw sets. "Why did you not inform Radmilla? She would have taken care of it."

"We did — she did…" I'm losing what's left of my voice and have to cough into my fist. "A couple times. But it doesn't matter how sternly she warns the vendors, they claim to deliver fresh produce to the castle. The staff claims they receive rotten stuff. No one takes responsibility. There's nothing we can do but try to…" I cough again and just leave it at that. Rambling will only hurt my throat and there's nothing left to say on the subject. Nothing but the one thing.

Looking into his slate-colored eyes, I say softly, "I wanted to plead with them directly so I could make dinner again. I like making dinner and I wanted to make it for you. But I can't serve you that which we were given."

His eyes lose focus momentarily and I wonder what he's thinking...but then his attention snaps back to me and he says softly, "You... You are cold." His head cocks at the slightest angle, making him look far, far too much like a boy.

"N-no, I'm not," I reply, my teeth clacking together.

"I can see that you're shivering. Your lies..."

"I'm *not* cold and I'm *not* lying, my Lord. I'm scared." I'm not really that, either, but I don't know exactly what I'm feeling in this moment. Like the rumblings of a distant heat far, far away, but still large enough to see on the horizon. It feels eclipsing.

His face flashes with anger. Fur sprouts across his chest again before thinning back to a dusting of black hair. I remember the weight of it rubbing against my skin as he fucked me from behind, like I'd ordered him to, nothing but animals. Nothing but equals. I feel that threatening heat on the horizon loom closer and then...he reaches out and snatches me by the hips, yanking me until my butt is all but hanging off of the edge of the stone bench. His thighs part around my legs so that my knees press against his groin and the very prominent erection there.

"My Lord again, Kiandah?" He stares at my lips for a moment too long, long enough for my inner Omega to daydream perilous things. "When we are alone, you don't need to call me Lord. And you *never* have reason to fear me, Kiandah."

"But you're angry with me…"

"Yes."

"What are you going to do to me?"

"So many things."

I suck in a sharp breath.

And then as quickly as the charged moment slammed into me, he releases me from its prison. He turns my palm over in his paw. "Your hands will recover well, so long as we are sure to clean them thoroughly." He gently trails his fingertips up my wrist, over my arms, along my clavicle to the buttons along the front of my tunic. He slices through the first with a claw. My shoulders tense. He pauses and inhales deeply, then exhales through flared nostrils that transform, momentarily, into a snout. "Is it bad?"

I don't have the faintest idea what he's talking about and can't make sense of his words at all through how hard my heart is pounding. We're sitting so close. We've been…*closer*, but not like this. Not with our eyes wide open and all of our senses so finely tuned to each other. I've never been this close to anyone before. "W-what?"

"What Ugaros and the other villagers did to you." His hand brushes over my forehead. Crusted blood flakes onto his fingers and I wince even though he didn't hurt me. His touch was too soft for that.

"Oh. No. It's not too bad. Just some bruises…"

His gaze switches between my eyes. It's too much, the power of his focus wholly on me. I could drown. "Are you lying to me?"

"I hope not."

The corner of his mouth twitches right before his claws slice quickly through the rest of the fabric. He fans my tunic open, exposing my torso to his gaze. My breasts aren't enormous like my sister Zelie's or even as large as Audet's, but Lord Yaron looks at them as if they're the first breasts he's ever seen in his life and he does not find them lacking. My dark brown nipples are hard as stones. I struggle to stop myself from arching…

"He touched your breasts?" Yaron's expression twists from something almost *light* to furious.

A single claw traces the bruised skin on the underside of my right breast. I shiver as my painfully hard nipples harden further. "I…didn't realize he had."

Yaron makes a brutish sound, half roar, half hiss. "Lift your hips."

"What?"

"Either stand or lift your hips, Kiandah. I need to remove your pants."

"I…" I don't move. He's seen me naked before but I was gone to the heat. I didn't have time to be self-conscious and I haven't had a proper bath in weeks. Not to mention what I've been through today.

"Now, Kiandah." He looks up at me, jaw clenched, the muscles within it pulsing. "You truly have not one self-preserving bone in your body, do you?"

I shake my head, then nod, then shrug and shiver again.

"You try to defend a dead man. You defend villagers who attacked and assaulted you. You defend a family that lied to you and committed treason. You defend even Radmilla who should have known that rancid food entering *my* home is something egregious that should have been brought straight to me. You defend everyone but yourself. And you go even further, Kiandah the selfless. You *command* my beast without hesitation. He loves to serve you. But you deny your Lord now." He comes close to me, closer and closer still. He brushes his stubbled jaw across my shoulder, his lips working their way in towards my neck. "I do not understand you or what cruel god created you and thrust you into my path."

He bites my neck very softly, but it releases a flood of desire within me and makes me moan aloud. "Up, Kiandah." He pats my hip twice. "You cannot bathe with your clothes on." He reaches behind me and turns off the water. The bath is immense, big enough for six, and full to the brim.

"I can bathe myself, my Lord…" He doesn't feel like Yaron right now. He feels too much, too unwieldy to handle.

"You can, but why would you when you have *your Lord* on his knees begging to do it for you?" His eyes…I can't look into them for long. His voice is a rumbly whisper that hits me in the thighs. If I could purr like he does sometimes, I would. I'm glad that I cannot. "Let me serve you, Kiandah. Stand for me."

It's too much. I'm powerless. I rise shakily from my seat and Yaron doesn't hesitate to cut the ties of my trousers and push them down over my hips. The filthy material pools around my feet. I don't dare look down to see his reaction. I keep my gaze fixed on the door at the far end of the room. My hands…I don't know what to do with my hands… I set them lightly on his shoulders, which twitch.

"Do you feel any pain?" he asks after a moment. His fingertips feather over some bruising around my pubic bone and right hip and rib — likely, where I hit the stone fountain. I flinch when he touches a scratch on the top of my thigh, not because it hurts, but because his hands are so hot.

I shake my head and he responds with a low sound. "I do not believe you would tell me if you did. Your desire to protect others is infuriating." Yaron's tone drops, filling with heat. His hands wrap around my hips and I can feel each of his hot breaths against my lower belly. "You would protect the scourge of the earth, even when there is no saving them. You would sacrifice your own bones to make me a meal worth eating."

"I…" His words sound wrong, so hostile, something to be rebuffed. "Is that so wrong?"

"You have power enough to protect yourself. I've *seen* it, Kiandah. You protected your family from me in the dungeons. You protected *me* from the undead in Paradise Hole. You could topple my throne and rule the Shadowlands if you so desired. You could make an ally of Mirage City or, better yet, overthrow the Fates who rule there. You could rule Gatamora."

I feel his words course through me in a funny way. It's not that I think he's mad or wrong or delusional. It's that…I *know* he's wrong and a little mad and only somewhat delusional. He is Lord Yaron and he doesn't lie. He is a rational, reasonable, beastly male. And these are the things he thinks of me so they must be right. But…they don't matter. Not even a little. So, while warmth may cascade across each of my cuts and bruises knowing that he sees me this way, I also feel…sorry for him.

I lift my right hand from his hot, powerful shoulder and stroke his hair. My fingers come back stained in blood and I frown softly down at it. "Your hair…" I try to clear my throat, but it's too scratchy. It's a wonder he can understand me at all. "It's greasy. When was the last time you washed it?"

His expression loses its cutting, murderous edge. His pupils blow wide to consume all the grey. "Are you avoiding your chambers? Is your refusal to share quarters with me what has kept you from it?" I tsk, clicking my tongue against the backs of my teeth.

"What are you doing?" He speaks through clenched teeth and I don't miss the fact that some of those teeth have transformed into fangs.

"Is that it? Have you been avoiding me? Did I guess correctly?" I cough a little, inhaling steam and the scent of blood and sweat from his skin. *Heavenly.*

"Yes."

"Do I disgust you that much?"

"You know that isn't the reason." His voice is hard, but he doesn't elaborate. Left with no answer, a small sadness fills me at whatever the true reason might be. My fingers, meanwhile, continue to trace the line of his head, so perfectly shaped, to the back of his neck before following the hard angle of his jaw to his chin.

His pulse is thrumming madly, desperately, and I feel it, this power he's speaking of. In his presence, it seems easier to reach. When I was on the road, I searched for it and found nothing. Now, I feel it like a ball of liquid magma nested in the pit of my stomach, moving and lurching. I could slip a ladle into it, and drag up a draught.

Curious and amazed, I lift my hand and with only the briefest thought of fire, I manifest pure flame. It appears as a sentient torch in the middle of my palm, no brighter than a candle, but blue at its heart. And it doesn't burn me.

"Kiandah," Yaron says, "you see your gift?"

I nod, and then I close my hand around it, dousing it for good. "To be powerful and to have power…" I shake my head. "You have it wrong, Lord Yaron. You can have one without the other. I may have power, but I don't want to use it to cause pain. I don't want to hurt anyone *ever*. I don't want to rule. I just want to live. And for everyone to live. Is that so hard to believe? That I may have power and choose not to use it? That is a power in itself, I think."

I draw away from him and see the most spellbound expression covering his face. He looks so much less like the Shadow Lord in this moment. A softness touches him, like the wisps of fog twisting through the air. I touch his cheek wishing, for one fleeting moment, something I have no right to wish.

But I don't dare give voice to it, because it can never be. There is no fantasy universe in which the Lord of the Shadowlands could belong to me.

"I suppose that is a lie… I say I don't want to rule. I do. It's just that the only thing I want to rule is you." I tilt my head to the side, letting him hear my truth, letting him weigh it, but not letting him respond to something we both know he doesn't want and that could never be.

My small smile wobbles and the power I felt vanishes. I rub my filthy palms together, finding them colder than they ought to be given the circumstances. I think my adrenaline is crashing and I shiver, then shiver again. "I am sorry, Yaron, that I don't have these ambitions," I say in a scratchy voice. "Really, all I truly want in this world is to cook for you." So much more is loaded into my final words that I quickly reach for more levity to break the moment. It's too heavy to bear. "And right now, to bathe." I offer him a small smile as I use his shoulder to steady myself, turn and lift one foot, intending to step into the massive pool.

But the moment my toes touch the hot water, my feet are jerked out from under me. I yelp and laugh as he scoops me up and steps into the bath himself. "You're still wearing pants, Yaron," I shout, looking up at his face with a smile, but Yaron doesn't return it.

Instead, his expression is strange — somber and strange — as he lowers us both into the tub. Hot, nearly scalding water envelops me and feels so fucking good. I whisper a moan and Yaron releases me onto the stone bench ringing the inside of the tub. I duck underneath the heat, letting it wrap all the way around me, burying its pins and needles in every follicle.

I come up for air with a tired grin in time to see Lord Yaron plastered against the opposite side of the tub, arms outstretched, hands clutching the lip of the bath in a white-knuckle grip. "Yaron?" I croak, then hiss, my smile falling. "Shit. I must have rubbed it too hard," I whisper. There's blood running from the cut on my eyebrow into my eye.

Yaron's on me in a second, a rag in hand, pressing it gently to the wound. He gathers me up and sits me on his lap where

I can feel the unmistakable rod of his erection digging into my lower back through the shreds of his trousers. And as he administers to me from so, so close, his fingers gently holding me around the waist, his chest a wall of heat against my weary bones, the rag light on my face, he says the last thing I would have ever expected to hear from him here, now, ever.

Voice low, he says to me, "I hope you know, Kiandah, that when the Shadowlands hosts its next Red Moon Festival and all of the other Alphas and their packs gather to claim you for their own, they will leave disappointed."

"I…you find me so disappointing, my Lord?"

"You know that is not what I mean at all."

I blink up at him, confused, his face so close to mine, his lips blood-red and perfect, dripping with water from the bath. I want to lick it off, but I can't. He is the Shadow Lord and we are not destined for each other. "I… You circumvent tradition?"

He nods.

"How?"

"I am the Shadow Lord. What I will, so it shall be."

"So, I'll be able to live on my own? Without a master? Is it because I am still a prisoner, my Lord?"

His brow furrows and his cheeks, already warm from the bath, flood with greater heat. "You misunderstand. The Alphas will leave disappointed because *I* intend to vie for you. You will be master to *me*."

YARON
SHADOW KEEP

THE LOOK THAT CROSSES KIANDAH'S FACE ISN'T AT ALL what I expected. Shock, elation — I expected these, yes, and these are the emotions she wears, at first. But the disappointment? She slowly pushes away from me and reaches for a bottle of soap on the ledge behind her. "It would be a great honor, my Lord," she says, voice sounding like a gash.

I frown. "Is that your answer?"

"You…" She concentrates on rubbing soap into her skin. "You didn't ask me a question."

"When I vie for you and…" — maim, claim, slaughter, annihilate — "…defeat the other Alphas who fight to have you for their own, will you accept my bond?"

"I can't." Her answer is immediate and the way she looks at me fills me with doubt.

She's looking at me like I'm her villain.

I remove my trousers and toss the wet bundle out of the bath and onto the floor in the pile of other bloody clothing.

My cock is fully erect and juts so high, the tip protrudes from the water when I tilt my hips up even slightly. Kiandah stares at it and then blinks again, more rapidly this time. I fight not to touch it, milk myself for her pleasure… And I will, but she must first command it — and she will again. Whatever I must do to make that happen, I will.

"Why?"

She stutters, a little frazzled, more than drained from the events of the day. I feel bad pushing her, but I need to know why she will reject me so that I can begin my plan to ensure she does not. Now that I have given voice to my desires aloud, those desires are already history. A *rewriting* of history, in fact. The Shadow Lord is taking a Lady. The *how* is the final missing part.

"When we…" She licks her lips. Her dark brown skin does not reveal her blush, but I know that she is blushing. "You said never again."

"I was wrong. Is the Lord of the Shadowlands not allowed to be wrong, on occasion?"

She blinks brightly, her eyelashes thick and curly and accentuating the lovely shape of her eyes. Large and tilted up towards her hairline, she looks like a mirage, a figment created by steam. I have to fight my beast back not to reach out and grab her. "No, I don't believe he is."

"What about Yaron? Is he?"

She finds the soap and pours more into her palm, massaging her shoulders and the top of her head. Someone threw something at her — feces of some kind. I could smell it on her a mile away. I thought it was the mud, but the smell came from the top and back of her head. Even prostrated as she was in the dirt, the mud would not have spattered so high. It had to have been a farmer. I go through the list of those that I know and vow to repay their dishonor in kind.

"I don't know. I don't know Yaron as well as I should."

I chuckle to myself. "You already know him better than most." Better than me. "I'd like to discover him with you, though. Through you."

Her pupils are blown but she still manages to sound coherent as she rejects me again. I'm not offended. She can reject me all she likes, but it doesn't matter. It's all but decided. I will win her, I will bond her and she will rule me forever. I am a battle strategist first and foremost.

"I can't accept, my Lord."

"Yaron. You call me Yaron." I wade across the pool and come within arm's reach of her, but not closer. I slowly pull the green-hued glass bottle from between her fingers. I pour soap into my own hands and rub it through my hair, hair that she criticized before for being greasy, though I know it was the blood on her fingers that made her nose wrinkle. Bloody is an understatement as to how I left Ugaros on the road.

"I have my suspicions, but I'd like to hear from you directly — why are you so determined to deny me?"

"Because you don't know what you're saying." She licks her lips. I stare. She looks away.

"You think I am confused?" I smirk fully then, the thought hilarious in its own right. No one has ever made such an assumption of me, not even when I was a child.

"You don't know me. You have my family trapped. My Omega bond is the only thing that calls to you."

I nod. "These are fair assumptions. Is that all?"

"I think they're reason enough."

"Perhaps. But then am I to assume that, if I get to know you, release your family from their bonds and prove to you that I do like you beyond the signature of your pheromones…" Which are *intoxicating*… "…you will consent to take me for your mate when the red moon rises?"

She sinks lower into the water, letting it come up to her chin, but she holds my gaze above it. I can see the reflection of her eyes in the stillness of the liquid, holding fast, unblinking, trying to root out my lies. She'll find none. Trying to root out my weaknesses. She'll find one.

"Why are you doing this?"

I open my mouth, but I don't answer right away. I wish I could tell her that I was swayed by her eclipsing beauty, but I have seen more beautiful females. I wish I could vow that my intent is purely the duty of a Lord to an at-risk Omega in his territory, but it isn't. There are other Omegas who've passed through the Shadowlands underneath my rule and I felt no need to bond myself to them.

I wish I could tell her that it was more than her laughter. That one riotous laugh she released in my presence that made me sure I'd kill every other male in Gatamora before I let them have it. It's mine. I don't even want them hearing it. But causing it? Hearing it every day? Watching the expression on her face as she melts slightly, eyes crinkling at the corners, cheeks rounding and bouncing up to her eyes, making them appear as slits… If another Alpha or pack were to claim that laugh, I would have to renounce my title, offer up my claim to these shadowed lands. Because I would be distracted every day for the rest of my existence.

I wish I could tell her it's more than her words, oaths of power delivered from a being who seems to reject the very notion of power itself. I wish I could tell her it's more than the way she challenges me and my values, what I believe to be right.

I wish I could tell her that her commands and her mastery over my beast don't make me mad and leave me wanting. I wish I could tell her that I'd kill everyone in the whole of Gatamora if I truly thought it possible for her to turn that knowing smile onto another male or pack of males and whisper those fateful words to them: *Good boy.*

I wish I could tell her it's something selfless and not selfish, but it isn't.

I am curious about her and I have a crush on her like a schoolboy. I am among the most powerful males in Gatamora at present and I am in awe of everything about her. That is her.

I don't know how to say what I want to say without scaring her off. I settle for something paltry, a vagary that's not a lie, but a partial truth, leaving so many more important truths still covered. "I want to know you," I tell her.

Her hands, which have been torturing me by working soap across her pert breasts, still. She's covering her chest and I want to snarl and rip her hands away so I can see her. I want to see all of her. "You're scaring me."

"No, I'm not. You were frightened before. I can scent little fear on you now." A little, but not a lot.

"I am scared. The Shadow Lord is clearly a madman," she answers, shocking the hell out of me.

I grin with one edge of my mouth and feel a thousand times lighter, and very close to laughter. I try to remember the last time I laughed...but can't. "Perhaps."

"You know that whatever you feel right now, whatever madness compels you to want to bond me, is only because of our time in the woods. It's only because I'm an Omega and you're an Alpha beast."

I cock my head and, for want of something to do with my hands other than grab her, continue to rub soap over my body, washing the Rider's blood off of me. I wonder absently if he's still breathing. He was alive when I left him.

"I will give you that, when you commanded me in the woods, you unlocked a secret side of me I have never met before. I like that side of me. I like who I am when I think of you. And I like who I am even more in your presence."

I smile sadly. "I have lived a long time as the judge, jury and executioner of a justice I have created, that I know. But..." I do not know how to phrase what I mean to say next. That I've been blinded by my desire for her... No, no, quite the opposite. That my blinders have been removed. I cannot approach every problem the same way anymore. I must force myself to think from the perspective of others. To see what they see. To see the shadows in between what is right and what is wrong. "But there is more for me to consider now. Things I have not seen that you place before me in the light. I'm starting to realize that the Shadow Lord may be even more effective by sharing another perspective — the perspective of one even more powerful."

"It's pheromones," she chokes, and I feel like a bastard forcing her to talk to me when her voice is so ragged. I can see the darker purple marks of meaty fingers against her brown skin. I wish there was a way to throttle her into giving up the names of everyone who touched her in anger today, and yet, even if I could, I suspect I'd lose part of her if I went after them like I did the Rider.

She stared too long at the blood on my clothes and hair earlier and, remembering that, I quickly duck under the water, wanting to be sure it's not spattering my face. I don't like when she looks at me like I'm a murderer or a Lord or a savage. I want her to look at me like she did in the woods, in the moment right before everything changed and our bodies came together.

Like I'm a male named Yaron. A male sent to do her bidding and nothing more.

"Then how do you explain the other Omegas who have come through the Shadowlands? How do you explain the days — weeks — I spent with a powerful unmated Omega on the North Island, the Fallen Beast Omega? The witch of the woods? I was close to her. I could scent a heat not long passed on her skin and yet…nothing. There was not a hint of attraction between us."

"But…" She sounds frustrated. She's persistent, this Omega, but she must know that the battle is already lost. She is not a warrior. She only has a warrior's heart. "But you left…"

"Left?"

"You never tried to talk to me after you brought me to your chambers, only checking on me or doing strange tours of your chambers that put me on edge… You never tried to actually say anything to me."

Did she want me to? I don't dare ask her that. Instead, I clear my throat of the desire, unbidden, rising within it. "Yes. Because I did not trust myself around you and at the time, I knew better than to test the limits of my self-control."

She waits for me to say more. I don't. I force her to ask, "And now?"

"And now I have made my decision."

"What decision?" she says, voice hollow and starved.

"I will not deny myself any longer. Only you can do that."

Her lower lip wobbles and her hands smooth over the curve of her head. She is a beautiful female, hair or not. Her features are elegantly arrayed. Overlarge eyes, a lower lip full to bursting, a cupid's bow that's pronounced and makes her mouth look drawn on by the hands of an artist, high cheek bones, a soft, pronounced jawline, ears small and delicate.

"How have you managed to remain unmated to now?" I ask, out of the blue.

She fiddles with more soap. She doesn't need it. We've been in the bath long enough. "Lack of interest."

"Lack of interest on your part or theirs?"

"Both."

I find that hard to believe but don't say as much. There must be more to it than that. "Your sisters also are unmated?"

She nods.

I release the valve at the bottom of the basin and she starts when water begins to slowly drain away. I step out of the tub and make no effort to conceal my erection. I take particular pleasure in watching her watch it, though it's clear she tries not to.

I return to her with a towel as I ponder the dynamic of her family. I have a question to ask her, but struggle to phrase it in a way that doesn't sound judgmental. She reaches for the towel, but I hold it away from her. She relents and steps out of the bath and into my arms because it's what I want and because no, she is no warrior. A protector, yes, but she lacks all the bloodlust that I have in spades and plan to use to win her heart.

"Do you think that your sisters are unmated because of your family?"

She tilts her head to the side and blinks at me slowly. She's tired. Beyond tired. But I don't want her to sleep. I want her here, present, with me. "You mean, my parents? They've been happily married for thirty years. They don't keep us from getting married."

I wrap the towel around her and dry her weary body gently. "I don't imagine they do. Not outwardly. But they have fostered a closeness within your family that I imagine may be difficult to replicate. Perhaps, the thought of losing that is what keeps..."

Kiandah turns within my arms, showing me her front. She has breasts perfectly proportional to her frame, a flat stomach with a softness beneath her belly button that I long to sink my teeth into. Her hips and thighs are thicker than they appear when she's clothed and I love that about her, too. She has thickening curls that cover her sex and that my cock strains towards. But the bruises...I'm gentle as I work the towel over them, careful not to hurt her. My people and I have done enough of that, already.

And then something in her tone snaps. She speaks quickly and stiffly, "My Lord, it doesn't have anything to do with family — why we're not married. We're not married because we're poor. Do you know how hard it is for women in the Shadowlands? Owenna hates cooking. She's tried to get jobs in the castle as a chambermaid and been rejected. Life might be okay for Betas in the Shadowlands but it's hard to...to *move* when you're a woman here. Meanwhile, Cyprus is offered jobs and daughters when we set foot outside of our home." She chuckles lightly, her eyes glazing as if recalling a particular memory. Meanwhile, I stand there, stunned.

"No one wants to marry a poor woman with no dowry from a family of cooks. Maybe, if we were exceptional beauties, it would be different. But now, we're killers so it doesn't matter at all." She coughs and lifts her arms over the edge of the towel, wrapping it around herself and taking herself away from me. She tilts her chin up, peering up at me as if challenging me.

I frown. "You believe it harder for a female in the Shadowlands than for a Beta?"

"It's not a belief. It's a *fact.* Perhaps, if you left your castle and talked to people, you'd know that."

I hiss, trying to batten my anger. That she suggests she knows my people better than I do...*of course she does.* "You're tired," I grit.

She tips her chin up, the haughty little wench. "Yes. But I'm not wrong."

"I will investigate your theory," I finally concede. "And I will ensure you receive fresh, clean produce and supplies in the kitchens from now on."

"Thank you, Yaron," she says, gaze still on me piercingly.

My cock doesn't mind the intensity of her dark brown stare at all. I reach out and cup the back of her neck. I pull her forward and she stumbles into me so that she's fully flush to my chest, my erection pressed between us. "I won't be sleeping in the throne room any longer."

Her brow furrows. "You've been sleeping in the throne room?"

"Yes."

"Why?"

"I told you, I was aiming to keep my distance." I dip my head. She doesn't cower or canter back.

"Yes, but…you could have just sent me to sleep with my family. It's what I wanted, anyway."

"Yes, I could have." I inch a little closer. "But I think I knew then already what I know now with certainty. Staying away was a battle I was always going to lose. I wanted you here among my things. I wanted to be fully wrapped around you. I still do."

Her pupils expand and lose focus. I smile very softly, my breath feathering her lips, her face. She smells like smoke and cinnamon and only a little like my soaps. I don't understand such a chemistry.

Just as she sways towards me, eyelashes fluttering, her body giving in, I pull away and deny us both. The first stage of my plan involves torture, yes. It's what I'm known for — all she knows me for, perhaps. I'll prove to her I'm all of what she thinks of me and so much more. This is my unspoken vow to her as I sweep her feet up once more and carry her to the sleeping chamber, to my bed. I slide her beneath the covers,

covers that smell like her, and take a seat on the edge of the mattress.

She blinks up at me, surprise on her face. Her gaze flashes once, twice, to my cock, which is very unhappy with the chill of the room and would very much like to warm back up in her heat. I fist my erection and completely ignore the small puff of air from her lips.

I want her to fuck me fucking desperately.

But I don't want her to just *want* to fuck me. I want her to *need* me with a violence that will give me my ultimate desire — her bond, as mine. Her everything forever.

"Rest," I tell her. "I'll return shortly. In the meantime, I'll send Okayo to stitch your brow."

After donning a tunic, trousers and boots, but leaving behind my cloak and axe, I leave her. I manage not to look back by concentrating on my next task and walking with purpose. I shut the door with a bang.

It takes me little time to find Okayo. He's not far, in the east wing corridor, pacing restlessly at the base of the stairs leading up to my private chambers. He comes to an abrupt stop when he sees me. "I heard the Omega was injured by a Rider outside of Orias." He's approaching me, but I advance on him and don't stop.

He stumbles, eyes flashing with surprise, but only fleetingly. He's not one to be surprised by me. Not often, anyways. "Did you attend to the Rider?" I say, backing him into the wall.

"Horace said his hands scented of the Omega. Even through all the blood. I took that as a bad sign and chose to leave him in the infirmary until I could confirm with you whether you wanted him relieved of his agony." He waits, his eyes meeting mine unblinkingly. Then he huffs out of the corner of his mouth and adds, "Well, it's not like there's any saving him, not in the state you left him in, my Lord."

"Good. How long will it take for him to die without assistance?"

Okayo shrugs. "Another hour? Maybe he's dead already. I came here right away when I heard what happened. I've been waiting. What took you so long?" He blinks again, shakes his head quickly and tries to move past me. "Never mind. Don't answer that."

I block my hand against his shoulder, preventing him from moving forward, towards my chambers and my Omega within them. "She has bruises on her ribs and hips, torn knees and palms, the big toe of her right foot is bloody around the nail, though she complains of none of it, and she has a cut above her right brow requiring stitching. I expect you to tend to all of it *respectfully*. She's just come from the bath and is naked in my bed. You will be respectful and appropriate."

Okayo must read something in my expression or tone because he swallows hard, looking uncharacteristically uncomfortable. "You know I like men."

"And women."

"Men more."

"She is different. Perfection. I don't want Horace or any of your other helpers anywhere near her. You'll tend to her alone. Am I clear?"

"As the wind."

And he's off. I watch his back disappear around the next corner and my mind flickers dangerously with images of him looming over her, their skin tones so closely matched, their limbs intertwining sinuously and seamlessly as they bring pleasure to one another in *my* bed. My Omega. *Mine.*

The slow rage that filters through my limbs is something I've never experienced before and I find that I...that I...

My god.

I like it.

The rage brings clarity. It sharpens my mind and my muscles. My beast feels calmer basking in that rage. I inhale and the breezy corridor smells more fragrant than it did. I can scent her on the wind. I can scent her on my own skin. Okayo will scent of her when he leaves my chambers and I will have a hard time not removing the skin from his body just so I can covet it. Thoughts of murder make my lips twitch.

"My Lord?"

I turn and see Radmilla standing there wearing a perturbed and peculiar expression. "Yes, Radmilla?"

"You're smiling." She frowns. "It's terrifying."

I chuckle.

Her eyes round in alarm.

I laugh a little harder. "All is well, Radmilla."

"Are you sure? You seem..."

I wait for her to finish, a slow rumbling coming from deep within me. She doesn't. Her pale lips slacken. She shakes her head and takes a tentative step forward. "I just wanted to apologize profusely. By the time I realized she was gone, it was too late. The guards at the gates saw her leave, but they had not received orders from you or me to confine her to the castle, so they allowed it. I have rectified their misconception. It will never happen again." She pauses before wringing her hands and continuing, "I heard the Omega was injured. For my failing to protect her, I would accept punishment, my Lord. If you wish…"

I inhale again, Kiandah's scent so clear. Crisp, crystal, perfection. Its draw is just as clear. I understand everything. What I need to do. The laws that need to be set. The festival that needs to happen. The Fates that need to be killed. The undead that need to be rooted out. The *Trash* that needs disposal first, before the rest. These are too many risks — not to my people, to *her.*

I speak on the exhale, voice calm, words hopefully reassuring. "You are not at fault for this. The fault is mine and, above that, those that aggressed the Omega when she was in the village. I am, however, displeased that the Omega's family has been receiving spoiled stock. How have they been preparing food for the keep uninterrupted?"

Radmilla's cheeks glow pink. "I stopped several spoiled tuns of grain and meat at the gates. Other stock made it in… through staff that condemn the Ubutu family in the same way the villagers condemned the Omega today. The Ubutu family hasn't complained about the spoiled goods they've received. Instead, they've made do with what they've been able to source in our stores — goods that have been canned and kept as reserves. I also believe they've been denying themselves meals in order to ensure there's enough for everyone else. I know that you have punished them for what they've done, but they also punish themselves."

I do not like her answer and my lips twist because of it.

"I will personally inspect every food store that comes to the castle from now on, my Lord, and I will ensure…"

I lift a hand. "No. You have too much on your plate to manage such tedium. I will handle this another way."

She nods. "What can I do, my Lord?"

"The body of the Crimson Rider, the one who attempted to rape Kiandah on the road. When he's dead, I want him dragged by hand to the village. I want him left next to the fountain undisturbed. I want it disseminated why he died and how. I will also take Kiandah and her family to the Orias market as soon as she's well enough. Together, we will speak to the suppliers and ensure that it is clear that the Ubutu family is not to receive spoiled goods. Her family will not miss another meal."

"Yes, my Lord."

"Walk with me." I turn around and head for the south wing of the castle, Radmilla rushing to keep up. "How go preparations for the festival?"

"I… They have been…progressing…since we last spoke."

"I'd like it ready immediately."

"Immediately."

"Immediately. Right away. Shall I provide additional definitions for you?" I lift a brow and her incredulous look turns flat at my sarcasm.

"Don't you get testy with me. I was running this keep when you were still in diapers, young master." She pushes her heavy braid over her shoulder and chuffs between her teeth.

"As soon as possible, Radmilla. I do not wish to miss the next blood moon."

"The next blood moon will be in four weeks' time. It would be appropriate to host the festival then. Though it seems far, it's going to be tight with the chaos in the kitchens."

"What will you need to enable the Omega's family to preside over the meal? The meal is the centerpiece of the festival, of course."

"Of course." Radmilla blinks at me as if she's never seen me before in her life. "In addition to clean stores, the kitchens are rather out of date. If we could allow in some contraband equipment from the North Island," she says on a whisper, "the kitchens could be prepared to accommodate the influx of food needed to supply the Red Moon Festival. As it stands now, the uhmm…traditional nature of the kitchen would render it impossible for the Ubutu family to preside over the full meal. We could, of course, outsource some of the preparations, but I don't doubt that it would be seen by Kiandah's family as an insult."

"You think you're rather clever, don't you, Radmilla?"

She's trying to fight a smile and look at me with innocence in her light green eyes. "Whatever do you mean, my Lord?"

"You know how I feel about the old ways." I admire and stick to them, short of a few exceptions. Kitchens have never been among them, but I suppose that is a rather flawed way of thinking as I do not cook anything. "You know how I feel about the North Islanders and their precious technologies." Their technologies are only meant to divide and conquer, all in the name of efficiency. They don't even meet one another's gazes anymore on the North Island, hiding as they do behind screen after screen.

"I know, my Lord. But modern plumbing and *safer* cooking practices are common staples of many South Island homes. To ask the most important cooks in the region to use fire and brimstone when they could use industrial grade North Island ovens and stoves to prepare food for hundreds of people is not unthinkable. The Lords who came before you will forgive you."

"I care little for their forgiveness. They were madmen, the lot." I rake my hand down my face, some of my earlier enthusiasm deflating at this change in topic. "And how quickly could you source such appliances?"

"Faster than you care to know, my Lord."

"Fine. You know who to speak to for coin." I don't like that at all, but I do not want to know more. "And how many builders can be spared? I want it up and running within the next ten days so that preparation for the festival can begin."

"I should be able to spare five builders from the southern highway lines. And that won't be a problem at all. There is also the question of the cooks themselves."

"Yes?"

"The Ubutu family was previously aided by over a dozen more cooks. Right now, they do all of the cooking among themselves. They are too few for everyday cooking if they are expected to feed the entire keep — your Riders are not small men and women — and they are far too few hands to manage the entire festival, particularly given that Kiandah is the one who comes up with most of their meal plans and many of their recipes and it does not seem you intend to give her back to them."

"I do not."

Radmilla is smiling, though the corners of her lips are pinched as she clearly tries not to. "So, how would you like to proceed then, my Lord? Many of those who worked with the

Ubutu family in the kitchens were detained and released after questioning."

I pinch the bridge of my nose, my pace slowing. "How many are needed?"

"If Kiandah is no longer working full time, then perhaps we start with the eight that were detained and released…"

"You said there were a dozen or more."

"Yes, but some did not survive the church fire."

The church fire. My nostrils flare. "See about hiring an additional fifteen to seventeen for the kitchens."

"Fifteen, my Lord?" She shakes her head. "Lord Talbot will not be happy with that."

"Particularly when you tell him to increase their wages."

"Wages?" Radmilla's voice goes up shrilly at the end. "You mean for the new kitchen staff, not for the Ubutu family…"

"I mean for them all. You know as well as I do that keeping the Ubutu family caged in my kitchens forever will not work. It is not the way things are done. Prisoners are kept in the dungeons or not at all."

The frown that crosses her face as we enter the south wing tightens the muscles across my chest. It is cooler here. Most of the castle is split into two levels except for the south and southeast wings, which are split into three. The lowermost level of the southeast wing is the lower dungeon where the Omega's family was kept, but only briefly, but in the south wing, the lowermost level is occupied by servants' quarters that haven't been used in two decades.

They are half underground and as I take the double helix staircase down to this lower level, the sound of clanging and clashing fills my ears. I follow the sounds of chaos to the end of the hall, which splits into a T. To the left, I hear singing, and when I step into the center of the intersection, I see fractured daylight filtering in through the slits that older generations called windows.

"Omegas say boom…" comes the cry from down the hall. I follow it towards the old palace kitchens, wondering if I've ever even been down here before. Maybe once, when I was a boy? No, not even then.

The corridor feels devoid of life, the stone walls and floor bare and free of decoration. Such a contrast to the vibrancy of the voices echoing within them. "What are you…" Radmilla's stopped walking at the T junction.

I turn to look back at her. "Yes?"

"You plan to free them?"

"Not without punishing them first." Her frown dips even further down her face, but before she can speak, I reach out and, in a move most uncharacteristic of me, I place my palm on her shoulder. "Trust me Radmilla, I do not intend to lose her."

Radmilla must be shocked, because for the first time in her life she doesn't answer me. I smirk and cock my chin towards the kitchens. "Come. You will accompany me to the kitchens?"

"To…fetch the Omega a meal, my Lord?" she guesses, struggling to understand what I'm doing here — what we're doing here.

I shake my head and look back at her over my shoulder as I near the door. "Not at all. You're here for me. For moral support."

She gawks and then stumbles in her effort to catch up to me as I take the long strides necessary to bring me to the open doorway in the left wall. There is no door set in the frame, just a large, gaping opening of rough-hewn rock. Stones are missing in several places.

I step into the kitchens, light washing over me stemming from the wide double doors, which are currently propped open. It seems that some foods — potatoes — are being either brought in, carried out or sorted. I feel…strangely nervous as I enter the vast space. I'm surprised by both the scale of it and how empty it feels, devoid of Radmilla's precious appliances, with only the one cooking fireplace against the far wall and several long stretches of disintegrating wooden tables for them to prepare food upon.

I frown. This won't do. This won't do at all.

The singing dies with my presence and I look around the chamber at the members of the Omega's family, meeting each of their gazes in turn. There is the youngest daughter. She stands closest to me and is kneading what I have to assume to be bread. I know nothing of food at all. She stiffens when she sees me and quickly begins smoothing down her skirts and rolling back her shoulders, but before she can fully preen and present herself, I flick my gaze to her brother.

There is fire in his gaze, a twin flame I see reflected in the eyes of his sister. Though hers is stronger, his is still bright green and fierce. I can work with that.

Next to him is another sister, though not the eldest. She has doe eyes, like Kiandah, and hair that falls down to her chest in twists. A sudden fleeting image interrupts my thoughts. *Kiandah, with hair down to her mid-back, wrapped in twists*

just like these. We're here in the castle and she's hiding behind a corner,
thinking I can't see her watching me out of the corner of my eye. She's
with a friend. They're both watching me and giggling like schoolgirls
because that's what they were. She was so much younger then.

I nearly stagger at the realization that this is not a dream
but a *memory*. I have seen Kiandah before in the castle. What
had she been doing there? I wish…my stare had lingered over
her longer…that she hadn't been a child… Had we both
been of age and had I noticed the fire within her then,
perhaps so much could have been avoided. Perhaps, her
family would not have gone to such lengths to better their
circumstances. Perhaps, I could have kept them all safe from
me and the judgement they are owed. Perhaps, I could have
kept Kiandah all to myself and so much time would not have
been lost between us.

Staring at this sister of hers with the long hair, I wonder if
she is older or younger than Kiandah. I cannot tell, for they
look so dissimilar, now especially without a hair color to bind
them. They do share the same skin tone, a skin tone shared
also by their mother, while their father, brother, and youngest
sister all hover on a spectrum of brown a few shades lighter.
The oldest sister has a skin tone slightly darker brown than all
the rest.

My gaze passes to her, but she will not look at me, and as I
look between her face and that of her mother and father,
sensing their guilt and sensing her rage, I wonder…who is
truly in charge here?

Not being able to answer that, I look toward the elders.
Kiandah's mother stands at the open doorway, a potato in
each hand, while her father feeds wood into the sticks in the

bottom of the fireplace. He has sweat on his brow, pouring down his face. They all look dirty and unwashed, like the servants one might find in Hjiel, where violence is prized and the strong oppress those weaker. Is this what I have made them? In the realm of shadows, have we all become savages?

Behind me, Radmilla softly clears her throat. My annoyance flashes into discomfort. I realize that I've been standing there silently intimidating them for the better part of a minute and that was not my intent. "Hello," I say. That sounds rather dumb though, doesn't it? I clasp my hands behind my back and take a step further into the space while the Ubutu family glances around uncertainly at one another.

"Apologies," I say, starting again. "I do not mean to interrupt your preparations for the evening meal."

"Don't worry, my Lord, the evening meal has already been prepared and taken to the great hall. We are beginning preparations for the morning meal. But they can wait," Kiandah's father says uncertainly. He stands up and wipes his hands off on the soot-soaked apron tied around his waist.

I stare at him, meeting his gaze, watching his discomfort with a mirrored discomfort of my own. "I…" I clear my throat. "I had not yet received my evening meal."

"Normally, Lady Radmilla comes to fetch it. We have it here." He gestures to his middle daughter, the one with the twists, and she steps aside to reveal a covered tray. It's a long tray, always laden with far more food than I could eat in a sitting. I end up throwing a lot of it away. Meanwhile, Kiandah fought for her life today to try to ensure that the castle has fresh stores. And I discard mine… The knot in my stomach twists like a knife plunged in up to the hilt.

Grimly, I say, "Have you all eaten dinner yet?"

"No, m'Lord."

I have five other questions ready to ask them, that I would ask them were they staff, but they aren't...even though they are...so I don't. I clear my throat. "Why don't you all dine from the tray you prepared for me? It seems large enough to accommodate a family and far too large for a single individual."

They look around at each other and I can feel Radmilla laughing at my back even though she doesn't make a sound and her amusement is likely not visible on her expression — but I can still feel it.

"You... What will you eat, my Lord?" Kiandah's father says.

"I actually came down here with a request. I would like to prepare a dish for the Omega...for Kiandah. I'd like to prepare it myself, but I am unfamiliar with cooking practices and could use some...help." Help. I don't think I've ever asked for *help* before from anyone for anything. "I can prepare for myself whatever I prepare for her."

The family seems momentarily frozen in time. Momentarily... And then the youngest sister snorts. "You want to prepare Kiandah food, Lord Yaron?" She laughs. "Why on earth would you want to prepare *her* food?"

I'm curious about the young one's tone. She is young, perhaps, that can explain the slight bite behind it. But I don't think so. Her jealousy runs deeper. Evenly, I answer her, "I intend to take Kiandah for my wife."

That shuts her up so fast, she chokes. "A w...wi..." She never finishes that thought and I don't wait for her to.

Meanwhile, Kiandah's mother shrieks. The sound startles me and I reach instinctively for my axe, even though I'm not wearing it. I pivot and see her rushing towards me. I worry for a moment she means to attack — it would be no less than what I would do, were the positions reversed. But when I lift my hand to repel her assault, she grabs my forearm and shakes it vigorously. She is a very, very short woman — shorter than Kiandah by half a foot — and has to lift up onto her tiptoes to reach my face. She grabs my cheeks and pinches them to the point of pain.

"My son! My son, a Lord? My daughter, a Lady! Welcome to the family!" She moves in like she's going to strangle me… or hug me…but her husband lunges from his position and races over to grab her by the shoulders. He drags her away from me while she bats at his hands.

"You can't grab Lord Yaron!" he hisses in her ear. "We'll be back in the dungeons before you can blink."

He's not right. But he has a point. Slowly, I nod and take a step towards them. He isn't a short male, but I'm still quite a bit taller. I'm not wearing my cloak, but I don't know how to shake the feeling that I'm still towering when I want to approach him as equals. "It's quite alright. I just…am surprised you would welcome me into your family so easily."

"She's just excited, m'Lord." He looks to the side, his displeasure apparent. With his wife, though? Or with me? "She's been wanting her daughters married off since they were born. A lord is far better than any of them can do, given the fact that we're just cooks, m'Lord." Just cooks. Poor. Few opportunities. Female. I don't like the words of the Omega echoing in my skull.

I nod, as if in understanding, though I'm not sure I fully do. "You would be pleased with a Lord marrying your daughters," I say to Kiandah's mother and father, "but would you be pleased with Kiandah marrying me?"

"Of course!" shouts her mother at a pitch that feels a little too high.

"Fuck no," her brother growls at the same time.

Her father says nothing. He doesn't need to. His eyes flit away before moving back to mine again.

I don't say anything for a moment. I am in a particularly torturous position. I am Lord over them and I intend to mate and bond and marry their daughter. It is only a matter of time. Yet that time could be *years* from now. Having the approval of her family could condense my timeline by months — no, that's not true. That's a simplification. If her family approved of me today, I would have her hand by tomorrow.

I nod, not needing to hear more. As is the case with any war, I will need a strategy, but this one will take time to devise. I've never fought a war for a *heart* before, let alone for many of them.

"I understand," I say. My heart beats hard and slow in my chest. So hard I can feel it in my eyes. "For now, let us begin with dinner for Kiandah. I would appreciate some direction as to what Kiandah might enjoy. She has had a trying day, after all."

"Trying?" Her oldest sister.

"Is she alright?" Her middle sister.

"She okay?" Her brother.

"What happened?" her father and mother say together.

"She likes Orias rice," her youngest sister says, voice high and strained. "I'm not a good cook like her, but I think I can show you how to make it."

I turn towards her and am curious about the terrified look on her face. It is very unlike her, the little I know of her thus far. She is a male peacock, this one, all plumage, and though I don't know her, I know her well enough not to trust her to have Kiandah's best interest at heart. So why does she offer her help now?

Curious, I turn towards her and nod slightly. "Please, proceed. And Radmilla," I say, turning to the woman who's been standing by the door silently laughing at me. "Have the builders come by to take measurements as soon as possible."

"Very well, my Lord." She moves to leave, but before she does, she pauses. The old dame has the audacity to wink at me. "And have fun."

The Omega's family chuckles, and strangely, Radmilla's insubordination seems to ease some of the tension in the room as I'm folded uneasily into their ranks. Working together with her mother, whose name I learn is Mercy, they show me how to make Orias rice. It's harder than I thought it would be to make rice, and this rice has many ingredients. Red pepper, bay leaves, onion, garlic and a dried pepper that Mercy doesn't let me touch, but handles herself while wearing gloves. There are many times when I sense that they'd like to correct something I'm doing, but Mercy is the only one who has the courage. She takes the knife from me after I chop the onions and redoes my work while I look on, frustrated that I've done it wrong. I'm not used to doing things wrong.

Zelie, the middle sister, suggests charred chicken wings to accompany the rice. I think that sounds awful — charred anything does, except for the bodies of Trash City I'd like to have hanging from the spikes on my gates — but I don't say so. Instead, I have her show me which spices to coat them in and then her father shows me how to rack the "oven" firepit and at which point to lay the chicken on. Meanwhile, Audet, the youngest sister, continues to stir the rice through to completion.

I dust my hands off on the rag Reginald, her father, hands me. I notice that his hands are scarred worse than mine. Lots of his wounds look like burns. "Radmilla has encouraged me to consider breaking tradition," I tell him, glancing from his scars to his face. "We will be upgrading the kitchens over the next ten days. The builders will be in and out. They will attempt to remain as out of your way as possible. You are free to give them direction as how best to assist you and where you'd like the machines placed. In advance of their arrival, if you'd like to come up with some sketches, or if you have particular machines you would like or other requirements, that could be helpful."

"Thank you, my Lord," Reginald says.

Then Cyprus cuts in, "If it's sketches we'll need, we need Kiandah for that. She's the only one of us that can draw. Her sketchbooks are in the old kitchens." He has his hands on the butcherblock countertop of the massive island that dominates the space. His left, free hand drums angrily near the pile of onions he's been dicing. His right hand still holds the knife. "Can you have one of your...people go get them, my Lord?" His tone is acerbic. I don't let myself rise to it, but nod.

"You will fetch them with one of my Riders, along with anything else you might need from your old home."

"It wasn't torched?"

"My Lord," I hiss.

"My Lord," he says quickly, color rising in his face. The hard slash of his brows hardens further.

I nod, trying not to be infuriated by his obvious insubordination. I need to win his respect. I have his sister. He is an Alpha and he is right to worry. I have not been able to keep her safe thus far. The thought sinks through me like a stone. I swallow hard and my voice comes out sharper than I intend as I answer him, "No. It was not torched. You may bring your things here. Any that you need. And any additional requirements you may have to make your living conditions more…tolerable, you may give to Radmilla. She will ensure they are procured, within reason."

Cyprus's eyes flash with surprise before narrowing. His hand twitches on the knife he holds. "And after we get her stuff, my Lord, can Kiandah come help us draw plans for the kitchens?"

"She is not confined to my chambers, if that is what you're asking," though I know it's not all he's asking. He wants to know if she's in trouble, if she's safe, if she's my prisoner, if he'll ever be able to see her again. Answers I'm not sure he deserves. I'm also not sure he doesn't. Carefully, I say, "But she is injured at the moment. I won't have her up and walking around freely for the next couple days, or until Lord Okayo gives her clearance to do so, whichever is longer."

"Injured how?" The tension in the room is palpable. Her family has stopped everything they're doing.

I sweep my gaze around at them, wondering... "She was pelted with rocks and animal feces, strangled, slapped and nearly raped."

"Raped?" Cyprus chokes. He rears back from the counter where he'd been working and the knife tumbles from his hand, clattering to the ground. "By who?"

"One of my Riders."

Cyprus's chest swells with unspent aggression. The Alpha within him cannot transform, but Alphas all have a predilection towards beastliness and physiologically appear more swollen when enraged. He appears slightly larger than he did and he was not a small male to begin with. He could be molded, shaped, and honed to a weapon. Hm...

"You let a Crimson Rider attack Kiandah?"

"Do not test me," I snarl. "Kiandah left the keep and was attacked, first by villagers — your *friends* — in retribution for crimes *you* committed and then was attacked on the road by one of mine. Him, I take responsibility for and he has been dealt with. But what I want to know is why she left the keep at all. Kiandah is a good girl, isn't she? She would not have left for no reason... She would not have even thought of it."

Cyprus looks down. Owenna is looking down. Her father is looking at the fire. Zelie and Mercy, however, both have gazes that stray. I turn to approach Audet, whose eyes remain fixed to the floor until I stand within arm's reach of her. She's got her fingers clasped. Behind me, her brother attempts to speak in her defense, "She didn't..."

I hold up my hand — he quiets immediately — and I wait. It takes her a long time to look up at my face. Long enough for my irritation to bubble to the surface. "Do not keep me, child. My *wife* is waiting."

Audet winces, then offers softly, "She wanted to go."

I hold my right wrist in my left hand behind my back. I flex my right hand several times before curling it into a tight fist. Restraint. *Restraint…* "I am…certain she did." I have to take a breath between each word, struggling as I am not to inflict pain. So much pain. I try to keep my words clear and pointed as I speak. This female may be younger than her sisters but she is no child. She is fully grown and *knew* what she asked of Kiandah. She knew the risks and she simply tossed her sister to the fire.

"Your sister would fall on her sword for you. And you used her love against her, for your own gain. I can guess that this is not the first time you have done this, and if allowed, I'm certain it will not be the last." I lower my face until I'm looking at Audet at eye level, bending near in half to do so. "But it will be the last."

Audet shivers. My nostrils flare. "You see, I have Kiandah's respect, but I do not yet have her love, as you do. This means that, for the time being, you hold great power over me. I cannot bring harm to you as I would were you any other creature in my city, in Gatamora, for having coerced Kiandah into leaving the safety of the keep…"

And then the female has the audacity. She interrupts me, stuttering, color in her cheeks high, "I didn't threaten her, if that's what you mean, my Lord. She left on her own…"

"And her life means more to me than yours," I snarl. I snatch her chin and squeeze it hard. "Correction. Your life means absolutely nothing to me while her life means…

everything. If she did not exist, you would be rotting in the lowest cells of my dungeons. If she had died on the road, I would have ripped out your insides, and if I am ever forced to make the choice between your life and Kiandah's safety, I will not hesitate, little girl. Do you understand me?"

She nods, the insolent welp.

"I want to hear it."

"I understand, my Lord." She's crying, tears tracking down her cheeks. She is a pretty woman, yes, that's clear, and I would gut her gladly if she ever crossed me.

I tilt my head very slightly to the side. "She was yours before today, but now she is mine. Tell me you understand."

"I understand, my Lord," she sputters out, blinking quickly to try to stem her tears.

I drop my pitch so that only she can hear, leaning in to whisper directly against her hair. "And if you pose a risk to Kiandah's life again, ask her for something that she has no ability to give, or ever *dare* try to separate her from me, I will have you killed savagely and make it look like an accident. Kiandah will never know it was me. And as your corpse is lowered into the ground and your soul joins those of your ancestors, she will use my shoulder to dry her tears and I will comfort her and tell her things like, 'Audet, such a pretty little girl, such a senseless tragedy.'"

Audet's tears burst forth and she nods feverishly. I take that response as sufficient, for now, but I'm not certain just how much Audet has heard me. Taking advantage of Kiandah has been ingrained in the spoiled princess since birth. I'm not sure a few threats will simply undo it. I need more robust assurances and so, when I stand, I turn to Cyprus.

"She would have been raped bloody and left for dead on the Orias highway line had I not been informed quickly by members of my staff that she had departed and had I not immediately set off to follow her."

The anger that barrels out of Cyprus is tangible to my beast and claws extend through my nailbeds. I drag them along the countertop as I reach Zelie, who is adding the final touches to Kiandah's tray of food, fingers fumbling desperately.

She freezes as I drum my claws across the board. "My Riders cannot be trusted when it comes to her. They are Alphas, or they are savages, or they are angry, or they are all of the above. I need eyes on her when mine cannot be spared." My fingers still and I turn away from Zelie to face her brother who is busy glaring at my back. "Would you wear a red cloak, Cyprus? Would you consider moving from the kitchens?"

Mercy gasps and claps a hand over her mouth. The older woman with too many laugh lines has desires for her children. And I am sorry it has taken so much of her lifetime to see them realized. A chance to don a red cloak, at this late age, is rare. My Riders are typically selected between six and sixteen. Alphas ascend in their earlier years and, by then, Betas' and Alphas' aptitudes for combat, battle strategy and border security will have made themselves known. To invite him to join their ranks now will cause a stir. Fortunately, I answer to no one.

Cyprus is giving me a peculiar look. He wants to hate me, but he cannot hide the desire in his eyes, which glitter at the possibilities. "You'd make me a Crimson Rider? Just like that?"

"Yes. You would of course go through an accelerated training regimen. If you survive it, then you'll receive your colors. If you don't, I'm no worse off for having rid the world of a suspected killer."

"You know I'm not."

I narrow my gaze at his insolent tone, but still I say, "No, you are not. But could you be?"

"My...my Lord?" he says, seeming to remember to whom he speaks. Showing me an ounce of the respect he'd denied me previously.

I turn to face him fully. "Could you slit the throat of an aggressor coming for Kiandah? Could you throw your body between her and the blade as she would do for you and has done for all of you at least twice over?"

"Of course," he says without hesitation, without blinking, and I sense truth.

"Good. And as you are her brother, her heat cycles will not affect you. You are best positioned for this task."

He snorts — insolence runs in this family. "To be her human shield?"

"If you cannot wield a sword, then a shield will do."

He smiles a little more fully at me then and I struggle not to return it.

"I can do that."

"You'll stick closely to her until the threat has passed. And when it is time to move you, you will not lose your colors. You will be folded into the Crimson ranks, wherever Dorsten seeks to place you. Do you accept?"

"Y-yes. Yes, of course."

"Yes, *what?*"

His gaze narrows. Yes, there's fire there. "Yes, my Lord."

"Report to Dorsten just before sunrise, when the sky is still dark. That is when the Riders begin first practice. You will have your work cut out for you."

He nods and clenches his fist, determination fueling him. His gaze is glazed and as it returns to me, I have a premonition of what he will say next. *Revenge...* "What happens if I catch another Rider trying to harm Kiandah, my Lord? Am I..." He swallows. "*Allowed* to kill them?"

"I'd like you to try to keep them breathing, but kill them if you must. I imagine you'll have to. It's difficult to keep a good fighter that you've maimed but alive, and all of my Riders will be better fighters than you."

He frowns. "Is that what you did to the other guy? Kept him alive after what he tried to do to Kia?"

I grin to show a mouth full of beastly and razor-sharp teeth. Cyprus takes a half step away from me. "Oh yes," I hiss. "I hope he lives. I hope he lives a long time and, if another Rider makes a similar attempt *knowing* what is in store for them, then I want them captured so I can take them to my dungeons where they will live out a very long, very painful lifetime."

Cyprus' face betrays his shock when he says, "Are you... mad?"

I bark out a laugh that surprises everyone in the room, myself included, and turn my back on him to collect the tray that Zelie has finished arranging so artfully. "Kiandah is hungry. I will be off. You, master Cyprus, will not trouble yourself with thoughts of revenge. Your allegiances now fall to Kiandah first, then to me as your Lord, then to your fellow Riders, then to your family, then to your people. Understand that and remember it when the time comes that those allegiances are called into question. And there will be a time." I sweep my gaze over the group, settling it on Owenna. "Owenna. Walk with me. Select a wine for your sister that you think she'd like best."

As Owenna retrieves a wine from the storage pantry, I bid farewell to her other family members. Her father grunts a goodbye, Mercy showers me with pats to the cheek and arms that I think are rather inappropriate but that I allow, Zelie whispers a soft goodbye and tells me to wish Kiandah well. Audet merely cringes and tries not to cry.

I carry the tray, laden with a large covered wooden bowl of the rice I helped prepare and another with a modest amount of chicken. I wasn't sure how much of the chicken they offered me because they could afford to or because they felt they had to, so I wasn't willing to take more than needed. Owenna holds a bottle of wine and a pitcher and looks as if she's walking across a bed of nails as she follows me out into the hall towards the central staircase.

We walk for some time in silence, long enough for the sounds of clean-up in the kitchen to fall away and for voices from the great hall to echo through the walls as supper begins in earnest.

Quietly, I say, "It is impressive the number of people your family has been able to feed these past days, even when denied access to clean food, tools and support staff."

Owenna doesn't reply right away and when she does, it surprises me. "I didn't believe we had a choice, my Lord."

I smile with one corner of my mouth and glance down at the female with her hair neatly arrayed in a short halo of curls around her face. It's a soft halo around a hardened face. Sharp lines she has not, but she carries a sharpness all the same.

"Is that why you have done what you've done? Because you did not feel you had a choice?" She does not reply. I do not need one. "That is what your sister believes because she is a very good girl, but that's not the truth, is it? You are charitable with your family, but your real ambitions lie in the realms of power. I do not doubt that, had you ascended as Omega in that church instead of Kiandah, my Riders and I would now be a pile of ash. I also don't doubt that if you had been the one to ascend, you might have considered new allies, like the Fates."

She stares straight ahead, her lips pursed as she places one foot before the other. She doesn't wear shoes. I wonder why. "Is there a question in that, my Lord?"

I laugh humorlessly and shake my head. "I have a theory that I want confirmed or denied. A dishonest reply will result in your return to the dungeons, alone this time, without your family. Do you understand me, Owenna?"

"Yes, Lord."

"It was you, not your siblings or your parents, who brokered the deal — whatever nefarious deal was made between your family and Trash City."

She stumbles. I shift the tray into one hand, despite its heft and awkward shape, and catch her elbow with my other. She jerks away from me, turning until her back is against the wall of the staircase. She stands with one foot on the stair below, as do I. I don't crowd her. I don't need to. She meets my gaze and my displeasure slices my stomach like a sword. The urge to gut her grows, but I flex my hand several times and force back my claws.

"It was me."

Disappointment throttles me — that one of my own villagers would thus betray me, but also that one of Kiandah's sisters would thus betray her. "How?"

"The story is complicated. There were whispers and rumors of North Islander refugees from Trash City on South Island shores. I was...connected with them. They weren't hard to find. Their leader Merlin used to walk the Night Market without a disguise. And then when the Alphas first started disappearing, she went to ground, but by then she'd already told me when to meet her and where."

"And where was that?"

She makes a rough sound and wipes her face on the inside of her arm, as both of her hands are occupied with wine and jug. "It changed every time. But they needed the kitchen cellar to embalm the bodies before they moved them. I never saw where they came from and I never asked, but..."

"But did you see where they were moved to?"

She freezes, turning to stone, her shoulders rolling up by her ears. "I..."

"You know how I feel about lies, Owenna."

She clenches her jaw and blinks at me slowly. Her eyes... they are the same color as Kiandah's, the same shape, but they look so different. Kiandah does not have that look. She does not have the capacity to generate it. I do not understand how a single creature can be so unique and distinct, even when born of the same blood and into the same family.

Owenna got all of Kiandah's sharp edges. Kiandah got all of Owenna's soft parts. Except for the bits of her that exist in the safety of my arms. I wonder…is Owenna a lamb when she takes a lover? That would be a sight to see, though not for me. I have only eyes for she who is master of me.

"The Cliffs of Oblivion is where Trash City takes the bodies."

"That is not true. We have scoured the cliffs and found nothing."

"Then your Riders are blind or not looking hard enough."

"Or they do not know where to look." I tilt my head and watch her eyes widen with knowing. She knows what I will say before I say it, what I have intended to ask of her for some time now. "But you do."

She shakes her head. "No. No, Lord Yaron. Merlin already thinks I betrayed them. She'll slit my throat…"

"Whatever you did to gain her trust the first time, I'm certain you'll be able to replicate."

"It's suicide…"

"And if you do," I say, speaking over her. "If you lead us to the bodies and to Trash City — for I'm certain the locations of both are one in the same — I will give you what that foul wretch could not."

Owenna stills. The bitch is greedy and covetous, cunning and agile. I had been hesitant in asking her this, concerned that her allegiance to Trash City would be strong and even more concerned that a deceitful bitch was the wrong person to ask into an alliance. However, I can see the calculation in her eyes...and no matter what Trash City once offered her, I have a price that she cannot say no to.

"If you bring Trash City to me, I will move you from the kitchens."

"To where?"

"Where would you like to go?"

"I want to wear a black cloak." Her confidence astounds me, as does her ask.

I cannot help the grin that sweeps my features even as I lie in cold blood, "But no one wears a black cloak in these realms."

Her gaze narrows and she clenches her fist around the wine in her hand. "You said you don't tolerate lies, my Lord."

I grin a little wider and cock my head. "Does your family know that you are a ruthless woman?"

"No."

"They mistake you for a simpleton." She doesn't respond. "How do you know of the Black Cloaks?" A small elite group that rank among my soldiers, typically recruited from Crimson Riders themselves, but occasionally, a villager will show potential. They are spies, and occasionally, assassins.

"Everyone knows of them."

"Not that they exist."

"Your denial, if anything, serves as confirmation."

Fire. Dear gods. Is her whole family infused with it? Kiandah is simply the visible spark. "You are a bold female. You think you deserve such an honor?"

"I never much understood concepts of honor, my Lord. I can't buy anything with it and alone, it has no power.

Information has power. That's what I want and I'm good at getting it. I want to be rewarded for my hard work."

It all comes together. "That is why you sought placements in the castle. And when you were denied, you found another provider. And since you are eager to join the Black Cloaks, it's clear you have no issue with slaughtering for your own gain."

"I didn't slaughter for Trash City. I transported the bodies. That's all." She may be lying. She may be. And I cannot tell. She is a dangerous female and if I did not have need of her, I would kill her myself, break her neck and throw her down the stairs right here, and tell Kiandah it was an accident.

I resume walking and hear Owenna move in line just behind me. A dangerous place for a female like that. "You will have your colors, Owenna, if you can bring Trash City to me or if you are able to ascertain actionable information as to the whereabouts of the bodies they've stolen. Anything less and you'll be bound to the kitchens forever. No one will ever know how clever you truly are." I turn down the hallway leading to my chambers. "Or how ruthless."

Owenna doesn't respond immediately, she doesn't need to. My terms are final, a threat, yes, but also an opportunity for us both. "Why me? Why offer me a chance to commit the same treason that once relegated me to the dungeons, this time for reward?"

"Because I am running out of time. I intend to take Kiandah for a wife and I want to do it knowing that she is safe. My Riders are too obvious in their searches and my Black Cloaks have thus far been unsuccessful. They've found whispers, but not their provenance. You are the only one I know that's alive, that's done business with Trash City directly. I could torture you for information on their whereabouts, but I believe a mutually beneficial solution may yield quicker results. And torture is a messy process. I don't think Kiandah would want to fuck me anymore if she discovered I'd ripped your intestines out through your belly button and strangled you with them..."

Owenna balks. "You...ancestors be...you can't talk about my sister like that in front of me. Regardless of what you think, she's still my little sister..."

"And she'll be my wife. I suppose I do owe you a debt of gratitude for that. If you hadn't traded your soul for a few pieces of silver, I'd never have been thrust into her path and would have lived and died without ever having tasted her, and the taste of her..." I suck in a breath through clenched teeth. "It is exquisite." We have climbed the stairs and made it to the east hall. Up ahead, the stairs climb to my private quarters. "We're almost there now. It goes without saying, you'll tell no one about our arrangement."

"I won't, my Lord."

"You have four weeks. I expect some results by the time the next blood moon rises, either on locating Trash City and where they've gone, or what has happened to the bodies they've absconded with."

She glares at me and it's a powerful thing. I cock my head to the side.

"How much do you know, Owenna? Do you know what's become of the corpses?"

"I don't for certain, but I have my suspicions."

She presses her lips together and I nod, deciding. "When you leave the keep, you will do so with an escort. My Crimson Rider Sipho will accompany you."

"He'll only slow me down and arouse suspicion."

"And yet, I believe you are a woman of wiles. I believe you will find a way to make it work regardless. Find me what I want, Owenna, and you will have it — power. Softer, but perhaps even more than mine."

Her eyes flash and she nods. I nod again in response as we begin our ascent to my chambers. "You and your family will join Kiandah and me in the village tomorrow where I plan to address your family's crimes. A contingent of Riders will come for you around noon. Be ready then."

Reaching my chamber doors, I turn from Owenna and shove the door open with my shoulder. I place the tray on the sideboard just inside of the room and turn to take the wine and jug from Owenna, but she pulls them back to her chest and tries to look around my body. "My Lord?"

"Yes?"

"Can I see her?"

Something softens in me towards this battle-hardened female, this viper in the grasses. I open the door, allowing her entry. She goes straight to the bed and places the wine on the small table abutting it. She stands next to Okayo, reaching past him to give her sister a prolonged hug before ascertaining whether or not she's okay.

She's fine. Okayo has finished with her stitching and has placed a small bandage above her eye and across her palms. I imagine she has others on her stomach, though perhaps the wounds were superficial. I am soothed by the warmth that radiates from between the two women as I approach. Okayo comes to me, his supplies packed away already.

"I was just waiting for your return," he says.

"She will live, then?"

"Very well, if I'm judging by the look on your face right now."

I shoot him a glare, but it's mocking.

He smiles and gives me an exaggerated bow before I roll my eyes and nod, dismissing him.

The two females talk a little bit longer while I prepare Kiandah a plate. "And he's treating you okay?" Owenna says, dropping her voice to as low a whisper as possible, not that it helps. She might as well be shouting to my beast's ears.

Kiandah doesn't answer, though I wish she would. I want to know how she'd answer that question, but she must give some sign or other because her sister says, "Good," while my back is turned.

When there is nothing left to say for the moment, at least in my presence, Owenna excuses herself with a promise to see her sister tomorrow at noon. She gives me a knowing look. I nod, dismissing her before returning to Kiandah.

"What was that about? Where did you go?" she says to me on a yawn as I bring her a plate of Orias rice and charred chicken. It's not as warm as I would like it to be by now, but it does not seem to matter much to her. *Content. Content with everything she has and everything she's given.*

It makes me want to give her the world.

I watch her eyes grow wide as she takes in the sight of the food and I use her distraction to my advantage and lean in. I slip my thumb beneath her chin and stroke my fingers along her jaw and soft earlobe. I tilt her face up to mine and watch her whisper words, my name, I don't care. I kiss those thoughts away from her. I devour her hungrily and am not surprised when it takes her a moment to melt. Her fire is stoked by my desire and, when I lavish her lower lip with my tongue, she parts her lips and meets me kiss for kiss.

Her tongue pushes into my mouth and tangles with mine. She tastes so fucking good. I growl. She gasps and, as if finally remembering that she and I are in a detente, she tries to pull back, but I hold her close, releasing her only when I'm ready. Before I'm ready, but when I'm *willing*.

In the closeness between us, filled with only the spicy scent of her food and the sweet smell of her breath, she says, "You are a naughty boy, Yaron, deserving of punishment, kissing me without permission."

By gods. I'm hard instantly. The smell of antiseptic and blood on her skin does nothing to quell the sudden surge of need that beats through me. "Yes."

"I've been thinking, while you were gone, how you should be punished."

I cannot even remember what it is I'm meant to be punished for. And I don't care at all. "And what did you decide?"

"Did my family make this for me?" she says, taking a bite from her tray before answering.

I debate telling her that I helped prepare the dish, then decide against. "Yes. What is my punishment, Kiandah?"

She smiles up at me, likely at the impatience in my voice. "I decided since you behave like such a beast, taking without permission, that you'll sleep at the foot of my bed tonight, like the beast that you are."

I grin. "In my beast form or as a man?"

"Beast, of course." She takes another bite of the rice and her eyelids flutter.

My heart is beating hard. I can feel my pulse in my erection. I can think of little other than fulfilling her wishes. All of them.

I take my own plate and finish it quickly before shedding my clothing while her gaze moves with surety over my nakedness, falling to my cock and driving me to the brink of madness. Then I transform, shifting quickly into my Berserker's true body, letting him take over.

The room shifts, everything taking on the silverish hue of night, illuminated by only the few sconces in the walls. Her jaw drops. The spoon she had been so diligently using to shovel rice into her mouth at a speed I found both hilarious and alarming hangs suspended in the air by her chin. She has seen me before as a beast, but in pieces. I don't think she's ever seen me before like this.

Fully formed. At her mercy — though she believes herself to be at mine. I prowl towards her, looming over her two human lengths high. I could not fit through the door of this room if I tried. I have an oversized bed to accomodate my beast's form, but it only just fits my entire beast. I've never tried to share it before. But as she sits there, I step one paw up onto the bed and then the other three. I switch back and forth once before curling up into as small a ball as possible near her feet. I cover all of the bed, all of her legs. My head settles to their left, my snout pressed up against her hip lovingly… threateningly.

She no longer seems very hungry and slides her tray onto the side table before scurrying back to the center of the bed. There, she slides under the covers. "Um…goodnight, Yaron. Can you…understand me?"

I laugh, though the sound comes out a growl in this physical state. I move my head next to her legs, annoyed to be separated from her skin by the blanket, but I'll allow it for this night and tomorrow I'll work to be a good boy again and win my way back into her graces. With our planned excursion to the village, it will not be hard.

She reaches down and strokes her finger across my wet nose. Her two hands would span its entire length with her fingers spread wide. She scratches the top of my snout and I lean into her touch. She falls asleep with her fingers tangled in my fur and, at some point in the night, I burrow beneath the covers and press my snout to her stomach. She wraps herself around my massive head to the best of her ability and calls to me in her dreams.

"Such a good boy…" she whispers, her words laced with lust and promises.

KIANDAH
ORIAS VILLAGE

I'M NOT SURE I'M GOING TO LIKE THE EXCURSION YARON has planned. I woke up this morning to find him wearing skin instead of fur, naked and wrapped around me. He'd been awake, the naughty, naughty boy, and unrepentantly cupping my bare, wet core. I'd heated immediately, but he had pulled away before I was fully awake, and acted like it never happened, leaving me in a state of want so painful I wondered if he wasn't a sadistic male. Or just a male determined to get what he wants. I'd been hard pressed not to tell him to forget his punishment and fuck me then and there.

But then he told me to get dressed and that we were going to the market. Again.

I'd been apprehensive when his mood changed. Now, sitting in the carriage while it jolts and jerks unsteadily down the Orias highway line, he looks like he'd rather be anywhere else. Yaron sits like a beast caged against the plush black seat cushion. He stares out of the window, occasionally making small growling sounds. He looks angry.

"What's wrong?" I blurt, not liking that I've asked. It's too informal. Too strange, talking to the Shadow Lord in this way.

Like he's thinking the same thing, his face turns to me, seated on the bench across from him, and his thick, black eyebrow lifts. Just the one, though. "Are you worrying about me, Kiandah?"

It feels like any answer I give here would be wrong, so I give him a truer one and shrug. "I suppose."

"Alas, was that all it took? Obeying your commands to sleep at your feet? Have I won your heart so easily?"

"No. I would worry like this about anyone."

His face changes and I feel a soft warmth pulse between us, then retreat. "I suppose you would, wouldn't you?" He goes back to staring out of the window and, sensing I'm not going to get a better answer than that and knowing better than to press the issue, I turn to stare out of the window, too.

Paradise Hole is looking bleaker than usual today, even though the sun is shining. Maybe it's because the sun is shining that it looks so much darker here on the ground. It's like Paradise Hole is sucking the light from the sky, trapping it in a canopy above our heads, refusing to let the darkness below out, to be released among such color. The sky is overcast on the horizon, but above our heads, it's blue.

"It's beautiful today," I offer lamely.

Yaron nods, but he stares out of the window for a while before answering. I don't need to have rutted him to know that he is painfully intentional in everything he does. I knew that already. So, I don't know why I'm still surprised when he doesn't reply with something trite and instead says, "I can count on both hands the number of sunny days I've witnessed since I was a boy. Most of them, I experienced in Echo's garden — the Fallen Earth Omega. It seemed that sunlight followed her." He tilts his head and settles back in his seat, staring at me. "Perhaps, it follows you, too."

"I feel like there's something you want to tell me about her." I feel jealousy twist in my gut like a knife and I don't know why. I know she's with the Dark City Berserker, but... Yaron speaks of her so highly. And now he's gone silent.

He doesn't answer for quite some time. I sit with my shoulders slightly hunched inward under his scrutiny. I don't like the invasive way he stares. I do, because I don't want his full concentration on anybody else, but I also am not strong enough to stand up under it. I feel rather threadbare seated here in nothing but his oversized clothing, unsure of where we're going with a terrible sense that I don't want to know and never want to arrive.

And then he leans forward in a surge. Wind rushes over me. It tastes like him. Like an expensive cologne, leatherbound books dusted with age, and ash. I never knew ash had a smell, but he smells of it. Like a fire after all the flames have burned away. "I cannot make sense of you. You present as this meek, terrified little girl, but by your heart, you are betrayed."

"M-my heart?"

"Yes. You have the heart of a warrior, standing alone on the plane of battle against an army of the undead. You carry the conviction that you can and will vanquish them all because you have the lives of those you love to protect." He keeps coming, sliding off of the bench onto his knees in the short carpeted space between us. He palms the side of my face, his hand large enough to cover it completely. I flinch as his fingers curl around my head — I shaved the sides into a fade this morning. I don't have access to any hair products, so it was the only thing I could think of to make it look presentable. His thumb rubs the short hair near my temple, making my toes curl.

"You present as a peasant." His brows furrow. The muscles at the edge of his jaw give a little pulse. "But when your love is on the line, you transform into a queen."

"Love?" I balk, nearly choking.

"Yes. The love you have for your family." His mouth curls up slyly, darkly. "The love you have for me."

"For you?" I sputter. "I…"

"You are already half in love with me. I know you half as well as I should, but I know you well enough to know this."

"You…I'm not…"

"Don't lie." His fingers curl around my ear. They're rough and callused so badly, it feels like his touch could cut. "Don't lie to me. Not in this. I won't force you to admit it, but you should prepare yourself, because one day I will. Soon."

I want to rip away from him and slap him and deny his accusations, but he has me feeling very small. Very *seen*. I don't know how often it's happened…that I've felt that. Growing up in a big family has its benefits…but one of the drawbacks is that we sometimes can all meld together. Siblings jostling for power, animalistic pack dynamics, and parents trying to maintain some kind of order. It makes it hard to have that intimacy.

This intimacy.

To be noticed.

To be explored.

I look down at my lap, trying to retreat, but he slides that thick, callused thumb down my cheek, over the corner of my lip, under my jaw, which he tips up. His look is pure condescension and pure fire. It frightens and angers me.

"You can't know that that's how I feel," I assert with force. My skin burns every place he strokes.

"I do."

"How?"

"I may only know you a little, but I know you wouldn't have taken me as you did in the hunter's hole if you did not want to. Your commands are a gift, a treasure that I plan to hoard. And if you so much as think of giving them to another or, gods forbid, they try to take from you again, I will not react well, Kiandah. I will not react well at all."

He drags his hand down my neck, over my chest, between my breasts until he reaches my hips. He grips them from both sides and scoots forward so that his chest is between my legs, my knees spread around him and locked there. I can't move my lower half. I can't feel my upper half. All of my concentration has surged downward.

"You can't do this," I whisper.

"Do what?"

"Use my Omega nature against me."

"Why not?"

"I can't say no."

"No. Do not use your Omega nature against *me*, Kiandah. You are unbonded. You can speak freely. Do not place blame where it does not belong to make yourself feel better that you are letting a male you are half in love with eat you out like a beast, even though you pretend that you don't like him at all."

I open my mouth, but I don't know which of his comments I'd have responded to first, if he'd given me the chance. But he doesn't. He hooks his hands underneath my knees, wrenches my hips forward, and then leans in and rips a hole through the crotch of my linen pants with his teeth. Warm air, his breath, caresses me.

I tense up, arch my back, stab my fingers through his hair. I push him back — no, no I don't. I drag him up against me and rock forward until I'm nearly sitting on his face. He bites me and I gasp, panicked that he's broken skin and bonded me, and I jerk back wildly, violently. My arms knock into the doors and my head knocks into the wall behind me. My feet kick and my toes smart when I kick the underside of the bench seat across from me. My hips are still locked into place by his arms until Yaron growls and releases my inner thigh from between his teeth. Teeth, not fangs. Blinking rapidly, I look down to see my fingers tangled in his hair and his nostrils flaring as he inhales very deeply at my center. He glances up at me with those violent and demanding eyes and I tense. Everything within me immolates.

He reaches towards me and I flinch, but he was only moving to touch my cheek. "One day, you will realize that you are more than a member of a family. One day you will realize that you are only a peasant in the gaze of the weak. It is on that day that you will command me to bond you." He leans up and forward, nose just barely grazing my cheek. "I look forward to that day."

He returns to his seat and turns his gaze to the world outside of the open window, but not before sparing one last glance at the open crotch of my pants and releasing a low, almost inaudible growl.

I shiver with need. Yaron smirks and I scrunch my nose, annoyed with him in a way I've only ever been annoyed at my brother. "I love my family."

He balks. "No one in their right mind would think otherwise."

"It's not wrong to have love for your family."

"No one would suggest that, either. However, do you not find it a little peculiar that a family full of pretty girls and boys would have no children? No partners? You're all of birthing age and yet, the family line has died with your generation."

I feel my face flame. "It's not dead yet. We're just taking our time."

"You may tell yourself whatever you like, but the facts still stand. I said it before and I will say it again — your family is so wrapped up in itself, it would be impossible for a partner to gain entry into that. The bonds are too strong. The walls too thick to scale. What mad man or woman would want to compete with a love like that?"

"You seem to want to try," I shoot back, tone nastier than I've ever heard.

Lord Yaron seems unfazed. He just smiles that cryptic smile. "I am Lord of the Shadowlands. I have no fear because I know I will not fail. You will give me what I want. I could keep your family in chains and still get what I want from you."

"I would never."

I feel the wagon start to slow, but as he speaks, he takes his time. "Your love is strong. Your ability to hate is weak. I could stab your father in the heart before your eyes and still make you fall in love with me."

I strike him before I realize what I've done. I feel heat in the backs of my eyes. In the back of my heart. My pulse is pattering fiercely and my mind won't slow down. "I shouldn't have done that…"

"No. And I look forward to punishing you for it."

"You're a bastard," I whisper.

He grins cockily with one edge of his mouth, just enough to flash his teeth. His canine is sharper than it should be and I feel myself grow warm. I hate him, I decide, *but only because he's right. I don't hate him. I really don't.* "For you, I will be the villain. A hero would have no chance with you."

"Why are you saying all this? Why are you being so *harsh* with me?" He was so gentle yesterday, obeying me as he did, bringing me my sister and food.

He gives me a look I cannot interpret at all as the wagon rolls to a final stop. Then in a flourish, he shoves the door open on a creak and walks out, leaving me sitting there alone. I have a choice — remain where I am or follow — and when I look out of the window, I see a crowd forming. We're near the main town square, the stone Berserker still lunging up out of the stone fountain at the sky, like he'll swallow the sun. It's disappeared again behind the clouds, but when I take a shaky step down from the carriage, I can still feel its residual warmth.

The people of Orias Village are gathered, but not in commerce or trade, like they were yesterday. The stalls have been cleared and the doors of the shops closed and barred. Everyone is outside, gathered here. There are so many people gathered in eager and curious bunches, I wonder if he hasn't summoned the entire village here.

They stand against the closed storefronts, low awnings shading some while the rest spill out into the square. Yaron and I aren't alone in the space cleared out beside the fountain, though. Crimson Riders cross the space and my family stands at the fountain's edge. I go to them.

"Kia…"

"Kandia…"

"My sweet baby…"

"Come here…" My brother lifts his arm and I step into him. He's warm despite the fact that he's not wearing a jacket. He's just wearing a thin tunic, same as me, and when I look down, I see that we all have bare feet. *We look like prisoners.*

I frown, feeling sad that this is how Lord Yaron would parade us in front of the town. He speaks of wanting to bond me, but if I were out in the crowd, this isn't how I would want to see my Lord parade his Lady in front of me and the rest of his people. Because they should be her people, too, shouldn't they?

My mom reaches across Cyprus to grip my hand. I hold her back, and together, we watch Lord Yaron walk a long line in front of us. His boots clatter on the cobblestones. The skies have once again darkened. His gaze passes over each member of my family before finally landing and lingering on me. Then he wrenches his gaze up to the crowd.

He moves towards the other villagers and begins to walk a long line around the circle they form around us. He's speaking to them directly, in ways he has done before but that I have only had the honor of being a part of twice — once when he was announced as our Berserker Lord all those years ago when I was six and he was fourteen, and again a year ago, or more now, when he came to warn us all about a dangerous animal that had been sighted on our shores. We didn't know then that they were *not* animals, but undead Alphas.

His voice pitches loud and carries with a booming force that I feel in the soles of my feet, echoing through the cobblestones. There is a reason that, when I first saw him even as a child, I could identify him immediately as our Lord. "I have gathered you all here to witness the trial of the Ubutu family." My blood turns to ice in my veins. *What?* Cyprus's arm tightens around my shoulders as I feel my legs start to wobble.

Whispers start up. Yaron speaks over them, "The Ubutu family has been involved with Trash City in carrying out nefarious deeds impacting all of Gatamora. They helped Trash City prepare the bodies of Alphas. Though the reason cannot be confirmed without a shadow of a doubt, I'm sure that we all suspect that these bodies were collected with the intention of being turned." His cloak trails behind him, fluttering in a breeze that I can't feel. The air feels static everywhere except for around him.

"For those of you who have not seen the undead with your own eyes, rest assured that the rumors of their existence are true. I have seen and fought them both on the North Island

and now here, on our shores." He sweeps his gaze over the crowd and I wonder at his reaction. He seems tense, angry, even, and I don't know why.

"My Crimson Riders and I have not been able to root them out, but if you have information that would help me keep you safe, please do not keep it to yourself. You will not be punished for holding information, if that is your concern. I am your Lord, yes, but I am also your protector. I am duty-bound to raze the undead from our shores. Inform one of my Riders if you know anything. They will be stationed around Orias Village over the coming days with the express intent of collecting any information you may have…"

A woman in the crowd whose face I know but whose name I can't remember stands with her arm around a younger woman. She speaks up, "Inform your Riders, my Lord? So that we can be raped? We heard that the Omega was assaulted as she was escorted from Orias Village only yesterday." The crowd's rumble picks up in volume. Yaron remains undeterred.

"She was. And the assailant has been dealt with." He lifts a scarred hand and beckons towards the carriages with two fingers. Two Riders emerge from between them, dragging something into the square that I don't understand at first… until villagers begin screaming.

Shrieks and groans from the crowd are punctuated by the sounds of vomiting. At least half a dozen people retch, one of them being Zelie, who stands on the other end of the row of my family. Owenna gives her comforting pats on the back and whispers to her in words I cannot hear.

My eyes are still unfocused, not understanding…the mass… "Is that…"

"Yes, Kia," Cyprus says to me. "Don't look."

I feel my own stomach lurch as understanding finally dawns on me. The man has had his hands and feet removed, he's been impaled in his…rear end…and the skin on his back has been flayed. His lungs have been removed. They sit on his shoulders. I close my eyes and bury my face in Cyprus's chest. He squeezes me tightly.

In my ear, he whispers, "He deserved it."

"No one deserves that," I croak. "Did…Lord Yaron do that?" I ask, already knowing the answer.

"Personally."

I feel nauseous. This is what he's capable of. I let him touch me with hands capable of pulling the skin off of someone. Another few voices release gut-wrenching screams.

And still, Yaron is unfazed by them. "There will be rewards for those who come forward with information pertaining to Trash City, its leader, Merlin, or the undead." The same Riders who dragged the *thing* forward on a bloody rope return from the chariot with a chest. One of them pulls open the lid, revealing treasures. Gold, silver and gemstones glitter. "And punishment for those who hold information and do not divulge it."

The juxtaposition of the *thing* and the treasure chest are stark and grotesque. The implication behind his words is clear. The crowd quiets amidst sniffles and whispers.

"However, punishment is to be handed out by me alone. And if I say that the Ubutu family is not to be punished, then I expect this proclamation to be followed. You are to treat

them as you would any other citizen of the Shadowlands."
He's approaching the blacksmith now and Olac does not
cower, but meets his gaze with a ravenous gaze of his own.
Lord Yaron is not much taller than Olac, who was the largest
man I'd ever seen and might still be. He has meat on him
Lord Yaron doesn't have, especially around his thick belly.
"Am I clear?" I hear him say to the crowd, though his gaze
doesn't move from Olac's.

Olac clenches his teeth. His hands are blackened, which
seems fitting as he gestures towards us hatefully. "You mean to
let them go unpunished? They *killed* my goddaughter."

"They did not raise the blade that killed her, but I
understand your grief. Your desire for revenge. You wish to
see them punished, yes? Beyond their confinement to the
castle?"

"Yes. You turned this foul man inside out for daring to
touch your precious Omega, yet you won't touch her for
doing far worse to a family in this village."

Yaron grabs Olac by the collar and wraps his fist in the
fabric of his shirt. He looks a breath away from the kill. "I
plan to take this precious Omega for my wife. And this
precious Omega is not a killer. She saved the lives of thirty
members of this village when *I* intended to kill them by
burning them alive within their precious church, under the
eyes of their ancestors.

"*That* is how I intended to punish her for what she did to
that family. *That* is how I intended to punish them all. I
packed innocent people into a church — people who had no
idea that Trash City was even on the South Island, let alone
scavenging for bodies — with every intention of burning

them all to the ground. Incinerating them. Listening to their flesh bubble, blister and burst. Five died that day, but *my precious Omega* saved the rest. Does that sound like the mark of a killer?"

Olac is looking defiant...yet unsure. And the crowd around him is in an uproar. They have been ever since Yaron declared he'd take me for his wife. Though I know he said as much already, I still stand in shock. Maybe, because he told me in such a private space where it felt like the world was different, between us — where there were no blistered or disemboweled bodies, no undead and no expectations, only peace and tension, curiosity and lust — I sort of...didn't believe him. And still...I know he cannot mean it. *Lady* of the Shadowlands? *Me?*

I frown and waver on my feet, using my brother's strength to comfort me while Audet shoots me a carnivorous look around Yaron's and my mom's bodies, a look that I cannot fault her for because it says just what I'm thinking — that I'm not worthy.

Meanwhile, Olac sputters out a response when prompted by Yaron. "Even-even the guilty will defend themselves when backed into a corner, my Lord. Just because she was successful at staying your hand doesn't mean her family's punishment should be over."

Yaron nods, as if expecting this answer. He releases Olac. "Very well. How would you have them punished? An attempted rape was not sufficient?"

Olac's fists clench as he tries to find his footing. His wife's hands come to his arm, steadying him, and I see her lips moving. *Enough.* Olac sags into her slightly. He shakes his head. "I am…I am… This is not who I am, my Lord. I must apologize to the Omega. I tried to stop the Rider from handling her when he made his intentions known, but I still let him leave. And before that, I put my hands on her when I should not have. My wife is right. She is the goodness in me when I am only my temper. I would gladly accept a punishment from you, my Lord. Whatever you deem appropriate…"

"No!" I shout, trying to lurch away from Cyprus, who grabs my shoulders and pulls me back. "No, please, Yaron." Yaron. I call him by his first name, which incites the crowd to excitement bordering on violence. There are some laughing, there are still some crying and screaming, there are cheers. There is so much emotion, I want it to stop. My bones are still weak, my flesh bruised, and my heart…it's been too much in too short a time…I can't breathe. "Yaron, *please.*"

He turns to look at me, his expression cold. He comes forward as I break free of Cyprus's grip, but only because he lets me. As I stumble forward, he catches me against his chest. He slides his hands around my throat and squeezes gently, a reminder of what Olac did…a threat… "My Lady," he breathes against my lips, but he doesn't kiss them. Instead, he brushes his softer than sin mouth over my nose and then my forehead. "Do not break my heart. I cannot stand your begging."

"Then I command you…don't hurt anyone else. Not for me." I grab the front of his tunic in shaking fists. I'm scared. My feet are cold.

He brushes his lips over my temple and his words, unlike his actions, are so, so soft. "You are master over me, Kiandah, but I am still Lord of this city. Rejoin your family and do not interfere again. I will not ask you twice."

Fury fires through me as he barks an order and Cyprus comes and takes me back to my kin. I clench my fists and cross my arms, *hating* Yaron as he approaches Olac again. My muscles are all locked and they're too tired for that. I feel lightheaded despite getting a good night's rest — the best I've had in a long time — and having eaten well last night and this morning. I think…my greatest fear is knowing that Yaron was right in the chariot — he does…he is capable of having my love. But I don't want to love a man who hurts other people like this…who is capable of such unrepentant and merciless violence.

"You are good to renounce your anger and request punishment. What do you see fit for yourself?"

Olac doesn't answer, but I see how his gaze nervously shifts to the pile of dead Rider, a thick carpet of blood leading back the way he came. "Whatever manner of punishment you select for yourself will also be delivered unto the Ubutu family."

Olac's eyes widen. "I… You are right, my Lord. The Omega has been through enough and, perhaps, isn't responsible for the crimes her family comm—"

But Yaron cuts him off. "A public flogging, perhaps? A good lashing?"

"Uhm, yes. That is customary."

"How many lashes for putting your hands around my Omega's neck?" Lord Yaron's hand opens and the tail end of a black whip tumbles out to hit the ground. I hate him for it. I hate him so much for that. He came prepared to lash my family.

"My Lord?"

"A number. How many?" He speaks to the crowd now. "How many lashes does this village deem appropriate for Olac for laying hands on the female that is to be your Shadow Lady?"

Several voices shout numbers, but I can't stop myself from shouting, "None!"

"One!" Cyprus says, shouting over me and drowning me out.

Yaron turns to look at Cyprus over his shoulder and nods once. "Very well." Turning back to Olac, he says, "Prepare yourself."

I clench and watch in horror as Olac nods and moves to the end of the square. His wife struggles to release his arm, but he reassures her. I find something absolutely *tragic* in that. I find it more tragic that Yaron could stop this, but doesn't. Instead, he positions himself at the opposite end of the clearing, raises his whip and only just waits for Olac to lift his shirt to fully expose his back before bringing the whip down. One strike, that's all. But it feels like a hundred.

The last public flogging happened when I was only ten. Yaron was eighteen then. He'd been Lord for only two years and his master of coin thought he could filch from the public coffers. A new Lord, a young Lord, Yaron had made an example of him. Eight lashes later from Yaron's own arm, he fainted. He died at lash twenty-two. My parents had let me watch the first lash fall, but had taken me away after the second and still, the sound that it had made was and is forever burned into my memory.

Yaron turns to face the village while Olac's wife rushes to him. Yaron points at the medic called Finn and gestures him towards Olac. The male responds immediately, carting supplies across the space in a small satchel. A chair is produced from somewhere within the crowd. Olac sits and Finn begins administering to him immediately while Yaron points his whip at my family. At me. It's only when Cyprus clenches my hand tighter that I realize I'm shaking.

"And how many lashes until the Ubutu family has learned their lesson?"

Silence.

"You all were so confident in their guilt moments ago, yet now you are silent? Tell me, how many each?"

"T-two?" a young woman says.

"None!" another shouts. Justine — I'd recognize her voice anywhere. I scramble to find her in the crowd and when I do, I meet her gaze and we exchange small, scared smiles. They do not all hate us. Some that know us will know our hearts and believe that the killing strokes were not delivered by our hands. By mine least of all. *Because I am not my family.*

"Two only?" Lord Yaron says, ignoring Justine. "You can do better than that."

"Three!" someone offers and I recognize that voice, too. It's the pig farmer, the one who threw shit at me. "No more! Any more than that and they'll bleed out. These are townspeople, not Crimson Riders! They cannot take more than that…"

"You care? You intend not to kill them?" Yaron's tone is condescending and cruel. The crowd is murmuring, unsure. "For such wickedness, I would think at least ten lashes apiece would do."

The pig farmer doesn't respond. Silence prevails. I can't believe it. My stomach is in my eyeballs now. That I haven't vomited is only a testament to the fact that my shock outweighs my terror. Yaron begins to turn away, but a voice from deep within the crowd says, "Fifteen."

A collective gasp echoes across the village. Fifteen lashes could be a death sentence. Cyprus will likely survive, but I don't know about the rest of us — of them. Yaron will show no mercy.

"Fifteen," Lord Yaron says softly. The boy who spoke steps through the crowd, which parts around him. The boy is pale with blond hair and bright eyes, red cheeks and hate seeping through his pores. He must have known the Alpha family intimately because he looks at Yaron with a gaze full of sadness and scorn.

"Fifteen it is, then." Yaron says. The crowd gasps. Several mouths utter protest, but they are washed away by the whooshing in my brain. I feel lightheaded and can only watch, stunned and betrayed, as Yaron steps towards the boy and says, "And you shall deliver them or name your champion."

"Olac," the boy says immediately. "He is stronger."

Yaron nods. "Good. Olac, come."

It is a brutal sight — Olac turning in his chair, a needle hung on a thread like a noose dangling from a loose tag of his flesh. He's sweating, I can see the way his rich brown skin glistens even from here. "My Lord, I cannot deliver so many lashes to each of them…"

"And you won't." Lord Yaron hands Olac the whip when the man rises to stand, wound still gaping open. "You will deliver their lashes to me."

The crowd goes crazy. My knees go weak. I start to fall. Cyprus catches me. "No…" My heart. My heart…

"My Lord, no!" Olac sputters and gasps. "I cannot be compelled to raise a hand to the Shadow Lord. Do not dishonor me so…"

"You will do as I say for this is my decree. I shall champion their lashes. You open your mouth to defy me again, I will give you the punishment I think you truly deserve." He tips the staff of his whip so subtly it could have been mistaken for a simple twitch. But I do not mistake it as such. I know that he is gesturing to the mess of a male he made out of that Rider and I know that Olac does, too. He is no fool and takes the baton when Yaron gives it to him.

Yaron turns and sheds his tunic, tossing it aside, but the boy who said *fifteen* still stands in the clearing, not in Yaron's path, but not well enough out of his way. He looks stunned, his jaw works. He tries, "My Lord, this isn't what I wanted at all…"

"But it is what is deserved. I will take the lashes they are owed because I failed to deliver your justice in the church, and subsequently let the family escape. And now the family that aided and abetted the Trash City scum that took Gwyn's life will be punished, for they will have to live forever with this humiliation, knowing that the scars I bear are for their crimes. For Gwyn, for how I failed her, too."

"S-scars, my Lord?" The young man shakes his head. "Why should you scar? Won't you heal quickly from this?"

"Not this time. Okayo," he barks. The male comes forward with a black syringe which he injects directly into Yaron's vein. "So that my blood does not coagulate," he hisses and the village is in upheaval. So many voices chiming for him to stop.

He continues past the boy and gestures with two fingers to his Riders. Two appear and flank him. He faces away from me, his back visible to me and my family and the riotous crowd. Several villagers try to storm forward to stop the atrocity we're about to witness, but Yaron directs his Riders to hold them back.

Meanwhile, I feel something stir in my chest that I can't put a name to. It feels like sludge, but hot. I step forward, away from Cyprus, afraid, but needing to do something. "Yaron."

"Stand down, Omega," he says, facing away from me. "The village had its chance to punish you yesterday, and so they did. Olac, begin. Ninety lashes for each member of the Ubutu family save Kiandah." He spreads his feet and grips the inner shoulders of the two Crimson Riders that stand before him. They grab his forearms with both of their hands and brace.

Olac takes a long time to deliver the first lash. It's the hardest to watch, to bear. The crowd has started to shift, to run, to return, to retreat, to swell. Many are cursing Olac. Many are cursing the boy whose name I hear shouted. Robert. But I don't blame him. I blame Yaron. This is barbaric.

I start forward and the sludge in my chest moves, hurtling down my arms. I raise my left hand as Olac raises the whip to deliver the tenth, twentieth? Lash. I've already lost count, my skin burning, my eyes blurred as I watch Yaron stand there and bear it. Already, Yaron's back is a mess of torn skin and bright abrasions. He hasn't so much as flinched through it all. He keeps his head down like he's staring at the ground just in front of his feet, and his hands planted on the shoulders of the soldiers before him who are both gritting their teeth.

Olac lifts the whip but when I exhale, I feel power roll out of me. My will is my command. A small tuft of blue smoke explodes from the tips of my fingers. The whip is gobbled up by a rogue flame. Olac shouts and drops the whip, and together, we all watch it catch fire at his feet. It burns far faster than it should, turning to ember by the time Yaron has looked over his shoulder to understand what caused the delay and the commotion. The ash from where the whip once was disperses in the breeze.

Yaron's expression is incalculable as he stares at it and then looks at me. "I said stand down, Omega," he hisses. He releases the Riders and advances on me. I stagger back. It's so silent. The entire village is shouting, but it feels like they've all vanished as he crushes my biceps in his strong grip. He lowers his head and speaks angrily through his teeth. "I will heal from these wounds. Slowly, but I will heal. You delay and prolong the inevitable. Stop, or I will reverse my decision and design a punishment just for you. You will not like it." He roughly shoves me back against my brother and calls for a new whip.

The flogging begins anew, this time to a chorus of silence. The muted sounds of the crowd are punctuated only by the occasional whimper or cry. His people bleed for him. They love him. *We* love him. We always have. Even when he flays and maims and imprisons, we love him for it. Because we lead good lives in the Shadowlands. We lead good lives...

Why did my family do this to us? To all of us?

I feel a hatred toward them I don't often experience as I watch Yaron take the brunt of our failings as villagers, as neighbors, as human fucking beings. I glance down the line of my family, first at Cyprus, nearest to me. His expression is set grimly. At my mom — sobbing. At Audet, shaking so badly she looks like she'll fall apart. At Owenna. Her face is blank — no, hollow — her eyes sunken and dark like she's seeing a ghost. At Zelie, hunched over, gagging at the sight and smell of flayed flesh. At my father, whose eyebrows are pulled together and whose face is darkened in rage.

His proud shoulders are pulled back as he steps forward and says, "Stop!"

Olac stops. Yaron's muscles are moving beneath his skin in a way that I don't like at all. He's clearly in pain. His beast is clearly trying to escape. He's having to endure this while also keeping his Berserker side contained. And he's bleeding. He's bleeding so much. The blood pours in rivulets down his back. I'm not even sure if, had Olac been trying to go easy on him, it would have mattered. The whip he's using is Lord Yaron's black whip. He makes them special. To hurt.

My eyes are hot and my fingers are pressed so tightly to my lips as I watch my father step forward and speak, not to Lord Yaron, but to the town. To Olac. To Robert. To everyone. "Enough!" He roars, lifting his hand and letting it fall. "For our honor, please. There are ten lashes left. Let me take them…"

Lord Yaron stiffens and straightens up. His fingers uncurl from the Riders' shoulders he'd been holding and they both wince as he finally releases them. Yaron turns to face my father, fury on his face that my father does not back down from.

"Please, my Lord. Let me take the remaining."

Yaron's nostril's flare and though his posture is lethal, his back a brutal landscape, his gaze is soft. He shakes his head just once, down at my father and says softly, firmly, "No."

My father takes a step back and touches the center of his chest. He steps away from Lord Yaron and speaks to the crowd once again. "Then let this be enough."

A pregnant pause. Lord Yaron nods and turns around to face Olac, who lowers his arm. The crowd seems to release a single gathered breath before falling silent once more.

"Are you satisfied?" Lord Yaron roars to the village, and then more quietly to Robert alone. "Are you satisfied? Do you think Gwyn would be happy seeing the Lady of the Shadowlands kicked through the streets or her Lord whipped like a dog?"

He takes the whip from Olac's hand and tosses it at Robert's feet. The boy bursts into tears and retreats to his parents. He'd looked like a man standing strong in his convictions. Now, with shaking hands, he looks so small. He meets my gaze across the square and looks away quickly.

Lord Yaron's chest is heaving. His blood drains from his back and soaks his trousers, which are dark, but not dark enough to disguise the blood loss. There's so much of it. I want to go to him, but I know it would not be welcome. He is raw, unbridled rage.

He sweeps his hand across his lower back, his palm coming back red. He holds it out to the village and all but roars as he says, "May this blood be enough to assure you that this family has paid their penance." He swipes his hand across his chest. The red palm print streaks across his abdomen, making him look like a god not of this world, but a god above us. Or maybe that is simply how I always viewed him.

"May *my* blood ensure that they do not step out of line again. And may this tome of violence finally close." He looks so huge, his body swollen with rage or pain or a combination of the two. His muscles glisten. The sun pokes its head through the clouds and brushes over his face before retreating in terror. "I should hope that you all remember the sound of the whip falling the next time you have your dealings with the Ubutu family." He lingers in front of the baker and the pig farmer, who stand together. "And provide them with clean food. It is not your job to punish them." He moves to Olac and concludes. "I am through here. Are you?"

"We understand, my Lord. The Ubutu family has paid their penance. I believe we all have." Olac looks down at his feet, his expression pained. His hands are flexing — with his own pain, or with the pain we all feel looking at Lord Yaron. I wonder if he'll ever forget what it felt like to flog the beloved Lord of our city.

Yaron sneers in disgust and turns away from the village. He starts towards my family. No, not them. He has eyes only for me and they are brutal slashes, everything about him untamed and scarier than my most vivid of nightmares and so utterly severe. I stand, surging away from my siblings and batting away Cyprus's reaching hands. I walk towards Yaron, fingers clenched violently underneath my chin in prayer — prayers I've been making to the ancestors since the whip was first revealed.

We meet, coming within reach of one another, but his fists are clenched. He speaks low enough for me alone to hear — at least, he tries to, but I never hear what he says. I don't stop walking and barrel straight into his chest.

A shocking puff of laughter leaves his lips as he canters back, clutching me to him — for balance or because he wants to, I'm not immediately sure. But then his hands form around my face and he moves my jaw so that I have to look up at him and his lips descend and he kisses me for everything I'm worth and I kiss him back with everything I'm worth and so much that I'm not. *Deserving.* I do not know what I deserve, because he makes me feel like I deserve…I deserve…to bask forever in his light.

He holds me beneath the bum, his large hand circling the underside of my thigh, his fingertips very close to the hole he tore in my pants earlier. His other hand slides around to grip the back of my neck. He clutches me to him like a lifeline, while my arms slide up his shoulders to carefully and lightly tug on the hairs at the nape of his neck.

His eyes close and the growl he releases is so beautiful. It's all for me. I see him better now and know that he is dangerous because when he said that he would win me and I said he could not, he knew. He's always two steps ahead. I might as well give him whatever he wants. To fight him is to lose. It's just inevitable.

"Will you come with me or would you like to remain with your family?" he whispers and I feel immediately guilty. *Does he really think I would not want to go with him after this?* Or maybe, he just thinks I would never choose anyone over my family. And I…never thought I would.

"Do you want me to stay with you, my Lord?"

"I would not have asked if I did not." He growls, "And don't call me Lord, Kiandah." Yaron is out of breath and his heart is pounding so hard I can feel it against my own breast. I try to disentangle myself from him, worry that I'm hurting him eclipsing my need to be close, but he only grips me tighter.

"Let me go to them, Yaron."

Disappointment drags his shoulders down. A fleeting pain twists the expression on his face. "Of course. I will come find you after Okayo deems me fit to…" He starts to release me, but it's my turn to grab him with the desperation of a drowning woman clinging to a flotation.

"No." I shake my head, reach up, lightly brush my fingertips over the blood spatter on his cheek. "Not to leave you. Just to say bye to them and make sure they're okay. Can you wait just a moment?"

He stares at my face, his eyes tracing its every curve. I would feel self-conscious if my body weren't so warm and wanting. I feel arousal pool in my stomach and surge down, slickening my folds. Yaron grunts.

"I'll only be a moment."

"I don't want to be parted from you for a moment," he says, sounding strange. I'm worried and elated. He sounds so…soft.

I nod, tears wetting my eyes, desire, desire, desire beating me like a whip against flesh, only so much more damaging. "Whatever you want, my King."

He hisses in a breath, sounding shocked. I smile a little and take him by the hand and we walk very slowly to where my family stands by the fountain. They rise, except for Audet, who sits crouched over her knees, looking so very small and scared in a way I've never seen her.

"I'm so sorry, Kia," she sniffs as she takes my free hand. "I never thought you would get hurt when I suggested you leave the keep…"

"It's alright…"

"And I'm sorry for how I've treated you. I…I'll do better. And not just because you'll be Lord Yaron's Lady. I just…I've always envied you."

"Envied me?" I say, feeling surprised by this revelation whispered by blubbering lips that are full and perfectly formed, just like the rest of my sister. She's always been the beautiful one.

"You are always so happy. I just…never felt…never understood how. It was like you knew something — had something — I didn't. I guess you always did. And now you definitely do. But I don't…I'm just…I'll work on it. I'm sorry, Kandia. I hope you know I do love you."

I bend down, not releasing Yaron's hand for a moment, even as I wrap my arms around Audet's hunched shoulders.

Against her pretty rush of curls, I tell her, "I will love you forever. No matter what. You're my sister."

She sniffles some more while I quickly give Cyprus and Zelie hugs. Owenna squeezes my shoulder and gives Yaron a funny look. My mother is crying. She's fussing and telling me what a poor wife I am, asking my weakened husband to hobble around like this. Yaron's puff of laughter reassures me and all of my soul because it sparks small smiles across all the members of my family. My father sticks out his hand to Yaron after giving me a hug.

Yaron takes it. My father pulls him in and Yaron, in a worrying display, stumbles. "I could not have parted with her for anyone more worthy. Thank you, my Lord. You do not understand the depth of my gratitude for what you've done for us."

"Taken a few licks?" Yaron says, trying to joke, but it isn't funny. He sounds downright pained.

My father does not rise to it, but releases Yaron's hand and bows a little more deeply. "Lord Yaron, you gave us back our lives today. Now go, Kia, get the poor lad some medical attention."

"Since Lord Yaron has cleared our names and we are in need of supplies," Owenna announces slowly, "I will do some shopping here in the market. Do you think it acceptable for me to ask Lord Sipho to provide me an escort?" she asks Yaron. They exchange an even funnier look.

Lord Yaron nods. "You may." And with that, she's off. He turns to me, looping his arm over my shoulders. I say bye to my family and help him as best I can to the chariot.

It's a surreal sensation, reentering the small, plush wagon. The sun is no longer shining, but it doesn't matter. The whole world tastes of sunlight.

"You're giving me a strange look, Kiandah. What are you thinking?"

I drop forward off of the bench across from Yaron and land on my knees. I place one of my hands atop his knee, and then the other. I spread his legs a little further and don't miss the sharp way he hisses or the hard way he swallows. "I'm thinking that you've been a very, very, very good boy, Yaron."

YARON
SHADOW KEEP

"IF I'D KNOWN YOU'D BE LIKE THIS, I'D HAVE LET THE blacksmith flog me days ago." She hasn't stopped touching me since the square. Her touch is heavenly. I'm lying on my stomach on the bed at her insistence while she cards her fingers through my hair and applies more cooling rags covered in healing salve and aloe to the deepest lacerations across my spine.

"I knew you did this on purpose. Taking so many lashes just to win over me and my family."

"I am sorry, Kiandah, that they had to endure any pain at my hand all."

"You did the right thing. At the church. In the dungeons. And here in the Orias marketplace, you did the only thing you could have, really. The villagers would never have given us back the respect we lost. You restored some of our honor. Now, we might have a chance to rekindle some relationships, get our jobs done, maybe even restore our friendships. Justine was rooting for us out there. She's one of my friends. I never thought she'd talk to me again after your Riders killed Tor."

I'm quiet. It's hard to know what to say next. I am filled with regret and yet, I am not sure I would have changed my actions if I could go back. "I am sorry, Kiandah, for those that you've lost at my hand."

She doesn't answer right away, and when she does, she redirects, "You know, I happen to like looking down at you like this, below me on the bed."

I smirk, thrown by the sudden power I hear in her tone. "And why is that?"

Her fingers are strong and sure against my scalp, distracting me from the pain of my wounds. "You can't meet my gaze and reduce me to rubble with that smoky stare." She bends down and whispers against the back of my hair. Her breath is warm and contrasts against the chill of the healing strips and I shiver. She laughs menacingly and I feel it when she says that I'm vulnerable. "It feels like you're at my mercy, injured like this…I like it. It fills me with visions of you at my mercy in other ways."

"Kiandah," I hiss. "Stop this. Do not use your power now when I cannot rise to match it."

She pulls back on a huff, but I can sense that she's smiling. We lapse back into a strained silence. I'm not sure it's strained on her end, but I can feel the tension on mine as she's left my question unanswered. *Do you forgive me?* "I… Your attempts to distract me will not be met with success. I want you to hear my apology for the wrongs I've committed against you, your family and your friends."

"And you want my forgiveness?"

Yes. "I want…whatever you are willing to give."

She sighs. "I think I'm starting to understand how you became one of the most feared Lords of Gatamora at such a young age. You don't lose. You know just what to say…"

"I do not lie. I do feel regret."

She pauses, as if trying to gather the right words, before she eventually says, "I don't know that you are sorry. I think that you are sorry I saw what you're capable of. But I'm not sure you feel regret in the same way I do. I think you regret only that you've had to take such drastic steps to fix things in such a way that when you ask for me under the blood moon, I won't be able to give any answer but one."

"And what answer is that?" I ask, heart beating hard rather than fast.

She leans in close once more, her lips brushing my temple. "You are a clever male, Yaron. You tell me what I'll say then."

"You cannot say no to me."

"No, I cannot."

"But do you want to say yes?"

Her hesitation fills me with madness. I grab her wrist and bring her callused hand to my mouth, brushing my lips over her hardened knuckles.

"I…do."

"However?" I snap.

"However, I…" Her fingers still against my scalp. She removes them and I curse my temper. "I'm still quite afraid of you. Your capacity for violence and brutality. I just…" She inhales deeply once again and exhales heavily, her cool breath fanning over all of my wounds. "I don't have anything to say, Yaron. A day ago, the whole town was convinced my family was a bunch of killers. It makes sense that the male who wants my hand would be, too. Justice is no excuse for death and yet…it does not change my feelings. Because you were right in the cab of that chariot. You could raise an arrow to my friends and a torch to my family and forgiveness would still find a way to trump my reason." Her fingers return to my arms this time, and she begins massaging me in firm ministrations.

It feels glorious — or it would, if I weren't so tense. Damn the wounds on my back, I flip over and move into a seat, startling her so that she slips off of her knees and lands on her hip with a squeak. "I want you to want me for who I am, not in spite of it."

She scowls. "I want you to lie back down and rest."

I growl. She narrows her eyes and points at the sheets. "Down, boy."

I growl louder, incapable of keeping my blood from surging south. "You speak to me like that and you're inviting my beast to rage."

"Keep him in your pants and maybe I'll see to him later."

I bark out a laugh and Kiandah's lips quirk. I begrudgingly lie back onto my stomach, mostly to cushion the erection she's just provoked. Luckily, movement makes the pain flare and it's possible to overcome my sudden need for her. A gift, when she ambles off of the bed a few moments later.

"What are you doing?"

"I'm going to fix you a meal."

"You're still injured from yesterday, Kiandah. We need to wait for Okayo to return with the rest of his supplies. You must rest in the meantime."

"He has already seen to me."

"And said your throat needs medication."

"The bruises look worse than they feel."

"Kiandah, sit."

"Worry about yourself. You're not healing properly because of the undead Alpha venom in your system." She makes an angry sound. "I cannot believe you willingly injected yourself with that." I plant my right cheek on the mattress and see her walking across the room away from me. I try to rise, but before I can so much as shift my arm, Kiandah pegs me with an angry stare. "If you get out of that bed, I will punish you, Lord Yaron. You will not like how," she says, repeating my own words. "Okayo says you need to keep still so you can keep your blood pressure low."

"Kiandah…" She's ignoring me entirely, sliding her arms into the sleeves of a fresh tunic. One of mine. I need to procure her clothing. The Lady of the Shadowlands can't be walking around the castle in a fucking shirt. "Put pants on, for your precious ancestors' sakes."

She rolls her eyes, but does as I ask, then she heads to the door, despite my instruction. "I'll be back shortly with Okayo, if he's not back before I return. Stay still. If I find you up and moving about the room when I return, I need not remind you that there will be consequences, Lord."

If I were feeling better, my beast would have certainly surfaced at that pronouncement. As it is, all I can do is listen to her and let her go. She is not a captive, she is not a slave to me. In fact, one could argue quite the opposite. I yearn for her approval, for her to find me just as she left me, but also for her punishment, to chase after her — but the trouble is, I really am tired...I yawn once and I fall asleep to the scent of Kiandah, still lingering on my sheets.

The sounds of voices rouse me some time later. Kiandah's light laughter is punctuated by a deeper voice saying, "...was nothing...my pleasure..."

I wake fully then and jerk back, only to have a heavy weight smack the back of my head. "Stay still," Okayo's throaty voice says from much closer. "I know what you're thinking and no, Kiandah is not thanking Dorsten for bending her over your half-dead corpse and fucking her..."

"Okayo," Dorsten's deep voice rings at the same time Kiandah shouts, "Ancestors bless. What are you two talking about?"

She comes closer and I still struggle to blink my eyes fully open. I'm exhausted. I'm not used to feeling this tired. This injured. And then I remember the undead venom in my veins and how I have felt this tired and exhausted once before, when I was bitten in Echo's garden, in the battle of the North Island against the reanimated corpses. But I did not have Kiandah's voice and touch to soothe me then.

"Lord Yaron was prepared to launch out of bed and strike Dorsten down for defiling your honor, but rather than risk burning the shit out of him, I decided to cut off that impulse at the knees."

"Defiling...burning... What are you talking about?" Kiandah's voice is near a shriek as she hands her tray to Dorsten standing at the door, eyes bugging out of his head.

"Uh…" Dorsten starts, moving to set the steaming tray of food on the table. "I will leave you all."

"What were you doing with Kiandah?" I ask him while Kiandah and Okayo argue over my back.

"You can't take that torch to him…"

"Oh, and are you a medical professional…"

Dorsten looks uncomfortable as he glances back over his shoulder, as if trying to decide whether to approach or retreat. It vaguely occurs to me that I should be annoyed that he's in my private chambers and that his gaze is focused too heavily on the Omega for my liking as I squint up and look at him. But I don't seem to be able to muster the energy other than to bark, "Dorsten."

He jolts. "I was escorting the Omega back from the kitchens. She prepared a meal for you and, as Cyprus is still being tended to by Finn, I wanted to ensure she was not left alone. But I will leave now and see how he progresses and if I cannot get him outfitted today in a red cloak."

"A red cloak?" Kiandah says, looking at Dorsten before something above me draws her attention. "No, don't!"

She lunges for Okayo and I laugh gruffly as the male squawks. "Stop it!"

She shouts, "Give me that!"

Dorsten jerks backwards and forwards, looking concerned, clearly trying to decide whether or not to intervene. "Uhm… yes, my Lady. Your…Lord Yaron has decided to give him a red cloak, conditional on his supervision of you until a time that he is no longer needed. At that point, he will be folded into the regular guard, should his training progress normally."

"You…did?" Kiandah says, the sounds of a struggle have me lifting my head to see Okayo and Kiandah *fighting* over a small, red-hot poker in Okayo's gloved fist.

"Good grief, stop this at once. Kiandah! Okayo!"

"Let go!" Okayo shouts.

Kiandah does, but she pushes him hard so that he falls backwards, tripping over the carpet, the red poker in his hand flying from his fist. "Ha!" she exclaims and then runs to retrieve it.

"Don't touch it — " Okayo warns just as my flesh jolts under the shredded barrier of my skin. I prepare to lunge for her, worried about her burning herself, but when she grabs the poker, her hand is engulfed in flame. She takes the firebrand easily into her fist and as the blue flames licking at the outside of her palm retreat, so too does the red color at the burning end of the tine.

She tosses it aside when it shines black once again. "You will listen to me next time, Okayo. I know what I'm talking about…" She returns to the bed to lean over me and inspect my back, but as she draws close enough to touch, I launch my right arm out and snatch Kiandah around the waist. She yelps as I drag her onto the bed. In a seat, I lay my head against her lap, nuzzling my nose into her belly. "Dorsten, you are dismissed. Kiandah, would you like to tell me why you are fighting my best healer?"

Kiandah huffs out a laugh and cards her fingers through my hair. "He's going to burn you horribly if he uses that tool. I have a better idea." I don't care what it is, so long as she keeps touching me.

"Okayo, the Lady has dismissed you. Be gone."

He scoffs, and it would be hilarious if it were accompanied by the sounds of him gathering his equipment and leaving, but it is not. "Okayo," I growl in warning.

"I am not leaving you bleeding all over the place like this. Why did you take so much of that fucking venom again, my Lord?"

"To make a point," I say sleepily.

Kiandah and Okayo both scoff. "You made a point, that cannot be denied." The stupid satin pants she wears now are in the way of me burying my snout between her legs, the sweet scent of her pussy ensnaring all of my focus. I'm distracted by that, so I simply snuggle closer while she and Okayo discuss something...important.

"Okayo," I have the awareness enough to ask, "did you drug me?"

"I'm listening to Lady Kiandah, my Lord."

"Okayo..." I start to lift up, but my arms are heavier than they should be and Kiandah is easily able to wrangle me back down while her fingers pick carefully over my back.

"My Lord, I think I can cauterize your wounds myself... with my hands..."

"Your gift is remarkable...but it still seems risky," Okayo butts in at the same time that I snarl, "Don't call me Lord, Kiandah."

They both ignore me. As if I'm not Lord of this castle at all. It's a rather jarring sensation. I've never been ignored. And in another way, it's quite liberating.

"Nothing can be as bad as that machete you were about to scald him with. Let me try." She sounds insistent and sure. Her alternate personality is showing and I'm pleased.

Normally, she reserves this personality for protecting her family, or ordering me to my knees.

Okayo grumbles, but relents. I feel a cool breeze against some of the skin on my back near my right shoulder a moment before warmth douses it. Warmth. Not scalding heat. Warmth free of pain. I relax against her thighs and close my eyes. Sleepily, I offer, "It doesn't matter if it doesn't work, Kiandah. Let Okayo butcher me with his machete. He's done worse to me than that."

But Okayo is silent. For once.

"Hm?" I say, rolling into the fleshiest part of her thigh and pinching it between my teeth. She swats the back of my head with her other hand and hisses. "You do that and the scarring will be even worse. Hold still, Yaron. Don't be a baby. It can't hurt that badly."

I'm confused and not able to think clearly with whatever Okayo gave me running through my system. Piecing her words together, it almost sounds like she's suggesting that what she's doing with her fingers is working...

"It's working, my Lord," Okayo says breathlessly. "It's incredible."

"It's working?" I ask.

"Yes. It seems to be," Kiandah mutters. "But shh. It takes concentration."

"Do you even know what you're doing? Or how you're doing it?" Okayo fires.

Kiandah doesn't sound as incensed by the question as she should. "Err..."

"Of course she does. My Omega is a creature of many talents." I close my eyes and settle against her, hoping she'll keep on touching me like she is.

"Am I hurting you, my Lord?"

"Not at all. The sensation is heavenly."

Okayo is firing off questions feverishly now. "What does it feel like?"

"Like fucking a cloud."

Kiandah barks out a laugh, which she follows up immediately with curses. "Gods of the shadows, Lord Okayo, what did you give him?"

"That's uhh…not important."

"Okayo…" I grumble, though I meant to sound more menacing than that.

The two chat over the healing properties my Omega wields with her fingertips while I loiter on the boundary line between drowsiness and ravenous contentment. Whatever she does takes forever and I'm fine with that. I hope it will never end. I haven't felt so at ease in a long time. I don't doubt that every ounce of tension has fled my body. That I didn't get up and immediately flay Dorsten for having had the privilege of making her laugh should have been my first indication that I am completely and utterly stoned.

I must drift off to sleep because when I wake, it's dark, the room is quiet and Kiandah is with me in bed. The sheets are fresh and I feel oddly clean, lying beneath them as I am. I can feel the bandages pull on my back as I reach for her, wrapping my hand around her leg above the knee.

She's staring at my face wearing a small, cryptic smile and I can't figure out if she killed me, and momentarily I am concerned that I've died and entered a blissful afterlife. It occurs to me on the next instant that I'm also okay with that. If this is the afterlife and Kiandah is here, there is nothing else for me to do except enjoy it.

Suddenly, she smiles bright. She has a slight gap between her front teeth. I have never noticed any other woman with this feature and I have never adored a feature more in a woman than I do this one, right now. "What are you thinking, Yaron? You have the strangest look on your face."

"I'm not certain I'm not dreaming." Or dead.

Kiandah laughs and it ricochets through my skull. It scars everything it grazes, changing the chemistry of my makeup irrevocably. "Did Okayo really give you so many drugs? You're looking like a fat, sleepy housecat."

"How about a lounging lion, satisfied after a kill?" I reach for her and she doesn't stop me from wrapping a heavy arm around her waist and pulling it flush to mine. I'm immediately annoyed by the tunic she's wearing and start picking at the dull black buttons.

"You do know that female lions do all the hunting for the pride, don't you?" she says, but she doesn't stop my fondling.

"Perhaps I'm a rabid lion, then."

"That I could believe. Yaron, what are you doing with my shirt?"

"I want it," I growl irritably, incapable of getting the buttons free with my claws. Why do I have claws again? My head is still lost in the fog.

"You want my shirt? Well, it is your shirt, so I suppose…"

"I don't want your shirt," I growl, irritated with my progress. Regaining control of my hands doesn't improve my work with the buttons. Finally, I just tear the whole thing apart. "I want it off."

"Yaron," she says on a laugh, trying to cover her breasts with her hands. I can't see them as well as I'd like without my beast's eyes and I'm not in control enough to access a single aspect of him without the rest. Curse Okayo... "You're not supposed to roll onto your back," she chastises when I lean over to do just that. "You're not well enough to have sex," she adds, which is a pity, because I'd been about to drag her body over mine and beg her to ride me to the sunrise.

I groan out my concession, sighing heavily as I sag back into the mattress.

Kiandah laughs lightly, but she doesn't move to retrieve her tattered shirt or any other. She just sits there, torturing me with the sight of her perfect breasts hanging heavy on her chest, tipped in hard nipples that, in this light, look like black diamonds.

"You'll stay until morning, yes?"

"I already promised you I wouldn't leave your side, didn't I?"

"Did you make that promise?"

"Maybe." She shifts a little closer to me. "So I'll stay. If you'll have me."

"I want to have all of you."

"You'll be begging soon enough, Lord Yaron."

I growl but it comes out as a puff of air. "I'll beg now."

"You can't even keep your eyes open."

"I would for you."

"You're lucky that I wouldn't ask you to. I want you to heal. And I need to rest." Her expression twists a little bit then, the shine of her humor dulling. "It wasn't as easy as I hoped it would be controlling the heat in my hands. I don't really understand the power. It seems to only work when I'm desperate, and when I saw Okayo with that barbaric wand he was going to use, I panicked. The flames came easily then. But as you got more relaxed and I did too, it flickered in and out. I…" She glances away. "I'm sorry. Okayo had to use his machine on some small sections of your back. I wasn't able to keep it up. I would…"

"Shh. You're learning, Kiandah. That you wanted to help me at all is more than I could have asked for."

"You are Lord of the Shadowlands. I'm yours to command."

"You know it doesn't work like that. You set a different precedent. One I'm happy to obey and abide by."

She snorts. "You are such a man."

"Am I? I thought I was a Lord."

"You're a brute, using your whip to try to win my hand."

I grin. "But it is working, is it not?"

"Let me go fetch Okayo to bring you more drugs. You're clearly delusional." She pretends to roll out of the bed only to have me easily pull her back. I laugh when she giggles wildly, and for a moment we simply laugh and are and exist.

She settles back on the pillows, looking down at me, letting me breathe in her smoky silhouette. I drag her very close until I can feel her breasts against my chest and her long, warm legs tangled with mine. She's hot to the touch. An echo of the flame that lives inside. I press a lingering kiss to her forehead and smooth my hand over her very short hair around the curve of her head. She's so perfect.

"You are right, though. I did have an ulterior motive in taking the lashes for you and your kin."

"Did you now?" she says slowly. She still sounds so relaxed, but I can feel fresh tension thread her limbs.

"Yes. I need your family's help."

"With what?"

"Finding the undead."

She freezes and I immediately curse Okayo and his horrible, wonderful drugs. They've loosened my tongue. I never meant to tell her any of this. The deal I brokered with Owenna was meant to stay between us. "You would use us for the very purpose you once condemned us for?"

I grunt rather than answer, sensing the moment sliding violently away from me like an avalanche.

I lock her legs to the bed with my own and dig my fingers into the curve of her waist, preventing her from leaving if she does not like what I've said or what I have further to say. "Yes."

"You are unbelievable."

"Thank you."

"That was not a compliment, my Lord," she sneers.

I growl and look up at her. "I'm out of options."

"There are plenty of options."

"I want to wed you under the blood moon knowing that you're safe."

She stills...and softens, rubbing her hand down her face. "I will help you, but you cannot involve the rest of my family. Promise me."

I am backed into a corner. Because I cannot make that promise. Owenna is already on the hunt. "I need rest. You need rest," I say. "We will talk about this further tomorrow. I want to take a trip to the ports…"

"Not tomorrow. No way will you be well enough — and not during the day…"

"What do you mean?"

"Well, you can't very well search for creatures of darkness in daylight, can you?"

The way she says it, so simply, makes me shudder. We've done some exploring at night, but not enough. There is a *knowing* in her gaze that compels me to say what I do next. That, and the drugs Okayo has me on. I offer her a confident, dare I say, cocky smirk and suggest, "You are already helping, then, Kiandah. Why don't you make up to me these scars I took by remaining in your rightful place in my bed and, when we're well enough, joining me to vanquish the undead at nightfall?"

She is silent for far too long before finally, harrumphing in a petulant way that makes me smile because it lets me know I've won. *Again*. She settles again beneath the covers, drawing them up over us both, and I revel in the feel of her warm body next to mine. It's like drinking a forest fire. Incinerating and painful and consuming. I bite down on her shoulder and she swats at my cheek. "You are incorrigible."

"Thank you."

She laughs begrudgingly. "You do not take insults well."

"I didn't hear an insult." She laughs harder and I use the opportunity to say, "Your brother will have to join us when we go hunting for monsters."

She opens her mouth, shuts it, then nods. "Because you gave him a red cloak to protect me?"

"Yes."

"Thank you for that. It is an exceptional honor."

"It was an obvious solution to the problem of the Crimson Rider who assaulted you." She shudders. I pull her closer on a growl. "You need a bodyguard that I trust not to touch you. Your brother fits the bill. He's got the same fire you do. He'll make a good Rider."

"It's…" She bites her lower lip. "He used to dress up in red capes all the time when we were children. He always wanted this. You…you don't know how you honor my family with this."

I hope she feels the same when she discovers Owenna's new rank, but I cannot share that with her until we are wed. Owenna's rank will remain what it is only because so few know of it. If she becomes compromised, her colors are lost, so only Lord and Lady of the Shadowlands can know, along with the other Black Cloaks operating with her in the darkness.

"Once you become my Lady and the undead army has been vanquished and I am certain that there will be no threat to you among my people, he will be absorbed into the Riders' regular ranks. Until then, I want him shadowing you anytime you move beyond these castle walls. No exceptions."

"And my brother was okay with this?"

Her surprise surprises me. "Of course. He wants to keep you safe." I growl as I nuzzle into her very short hair. Her curls are barely regrown, but are so soft against her scalp. Her head is so small and perfectly shaped. I open my mouth to tell her how much I love her hair and the smoothness of her skin and see if she wouldn't mind a quick fuck, just to help the both of us go to sleep, but she spares herself — us both — by speaking first.

"If I stay all night, *my Lord*," she says teasingly, in a way that annoys me and makes me smile at the same time. "Then there will be nothing you can say to stop me from coming with you to look for the undead when you're clearheaded and no longer in pain."

"Make it every night and we have a deal, my queen."

She reaches her way around my body and awkwardly takes and shakes my hand. I smile. "Deal, except if I'm cross with you. I reserve the right to kick you out of your bed — our bed. It's mine now if I'm being invited to share it indefinitely."

I smile, feeling lighter than I ever have, and breathe in her wonderful scent. "Whatever you say, my queen. Whatever you say…" And I drift off to the sweetest dreams I can remember having in all of my long days.

YARON
SHADOW KEEP

"**You must be out of your mind, Kiandah, if you** think you'll be joining a war party to hunt for undead Alphas."

Her lips are tightened to a tiny point. She shoves her finger in my stomach as we square off against one another. "You promised."

"I was high out of my mind." I hold my arms out and let them fall. I feel incensed and flustered, but Kiandah doesn't seem fazed at all.

In fact, since the lashings four days ago, she seems so much more confident. I thought we'd have been able to move sooner, but my body healed slower than I anticipated. In the meantime, her confidence has sweltered like the fire she wields. Though that had been one of my hopes, I'm no longer certain that a confident Kiandah is a good thing. A confident Kiandah is bolder in her desires to save and protect and seems so confident in her ability to do so, while I feel increasingly unsure about my ability to protect her in her quests. I already have failed her so many times. It's better if she stays here. But she won't take no for an answer.

She's royally pissing me off.

"Are you a liar, Lord Yaron?" She advances on me and moves to push my chest. I capture her wrist before she can touch me.

My gaze narrows and the sudden surge of anger I feel rattles me. She must feel it in the pressure of my fingers on hers, or her Omega must sense it, because she tenses, bracing. "You continue with such accusations and I might throw you into the dungeons," I tell her, "or over my knee."

"If you release my arm and keep your word, Lord Yaron, I might just throw you over mine." Her hand forms a fist, tendons and muscles straining beneath my palm. She takes a half step towards me, almost closing the distance between us entirely. The vision is too much. I jerk away from her roughly and show her my back. I adjust myself in my riding trousers, wanting…wishing for… I'm slapped in the face by a memory of her moans, the sounds she made when I rutted into her that very first time. I feel flush with heat.

And she must sense everything I'm feeling. When I glance back, her pupils have dilated. Her tongue wets her lips.

"Kiandah, don't." I storm across the chamber, past the inane pieces of furniture decorating the sitting area in the center of the space, to my closet. I retrieve a cloak. I spend a long time retrieving that cloak.

Kiandah, no sense for self-preservation, slowly follows me. "You said you invited my brother to join the hunt because he's a Rider now…"

"His job is *you*. He'll remain in the castle if you remain in the castle, which you will. And if I hear that you have set foot outside of the grounds, his cloak will be stripped and I will..." Chain you to my bed...that's what I'd been prepared to say, but my mind cannot help but conjure up the memory of what happened to the Lord of Dark City when he did just that to his Omega. He almost lost her. I can still recall the despair in his gaze, the longing he'd held as he stared after the female he loved most in the world and who hated his guts — who wanted to gut him herself. Granted, she eventually overcame her revulsion, but...what if I'm not so fortunate?

"Yes?" Kiandah barks, her hip jutted out, her tongue pressed to the inside of her cheek.

Fire. She carries so much of it today, so visibly, and even though my back is still tender, I cannot come to regret the decision I made just to see her defy me like this.

"What?" Her expression chills and she stops tapping her foot on the floor. She angles her shoulders away from me. "Why are you smiling at me like that?"

"Like what?"

"I don't know. It's a little creepy."

I smile more broadly.

She takes a step away from me and my beast exalts. He wants to chase. But if he catches her, it means nothing good for her at all. I am too poorly restrained these days. The lashing I took must have broken something. I don't feel at all the same. "Yaron, say something."

I want to fuck you. Forget the fucking undead. "You aren't coming."

"I am. With or without your permission."

"Why are you so insistent? Do you know something I don't? Are you more involved with Trash City than your little innocent act has led me to believe?"

Hurt flashes in her gaze, filling me with a momentary guilt. It's fleeting, however. Her hurt is a powerful force and I refuse to allow her to manipulate me with it. "You know I'm not. I just..." Her teeth worry her lower lip. It's out of proportion with her upper lip, which is a perfect, sharp bow, and too large for her face. Makes me salivate. I want nothing more than to sink my fangs into it and watch blood flower over that pretty brown edge. "I made a promise."

"To whom?"

"Someone in the village."

"To Robert?"

"The boy? Was he...lovers with the girl?"

"Yes. Her boyfriend. Quite in love, or as much as one can be at that young age."

"I think that's not giving him enough credit. Emotions are so strong at that age, maybe his love is more real and powerful than any of them."

"Is that a challenge?" I feel myself grow hot and hateful. I hate that my skin is as pale as it is, for it can betray my emotions in bright flares of startling red color. It's rare, but around her, I feel my heat betray me constantly.

She tenses her shoulders by her ears and juts her pretty little lower lip even further out. "Don't try to change the subject or confuse me. I made a promise..."

"If not to Robert, then it had to have been to one of the villagers. Tell me who it was — the one who threw feces at you or the one who tried to strangle you?" She recoils, but I don't feel guilty in the slightest. "You aren't coming, Kiandah, and that's final."

"I am, and *that's* final, Yaron. The only question is whether I go with or without you." She steps forward and places her hand on my forearm. I cannot help the rush of warmth that flowers on my skin beneath her fingertips. "I won't do anything stupid or crazy. I just want to help. You *asked me* for help. Let me. We'll just talk to some people. Peasants are more likely to talk to me than to you. I might be able to get answers you can't."

"Many of them will still hate you. Why would they want to talk to you?"

"People say stupid things to people they hate. But to people they fear, they say nothing at all." She's right. Damn her. "And besides," she says more loudly when I don't speak. She takes two steps away from me and holds up her hands, fingers gesturing down at her garments. "You keep calling me your Lady, but is this really how you'd dress your Lady? If we're headed to the ports, we can stop at the vendors there. I need clothes befitting a cook, at the very least, not a whore."

I lunge forward and grab her throat. I can't help it. I'd thought Dragnovic weak and a fool for his impulsive and tempestuous behavior around his Omega, but I'm starting to grow concerned that my behavior is far worse than his ever was. She's making me a beast of me, regardless of what skin I'm wearing.

"Do not manipulate me, Kiandah."

"It's true," she says, her so recently battered throat working beneath my palm. She licks her lips. "You know it's true. I've had nothing to wear this whole time but your clothes. I don't even have underwear or a bra."

"What makes you think I'm going to purchase either underwear or a bra for you at the markets?"

"But you are going to take me, aren't you?" A smile tugs her mouth up at the corner, just the one. She knows she's got me. She knows she's won.

I curse and step away from her at the same time that there's a knock on the door. I leave her and open the door to find Cyprus there, Zelie beside him. Surprised, I glance between them, my gaze lingering over Cyprus. "What are you doing here?"

Cyprus looks just as surprised by my question as I am by his presence. "I understood you wanted me to join you and Kiandah at the ports."

"When did I give such an order?"

"To Malik? When you were first brought in? I... Am I mistaken?" He shines in his red cloak, but right now, he shuffles, looking around me at his sister in discomfort.

"I..." I start, and then sag. "No. You are not mistaken."

Kiandah makes a squeaking sound behind me and rushes forward. She hugs both of her siblings and I try not to be angry that she's touching anyone but me. "Zelie, so good to see you well. What are you doing here?"

Zelie tucks her long twists over her shoulder and glances at me, her gaze dropping to my bare chest before she blushes. She tries to drop her voice, but I don't move to give the females any additional privacy. "Hey, Kandia." They have so many nicknames for her, I feel put out not knowing all of them, and not having more of my own. "I just was coming to see you off and to see if you wouldn't mind picking up more batiks? We're…" She glances at me, her blush deepening, before returning her gaze to her sister and saying even more quietly, "You know, if you can. I know you don't have any money, but if you are able to…get us some fabric, we could use it. You know…" She makes a small, surreptitious gesture to the garment she's wearing — the almost exact same gesture Kiandah made moments earlier.

I glance down at what the sister is wearing — a simple, burlap shift sporting threadbare patches. I know my face is likely red and splotchy as I look down at this interaction. I am ashamed. I should not be, for a plethora of reasons, but I am. Shame by proxy. It is unpleasant.

"How much?" Kiandah looks concerned. She's picking at her bottom lip in a way I don't like.

"Well, I think my dress can hold a little longer and Cyprus has been newly outfitted by the training guards. Audet's dress is…"

I slap Kiandah's hand away from her mouth, more irately than I intended to and she swats my hand back. Cyprus's mouth parts in shock at our interaction, but he's a clever male and doesn't give it voice. "We'll procure whatever you need. Return to your family and make a list — not only your clothing requirements but anything you need to improve your living conditions. Cyprus will bring it. Bring the list with you when we convene at the stables."

"Truly?" Zelie says, gaze shifting nervously to mine. "My Lord. Apologies."

"Yes. Don't cut corners because you're worried about cost. Tell me what you need, both for yourselves and for the kitchens. We will procure as much as we can with what time the day allows."

Zelie shifts her weight between her feet. She dares me another look. "I don't think I can accept that. After what you've done for us, my Lord."

"Accept it, you will. You are royal cooks, staff of Shadow Keep. It is a disgrace to me to have underserved you."

"You haven't," Zelie and Kiandah say in unison.

They're watching each other with big brown eyes that they share, communicating in silence in a way I don't like. I want Kiandah's words. All of them. Spoken or otherwise. They're mine. She's *mine*.

I don't know why I'm feeling so sensitive. Must be blood loss or residual venom still lingering in my veins. I shake my head. Cyprus says softly, "You haven't, my Lord," he offers even though — or perhaps, because, the words sound so unwilling, the moment feels rather big.

I am uncomfortable and so is he. We make brief eye contact before I nod my head. He bows sharply. "We will…be off then, my Lord."

"Very well. Be ready to depart within the hour." I quickly turn from them and close the door. I lean against it, breath caught in my throat. My discomfort spreads as I slowly swivel my gaze back to Kiandah, but the moment our eyes connect, it dissolves like dust in water. The look on her face erases it.

She's looking at me like I'm her hero.

A sudden need floods my bones, but it is subtle enough to overcome. Just subtle enough. "I…" I start to say, but she places her hand on my chest, right beneath my throat.

"Thank you, Yaron."

Rage at how I've been manipulated fills me. Rage and want. I want to fall to her knees now and push her to her absolute limits before denying her what she needs from me, what only I can give her. I close the space between us and place my hand on her neck in a similar, but more threatening position. I duck my head. "If you do anything to get yourself hurt today, Kiandah, I will kill you."

"Comforting." She purses her lips and looks like she'd like to say more, but doesn't. We get ready in a tense, impenetrable silence before I escort Kiandah to the stables.

The stables are located on the western side of the castle. We walk through the courtyard of the keep to get there. Eyes track Kiandah and me everywhere. They see me, but they linger over Kiandah. A group of four older women — castle staff — carrying a basket of fresh linens between them are staring with particular vehemence. I slide my hand across Kiandah's lower back. She stiffens, looking up at me, but I'm more interested in the way the women all grin and devolve into titters like schoolgirls when I raise my eyebrow in their direction as if challenging them to question this… Though as I stare, I realize I don't think that is their intention at all. They look…*pleased* at the sight of Kiandah with me. Huh.

"We'll take horses today," I tell her as the scent of the stables precedes the sight of them. "The chariot would be too conspicuous."

She scoffs, smiling slightly. "*You* are too conspicuous. Your mode of transport doesn't change that."

"You're right, but unfortunately the carriages have a hard time following the highway lines through Paradise Hole. The swamp has overrun the roads and we're likely to get stuck out there." That is only part of the reason. The larger part is that I can't risk taking a slower transportation if we are set upon by undead or if Trash City is prepared to ambush. But I don't say that.

Dorsten is busy conversing with the stableman, the two of them trying to determine the horse best suited for Kiandah. "Are you an experienced rider?" he asks her over his shoulder while he secures the ties of Brega's saddle. Brega huffs in impatience, ready to depart. While Brega has been allowed run of the pastures while I've been away, he hasn't been ridden. I am the only one he allows that honor. And I can sense he's battle-hungry yet.

I didn't hear Kiandah's answer, or if she gave one at all.

Dorsten continues, adjusting the final latch before lifting the reins in my direction. "My Lord." I reach forward. Kiandah tries to step out of my path, but I prod her forward. Dorsten speaks to her next. "We have a smaller horse that would be well suited for your size, but she requires a firm hand."

"Oh no…" Kiandah takes a step back, bumping into my chest. "That is generous, Lord Dorsten, but I have never ridden a horse before."

I mine for strength. Her little vulnerabilities kill me. Though her brother has undoubtedly been introduced to horses well enough to ride one now, either this past week or prior, and we have more than enough time to give her basic training today, I don't want to. I do my best not to betray my reaction as I slip my riding gloves on.

"No matter. Brega is more than capable of carrying us both. Let us not delay."

I guide Brega out of the stables on foot and into the courtyard. People, people, everywhere. Their eyes track us from every vantage and I am both honored and proud to show Kiandah off and embarrassed that their Lady is displayed such. Covered in bruises and scabs, wearing a tunic beneath a cloak much too big for her.

The season is turning colder and while the trees still hold their leaves, they have begun to turn harsher colors. Redder colors. It does nothing to decrease the sense of foreboding I feel as the gates open and I prepare to venture with Kiandah into the unknown. These are my lands, but I hardly feel like I know them anymore. The Fates have changed everything.

My pride at showing her off as mine, my shame at how she's displayed, my crippling lust as I imagine the feel of her body pressed to mine atop Brega, and my sudden irritation that I was swayed by her pretty smiles earlier and allowed her to come at all compete for dominance in the pit of my stomach.

My voice is not as charitable as it should be when I speak next and hiss, "Get on the horse, Kiandah. No matter what happens, I want you close." I vault up onto Brega's back and extend a hand down to her.

She doesn't meet my gaze as she wraps her fingers around my wrist and I do the same to hers. "As you command, your Lordship." Her heat is fiery as it flares. My lips twitch in a barely restrained grin as I haul her up and place her on the horse in front of me, push the sweet scent of her skin from my mind and prod Brega forward.

We are joined by a small contingent of ten Riders, her brother among them. As Brega plods past him down the row of Riders, she smirks, "Wow. Who knew red was your color, Cyprus?"

He attempts to maintain a stony expression, but his mouth still quirks.

"Apologies, my Lady, but Cyprus is still in training," Dorsten answers on his behalf. "He isn't permitted to converse openly with you."

"Oh. Right. Of course, Lord Dorsten."

Dorsten's pale cheeks redden for no reason I can determine. I don't like it though, and worry that I will not only have to keep my eyes open for undead and Trash City, but for other Alphas like him. I snap Brega's reins and we start toward the gates. Uneventful, the trip will be. I'm sure of it.

I intend to be sure of it. I will that into existence.

KIANDAH
THE NIGHT MARKET

I HATE RIDING HORSES, I DECIDE AFTER ABOUT TEN minutes on Brega's back. My ass is sore and my inner thighs are chafing, but I don't dare say one word about it. Yaron's been in a foul mood ever since we left the castle, crossed Orias and reached the highway line crossroads.

Here, four highway lines intersect. The one south of us now that we traveled upon to get here is the Orias highway line and leads through Orias back to the keep. To our right, heading east is the Undoline highway line. To our left, heading west, is the Shadow Ridge highway line which leads to the Cliffs of Oblivion and some of the Shadowlands mining towns just south of them. And to our north, eventually reaching the ports, the Orias highway line continues through the rotten woods of Paradise Hole.

The Crimson Riders are all silent as the woods close in around us and the hard, packed soil of the highway line turns to mud. There is no camaraderie between them. Instead they march in two parallel lines of five Riders each while Lord

Yaron and I ride our horse in the middle. It doesn't help my unease any, though.

I've been to the ports before, but I don't like going. I don't like crossing through Paradise Hole. The sensation can best be described as ominous and, after our last encounter with the undead in the woods, I feel on the verge of panic.

"You can relax." Yaron's grunt is terse, but his chest continues rumbling against my back in a way I find immensely soothing.

"Hard to relax here." I glance to the left and right into the dark woods. Black roots crisscross over the highway line before us, rendering it almost invisible. The highway lines were originally built wide enough for three carriages to fit side by side, but here, our three lines of horses — not carriages — have been reduced to two and, in some places, we have to march single file.

"I can assure you, we are alone."

His hand slides around my body, through the slit in my cloak across my lower belly. The fabric of his tunic feels very thin all of a sudden and his hand feels so warm. Warm enough to melt beneath. I inhale and the sharp scent of Paradise Hole's musty, misty forest assaults me with a memory of a time when he told me he did not want me and never would moments before he threw me to the ground at his feet. *Present for me.*

"Whatever you are thinking, stop it," he whispers in my ear. "Not only are there other Alphas present, but I have no intention of repeating my poor performance the last time we were in Paradise Hole together."

I drop my voice, worried about being overheard. Cyprus rides near the back of the group, but still, I'd willingly launch myself from a canon before having a conversation about sex in front of my brother. "Poor? I found your performance quite…adequate."

Yaron's fingers tense and I feel the sting of his nails as they form claws and prick my stomach through my tunic. "Adequate?"

I try really hard to keep from smiling. It's so hard. "Yes. Perfectly satisfactory, my Lord." I give the back of his palm a couple condescending pats.

His hand jerks me to him even harder, pulling my ass to his groin, his heat clashing over mine. His shoulders curl around me. He brings his face down to my cheek. I feel caught in his shadow, alone even though we're surrounded by people. "Do you mock me?"

"Teasing you, my Lord. Do you not understand the difference?"

"Teasing is something done between children." His fingers crawl down my body and I try to wriggle back, away from him, but there's nowhere to go.

I grab his wrist. "Yaron…" I hiss, but it's too late. He's already cupped my core. His thick fingers can feel everything through the fabric, and they push ruthlessly at the thin cloth barrier, massaging my entrance, fingering everywhere around my clit, brushing softly over it. "Yaron!" I feel suddenly flush. My mind goes hazy. The Alpha riding directly in front of us coughs.

"If you intend to tease, you must be prepared for me to tease back." He removes his hand all at once and the cool that follows the warmth of his palm comes as a shock. I feel tingly all over. Desire bounces between my bones. I shove my elbow back into his abdomen hard and he emits a soft *oomph*.

"You do that again, I'll light your underwear on fire," I whisper.

He barks out a laugh. The sound is so startling that the Alpha in line in front of us whips around, her hand on the sword at her belt. Her eyebrows are raised and her pale skin is flushed. "It's okay, Mara," Yaron says, holding me tight, but this time, thankfully, outside of the cloak. "The Lady Kiandah means me no harm." Ah. He thinks she's surprised because I elbowed him. No, no, no, my Lord. She's surprised for the same reason I am. I doubt she's ever heard him laugh before either.

His erection digs into my back as we continue through Paradise Hole, emerging finally through the dark trees into a darkening world. Elation skitters over my skin. The sight of the sea blows me away every time. I will never get used to it.

"What is it?" he says to me, his breath warm.

"It's so beautiful. Zaoul. The stars. The ports and the ships bobbing in the sea. The lights from the Night Market. I've only been twice before. Once, when I was really small, and again a few years ago. I love the way it feels."

"And how does it feel?" He brushes his fingers against the side of my face, over my ear, like he's tucking back hair that isn't there. But I don't mind it. I minded it once, but I'm starting to get used to having very, very short hair. Yaron's soft, loving touches are helping.

"Like magic." I glance at his face over my shoulder. I can't keep myself from looking at his lips. "You know, if your guards weren't here, I'd almost say this feels a little like a date."

Lord Yaron practically leaps away from me. He swings a leg over the back of his horse and drops to the ground quickly enough to startle both me and Brega, who rears back. My hands scramble over the saddle, which feels so huge beneath me without Yaron there to dominate the space. My fingers twist in Brega's mane, clinging for survival. He doesn't seem to like that much, either, and lifts his front hooves into the air. I squeeze my aching inner thighs together around the massive stallion and just when I think I'm about to go slumping off the side, Yaron grabs the reins and whispers something softly to his horse that calms the creature.

"Yaron?" I say, heart beating erratically. I press my palm over my chest to try to calm it.

Yaron doesn't answer and I can't see him well enough around Brega's neck and I'm too scared to lean over. His Riders have scattered from formation and are slow to return to it. They're looking between us. Some have their hands on their weapons. I search the back of the queue for Cyprus, who has one eyebrow cocked and is asking me what happened and if everything is okay. I shrug and nod, and he nods in return, casting his gaze back out towards the markets as a loud bout of laughter and shouting picks up near the well-illuminated entrance — a market staple.

"Apologies," Yaron mumbles up to me gruffly, stepping back around his horse and to my side. He has a funny expression.

"Are you okay?"

"Fine. Shall we go to the market to gather supplies for your family first?"

"Like this?" I glance around at the Riders in militant formation around us. "We won't be able to talk to anyone about anything if that's our goal tonight."

Yaron seems to struggle to look up at me. I'd be concerned if I weren't also so determined. Yaron only begrudgingly let me come on this trip and, judging by his erratic behavior, I don't know if he'd let me come again. I want to make it worth it.

"We should shop first. Worry about our garbage friends later."

I snort at his description, and at his suggestion. "I take it you've shopped at the Night Market even fewer times than I have. You can't go through with a horse. It's labyrinthine and narrow. And no one will want to talk if there are a million Riders around. It would be best if we split up. I can go through with my brother and…"

"No." His tone brooks few arguments. His gaze none at all. "You'll travel with me and we will have a tail. Your brother and one other more experienced Rider. Mara," he barks, relaying to her the plan. She's the only female in our brigade, I note with slight apprehension. Not that I think all Riders are like the man who tried to take me on the road, but having more women in the group would make me feel safer. Even if they are Alphas.

"Do you need assistance dismounting, my Lady?" Mara asks me as she passes by. She is a white woman with blonde hair and a large birthmark below her right eye in the shape of a strawberry. She's very pretty and I feel a little flushed as she lifts both arms to help me down.

"Mara," Yaron barks. "Step away."

She gives me a wink and a grin, which totally disappear when she spins on her heel to face Lord Yaron. "My Lord." She offers him a slight bow and I notice that the other Riders are all making eyes at each other, subtle expressions of laughter passed between them. Lord Yaron should know a bit more about teasing, I think, because I'm pretty sure his Riders tease him all the time.

Yaron's hands fit around my hips as I swing my leg over Brega's back. As I wobble atop the horse, Yaron steps closer, his grip on my hips tightening near to the point of pain. His eyes are at my knees and he suddenly huffs and rests his forehead against them. "It will be best if we do not speak while touring the market."

I stroke the top of his hair, concerned, but I nod, not wanting to ask him what's wrong in public. "Alright," I agree with a frown, because it's really not alright. *A date was too much to hope for.*

I try not to feel disappointed as he lowers me from Brega's back, making sure that the entire front of my body runs the length of the entire front of his body. I am able to stay quiet through that. I'm able to stay quiet as we walk down the boardwalk, through the chorus of shouts and orders relayed between merchants and boat captains as wares are loaded and unloaded and taken to new wagons destined for Hjiel and other places on the South Island. I'm quiet still as we walk side by side up to the towering entryway to the Night Market — two poles standing like totems with snarling faces carved into their aged wooden exteriors, colored lanterns strung between them on long thick ropes like vines. And I'm quiet as we step beneath them into a world of life and light.

And that's where my silence ends. I squeal, "They have saffron!" I'm bouncing on the balls of my feet as I approach the first merchant, a spice vendor with piles of the bright yellow-orange herb in various wooden casks. The fragrances from his stall and so many others clash in an overwhelming combination that makes me want to spin in circles and dance. I love it all. I grab Yaron's sleeve and drag him forward. "They bring it all the way from Ruby City. It's wonderful in curries and breads and soups. Ooh! I can make you a saffron rice dish to die for. Can we get some?"

Yaron is frowning at me, but it's a strange frown because it doesn't quite reach his eyes. His eyes are glittering with mischief — or something. I'm not sure I understand this male who's here with me now, but I'm too eager to investigate it. Especially when he nods. I clap my hands and shop.

We move on to a second spice vendor but by the third, he harrumphs. "You can't possibly need curry spice and curry powder."

"There's a difference!"

"What is the difference?"

"One's a spice and one's a powder."

His stoic expression breaks. He smiles and rolls his eyes. "Whatever the Lady wants," he tells the vendor, who takes that to heart. He starts showing me everything he's ever grown, harvested and caught and when he's finished selling me a small garrison of spices, he waves over his brother, a fisherman, to show me his latest catch.

"I think you were wrong," Yaron says, ducking down to speak in my ear just after he instructs Mara and Cyprus to ferry back the items we've bought thus far. "We do need all of the Crimson Riders with us in the market. You're going to spend the coffers dry, my love."

My love. I trip over a cobblestone and Yaron curses as he lunges forward to grab me above the elbow before I can faceplant in a pyramid of lemons. "Am I going to have to tether you to me, Kiandah, or are you able to walk for yourself?" He curses again when he looks down at my feet. "We are done with the food..."

"But...but we haven't even been to the Rookery sweet meats stall yet!"

"Is that what that stench is? No, Kiandah," he says, shaking me gently and placing me back on my feet. He takes the baskets from my arms and passes them off to my brother when he returns. Cyprus looks at the basket, shoulders sagged, rolls his eyes and clenches his teeth — he's been shopping with me before, and he hates it. "We are going to get you better shoes." I'm wearing borrowed boots that clatter when I walk. I don't know whose they are, but they were given to me by Radmilla and are a size or two too large.

"If we *must*, my Lord," I say, trying not to sound as excited as I feel.

Cyprus makes a choking sound and Yaron turns to look over his shoulder at my brother. He gives him an inquisitive glance. "Tell me that shopping for clothing with this one is less maddening than shopping for food."

Cyprus must have gotten orders not to speak at all on this trip because all he does is purse his lips into a line so thin, his full lips become an invisible smear. Yaron frowns. I laugh at the two of them and clap my hands together. Feeling light, not just because we're going shoe shopping but because they're making fun of me. Both of them. Together.

I grab Yaron's hand and he starts, feet light as he lets me drag him toward the stalls selling anything you could ever hope to have in leather. "Well, if you are buying…" I wink at him over my shoulder. His expression is stern and confused and I like this off-balanced version of Yaron. "I also need new aprons, boots, and shoes for my entire family."

"Do you know their sizes?"

"Yes. I wouldn't be a good sister if I didn't."

"I'm certain that since you saved them from a burning building, that's not the case."

I scoff. "Are you making jokes about burning down a church?" He frowns harder and when he opens his mouth, I sense he'll say something profound, something I can't handle. "Do you need anything from the leather workers for yourself, Yaron?" I quickly interrupt.

He considers, successfully distracted. "Perhaps a new set of boots and vambraces. My best sets were destroyed when we…" His gaze grows hazy. My mind races. I yank on his wrist and he looks back at me and takes a long step to close the distance between us.

"Are you truly so unaffected?" he hisses.

I hesitate, unsure of what he means. "I…" He brushes his knuckles over the back of my cheek. "I feel…" I start to tell him that I am affected, but I'm not sure that's what he means. Of course, he has to know that I'm affected. I mean — isn't it obvious? I shake my head, try again, "I don't feel like I did in the forest, if that's what you're asking."

So out of control. So completely insane. I would have fucked anyone then, I'm sure, but I wanted it twice as much because it was him. I wanted him more than I'd ever wanted anything in my life. So much that it had hurt so badly, I couldn't have done anything else other than what I did. Took everything from him, to the point that it nearly killed me. Now, I want him, but I can use my whole head to decide the when and the how. I'm not going to fall to the ground here and…

"I understand," he says, but he withdraws his hand so abruptly, it leaves me feeling like I've done something wrong.

That feeling grows more pronounced as we shop in a tense silence, so much less pleasant than the light banter we exchanged before. I buy myself new shoes and shoes for the other members of my family that I know they'd like, and after swapping out my oversized boots with the short booties made for me on the spot in the leather shop, Yaron leads me to the fabric stalls.

"Batiks!" I exclaim when I see the beautiful, starched cotton fabrics, dyed in varying shades. I haggle with the vendor, arguing with them over which ones are real wax and which are synthetic fakes commonly produced in Glass Flats, but also in the Rookery. Real wax batiks only come from the Shadowlands and Ruby City now, though Mirage City used to be our largest supplier before the Fates were found to be controlling the city and trade stopped between Mirage City and the South Island.

Eventually, we settle on a price for the real wax fabrics and a few pieces of Ankara textiles and mudcloths. The female merchant, who I hadn't even noticed because she wasn't handling the negotiations, then takes me into the back to be measured and fitted.

I head into the stall, leaving Yaron out front looking stressed and grumpy. The female chuckles when she shuts the curtain between us and the outside world. Everything quiets. It's like we've entered another universe.

"So it's true," she says the moment we're alone. I wonder if Yaron can even hear us with how loud the market is. That makes me a little nervous, but I remember now that we did come to snoop. I suppose striking up conversations with random vendors is part of that and it's much easier to do without him looming over me.

"So what's true, miss?"

"It's Zanele," she says.

"Kiandah," I reply just as quickly. The woman looks young, though my guess is that she's around my age or older. She has long braids that fall to her waist and I try not to clench my teeth in envy as I remember what my hair looked like before.

She smiles at me and I feel instantly guilty that I've been caught thinking negatively towards her, especially when she drops her tone and says, "They say Lord Yaron has been tempted as no other Shadow Lord has been tempted before. They say a great and powerful Omega has brought him to his knees. That he took lashes for her. That he worships the ground at her feet…"

I laugh. I just can't help it. Zanele laughs, too, knowing she's spinning yarns. I shake my head as I wipe the moisture from my eyes and she resumes measuring me and making little adjustments to the stiff, brightly colored fabric she has wrapped around my waist. "I think someone's been telling you tall tales."

"Or someone is being modest, *my Lady*. I haven't seen Lord Yaron in the Night Market before and I've never seen him do his own shopping." She giggles again and I laugh with her, thinking of poor, sweet, homicidal Yaron standing outside a batiks stall grumpily waiting for me. "I think he really likes you, miss."

My face warms. "It's because I'm an Omega."

"I don't know." Her voice rises at the end, teasingly, but not in a mean way. In a way that sends feeling all the way down to the soles of my feet and the tips of my toes. "Omegas have passed through the Shadowlands before and he was not tempted by them."

"You're making me blush, sha," I say, using the old Orias word for sister.

"I don't think it's *me* making you blush, sha-lee," she replies, the Undoline derivative.

I perk up. "You're from Undoline."

"Born and raised."

"I didn't notice your accent."

"I work at the Night Market three days, then I go back to Undoline the rest of the week to help prepare the fabrics. It comes and goes, depending."

"I'd stay put, if I were you, given what's gone on here with Trash City." I didn't even mean to prod in that direction. The words simply came to me. And, having said them, I realize that I'm in a position now to push. "Has Undoline had any of the problems with Trash City or the undead army we've had in Orias?"

Zanele's brown eyes flash. She's hunkered down in a crouch, applying pins to the legs of my new trousers. I feel like I'm sweating. Cold, but sweating, even though the weather near the ports is balmy and pleasant, even at night. The waters of Zaoul are warm on the east side of the islands, cold on the west. Here in the strait between the two islands, the warm and cool waters clash.

I wait, staring at her expectantly in a way that I hope appears innocent. "Pardon me for saying, sha-lee, but didn't your family work with the traitors of Trash City to kill Alphas?"

I wince and shake my head. "Is that what people think?"

"Are they wrong?"

"I…" Ancestors save me, it's what I have to believe. "My family didn't kill anyone, but…" But I need her to tell me what she knows. "But my parents and oldest sister were working with them to supply bodies for the undead army. I… Lord Yaron absolved us. But at great cost. What we did — " *I am not my family.* " what they did — was wrong. So wrong. They shamed me." I shake my head, realizing what I've said and recoiling from it. "I…I'm sorry. I've never said that out loud before."

She shudders visibly, but she nods, too. "Have you seen them with your own eyes?"

"The undead?"

She nods.

I shudder. "They're horrible. Have you?"

She gives me a funny look and then she drops her voice even more. "I have. Three times. Once near Shadow Ridge — my husband and I were on our way to Heatherlen to deliver a special order when our cart broke down. We saw shapes in the woods and hid in a ditch, fearing thieves and robbers. What stalked by us, mere feet away, was so much worse. At least a dozen undead." She cringes. "It was awful."

"The ancestors must have been with you that night, for your cart to break down before they caught up to you," I whisper to her as she stands, undressing me once more and setting the patterns aside to work on later. She pulls a simple, floor-length black dress from a chest on the floor and drapes it over my head. From there, she returns to the ground to work on the hem.

"And twice more, I saw creatures that I believe were undead, near the ports when I was packing up my stall late. They were far away though, near the water, so I can't be one hundred percent sure. It could have simply been brazen creatures of Zaoul."

"Almost as terrifying."

She snorts. "Almost."

"Was anyone with them when you saw them near Shadow Ridge? They couldn't have been traveling alone. When I saw them in the woods of Paradise Hole, they didn't seem capable of making decisions themselves. They had to have been led."

"Oh, they were."

"By who?" I scoff, outraged and flabbergasted. "Who would willingly do such a thing?"

But, her confident hands still on the fabric, she gives me a curious look. "Sha-lee, you don't think yours is the *only* family working with Trash City, do you?"

I quiet and feel suddenly very small. Like an ant. I just... what she's suggesting...I can't fathom it. "But...but who would want to work with Trash City to make monsters?"

She shakes her head and I know I'm wrong for even having asked. My sister did. My parents did. "The desperate or the greedy, I suppose, but mostly the former, I should think. Trash City has preyed on families of women, single women, single mothers. We may be free as Betas — hell, I'm even married to an Alpha — but you know, you must know as well as anyone, how hard it is in the realm of shadows for women. We don't get the same opportunities, the same chances. You got lucky, miss, ascending as an Omega. You'll live in the lap of luxury and never have to work again. But for those whose husbands have died or who never had one to begin with, it's hard. Do you know that it's *still* a law that in order to set up and take down a stall in the Night Market, women need a chaperone?" She makes a disgusted sound in the back of her throat.

I am still stunned, reeling. Even as she fits me into a corset and cinches the waist. She's got me outfitted in a black shift, a black outer dress, black underpants, and a corset that's one of the loveliest patterns I've ever seen. A traditional fabric, it's been starched and dyed maroon against a darker maroon. The darker maroon shimmers.

"I never considered why my brother and father had to do some things, collect certain shipments and the like. It makes sense why women would want to work with Trash City for coin, especially if the Fates are behind them."

"Is that true?"

"I'm not sure," I reply honestly. "Yaron hasn't talked to me about them. He doesn't talk to me much about anything. I think…" I shake my head. "Never mind."

"What?"

I smile at her, but it feels sad and small and self-pitying. "Maybe, it's like you said. Maybe, he likes me even though I'm not an Alpha, but as a woman he doesn't trust me enough to talk to me, you know, as an equal."

She doesn't say anything to that.

I shake my head. "Sorry. I don't mean to burden you. I just…was curious what you'd heard, and if you knew where I could find Trash City. I'd like to give that wench that leads them a piece of my mind and atone for my family's crimes. It's one thing to want to support the women of the Shadowlands. It's another to tempt them with gold to turn on their own people and abet murder. And I don't care who they're working for — raising an army like they have is wrong, no matter the motivation."

She nods. "I couldn't agree with you more, sha-lee. They couldn't tempt me with all the gold in Glass Flats," she says, referring to the richest of the cities.

"Me either." I frown. "But I also like my job. I'm a good cook and I like working. Even if I'm just a poor woman, and a Beta…well, before."

She smiles at me and the levity returns between us. "I do, too. It's incredible seeing the way my designs transform people. Are you ready to see yourself?"

I nod. "Yes. This fabric is stunning."

"*You* are stunning. Come, sha-lee. Look." She spins me around and for a split second I wonder who that pretty woman is in the doorway before I realize that's a mirror and the woman is me. "You like?"

My jaw drops. "Zanele, I…" I can't speak.

She laughs. "You look gorgeous. Here, let me just apply a little makeup to accentuate the eyes. I like your hair, by the way."

I look down at my booted feet, nervous and shocked. "Thank you, sha. My hair used to look like yours until I burned it all off. It's begun to regrow, you can see here," I say, gesturing to the fuzzies that have taken up on the top of my head and the sides that I shaved into a fade. "I miss my long curls, though."

"You burned it all off?" She balks, then seems to consider. "Ohhh…oh ancestors be, you really are a Fire Omega?"

I nod.

"I guess I didn't realize your hair would also…" She starts to laugh.

I don't mean to, but I start to laugh with her. "Stop that. It was traumatic! You know how it is for us Orias and Undoline women. Our hair doesn't grow fast. It'll take me years to regrow my hair, if it ever does."

"You aren't beautiful because of what grows on your head," she tsks, and the words are so flippant and direct and raw and honest that I'm momentarily taken aback. "Now here. You're all finished. Go out there and you'll see that it doesn't matter how much or little hair you have because our good Lord is going to lose his mind when he sees you like this.

And after you have him all worked up, you're going to go to The Sea Witch and book a room and let him ravage you and *then*…" She drops her tone and lifts up onto her tiptoes so she can whisper directly into my ear, so close that not a word is lost to the wind. "When he's good and asleep, you're going to go down to the bar and have a fiery word with Madame Zenobia."

I raise my eyebrows and stare into my own eyes framed by freshly lacquered black lashes. A silent communication passes between us.

She nods in confirmation. "*Yes*. And I want the monsters *gone*, sha-lee. Can you promise me that?"

I turn to face her, woman to woman, and tell her words that I can't possibly hope to mean, but I do. "I promise you."

Her lips quirk. "You are the right choice, then."

"For what?"

"To lead us."

"Don't be ridiculous."

Zanele raises and eyebrow and grins big enough to show all of her teeth. "Sha, dressed like that, there isn't a soul in the Shadowlands who wouldn't follow you."

We devolve to laughter after that.

KIANDAH
THE NIGHT MARKET

I STEP OUT OF ZANELE'S STALL WITH A FLOURISH. Alright, Zanele's all flourish. I'm more stumble, trip, right myself and smile awkwardly. But Zanele was clearly mistaken about how pretty I looked because Lord Yaron, standing there all regal and annoyed with his hands behind his back, turns and, seeing me, he blinks once. His nostrils flare, but other than that he doesn't react at all, making me feel instantly uncomfortable.

Meanwhile, Cyprus smiles at me and winks. I smile back, appreciating at least my own brother's approval.

"The rest of your clothing will be delivered to the castle within the fortnight, my Lady!"

"Your fee will be doubled if you can make it four days," Yaron interrupts.

Zanele gawks at Lord Yaron before dropping her gaze to his feet. "That will be more than acceptable, my Lord."

"And I have one additional request."

Zanele gives him a curious look as he stalks past me *without looking at me* and effectively corals her back into the fitting room. The two of them disappear behind the curtain and I don't like the cold spike of pressure in my abdomen as I stand in the mouth of the stall, looking out at the people milling past. Lots of people are looking at me, some appreciatively, others condemningly, but mostly curiously and I feel very exposed. My shoulders curl. My brother frowns. He's looking at the curtain Yaron disappeared behind.

Yaron emerges a few moments later — it feels like it takes a long time. His hand is on his belt. I look down. Zanele doesn't emerge with him and I frown. Not that I think he just took her back there to have sex with her or anything. I mean, of course he wouldn't do that. Even if she is beautiful. She's married. And he is…he likes me. Right?

"Are we finished in the markets, Kiandah?" Yaron's voice is rough.

I glance up at him and force a smile. "Did Zanele frighten you off shopping?"

"*You* have frightened me off of shopping. I didn't think it was possible to spend so long in the markets." His gaze drops to my bodice — the corset hugs my curves and creates even more curve where there was otherwise very little. I think I've lost a little weight, too, since being in Yaron's quarters. I'm not spending as much time in the kitchens and I don't feel as full as I did before. Audet always said I had the body of an eleven-year-old boy. I know, based on what she's told me recently, that a lot of what she said came from a place of jealousy, but she's probably right now. Minus my butt.

I cross my arms over my chest and shuffle away from him, glancing back at the curtain. Zanele still hasn't reemerged. "Um. Yes, I think I'm done shopping." I glance up at the sky, the color of pitch. There grey clouds have come once again, absconding with the starlight. "If you are?"

"There is only one final item I need to procure. Then I'll see you fed before we return to Shadow Keep."

I place my hand on his arm. His skin is warm, even through his new black leather vambrace. Patterns have been embossed into the leather. I can't make them out in the hazy torchlight of the stall. I can't wait to look at them tomorrow. Maybe, when he's out of his room, I can shade them in relief on a piece of parchment.

"You know, I actually had another idea. If you're up for it. Probably not, but in case, I was just thinking we could potentially um…"

Lord Yaron turns to face me. The darkness of the sky frames his dark hair. The strips of grey at his temples hang down in his face, begging me to tuck them behind his ears. His hair has grown out. He has scruff on his cheeks and chin and looks rather wild. His eyes are bright and assessing. My throat dries. I feel destabilized and the feeling becomes more severe when he cups the side of my face.

"What is it, Kiandah?"

Surprised, I blink and step away. His hand falls and so does the expression on his face. His fingers flex and clench. I feel like I've done something wrong again. "I-I was thinking we shouldn't try to make it back through Paradise Hole tonight. Maybe we should stay at The Sea Witch. It's an inn just north of the market, closer to the ports."

He raises an eyebrow and gives me a funny look. "Zaoul's Mistress is, shockingly, the nicer inn between the two. If you'd like to stay overnight, perhaps, we should rather stay there."

I step close to him and beckon him to lower with the crook of a finger. His nostrils flare as he obeys. "For our other project...The Sea Witch may make more sense. Unless you would like to stay at the nicer one. I'm happy to stay at The Sea Witch by myself or with Cyprus. It might be easier anyway to get...informati..." The look on Yaron's face is intended to scald and even I, a fire Omega, feel its heat. "Never mind?" I say, voice very small.

"Do not suggest sleeping without me again. Did we not discuss this several nights ago?"

I nod rapidly, just to avoid having this conversation out here, in front of so many strangers...and my brother. Cyprus is glaring at Lord Yaron now and I feel heat flame in my cheeks. "Let's go then?"

He continues to glare at me for a beat, then nods. I move out ahead of him and am startled when he grabs my inner elbow. His glare is even more severe than it was before. He glances down. I glance down. He's offered me his arm. I feel warmth in my chest and in my cheeks and in...other places as I coil my fingers along the underside of his forearm. He tightens his arm against his chest, pulling me close to him as he escorts me back through the market.

We take a turn before reaching the final stalls, which boast weapons and other metalware, veering back in the direction of the spice merchants. We're in a bit of a strange area of the market, one I've never been to before. It boasts exotic and precious goods, all of them outside of my family's budget and cooking needs.

There are armed personnel outside of most of the stalls in this section and they don't seem to eye Yaron with much interest. I get the feeling that they might be hired mercenaries who respect his Lordship as much or rather, as little, as they respect anyone else.

Lord Yaron stops outside of a stall whose contents are blocked from sight by a black curtain. A man stands out front. He's older, white, and wears a blank expression as Yaron approaches.

"I'm here to pick up from Ivreness."

"Have you placed an order?"

"Yes. I sent someone ahead."

The man grumbles something under his breath sounding like *little Lords and their pretty coppers* but I don't hear the rest. Yaron's lips purse and he pulls me tighter to him and I do my best to ignore the way his hard chest feels against my arm. The man doesn't return, but a woman does. She's got medium brown skin that's utterly flawless and jet-black hair that falls in smooth waves to her lower back. She might be ten years Yaron's senior, but I wouldn't blame him at all if he took her for a lover or even more than that. She's absolutely stunning.

"So this is who it's for, I'm guessing?" she says with a grin as she hands over a small gold jar.

Yaron grunts.

She looks me over once more, assessing me in a way I'm not certain I like…until she says, "Oh yes. I can see it." And just like that, I'm irrationally pleased. "I made it to your specifications."

"Thank you, Ivreness." Yaron reaches beneath his cloak and produces a pouch which jingles loudly when he hands it over. He hasn't paid for anything himself yet. He has his Riders for that. But this he buys himself. Hm. Curious. I crane my neck and stand up on my tip toes, leaning across him to try to see it, but he just tucks the little gold jar quickly into his cloak's inner pocket.

"It'll shine like the sun, even in the dark." Yaron is nodding at Ivreness's words, even as she turns away from him. "It's also edible, as you asked."

"What's she talking about, Yaron?" I ask him.

But his cheeks are splotchy with red as he mutters gruffly, "Nothing."

He doesn't speak to me again until we're out of the Night Market, traversing the ports and approaching another lively section of town. A few low buildings made of wood are illuminated by bright lanterns. People mill about in the small square, laughing and shouting and drinking. A cluster of couples are dancing near the entrance of the first inn we pass, or, well... I suppose it isn't so much an inn as it is a brothel.

Women with their bosoms out hang from the balconies, clambering for Yaron's attention. He ignores them, but I look up and they laugh shrilly when they get my attention. "Shadow Lady, come join us with or without your Lord!" They shriek with a laughter that's infectious. I can't help it. As Yaron tows me along, I laugh, too.

"Don't encourage them," he mumbles.

"They seem nice."

He balks and shakes his head. "You'd like to join them, then?"

"I didn't say that."

His lips twitch with an unreleased smile as he tows me another few buildings down where the wide-open doorway of The Sea Witch beckons wayward travelers. We step inside and not a soul looks up. Well, maybe a soul or two, but the vast majority of the bar is too deep into their drink to notice the entrance of the Shadow Lord and his companions.

"Stay close to me, Kiandah." He has to speak directly into my ear to be heard as he leads me towards the bar that spans the entire left wall.

"No one will want to talk to me about Trash City with you standing right next to me."

"Is that why we're here?"

"Perhaps."

"What did the fabric merchant say to you?"

"That…" I debate how honest to be with Yaron and decide to go with *mostly* honest. "That we should come here. That other villagers that have worked with Trash City in the past have come through here before."

"There are *more* families that have worked with Trash City?" His fury reminds me why I went with *mostly* honest. If he was willing to burn down an entire church to kill my family for our involvement, I don't doubt that he would burn this tavern down with twenty times as many people in it to condemn the tavern's guilty owner.

"I don't know for sure. I don't know any myself. I didn't even know my family was working with Trash City…ouch." I glare at the burly male who just ran into me, sloshing beer on my arm. I'm about to tell him off when Yaron starts to turn. "Yaron…" I warn, lifting my hands to ensure he doesn't decapitate the man for a little push and a little spill.

But Yaron is denied his chance for revenge when the unrepentant drunk man is yanked off of his feet and tossed towards the exit by my brother. He glares as the man totters into another couple. One of the two men that form the couple grabs the drunk before he can run them over. He pitches him further towards the exit, where he lands face down on his belly across the threshold.

My brother rolls his eyes and shakes his head. Yaron abruptly pushes me towards my brother. "Take her upstairs. I will join you shortly with keys to our rooms."

"You don't want me to handle this, my Lord?" Mara says.

"I think I can manage this simple task, Mara."

She nods. "Of course." And abruptly turns on her heel and starts towards the staircase. My brother and I follow.

The next level up is entirely exposed, rooms running along the walls of the inn, the center open and looking down on the boisterous crowd below. We continue to the third and final floor of the inn. Here, the world is almost as loud as it is downstairs given how thin the walls and floorboards are. A drunk man is salivating over what appears to be an equally drunk woman. I think they might actually be fucking against the far wall. My brother slaps his hands over my eyes and I fight him off, laughing. Meanwhile, Mara whistles incredibly loudly and is intimidating enough for the couple to stumble out of sight down the far hallway.

"I don't feel comfortable leaving our Lord down there on his own," Mara says, glancing over her shoulder at the staircase. "I'm going to check on him."

I open my mouth to tell her that he's easily the scariest creature in this place, but I decide against it and let her do her job. She disappears, leaving me alone with my brother for the first time all day. In weeks. Maybe, since we were ten years old and we decided to play a prank on Owenna that got us grounded for two weeks. Granted, being grounded didn't have much weight. We just continued to perform the same humdrum tasks we'd done the previous day, only this time, we were forced to do them together. It was nice in its own way.

"What are you thinking about?" Cyprus says to me, leaning against the opposite wall. He's smiling a little deviously in a way that's so characteristically *him*, I smile.

"That time we painted the inside of Owenna's shoes with saffron oil."

"Oh yeah." Cyprus chuckles, "The soles of her feet were yellow for weeks." I laugh with him, feeling light, feeling hopeful. I haven't felt like this in so long the sensation has become foreign. "Mama and Papa were so mad at us. Saffron is so expensive."

"And so is leather. They had to buy Owenna new shoes."

"Not a problem for *you* now." He has a *tone* that Mama would whoop him for and that I don't like at all. I kick his shoe — try to — but he evades my strike. I huff and lean back while he goes on, "And my guess, based on the way he looks at you, is that you won't have that problem ever again."

I feel warmth in my face when Cyprus lifts an eyebrow. "Stop that."

He shakes his head and roughly rubs his face. "What did you do to him, Kia? Never seen a male so singularly focused on anyone. Maybe Papa was like that with Mama at the beginning. He'd do anything for her."

His words should make me smile, but with Zanele's words in my ear now, they don't. I whisper, "Like work with Trash City."

Cyprus frowns, getting a faraway look in his hazel eyes. Same eyes that Audet has. Same eyes as my father's. "Yeah. Like that."

I feel bad for ruining the moment and quickly grunt, "I didn't do anything to him. It's just the Omega bond. The pheromones are confusing him." I know it's a lie, but I'm certainly not about to delve into the details of whatever is happening between Yaron and I with my twin brother.

"It's definitely not that. At least, it's not all that. You did something to him, bewitched him with your feminine wiles." He shrivels his nose in distaste and I laugh and lift my leg, pretending to kick him in the groin this time. He bats my foot out of the air.

"I didn't do anything, I'm telling you."

"You did. A Shadow Lord's never taken a Lady before."

"I didn't."

"You did. Think hard."

"Well…"

"Yes?"

"I…" I glance at the stairs, gnawing my lower and upper lip together. "Before he took those lashes for our family…I denied him."

"Shit. Well that would do it."

"Yeah. I just…" I wring my hands together, listening for feet on the stairs. "I thought he would know that I obviously would accept him now, but he isn't acting like it…"

"Don't say it, Kia. Don't accept his hand. Are you crazy?"

"Are *you* crazy? I…thought you were starting to like him."

"Like him? I'm not so easily swayed as the rest of the damn family. I haven't forgotten what he did to us in that church and you're my favorite sister…"

"I'm your twin, you have to say that…"

"…and you deserve better than that murdering jackass." He glances to the left and to the right, worried about the ears that might overhear our exchange.

"He's *Lord* of the Shadowlands. I don't think Mama would agree with you."

"Mama's got four daughters that she thinks are only going to be successful in life and give her grandchildren if they're married off to wealthy men. She's desperate."

I frown again as the conversation veers quickly back into dark territory. "Yeah. Desperate."

"Seriously. Don't worry about that shit. Forget about all the shit with Trash City and our family and the dungeons and the church and the lashes and everything we've been through these past weeks. You don't have to like him because of that."

"I don't have to hate him because of that, either."

Cyprus looks unamused by and unimpressed with me. He opens his mouth, but I cut my fingers across my throat harshly at the sound of pounding feet on the stairwell. Mara reappears a moment later. "Our Lord is still busy with the innkeep, but he's given me keys. Apparently, they only had two suitable rooms available, so we will be sharing."

I glance down the hallway. While the lower floor boasted customers hanging from the rafters, up here, it seems mostly empty. "Really?"

"Yes. Follow me. I'll show you to your and Lord Yaron's room."

"I think I should room with my sister," Cyprus says and I'm surprised by the authoritative tone of his voice.

Mara must be, too, because she jerks up. It takes her a moment to respond. She glances between us. "I believe it would be our Lord's preference to room with his Lady."

"She is not his Lady. She is unmarried and Lord Yaron hasn't won her yet in the Red Moon Festival."

Mara gawks. She looks between me and my brother and then furrows her brow, pivoting towards me. "My Lady, I apologize. I did not mean to assume that you would be sleeping with Lord Yaron." I blush at her wording, but only because she blushes, too. "If it is your desire to room, rather, with your brother, I would not deny you that right. I am more than capable of rooming with our Lord." Her cheeks flare bright red at that and I might have laughed if I weren't also so uncomfortable.

Cyprus is shooting me death glares and I feel totally exposed. "I, um…" I don't feel worried about Mara and Yaron together in a room…but I do feel worried about what Yaron will think if I choose to room with my brother over him…and I feel worried not about what my brother will think if I choose to sleep in the same room as Yaron, but because he's chosen to speak up for the first time today and I want to support him.

"I…yes. My brother is um…he's correct. I suppose, it would be the proper thing to do to room with Cyprus rather than Ya…our Lord."

We all stand there uncomfortably exchanging glances before Mara glances down at the two sets of keys in her hands and huffs, "Alright. Follow me."

She walks to the end of the hall and follows the path the drunk couple made to the right. That hallway dead ends and Mara uses one of the keys to open the door. "You two will be staying here, then. This is the smaller of the two rooms. Lord Yaron and I," she swallows, "will be staying three doors down, should you need us for anything."

"I'm pretty hungry. Should we go down to the tavern now or wait for Lord Yaron to return?"

"No!" Mara practically leaps at me, as if trying to physically restrain me from fighting my way past her to the mayhem downstairs in order to get some stale bread and watered down soup. But I haven't moved anywhere. Mara gives me a gentle squeeze and, as if seeing how violently she's holding me, blushes harder and retreats. "Lord Yaron specifically did not want you to return to the tavern. He'll have food and a bath sent up."

"Oh. Okay," I say, turning towards Cyprus, who holds the door open for me. We bid Mara a goodnight. The door clicks shut, the latch clearly sticky. The moment he gets it closed and locked, however, I square off to face him in a room so small it makes our family's old quarters look like a castle. There's also only one bed. For the ancestors' sake.

"First, I'm not staying in this room. The whole reason we're here is to talk to Madame Zenobia about her dealings with Trash City and see if any of the other customers know anything that could help us find them. Second, I'm not sharing a bed with you. You'll have to sleep on the floor."

"Wait, why should I sleep on the floor?"

"You sound like you're twelve, don't mope. I'm your big sister, so I get the bed."

"You're my big sister by seconds."

"Yes. Still your elder, have respect."

"No, you're my big sister. You're supposed to take care of me so you should cede the bed."

I wait, and then I sprint. "Whoever gets there first gets the bed!" I leap, and mid-leap, Cyprus shoves me to the side. I hit the bed and bounce off of the hard, lumpy mattress onto the floor. I land laughing.

"Looks like you lost."

"Looks like you cheated."

"There were no rules." I stand up and Cyprus is lounging back on the bed, his hands behind his head, his red cloak looking more like a comfortable bedspread than the actual disheveled wisp of a sheet stretched across the lumpy mattress beneath him.

I point at him with my face scrunched and one eyebrow closed. "And when you pushed me, I hit the bed first, so there." I bend down and push his side, trying to shove him off of the bed. He starts to laugh when all of a sudden there's a loud banging in the hallway. A moment later, our *locked* door explodes open.

"What the fuck is this?" Lord Yaron roars.

Cyprus rolls off of the bed faster than he's ever moved. He stands straight and tall, gaze cast slightly down at the floor. I rush around the bed quickly and stand in line with Cyprus like a schoolchild ready to be admonished — an actual trained response from all the times we've gotten into trouble and been made to stand just like this before our parents. I have to fight the urge to look at the floor. I also have to fight the urge to laugh.

Cyprus coughs into his fist. "Sorry, my Lord. We were just roughhousing."

Yaron snarls, "There is to be no roughhousing with Kiandah, Cyprus…"

"Fine," I blurt, cutting him off, irritated. "I was roughhousing with my brother. I was trying to push him off of the bed."

"And why on earth were you trying to get on his bed? Why are you in this room?"

"I was going to share the room with my brother."

Yaron's sharp grey eyes narrow. His hand clenches on the brass doorknob. All of the muscles in his hand stand out in relief and the dark mixed leather and fabric of his clothing and cloak make him look truly like a shadow about to take flight…and launch directly at me. I swallow hard and start, "I…"

"I didn't feel it appropriate for my unmated sister to share a room with an unmarried male who isn't kin, my Lord."

Yaron looks like he's a step from murdering Cyprus, who stands there unrepentant, meeting Yaron's gaze with a glare of his own. "You dare. She is *mine*."

"I am my own," I pout. "But to spare Cyprus losing his head, I'll go with you to your room, so long as you have food. I'm hungry, Yaron," I say, approaching him and stepping well within his personal space. I place a hand on his chest, the other going to his hand on the doorknob.

He falters in his rage, looking down at me with an expression that's equally hot, but listing in another direction. I push a little and he gives like parchment paper. To my brother, he spits, "You may not approve of me with your sister, but do not come between us ever again. You will regret it. My dungeons are still hungry."

Cyprus's face twitches a thousand times in seconds, but he bows jerkily and gives me a hot glare before taking a step backwards.

"Kiandah, come." Yaron's voice says he is not to be trifled with and I don't mean to enrage him further now. So I obey.

Mara is standing in the hallway holding a covered tray of food, pretending not to listen. Her cheeks are burning pink as she slinks past us like a whipped dog and into my brother's room, closing the door behind her.

"You do not threaten my brother," I spit, stabbing my finger into Yaron's chest as he pushes me into the room and stalks after me.

He slams the door shut behind him and the whole wooden wall shakes. "What were you thinking? That I'd share a bed with one of my Crimson Riders while you shared a bed with an unmarried male three rooms away?" He towers over me, forcing me back with his size alone, but I'm too appalled to be intimidated.

I shove his chest as hard as I can, and though I end up toppling back, the post of the bed smacking into my outer thigh, he at least stops his advance. "May the old gods help you. He's my *brother*, Yaron. Get a grip!"

"What did I say, Kiandah? You will not suggest sleeping without me again, let alone sharing a room with another male. I don't give a fuck if he's your brother." He reaches up to the clasps of his cloak and unfastens them. In a rage, he tosses the heavy fabric aside. It lands in a chair, which clearly lacked some structural integrity because the front legs give out and the whole thing goes clattering to the ground. I jump. Yaron doesn't look at it. He doesn't look anywhere but at my face.

"I…" I lick my lips and clench my fists, feeling quite warm. "I know, I just… My brother is just being protective. I'm still an unclaimed Omega and an unmarried woman. I thought, you know, for appearances' sake, it might be a good idea not to stay with you in public."

Yaron roughly cards his fingers through his hair. It hangs long, past his jaw, and when it falls forward, partly covering his eyes, it makes him look lethal. I swallow hard. He unclenches his fist and takes a step away from me. He opens his mouth to speak, but before he can, there's a loud knock.

He huffs and waits a beat before opening the door. "Good evening, m'Lord, m'Lady," a woman says in a thick Dark City accent as she enters our chambers. "I'm Madame Zenobia. Only the best service for our esteemed guests. So fortunate we are to have you join us this evenin'. And you couldn'ta picked a better night. We have quite the crowd downstairs. You should come join us after you finish your business." She snickers and meets my gaze with a wink.

I smile, feeling my heart patter a little faster. She talks a mile a minute. I hope that means she might be forthcoming with information and what she knows about Trash City. But I can't ask her now. I glance at Yaron, who's standing in the shadows against the opposite wall while Zenobia and a team of helpers enter the room. His arms are crossed and he looks like he's about to erupt in flames himself.

"Got your meal you requested, m'Lord. Specially prepared by cooks recently arrived from the North Island. They specialize in delicacies from The Guild. I've got hand-filled mole rat dumplings and jeweled carrots and tejmond spiced milk bread. A little Rookery gateau for you for dessert, though I imagine you're excited for a different kind of dessert." She winks at him this time and I snort, trying to stifle a laugh. I glance at Yaron, expecting to see him laughing, too, but if anything, his previous rage seems to be darkening.

Madame Zenobia doesn't seem to notice or care and tosses back her rather scraggly-looking freeform locs and tugs down her deliriously low-cut blouse. She looks between the two of us as she orders the helpers around our room carrying a large bronze tub. "Don't you both go getting in here together now. It'll barely fit you alone, m'Lord — yes, just fill it up halfway, Starla," she directs one of her women. "And my floors aren't what they used to be. You bring the establishment down, you buy it!" She wags her finger at Yaron as the helpers fill the tub up with steaming pails of water. As rapidly as they all filed in, they all file out.

Madame Zenobia hangs on the doorknob. It looks a little warped under her long fingers. "Other'n that, have a great stay at the Sea Witch Inn. I hope to be able to report ten months from now, a little Lord or Lady was brewed up here." She titters. "And don't worry, you can be as loud as you want to be. Only three other occupied rooms on this floor, there are. Enjoy yourselves, m'Lord and Ladyship! You'll find two extra bottles of wine in that basket there, if you'll be needin' 'em..." She's still prattling to herself as she departs and shuts the door behind her.

"Mara said you told her there were only two rooms left at the inn," I say as soon as she's gone.

Yaron looks like a feast for the eyes, dangerous — but not like he'll hurt me. "Mara is correct. There are only two rooms available in the entire inn, I'm sure of it."

His gaze shifts down from mine, raking over my mouth, my chin, my throat, my chest, my bodice, my corset...and then lower. Yaron inhales sharply, as if he'd forgotten to breathe. He returns his gaze to mine and I realize only then that *I'm* the one not breathing.

"Hm." I feel my weight shift into my heels and I stumble half a step back. My hand searches for the bed post and, finding it, fumbles over the rough rounded edge. I wet my lips and his gaze snags on my mouth. I still haven't taken a breath. I feel like I'm going to get lightheaded soon. Maybe, I already am. I'm focused entirely too much on the hard cut of Yaron's shoulders in his patchwork leather armor. He seems like he's emitting heat, or something. Whatever it is, it's drawing me forward, making me feel like I'm standing at the top of a slope and he's at the bottom. There's nowhere to go.

"I know you said you don't feel the same way about me that you did in the forest, but I fully intend to change your mind." Wait. What? "I know that it will take time, that a single lashing won't change your feelings irrevocably, but I thought," he pauses. "I sensed, perhaps incorrectly, that you were receptive and I know that I've made my intentions clear. I would like to remain close to you while we are beyond the castle walls, but I can also be made to see reason. If you would like more space when we return to the castle, I will leave you our chambers and return to sleeping in the throne room. However long you'd like. However long it takes. For tonight, I'll sleep on the floor."

"Oh." I shake my head quickly and practically gasp in my breath. My lungs, full as they are, cause my breasts to push against my corset. Yaron's gaze drops to it momentarily before jerking back up. "Are you…is this…you don't want…"

"Of course I fucking want…"

"Don't curse at me," I snap and then I smile a little shakily and frown a little more shakily. "I just…I'm sorry. I think I haven't made myself clear with you. You perceive me indifferent, but that's not true. When you asked me earlier, out in the market, I didn't mean to imply that I wasn't attracted to you. What I meant was that I don't feel like I did out in the woods — out of control. That was my first heat.

"I'd never had a heat before and it was intense. Good, but also scary. I couldn't have stopped myself from presenting for anyone, I don't think. Out in the market, I meant that I don't feel a heat coming on. That's all. What I told you yesterday in the carriage was what's true. I…you…it's whatever you want, Lord Yaron. I feel…*strongly* for you. That's…"

Yaron's expression has grown hooded and so severe as to be bloodcurdling, but other than that, he hasn't reacted at all. The only change is that heat, that pulse, that scent that he carries with him always… It's gotten stronger.

"But…"

"But?"

"I…you've been a little erratic today. First, jumped away from me on the horse when I even dared suggest we date."

"Of course I did," Yaron all but snaps, making me feel hot in the face. And then he drops his axe — his metaphorical one, anyway. "How could I have ever thought I, a humble lord, would be in a position to date *you?* The thought overwhelmed me."

"O-overwhelmed, my Lord?"

"Overwhelmed," he answers just as hesitantly. He doesn't speak for a moment, then blurts all at once, "The thought of dating you did things to me here." He touches the center of his chest. "Explosive, terrible, tremendous things. Because I want to devour you. And as I've already said, I'm not a male who gets to date. So, to go on a date with you, it…" His voice catches and I all but burst into flames. "Yes. It overwhelmed me."

Oh my heart. My fluttering heart. My lips are slack and part lamely as I stare at him, stunned.

Yaron changes the subject, clearly uncomfortable. "What else?"

"Wh-what?"

"You said I was erratic and then mentioned the horse firstly. Was there another instance?"

The flame in my burning cheeks fans down my neck and over the top of my head. My jaw works. "I…I just…it's nothing. Stupid."

"Tell me anyway."

"I just…when you disappeared with Zanele in her stall in the market…" I feel like an idiot as I say, "She's…very beautiful."

Yaron suddenly falls perilously still. His limbs all lock and his eyes widen before closing entirely. "You were jealous?"

"I'm sorry, Yaron." My voice shakes. "Have I insulted you?"

He shakes his head once, more of a spasm than a real acknowledgement.

"Am I repeating myself?"

Another jerking shake.

"Are you…listening to me?"

He nods.

"So, what were you doing with her, then?"

"Commissioning the robes you'll wear for me under the light of the red moon." His eyes open and his gaze pierces me like a spear, impaling me in place.

"Oh." Oh ancestors strike me down… Embarassment doesn't begin to describe the Omega I've become… "I'm sorry, Yaron. I feel…um. Never mind. About all of it — any of it. Anyways, what were we doing? Should we…eat, then? The rat sounds particularly delightful…"

"Would you have presented for anyone? Out in the woods?" His voice is gravel, a spike-studded rope soaked in pitch and set aflame.

"I…" I roll my foot and wonder if it would give him the wrong idea if I slipped my foot out of my boot. Right now, one wrong move feels like it could send the inn crumbling to pieces around us. Carefully, like I'm trying to talk down a wild animal or a serial killer on a rampage — *I suppose he's both* — I slowly say, "I don't know if I could have prevented it."

He covers his mouth with his hand and I notice that he has claws tipping three of his fingers. His thumb, ring and pinky fingers. But his middle and pointer fingers are still tipped by blunted nails. My mind fires with a vision of him touching me with those two fingers, deep, deep inside...

"But..." My throat threatens to close. The room is closing around us. "I'm glad it was you. Even if I hated and feard you then, I'm still glad it was you...if...I...if it had to be anyone, I would have wanted it to be you...I think," I conclude lamely.

But he seems to be only half listening because he rapidly fires out, "Are you attracted to me?"

It's my turn to nod silently. Because if I open my mouth, I'll confess something I never intend to, *ever*. That I've *always* been attracted to him. Even when I hated him. Even when I hated him more than anything, I still thought he was the most attractive male in the world. I was attracted to him before the before the before.

"I don't want to frighten you." He grabs his belt so suddenly I jump. He growls, bows his head and speaks to the floor. "Fuck..."

"If this is you trying not to frighten me, you're doing a pretty bad job, Yaron." I smile, trying to joke. He doesn't rise to it at *all*. "Yaron?"

"I'm feeling strangely close to rut in your presence." He rubs his face again. "And yes, I do mean in your presence. I would not fall into rut for anyone else."

Warmth sizzles through me, but it's *normal,* more contained. It isn't uncontrollable. I'm not salivating and falling to the ground, though…I wonder if I should be? "Isn't it…shouldn't I…is that possible? For you to be in rut without me being in heat?"

"Normally a heat triggers a rut. In same sex couples it is obviously different. I suppose my rut could…" His voice lifts in a hope that's dashed the moment he looks back at me. "But you don't feel it." He makes a brutish sound and looks to the left. "I cannot explain this and I'm sorry, but I don't know how to be near you, and I sure as fuck can't let you leave."

My breath catches in my throat. I can't swallow. I feel my breasts tingle against the underside of my corset. The ultra-soft fabric of my dress feels abrasive against my nipples. My underpants are tight around my waist and ankles. My hunger is forgotten. I'm too hot and have the urge to rip off everything I'm wearing and everything he's wearing.

My mouth is dry, but I part my lips anyways and speak. "Are you…in pain? I just remember when I went into heat, it hurt."

He grunts-laughs and shakes his head again. He pulls on a leather chestpiece — the harness he wears for his axe. It falls. His hand snatches out and grabs the axe handle before it hits the floor and then he places it gingerly against the wall. "It doesn't cause pain yet, but I sense its imminent arrival."

"Maybe I can help you, Yaron."

Everything freezes. Him. Me. The stale, slightly moldy-smelling air between us. "Are you offering what I think you are?"

"Maybe…"

"No. Not maybe. Yes or no. This is not the time to be coy with me, Kiandah." He bares his teeth and growls low.

"Yes!" I all but shout the word. "Yes. Yes, I'm offering." I sound like an idiot. "It's only fair, after all."

"Yes." His hand curls into a fist at the buckle of his belt. "It would be fair." His nostrils flare and his pupils have fully dilated. He sounds like he's so barely restrained that I'm surprised he doesn't just charge at me and take me down until I realize…he's waiting.

Liquid steel floods my spine and I remember who I am and who he is and what he's learned to want. "So, what are you waiting for? Get on your knees, my Lord." His hand drops from his belt to the growing bulge beneath it. He palms himself and I shake my head quickly. "Ah ah ah…no touching what's mine, Yaron."

"Fuck." He falls to his knees with a loud thud. "I don't have long." He speaks like he's in pain even though he denies it.

"Then when you crawl, I suggest you do so *quickly*."

Lord Yaron does not hesitate. Alright, he hesitates for the first second, and then not another second more. He drops to all fours. The sight…dear gods of sin…the sight of it. This Lord crawling to me like a beggar to a queen. His shoulders move powerfully and I admire them, wishing the fabric of his shirt was gone so I could appreciate them even more. And then, I realize…that I can make that happen. All I have to do is ask for it.

"Stop."

He stops on the instant. His gaze is pinned to mine. It's never left. He licks his lips and they shine blood-red as he rises up onto his knees to bare for me his torso and chest. "What do you command, my queen?"

My pulse is racing. My heart...my lungs. I can barely breathe. I fall back onto the bed, perching on the edge with my legs slightly spread. I can't quite assume the power pose I was going for because my feet don't touch the ground. Slowly, I kick off my boots. They thunk to the ground one at a time.

"Take off your shirt." He draws his tunic out of his trousers. When he reaches for his belt, I stop him. "No. Leave your belt and pants and boots."

He nods and slowly, so fucking slowly, he removes his tunic. It's a strange construction, layered flaps of textured leather and roughspun cotton. I don't care what it's made out of, though, I only care how it looks, and even more, how it looks when his bare chest comes into view.

I'm startled. I have seen him without a shirt on before, but I don't think I've ever seen him like *this*. I've never been so, so...concentrated on him like this before. He's not sacrificing for me and I'm not withering before him. He's just...*displayed.* Positioned for my perusal. For my own personal use. However I see fit. Gods, I want to touch him. I want to touch him in so many ways.

He tosses the garment to the side and I don't miss the way the muscles pulse beneath his chest — his beast, struggling to restrain itself. I crook my finger and he comes forward again. It takes him only two strong prowls, his body moving like a panther in the dark, before he reaches the edge of the bed. His torso lifts, his shoulders positioned between my knees. He hooks his biceps beneath my thighs and slides his hands onto the bed, up my outer hips. He grabs me forcefully. My lips part and a gasp escapes them.

Yaron kisses my inner knees. Each one. The left first, and then the right. He bites the fabric of my pantaloons, nipping dangerously at my skin through them. "A few days ago, you flinched from me when I was in such a position. Is it your intention to flinch from me today?" he says, his warm breath heating me up everywhere.

"No, Yaron. Today, I will give you what you need and what we both desire."

He bites my inner thigh through my pants. Harder this time. My eyes roll back in my head. My head rolls back on my neck. My arms are trembling as they attempt to support the weight of my torso and not simply flop back and let him take me. "Is it because I took those lashes that you reward me with this?" His fingers dig into my outer thighs. Three clawed nails tip each hand, two blunt ones that dig into me harder, but hurt less than the rest.

I'm about to scream at him to fuck me, but I bite my bottom lip, needing to maintain the illusion of control. I'm not in control. I'm not *out of control*, but I am not in control here. "In part."

"What's the rest? Don't tell me it's pity for my pain…"

"Why not?"

"I don't want your pity. I want your heart."

I reach down between my thighs and grab a fistful of his hair. I yank on it hard enough for him to hiss and tip his head back. I look down at him, meeting his gaze boldly, and say, "You'll take whatever I see fit to give you, Lord of the

Shadowlands. Now make me come. If you do a good enough job, I might take it upon myself to reciprocate."

I've barely got the words out before Yaron tosses my skirts up to my chest and yanks down hard on my waist, dragging me to the edge of the bed so that my ass half hangs over the edge while my thighs brace on his shoulders, heels twitching against his shoulder blades.

He doesn't tease me. He doesn't coax me into submission. He does what he's told. His mouth latches onto my pussy through the thin fabric of my trousers. He soothes my labia with the flat of his tongue. It's hot and wet but, through the fabric of my pants, not nearly so wet as I am. "You say you're not out of control, Omega, but you're dripping for me," he says, voice raspy and so, so low. "You taste divine." He makes me so hot. He's rumbling so hard, everything about him is shaking.

I'm about to command him to shut the fuck up and take that cunt like a good boy, but he beats me to the finish. A tearing sound is followed by a blessed coolness as he blows softly against my sex, bared to him now. I bite my bottom lip as I watch him look up the length of my body and worship my lower lips with his tongue.

"Yaron," I whisper.

His eyes flare. He plunges his tongue deep within me and when I moan, he does it again. And again. And again and again. My heels are seeking purchase, looking to rock and take control, but he doesn't give it to me. Instead, he uses the breadth of his shoulders to force my legs farther apart so that I'm completely at his mercy. I want to open my mouth to challenge him, to put myself back behind the reins, but he's a cruel torturer and every time he slows down enough for my mind to catch back up to clarity, he does something to throw me back over the edge.

My elbows give and my spine hits the mattress. My fists clutch the flimsy sheets and my face screws up as he holds me on the cusp of an orgasm, on the edge of despair. "Yaron!" I shout as his tongue runs roughly over my folds, laving my clit, worshipping it. He dips his tongue inside my body and I lie there panting as his two declawed fingers slip inside of me, his tongue never leaving me.

The fullness is heavenly. His tongue slips free of my body and starts to work faster, circling back up over my clit. His free hand is roaming over my outer thigh, beneath the folds of my skirts and the torn fabric of my useless fucking pants. I want to kill Zanele for insisting I wear them right now, never more so than when he fists the fabric he finds at my waist and tightens it, simultaneously pressing down on my belly so I can feel his fingers working inside of me even more.

I can't hold on. I grab his hair and I'm screaming as I burst. The orgasm slaps me, spasming through me. I can barely hold on. I can't hold on. I'm not holding on…

I'm gasping and when he purrs against my wet, sensitive flesh, the reverberations echo through me, forcing my orgasm to spiral into a second, or maybe just keep spiraling. I can't tell. I can't feel anything but everything. The wickedness of his tongue is unending. He flicks it against my clit like a lash, culling more from me than I knew I could give and more than he has a right to take. His fingers are pumping furiously into me and out of me and just when I think I can't give anymore, he stands, bringing my whole lower half with him and changing the angle.

I can't breathe as he pushes me again to a final pinnacle of destruction, and when I come down, the room spins. Everything is hazy. The first thing and the only thing I'm able to focus on is the mania in his eyes. They're electric, glowing like moonstones when he tilts his head to the right, before returning to grey. He prowls over me, grabbing me around the back of the neck and yanking my body further onto the bed. I'm limp, unmoving, limbs all splayed.

His two fingers covered in my slick find my lips and pass them, shoving all the way to the back of my throat. I am undaunted and suck *hard*, tasting myself upon them. Even though I'm near to gagging, it's Yaron who chokes. He yanks his hand back, fingers scraping on my teeth, and reaches for the front of my corset with a devilish gleam in his eye.

I grab his wrist, panting, and twist his hand back. "Don't you dare. Flip me over, unlace me. Don't you dare destroy this corset."

He growls, an animal in his throat, no words to be found. But he does as I ask, flipping me onto my stomach. He works through the laces quickly and I'm hoping he used his nails and not his claws to untangle them. I'm breathing hard, feeling strangely nervous as he pulls me up into a seat and yanks my corset off and my dress down. His gaze rakes hungrily over my breasts when I shift around. He grabs his belt.

"Don't," I say, regaining my balance a little bit. A very little bit. My head...I can barely breathe or think, but I want…more. I lick my lips. I'm breathing so hard. He's frozen in time, not breathing at all.

He's waiting, but I can tell I've exhausted the limits of my power. I cannot make him wait long. I point, almost frantically, at the lone pillow on the bed. "Get on the bed. Lie down."

With a rough grunt, he tosses himself onto his back, torso slightly lifted as he watches me slide to my feet on the floor. The dress I wear beneath my now-missing corset and over my now-torn pantaloons pools at my feet, leaving me naked to prowl over him on the bed. I go to his feet and slowly unlace his boots. The lantern light in the room is brighter than it ought to be, so he can see every inch of me. His gaze lingers over my hands, shaking with desire. His chest is rising and falling in waves. His fangs are poking out to press against his bottom lip and he is tantalizingly stroking each sharpened tip with his tongue.

I toss one boot aside, and then the next, and then I crawl up onto the bed between his legs and sit back, reaching for his belt. I undo it slowly, struggling the first time with the latch. His cock springs free, thick and proud, while his knot bulges at its base when I drag his trousers down over his hips. His knot…it makes my mouth water and the rest of me feel a little apprehensive. It looks a lot thicker than it should, like it's already partially inflated. Thick and ridged and forming all the way around the base of his erection, it looks like he's smuggling marbles. His erection is smooth and hot, radiating heat that draws me forward. Its impressive length is only topped by the fact that it's thick and veined and straining, the blood-red tip all but begging for me.

"If you don't touch it soon, I cannot be responsible for what happens next." His voice is wobbly, almost frightened.

I nod, understanding, feeling panicked myself. "Are you mine, my Lord?"

"Yes."

I slide my hands up his thighs, inching them higher and higher in tandem. Feeling his skin, rough and sprinkled with black hairs, is electrifying. "Tell me. Tell me who you belong to."

"My Lady Kiandah. I'm yours. Now please." He licks his lips, breathless. "Please, Kiandah."

"Hold onto the headboard." Calling it that is a bit of a stretch considering that I'm fairly certain it's not attached to the bed, but simply propped up behind the bed and leaning against the wall. The wood is rough and scratchy, but he's a good boy and lifts his arms above his head, revealing the smooth undersides of his biceps. I lean up even further, planting my hands on either side of his ribs. I scratch my nails down his rib cage, from his pecs all the way down to his hips.

I lean over him and lick a line up from his belly button to his sternum, tasting his masculine flavor. He hisses. His thighs stiffen, the muscles beneath them harder than stone. Moving up the bed, I flatten myself to him, my elbows coming down onto the flat, scratchy pillow. My forearms frame his face. He feels so huge beneath me, my knees coming down onto the bed on either side of his ribs, where my hands just were. My pussy is spread open, the cool air splashing against my dripping core, wet with so much slick. I drag it over his stomach at the same time that my lips light down onto his.

He moans into my mouth, his tongue diving past the barrier of my teeth, invading my heat. I feel the strong weight of his hand on the back of my head, the pressure on my lips bruising. Another hand comes around my waist, his nails digging into my bare skin. I can feel the prick of his claws. I should push him away…he's breaking rules, and I had a whole plan to have him in my mouth and to ride him to the morning…but I feel awash with a sudden surge of heat and energy and I feel my own hands tighten on his hair and neck.

I scratch him across his chest. His fingers on my waist inch across my back, over the curve of my ass. He presses at my rosebud testingly before shoving his middle finger inside of my tightest hole up to the second knuckle with no warning and no lubrication. I arch up and gasp, but his hands are uncompromising. He pulls me back down to his mouth and I know that I made a mistake. I waited too long, tried to take too much. I'm overwhelmed, outmatched.

My eyes flutter closed. I cannot open them. I feel my heart pounding against his chest. I feel my armor crack and my castle crumble. I attack his lips with mine, fighting for dominance and then I simply pull back and hand it over. "Do it," I whisper in needy breaths. I kiss his bottom lip while his finger pulls free of my ass.

"What?" he says, his voice shaking. I feel…too many things at the sound of that tenuous control. He sounds so young. Like a young man touching a woman for the very first time.

I moan and brush his cheek with my cheek. "Anything. Whatever you want, Yaron. Let me be yours, as you are mine.

If only for the night." Because tomorrow, I'm taking this control back.

He grabs the underside of my jaw abruptly, his fingers digging into my cheek *hard*. At the same time, his other hand circles underneath my thigh and his thick fingers spear my pussy. I gasp and his fingers on my jaw tighten, forcing my mouth to open even more.

"Don't you dare," he hisses. "Don't make me a time-bound offer. I want it all and I want it forever." I made another mistake. He's made another misinterpretation of what I've said. He thinks I mean to deny him tomorrow? It's an almost laughable thought given that I haven't been able to deny him to now.

He sits up slightly and he *spits* into my open mouth when I open it to correct him. Gawking, I'm too stunned at what he's just done to speak — and then I can't when he slides one of his hands over my mouth while his other drops down slightly to my throat, which he squeezes, forcing me to swallow.

"Do I have you for the night?" he says, his eyes narrowed and gleaming like moonstone. There is no grey to be seen.

I nod vigorously.

"Do I have you for the night *only?*"

I shake my head, a little scared. He seems lethal. Like he'll do something drastic if he doesn't get what he wants. He licks his lips. My gaze drops to them. My fingernails curl into his chest, hoping to cause pain. Like he's causing me pain. "Tell me I have you forever."

I'm breathing hard, panting. What he's asking me is so monumental. Too much. To say yes, now, like this… But I can't say no. Because I don't want to. Not now, and certainly not under the light of the red moon. I know that Cyprus worries that Yaron's not good enough — that he might not be *good* at all — but there's that word again that makes me feel so small...*deserving. Am I enough?*

I can't speak to ask him any of these things or to say anything to him at all. All I can do is nod and stare into his eyes, meaning it. His hand is still over my mouth until he exhales so violently against my cheek, his whole body shudders. "Thank the gods." He wrenches me down beneath him, removing his hands from my face, his touch becoming violent. He grabs my hips and pistons his own to meet mine, impaling me on his length in one clean movement.

I scream. It's a warbling, unattractive sound that seems to bring Yaron to the point of breaking. His back arches and he closes his eyes...and then he moans deep and from the belly as his hips start to pump more rhythmically. His shaft moves clean in and out of me on every stroke and the sensations... my gods...his knot slamming against my entrance...it's...my *gods.*

He doesn't stop fucking me. He doesn't stop kissing me. He drinks from my lips like a drowning man. My hands scramble for purchase on his sweaty back, against which I feel the thin threads of too many scars. I carefully withdraw my touch from his healing back, holding his neck and his arms while emotion rises up within me so brilliantly.

"Yaron," I moan, eyes getting misty.

He starts to slow, his eyebrows knitting. "Am I hurting you?"

"No...gods no...please...I just...I feel for you..."

It's not what I mean to say, but he seems to know what I mean because he nods, and when he picks up speed again, his motions are more deliberate. "I feel for you, too, Kiandah…"

"I miss you," I blurt, but that's not right, either. I'm frustrated with my words and their limitations. What I feel is only *similar* to the sensation of missing someone, that pain, that longing, but it's coupled with a happiness so big it feels scary. Like my hands are too small to properly fit around and grip it. *Like another very impressively sized piece of him…*

"I am right here. I will always be here…for you… Kiandah." His eyes roll back into his skull as he starts to build speed and intensity. "I do not know how I lived so much of my life without you."

"Oh…oh bloody hells, Yaron!" I cry out as the first orgasm takes me unexpectedly. I didn't mean to detonate like that. I thought this was about him. But the way his hips meet mine, the friction against my clit, the way he so evidently means what he says… He's using his knees to keep my legs pinned. I can't do anything but try to get my ankles down and brace.

"Yaron…Yaron, I…" *I will say yes to you, under the light of the red moon, every day till then, and every day thereafter.*

"You told me…to use you…however…I…want…"

"Yes, Shadow Lord," I scream as the base of my pussy is stimulated by his knot rocking against it.

"Kiandah, you have no idea…how close…I…am…to losing…control…of everything… I can't…" He doesn't stop. He just keeps rutting into me. I kiss him hard. He kisses me back. Our mouths part only long enough for us to gather sacred breaths. He growls, words whispered in the tiny gasps and gaps between our dueling tongues, fangs, lips, teeth, "You're so hot it's like drinking the fucking sun."

I'm hanging on for dear life, wondering if he's close or if I'm going to combust again before he finishes inside of me, and as I climb that hill and near its crest, I gasp, "I would take you under any sun or any moon. All of them. Forever."

"Fuck. Don't. I can't..." He makes a primal sound and I don't miss the way his eyes glisten.

I'm bouncing on his length, fingers slipping over the sweat on his shoulders, shaking under the force of each of his thrusts. I know my pussy's going to be sore in the morning but in this moment, I couldn't care any less.

"I need more," I gasp. The angle has lost that delicious friction on my clit and Yaron doesn't need more direction than that. He grinds his hips against me, slowing his pace in favor of rubbing slow circles with his hips, working that knot against me...until my slick accepts him inside of me fully.

"Yaron!"

His hips close the gap with mine and his pubic hair rubs roughly over my clit and I see stars. I float into ether. I become undone, and when some semblance of myself returns to this planet, I hear him whisper, "Please...Kiandah...have mercy on me..."

My head tosses back, gyrating in small motions on his knot in the only way that I can. My lower lip trembles as his free hand finds my breast and clumsily flicks my nipple. He looks like he's suffering. He's sweating more than he should be, even in this small, stuffy room. Yes, he's suffering and he needs me to rescue him.

"Come for me. I give you permission, my Lord." I pump my hips up, the fullness of his half-inflated knot suddenly nothing compared to his knot when it expands.

"Thank you, my queen," he roars raggedly, his back arching, his fist flying up over his head to brace against the headboard. His whole body stiffens, his thighs tightening to the point that it lifts his hips — and me on them — up entirely. I hang onto his neck as his knot inflates to its full size and I scream in rapture as the orgasm wracks and wrecks me, the good little Omega that I am.

My eyes roll back and I'm distantly aware of a surging heat filling my body, and I'm also caught in a riptide of emotion that makes it possible for any and all of my concerns that we are once again not using protection to fall away. I yank his body down onto mine even though he's trying not to crush me, needing his heat against my core, needing the comfort of him. I nuzzle into his smooth skin, feeling way too much at home here.

I can feel my core spasming around his girth, squeezing him to death while he empties into me. His cock twitches deep inside my body and I feel a rush of heat as he groans, still sounding pained as his hips lose rhythm and slam upwards into me.

"Fuck, Kiandah..." His arms have circled my body, awkward lumps between me and the mattress that I don't mind at all because he's clutching me with such violent tenderness it makes me want to cry. "I want you..."

"You have me, Yaron." He moans again, his hips bucking once more and holding. His knot is massive inside my body, but it feels right. It can only feel right as I bathe and bask in his heat and he comes and comes and comes on waves of pleasure that seem unending until eventually, he releases his breath and relaxes his hands.

The tension leaves him all at once like a ghost from the recently deceased and he falls, the wave finally mellowing out into still water. I don't move as he repositions us, pulling me on top of him so that he can slump fully into the mattress, but I do lift my face at the feeling that I'm being watched. His eyes are hooded. He's got his lower lip trapped between his teeth.

"I…" he starts, but I'm too worked up. If he says…what I think he means to say to me now…I'll sob and I don't feel like crying. I tilt my lips up a little more and he is distracted by them. A good boy, he knows what I want.

He kisses me and the kiss is soft now, so painfully sweet. He tastes my mouth again and again just as I taste him, like these are our final moments. I don't know why everything feels so desperate all of a sudden, but my fingers curl against his pec and his hands on my lower back are rubbing obsessive, possessive circles, occasionally digging into my ass as his cock jerks again inside of me.

His knot will stay inflated for a while and I have no intention of trying to hurt myself by removing it, so I get comfortable, and then get even more comfortable when he manages to awkwardly use his feet and hands to free the blanket from the foot of the bed and drag it over us both.

"I could lie like this forever," he says, eyes closed, a soft yet strained smile on his face.

"Your knot warm in my body, your seed filling me to the point of inflating my belly?"

His eyes fly open and they flash opal before settling to grey once more. "Don't rile me, Kiandah." He grins wolfishly. "Or I may truly have to buy this inn because I'll take you until we ruin it like we did the hunter's hole."

I smile, even though I likely shouldn't. That heat was so intense, I barely survived. "You wouldn't be such a bad boy. No, Lord Yaron. You're my good boy." I stroke the side of his face with my chipped nails, wondering how a poor woman from Orias Village got lucky enough to lie here like this. And wondering in disbelief if he really, truly does mean to take my hand in front of everyone at the Red Moon Festival.

"I like being yours." His head lies back against the nonexistent pillow and he continues to stroke me gently all over. "I...I never imagined that I would belong to someone."

His words wound me. I close my eyes and press my cheek to his skin, exhale against his chest. My finger circles his nipple and he twitches, like I've tickled him.

"To be honest, I never even imagined what it would be *like* to belong to someone. It was never done, so it never felt like it was an option for the Shadow Lord. It never even crossed my mind as a possibility."

"I kind of, in a strange way, know how you feel."

"Hmm," he says contentedly and cryptically.

"Hmm?"

"Yes, hmm."

"Don't sound so pleased."

"Why would I not be pleased? If you ever wanted to belong to someone or several someones, I'd have to launch a killing spree. Your answer spares many lives and me much effort."

I flick the nipple I'd just been stroking. He hisses and then chuckles, sounding so...so easy I can't help but ignore his promises of murder. Changing the subject, he says, "Are you in pain?"

I don't tell him the truth, but lie. "Not at all." A little.

"I cannot tell if you're lying to me and you're making me worry. I don't want to hurt you, Kiandah. I never want to hurt you. Even if you deny me at the Red Moon Festival, I would not want to see you harmed. You are a special person. Caring to the point of being stupidly self-sacrificing. Domineering to the point of being sadistic." He grabs a fistful of my ass and I retaliate by pinching his ribs. He hisses and a low growl picks up in his throat that is no longer man, but all beast. "Beautiful to the point of being hard to look at."

"That's not true," I whisper back on a laugh. "None of it is."

"Humble," he continues, like he hasn't heard me one bit. "To the point of being nauseating."

I laugh and slap him lightly, then kiss his pec beneath my cheek before settling back in and closing my eyes. His cock hasn't jerked inside of me in a while. I wonder if he's close to finishing. "And what about you?"

"What about me?"

"You're all of those things, too."

He scoffs, "I forgot to add that you are clearly blind, too. If you think I am humble or self-sacrificing or caring or domineering, then you must have forgotten the blood-spattered walls of my dungeons and the fact that I crawled on the ground to your feet just now, and it wasn't the first time."

His words shouldn't make me smile, but I do. "You don't deny that you are attractive though."

"As I said, I am not a humble male. I know what I look like. Do you?"

I think about it, chewing on my lower lip as my eyes close and I picture my own face behind my eyelids. Strangely, the first faces I see aren't mine, but my sisters'. And then the images swirl apart and rematerialize into a memory of Yaron kneeling on the ground of the hunter's hole before me, and then again, his head tucked between my thighs on the bed. And it's not what I see in that instant, but what I feel. I feel beautiful in ways I never have.

"I'm not sure. I think I...I think I see myself better through you."

He's quiet for a moment and the sounds from all the way in the tavern suddenly trickle in as I begin to lose consciousness. "I don't know what I see anymore, Kiandah. It seems as if all I can see anymore is you."

I suck in a little breath, but it sounds loud. I freeze, hoping he doesn't expect a reaction because I don't know what reaction I'd give. I feel heat in my eyes and in my cheeks and an overwhelming desire to kiss him. I lift up. He's already there. He kisses me deeply and rolls us onto our sides. He wraps an arm and leg around me and tucks me in tight. I try to tuck him back, but he's too big. I feel like he's my shield now, and I want to be that for him.

"I want..."

"Are you..." he says at the same time. He clears his throat slightly. "Go on. What do you want?"

To protect you. "Nothing."

He doesn't believe me, but when I don't give him more, he grunts, "Are you hungry?"

"No. I want to sleep with you." I circle my arms around him as much as I can and squeeze him tight, afraid to let him go.

"You will. Every night."

I smile, filled with a ballooning and terrible hope. "I had a really nice time shopping with you in the market."

"I did, too."

"Really? I thought a couple times you'd throw a tantrum."

"I don't tantrum."

"Mmm…you do a little bit." I laugh when he tickles my side, and then I sigh, "It was a really fun date."

"Kiandah, please." His voice is strangled and hoarse. He tries to look away from my face, but there's nowhere to look. "We should both sleep."

"You don't seem sleepy." I say on a yawn, my eyes feeling hotter than they should.

He sounds so nervous. Like the boy I wonder if he ever had a chance to be, but gather that he didn't. And I…like to be the one that he shares this side of him with. The only one. "I…I don't know. I feel like I could fuck you all over again."

I guffaw. "You might break me, my Lord."

"I know." He kisses the top of my head. "Sleep. I should feel more…settled once my knot deflates."

Wanting to ask him more about dating and if he'd like to go on another, I decide to give him reprieve as another thought occurs to me instead. Shyly, I say, "I…I'll need some root of wormwood tea after this."

"No need. I've been taking the elixir for weeks and you don't seem to have entered your heat, besides. My seed won't get you pregnant. Not this time."

Not this time.

I hang on those words, feeling an exhilarated rush at the sound of them. "Do you...do you want children?"

"I want your children. I want children with you."

"You have to stop."

"Stop what?"

"Saying these things."

"Why? Do they so greatly offend you?"

I shake my head and lean forward in the quiet that exists between us, where there is only us, only truth. "No." I stroke my fingers through his chest hair and whisper so low that he wouldn't be able to hear me if he were any other man. But he's not. "They make me fall in love with you."

Yaron shudders and stiffens and makes a rough sound followed by a low, low purr. It comes from deep within his chest, seeming to emanate from the place beneath my hand. "You...cannot say such things either, Kiandah. Not now when I'm so...unstable." His voice breaks, sounding even more strained. He kisses the top of my head roughly once more and says, "Enough. Sleep now before something terrible happens."

I huff out a laugh in a voice just as shaky as his was and close my eyes. Sleep comes for me quickly, lulled away as I am by the furious pounding of his heart, but it does not stay long.

KIANDAH
THE SEA WITCH

I OPEN MY EYES, CONFUSED AND DISORIENTED BUT very aware of a cramp in my stomach. My thoughts fire. *Where am I? I work in the kitchens. Then, why am I so hungry?*

My left leg twitches and I flinch at the sensation of a mostly soft penis slipping out of my soft inner lips. There's a coolness there every time my legs scissor apart as air brushes over the copious amounts of Berserker cum and Omega slick all over me. I carefully extricate my limbs from the tangle of Yaron's and squeeze my legs together as hard as I can. I roll away from Yaron to the edge of the bed.

I blink, clearing cobwebs from my eyelashes. My stomach growls again and I bowl over, feeling starved. I haven't eaten since lunch and that session with Yaron was a real workout. I want to sleep and my head feels foggy… Maybe, I'll just eat quickly and then return to bed. Or…

I glance at Yaron. He's out cold, just as Zanele predicted. I turn her words over. Will I ever get a better opportunity to talk to Madame Zenobia? That's if she's even still awake. I listen carefully, hearing Yaron's shallow breath first, and then I extend my hearing father out. Oh yeah, Zenobia's still awake.

The bar sounds exactly the same as it did before, a muffled chaos, even from two stories away. It doesn't sound like any time has passed at all. Maybe I was only asleep minutes. I frown. I do really need to sleep. I've been exhausted lately, the stress of trying to keep everyone I love alive a lot for me, a wallflower. I frown harder, thinking about how Yaron sees me. How I see myself now, through him.

I might have been happy as a wallflower, but whoever she was, the girl in the kitchens, was set ablaze.

I don't know who was born of the ashes, this woman that remains, but — I swallow, gaze raking over Yaron's face, its sharp perfection making me tremble — I know that Yaron seems to like her. I also know that Yaron would not be happy at all with me if I left the room unattended.

I slide out from beneath the covers where our limbs had been intertwined, stuck together by desire and a thin sheen of sweat. It's cool in the room — the window's cracked open — and I quickly scamper over to my dress, which is still intact despite Yaron's best efforts. I pull it on, fastening the corset in the front and then working it around so that the laces hang down in the back. I slip my booties on my feet and close the window, which creaks. I pick a few items off of the tray, but it's cold now and I feel like warm food. It's only two floors away...

I head to the door. Yaron's cloak lies in a heap on the floor. I pick it up and think of throwing it on, then immediately dismiss the idea. While wearing his cloak would not be catastrophic in itself, wearing *this* cloak would be treasonous as it is held together at the throat by his sigil. I pull the clasp around and give it a close inspection. My thumb runs over the worn metal as I take in all the darkened grooves and the patterns they make. I smile shakily.

I'd expected a beast, his Berserker's form, a snout, fangs, claws, his axe…instead, what I see shocks me… Well, it should…but it doesn't at all. His sigil, the clasp he's worn ever since I first saw him and well before that, the moment he ascended and his cloak and clasp were given to him in silver and in black—

It's covered in flames. Twin logs engulfed in fire, flames rising up to consume the rest of the clasp. It's beautiful. It's *mine*, just like the male who wears it.

Feeling ballsy and light, I drop the clasp and the cloak, head for the door and step through it out into the hall. I take a deep breath and lean my weight against the door at my back, my heart full of longing and hope. I glance towards the stairs and reaffirm my resolution to get answers, to help. I take a step. A throat clears loudly behind me. I turn, expecting to see another inn patron only to see my brother standing there with his arms crossed, a surly expression on his face.

The way he's looking at me breaks me out of the spell Yaron had me under and I immediately laugh, then choke as I try to restrain it. I clap a hand over my mouth and collapse against the wall, working hard to calm myself.

My brother's expression tightens, but his shoulders are slumped in defeat and when he pushes off of the wall and stalks towards me, his smile is a little *too* forced for me to think he's really mad. "You think I don't know what you two were doing in there?"

"Do I seem ashamed?" I'm not ashamed. Not in the least. As my brother's frown deepens, I laugh some more, then reach forward and pat his chest only a little condescendingly. "Sorry, I don't mean to provoke you. And I'm sorry if you heard anything."

"The whole fucking inn heard everything." He steps up close to me and glances at the closed door. "Is he at least protecting you?" he says more softly.

I struggle to meet my brother's gaze when he says that, understanding the implication of his words. Lord Yaron told me that he's taking the wormwood root elixir and I believe him. "Yes," I nod.

My brother slides closer and drops his tone even more. I can smell his skin, so familiar and yet…different now that we're out of the kitchens, out of Orias, out of our home. His cloak carries a scent of its own, something woody and fresh, like moss. "And you're…it's…" he clears his throat. "You're willing?"

"Yep. Yes. Yes, Cyprus. Yes, it is. I am. I promise."

He straightens up, moving away from me at the same time that I move away from him. We both cough and kind of chuckle and shuffle awkwardly in the hallway.

"And so uhh…"

"Did you hear…"

We both start at the same time. He shakes his head and waves me to continue.

"Did you abandon Mara?"

"I told her I needed some air. That was a while ago. I haven't…it's…close quarters…" Cyprus's voice breaks and I laugh.

"Cyprus, are you blushing?"

"No," he scowls, glancing again at my door. "And I could ask you the same question anyways. What are you doing out of your room? He send you to fetch him another flagon of wine or did he just demand space from you after he finished?"

"Don't be crass, Cyprus, and keep your voice down. He's asleep now but he has exceptional hearing. Come on." I wave him to follow me, a little relieved if I'm being honest with myself. I hadn't realized I'd been scared to approach Madame Zenobia alone until Cyprus appeared. Now, I'm not scared. Now, I feel brave.

We head down the stairs while I explain the salient points of my conversation with Zanele to Cyprus. He's nodding along by the time we reach the bustling bar floor. Again, I'm grateful he's with me when he pushes ahead, his height and Alpha pheromones helping carve a path through the drunken, singing, dancing chaos to the long stretch of bar. Zenobia is the only person working the entire establishment, it would seem, though I know that can't be right.

My brother and I make surprisingly easy small talk as we wait for her to make it to our end of the bar. It takes her a *while*. I'd have thought that the color of his cloak or the fact that we traveled here with Lord Yaron might have piqued her interest, but Madame Zenobia treats us just like she treats every other drunk at the bar.

A band plays loudly and when she arrives before us, we have to shout to be heard. Before I place an order for food, I ask her what they have.

"We have what we have."

"Alright, I'll have whatever you have."

"We might not have that by the time I get back there. You're not the only ones here if you haven't noticed. I might have to give you the other thing." She cocks her head and her jet-black hair slips over her shoulder in thick locs. It's streaked with grey, her round face and lighter brown skin covered in lines that betray age and hardship and laughter.

"We'll take two of the other thing," Cyprus says.

Madame Zenobia gives him a funny look and waddles off without saying anything else. She returns a short eternity later, in which time I am *shocked* we haven't been found out by either Yaron or Mara, but I suppose Mara must also find their quarters *close* and Yaron most certainly needs the rest.

"Enjoy. Though you better pay properly for this," she says as she slides our plates across the table along with several overflowing glasses of wine. "Not like your precious Lord skimping on coin by taking two rooms instead of four."

"I thought there were only two rooms left?" I say, pulling my plate closer. The smells are decadent. Goose, I think. The cuts are odd and I'm certain there's a portion of neck in there, too, but the cardamom and cranberries she's spiced it with made up for everything else, I conclude as I take my first bite and moan appreciatively.

Zenobia smirks, either at my words or the sound I've made. "That what your precious Lord told you, because I distinctly remember telling you otherwise, little lady?" She speaks the moniker with a lowercase L, I can feel it.

"It is." My voice lifts, like my eyebrows, questioningly.

She chuckles and runs an already filthy rag over the wooden bar, patchy with gloss. "Almost the entire third floor where you and your Lord are staying is empty. Those are the pricey suites. Patrons come here for the booze and the whoring. They don't want to waste precious coin on starched sheets."

"That fucking…" Cyprus starts, then grumbles something about Yaron not trusting him enough to let him sleep in his own room, but I'm too distracted by the expression on Zenobia's face. It appears menacing, somehow.

"Why do you keep calling him *my* Lord?" I ask, probably only because I have a little bit of wine and food in me now. "Isn't he our Lord?"

Zenobia's look deadens. The edges of my vision go dark and she somehow sucks not just the light, but the sound out of the room with it. "No man is Lord over me, witch."

"Hey." Cyprus bangs his fist on the counter. Zenobia looks unimpressed. "Watch your…"

"What makes you think he lords over me?" I shoot Cyprus a look to shut the fuck up.

"You think we couldn't hear the sounds you two made? Ha. I had several patrons concerned you'd bring the entire inn down." She laughs and I don't tell her that Lord Yaron was prepared to do just that. I also don't ask why she doesn't tend to her other patrons and stays here with us.

I feel a tingling in my palms. My sore bones are renewed by that energy. I lean forward and meet her gaze steadily. I am sure when I tell her, "If you think it is *me* who bows to *him* when we are behind closed doors, you are mistaken."

Her eyes round slightly, and her lips slacken. She looks older for a moment, a little kinder. More like an ember and less like a flame. And then she snaps back with a frown. "You are his whore and you are his whipping boy. There are none in the Shadowlands who defy him."

"We did," Cyprus says.

Zenobia hisses, "A few bodies here and there? I doubt Trash City paid well for that."

"And that's all that matters, isn't it, the coin?" I answer back.

She gives me a scathing, assessing look. "You should know better than anyone. A woman *and* an Omega? You were born to be owned."

"I am my own."

Zenobia glares. Our faces press closer and closer together. "The Omegas that rule the North Island would do well to teach you their ways."

"They bring only destruction. Is that what you want?"

"I want off of this cold rock ruled by men and horses."

"You think another master would be better because she's a woman?"

She scoffs, "You think payment is the only thing I'm taking from them in exchange for what I provide? If that was all you received, then you truly are a useless family. They will cast you aside like all the rest after you have served their purpose. You had your chance to be at their right hand and denied it." She makes a disgusted sound, reaches beneath the bar and pulls out a bottle of amber liquid and three murky glasses.

She fills them to the brim. "You two should treasure this, because you'll be dust like all the rest of them under the light of the red moon. Your fire will not save you when war comes to your little Lord's doorstep."

I'm surprised to hear her speak so openly of war. Like she knows what's coming — like she knows so much more than Lord Yaron or any of his allies. "War may come, but what makes you think that the Fates are destined to win?" I rise up in my seat, feeling an irrational rage that she would dare threaten me and Lord Yaron and turn her back on the Shadowlands so easily. "They struck at Dark City and were defeated in Paradise Hole by two Omegas and two Berserkers and their warriors. Lord Yaron was among them, or have you forgotten that? They didn't even manage to take that city and it's the youngest of them."

Zenobia blinks at me once, twice, and on the third time she grins. Her pink tongue peeks out to wet her lips. She laughs and it's a hollow, hateful-sounding thing. "My girl, has your Lord truly so little faith in you that he's not sharing what he knows? Or…by the Fates…"

She hacks out a laugh, then reaches back beneath the bar and pours us each another amber glass. She slings hers back. Her eyes sparkle with glee when she rights herself, her black and silver locs glittering like onyx under the orange torchlight.

"Were the ports and traders truly so easily corrupted? Lord Yaron's allegiances were thin, that I knew, but *this* thin, I did not. If he does not know, then the South Island has lost already. You'd do well to take your little traitorous family and head to Hjiel. Maybe, if the Fates have forgotten your treachery, by the time they make it down there, they'll have forgotten you and you'll be spared — your family, anyway. I don't doubt they'll be able to make great use of your gifts..."

I refuse to be riled by her threats. She has information and I need it. "Know what?"

But Zenobia shakes her head and starts to turn. Cyprus stands, his seat falling back and crashing into a patron who tries to confront him, but I won't stand for that. I lift a hand and sparks flare between my fingertips. The man hastens away from me, his Alpha essence cowering, rather than compelled.

"Know what, you old crone?" Cyprus shouts after her.

Zenobia rises to the bait, her hatred of us, of everything, of the world, causing her to give in. Or perhaps, simply her interest in my gifts. She's still watching my fingers even though the light has flared and gone, and almost absently says, "The Fates and their undead army are positioned to take the ports. Should be any day now. Then they'll have successfully separated the North and South Islands."

I shake my head but it's Cyprus who snarls, "Mirage City may control the closest ports, but Ruby City controls the other. Everyone knows Ruby City is an ally to our Lord."

Her eyes are large when she blinks at us in disbelief. "My dear, sweet, sweet children..." She shakes her head and wipes amber liquid from her bottom lip. "I do not even know how it is possible that you have not heard."

I start to get a sick, sick, sick feeling in the pit of my stomach and I no longer feel so confident as I whisper, "Heard what?"

"Ruby City has already fallen."

YARON
THE SEA WITCH

SOMETHING SOFTLY WAKES ME, A MOVEMENT AGAINST my temple. But just as quickly as it comes, it retreats, leaving me restless. Consciousness comes upon me, though I rebel against it because awake now, I do not feel well. I do not feel well at all. My skin is hot and itchy and my scalp feels *tight*. I'm erect, like I've been stuck in a whorehouse all night and been told to watch but not allowed to touch anything. And in this nightmare, every fucking whore is Kiandah.

I reach for her instinctively, a desperation luring me towards the idea that she isn't there, that she won't be there, that she left in the night without me, but my hand comes down on warm, smooth flesh, an arm much thinner than mine but just as powerful. Maybe more so. I know I took her too roughly last night and shouldn't take her again but I'm going to have to. Nothing could stop me.

I roll towards her and don't bother opening my eyes. I lean into her mouth, finding it instinctively in the darkness behind my eyelids, and I kiss her roughly.

And I jerk back just as roughly.

The smell.

My eyes fly open and see her face. Her lips are mouthing words that look like *my Lord*, but I don't give a fuck what she is trying to say to me.

The *smell*.

Not an unpleasant smell, to be sure, but one decadent and divine. Spices and wine mixed in with the natural aroma of her skin, a scent utterly incapable of being replicated by anyone else, but…she didn't smell like this when we fell asleep last night.

She's already speaking, but I speak over her, voice a dangerous and unsteady pitch, "Did you leave the room while I slept?"

She's not wearing her corset, but she's wearing her dress. My cloak and her shoes are not where they were cast wantonly last night, but lie situated before and folded over the back of the broken chair beneath the window, through which dewy morning air and the colors of a dreary daylight filter in lackadaisically, as if I'm not about to fucking *die*.

"My Lord, I need to speak with you about something very important…" Her lips are swollen with the memory of mine and close enough to scent. She's blinking quickly, looking defenseless, entirely too vulnerable and so fuckable I can't think straight. I want her mouth on me and I want to beg for it. I cut her off with a brutal kiss, which she tears away from me, gasping.

"Yaron…" She half laughs, then shakes her head and tries to push away from me. "It's important. I've been trying to rouse you, but you were out cold and I wasn't sure how to proceed..."

I don't give a fuck about any of that. "Did you leave the room while I slept?" I repeat, yanking her onto her back and moving up onto my knees beneath her thighs. I throw her dress up to her chest, exposing her splayed legs and the black, glossy curls between them. I palm her core.

She gasps. "Yaron...I'm serious..."

"You're swollen still from last night. If you tell me that you did not seduce me, fuck me and leave the bed shortly after I succumbed to sleep, then I will let your body rest. But if you tell me that you left the bed, betraying my trust, and ventured off into this dangerous inn unprotected, then I will punish you here and now and there will be no commanding me otherwise."

Her lips part. Her pupils dilate. Her chest rises and falls rapidly. I yank down on the collar of her dress but she grabs my hand in both of hers and whispers, "Please don't. I don't have any others."

Guilt and pride and rage and other emotions I don't expect climb up from my heels, scraping their talons on the backs of my thighs and burying themselves in my balls and shaft and knot. It's pulsing. My cock beads with precum. I lower it to her swollen lips, which are already wet enough for me to drive into her smoothly. I shouldn't, but I will. Borne by panic and rage and feelings of betrayal, my need is all-consuming.

"Tell me. Tell me now, Kiandah."

"I..."

"Don't lie."

She shakes her head, but is struggling to catch her breath, "I have something to tell you…Just please listen."

"You left the room." It's not a question.

She fails the test.

I thrust forward, thighs slapping against the backs of hers. Her head tips back and all thoughts of whatever urgent thing she needed to tell me are lost as I take her to the edge, rutting her mercilessly until we are nothing more than a tangle of limbs cemented in sweat and slick, my knot once again fully inflated inside of her.

"Fuck, Yaron…the way you make me feel," she cries, "like I'm flying…"

"Then, I should stop," I say, with no intention of doing so.

She gasps, "Don't you dare."

I grab her jaw and squeeze her cheeks. I nip at them, struggling not to hurt her. The desire to cause pain fills my limbs — but not her pain. I don't want that. And already she's wincing, clearly uncomfortable. I should apologize but I can't seem to do that, either. I feel heat feverishly wash up and over me. A tidal wave too powerful to stand through, it takes me down. I hang my head against her collar, the blanket snaked around our legs, constricting and binding us together.

"I am not pleased, Kiandah," I say against her neck. "You do something like this again and I will punish you in earnest." I palm her breast, careful to keep her dress intact as she requested. I want her again. The urgency is unforgiving and I feel a spike of genuine fear. It isn't right. If I take her this roughly as many times as I'd like, I'll break her for sure and I have no designs of rutting this Omega to death.

I want this Omega forever.

She's breathing hard, the muscles in her neck stiff as she tries to look at me. She makes a face and I carefully gather her against me, my hand on her lower back. I can feel her inner thighs trembling and another wave of sick, sick lust washes away the guilt I feel. I lean down and my teeth rapidly latch onto the smooth skin between her shoulder and her neck.

She jolts. "Are you going to bond me, Yaron?"

"Yes," I hiss, digging my toes into the bed and pushing my knot even further into her. "But not today. Naughty girls don't get Berserker bonds."

"I wasn't unprotected, Yaron. Cyprus was with me."

The words I had hoped she wouldn't say come tumbling out of her mouth. I grab her by the neck and squeeze. My rage wants an outlet — to fuck her — but I just did that and now my unspent energy has nowhere to go. It rattles around in the cage of my bones, making me wild.

"I want you to tell me every single move you made, every step you took, every person with whom you spoke, and only then will I decide how long to hang Mara and your brother by their heels in my dungeons."

She shoves my shoulders with both of her hands. They're hot enough to cause my beast concern. His instincts war — to fight to protect us, but never to fight against *her*. I growl low in my throat. I know that to threaten her family so brazenly like this is to play with an open flame. I should have just kept my plans for her brother to myself.

"Don't push me away." I grab her forearm and slide my other hand around the small of her back. "You'll hurt yourself, and right now, that's my job."

"You're not listening."

"You have my attention," I say, but the words are aspirational as I press my knot further into her again. It still hasn't deflated. I want to rut her with it, but I can't. Fuck me. Fuck her. Fuck this.

"Then *listen* to me." I *can't*. "What I did isn't important. What I discovered is. My Lord." She grabs my face with both of her hands, pressing my cheeks. Her eyes bore into me. "Ruby City fell the night before last. Word reached Zenobia yesterday through sources she wouldn't divulge. Cyprus and I spoke to her last night while you slept. When I couldn't rouse you, I…I acted in your stead." Her gaze deflects. "I sent Mara and Cyprus back to the keep to convene with the other Crimson Riders. I also had letters sent in your name to all of the other Berserkers — Dark City, the Rookery, Hjiel, the Guild, Gold City, Glass Flats and the Town of Teeth — informing them of the attack. I'm so sorry, but I used your crest to seal the letters." She points to my cloak while the shock wars with the lust running rampant through me.

Biting her lips again, she continues frantically, "Mara and Dorsten said that I should. I know I overstepped, but I didn't write them to do anything. I just thought it was really important that the other cities know right away so they can defend themselves in case the Fates of Mirage City come for them next. And it was so confusing because Mara and the other Crimson Riders that she hailed kept calling me Shadow Lady, your Lady, and no one blinked or second guessed me when I made my suggestions. I just…I'm a peasant. It feels so wrong and I'm scared, Yaron, and I panicked. I didn't know what to do. If you need to put me in the dungeons for it, I'll understand…"

I kiss her hard to shut her up and also because my emotions are spiking again and my knot feels like it's expanding even more, though that can't be possible. My erection hasn't faded in the slightest. My mind is a haze, my thoughts a snare. I'm fighting to care that one city has overtaken another and that both are our closest neighbors across the sea, that the undead army has grown that substantially, that the Fates have grown that bold.

I realize I've deepened the kiss when she whimpers slightly. At the same time, Kiandah pushes me away. The conflict does nothing but exacerbate my current state. If she had not pushed me, I'd never have been able to tear myself free from her.

"Yaron! I'm not joking." Her voice is shrill and I've never heard it shrill before. She's panting and her breasts brush against my chest on each inhale.

I shake my head, trying to drag my gaze away from the sight of her, trying to get my erection and my knot down through sheer force of will. "I didn't think you were."

"We need to get out of bed."

I growl. My beast growls. I don't restrain him. "I don't…" *Think I can.* I can't. *Can't.* I have to stay here. *We* have to stay here. Gatamora be damned. Let the Fates have it…

Fuck.

I swallow and push away from her, a brush of cool air on my chest enough to rouse a very weak, very distant part of my consciousness telling me that I'm losing my mind. "How did you…come across this information?"

This is why Shadow Lords do not take Ladies. This was a terrible mistake. A decision I wouldn't reverse for anything.

I blink rapidly and lift her hips as I move onto my knees, keeping her joined with me. She winces in pain and moans in rapture in a way that makes my blood surge through my body. Causing her this pleasure-pain is doing terrible things to me, because I feel exactly the same way she does. And the burn makes the ecstasy fucking exquisite.

I shake my head, forcing my beast forward, concentrating on animating my mane, my fangs, my snout one at a time and then retracting them with the same precision and care. The exercise helps clear my mind enough to start to feel my knot going down. I grip her hips, the claws on my thumbs creating dents in the soft skin between her hip bones.

"Yaron?"

"Do not speak." My tone is harsher than I mean for it to be, but I don't apologize and I don't look at her.

I think of terrible, undead things as I feel my knot slowly, *slowly* recede, the ridges and bumps used to seal our connection and keep my seed within her body deflating into a single ring around the base of my erection, which I am able to then pull out of her tight, swollen heat. The cool air brushes the length of my penis and I growl, opening my eyes to the sight of white, syrupy seed gushing from her pretty brown lips.

My eager thumbs move down, massaging their way through her slick. She's swollen and hot, her lips looking ravaged and delicious when I spread them. I want to suck them into my mouth, tasting my cum and her flavor on them.

I want to transform into my beast just so I can stick the full length of my tongue deep into her body. *Fuck.*

"Command me to step away from you," I bark just as my arms start to tremble.

"What?"

"Do it!"

Her foot stamps in the center of my chest. She kicks me *hard* and I topple backwards onto my ass. The surprise of it distracts me from my goal and I meet her gaze. She's glaring at me firmly, fixedly. "Get off the bed, beast. Go sit in the chair in the corner and stay there until I tell you otherwise."

"The chair is broken."

"Then kneel."

I'm moving before I know what's hit me, her foot first, and then her command. My beast whimpers through my throat as I retreat from her and kneel beside the too-small chair. I yank my cloak from it and the buckle hits the floor with a heavy clunk. I fist it, letting the metal dig into my palms.

Kiandah sits up in the bed and pushes her dress down to cover herself. "Would you throw me a towel?" She gestures to the small table beside the chair and the copper basin atop it.

I toss her a damp cloth, wanting nothing more than to clean her myself, but I don't have the strength to be close to her. My erection is still prominent and driving me mad. I fight past the sensations seeing her clean herself stirs and say, "How certain are you of Ruby City's fall?"

"I wasn't, at first. But after prompting her, Madame Zenobia confessed that a ship arrived at the ports yesterday afternoon with refugees from Ruby City. Madame Zenobia is housing them. We met with them — Cyprus, Mara and I —

and then with Dorsten, Renard and Malik when they came later. Their story is too believable to be faked. We also made sure to speak with some of them separately and their stories aligned."

"And how did they say Ruby City fell?"

"Apparently, the undead came in the night by the hundreds. They targeted the ports and the Ruby City fortress, overtaking both in a matter of hours."

"The fortress is just that, it would not be so easy to overtake."

"Apparently the Fates were with them. One of the boys said he saw one single Fate at the fortress. Soldiers were there, guards ready to defend Ruby City, but he said the ground opened up and the sands swallowed them whole. The Fate didn't even need the undead. She just walked through."

Adoqhina. The Earth Fate. Having seen her power in action, I can believe she was capable of this and more. "And what of Ruby City's Berserker, N'dogo, and her Omega?"

She shakes her head slowly and, cleaned up, slides off of the bed. Her knees buckle momentarily and she catches herself on the headboard. I flinch, wanting to close the distance, but I'm afraid. Clarity is difficult to clutch in my claws and I am clearer now than I've been at any point in the lust-fueled haze of the past twelve hours. I must cling to it like salvation, because it might just be. If I fall, the Shadowlands may follow me.

"The refugees don't know. Madame Zenobia is asking for payment from you to house them here. I told her we'd pay it." She looks down quickly, shame in her gaze that I hate. "That you'd pay it. I'm sorry."

"You apologize to me for nothing," I say, recognizing immediately that that's not correct. "No. You apologize for leaving our bed. You could have been killed."

"You asked me to help you find out about Trash City and the Fates and the undead. I did." The firm set of her jaw and the jutting of her lower lip cause me to narrow my gaze and curl my toes into the floorboards. I can feel my claws bore into the soft wood.

"Do not test me, Kiandah. I am not well enough for it."

"You're not well?" Her incensed outrage falls immediately, a rush of concern taking its place. She rushes forward. "What's wrong?"

"Do not come near me," I bark louder than I mean to. "I cannot be close to you."

A look of hurt changes her expression once more, and though I want to correct her misunderstanding, I don't. "Get dressed and gather your things. I want to meet with these refugees myself."

YARON
SHADOW KEEP

TWELVE RUBY CITY REFUGEES WERE GATHERED AT that shit inn, all Alphas, all from different parts of Ruby City, mostly very young or very old, but some in between. A young girl with her grandparents were the only ones who knew one another. The rest arrived alone, separated from everything and everyone they knew. When I asked them how they managed to escape, their stories aligned and rang true.

They fled to the ports, which were under the control of the undead who — it is supposed, but not certain — must have burned the boats they arrived on, for there were none there. The refugees found only a single skipper at the southernmost edge of the port city, where only black market deals take place. I did not ask how they knew it was there and none offered to confess to it. That is fine. They are not to be condemned by my hand for their past actions, and with no more Ruby City Berserker to offend, their criminal records — their entire histories — have been erased clean on these shadowy shores. That they made it out at all is a gift to me.

Of the refugees who gathered — many more than twelve, or so they say — they piled as many onto the skipper as they could and set it asea, the rest of their families remaining behind in the city. The twelve then had no choice but to give their lives up to Zaoul. Zaoul treated them with grace, unusual for the turbulent sea, filled with creatures known to down ships much larger than that one.

They said they landed on a beach south of the ports and that some fisherwomen helped escort them to the inn. That they were likely illegally fishing off of the coast — fishermen and women aren't permitted to fish without registering at the ports — explains why the kind-hearted women didn't stick around to collect a reward and also explains Madame Zenobia's insistence that she be compensated for housing them given that the fisherwomen didn't.

Their stories aligned and yet...it was filled with coincidences. Zaoul is not known to be kind. And that they managed to escape the city at all, only Alphas among them, seems just as suspect. Yet I could not see signs of deceit in any of their faces, in any of their voices. They looked haggard, ragged clothes stained with signs of struggle, blood and salty sea water. No, they told truths.

I had two of my Riders escort them back to the keep, placed triple my reserve guard at the ports, released two patrol ships, sent additional letters to Hjiel and Gold City requesting a convening of the Berserkers of the South Island, and an additional two letters to Dark City.

The first, to assure that they reinforce their borders — they are now the next line of defense against the southern cities on the North Island and their plan to build a new port needs enacting *now*. We are cut off from one another without it.

The second, to request that they begin amassing their forces. They will need to enlist Glass Flats and the Rookery, at the very least, and take up arms to take back Ruby City. I fear that if Ruby City is not won back soon, then Gang Mountain will be bought like mercenaries by the Fates, thus tripling their army.

I fear for the people of Ruby City, the Alphas in particular. I fear that this entire time I've spent lusting after my Omega could have been spent convening the other cities to overthrow Mirage City and reinstate a ruling Berserker there, where there are now only witches and zombies.

I fear that even though I know better now and am filled with many regrets, my lust refuses to dissipate, even in small measure. Insanity reigns. Temptation lurks in every corner of my mind. Hunger clutches me like a monster in the night.

Returned to the castle, Kiandah safely in our room, a small horde of guards stationed at the entrance to our wing, her brother stationed outside of her door, I find Okayo in his clinic bent over some medicinal concoction, a pair of telescoping spectacles perched on the tip of his button nose. I slam the door shut behind me.

"What is wrong with me?"

Okayo lifts his head. "I wouldn't even know where to start." Irritation blots out my desire to grin. Okayo's grin falls by consequence. He frowns. "You mean it? You're unwell?"

"I've had an erection for two fucking days."

Okayo looks down at my crotch. His eyes widen behind his glasses, the lenses already making his eyes as big as oranges. He looks absurd. "Oh."

I run my fingers roughly through my hair, wanting to rip it all out. "I have felt lustful towards my Omega for days now, but in the past twelve hours, I've felt dangerously close to rut. Meanwhile, she doesn't seem to be affected at all. I'm worried. The distraction makes me want to burn the whole damn city to the ground just to be done with it. The undead army feels like a nuisance, something in the way of what I want. My desire to vanquish the Fates is fueled entirely now by how annoyed I am that they are distracting my Omega from wanting to fuck me and I can't fucking stand that."

My hands are on the back of a chair covered in rather alarming-looking leather straps. A vision assaults me of Kiandah strapping me down in this chair and doing whatever the fuck she wants to me, and I feel precum pulse from the tip of my cock and wet the underside of my trousers.

I roar. I pick up the chair and throw it against the wall beside the door. When I turn around, Okayo's got his glasses pushed up on the top of his head, making them look like futuristic horns, and his mouth hangs open in a soft O.

"Oh." He swallows hard. "Well, then. It would seem that Horace was right. Horace, would you come out here?" he shouts to the hole in the wall behind him, a small opening covered by a faded crimson curtain.

"No, thank you," comes Horace's raspy reply from behind the veil.

I start at the sound of him. I hadn't heard him until now. I can't hear fucking anything over the sound of the rushing blood in my ears and roaring lust in my veins and I didn't mean to disclose this weakness before anyone but Okayo. I'm fucking furious. *More* furious.

"Horace," Okayo says, abandoning his instruments and turning to rip the curtain back. Horace is standing with his arms tucked into his chest, his black hair looking ragged and his round face more than a little rubicund. He's trying to look anywhere but at me.

Okayo speaks to him like nothing's amiss. "Tell Lord Yaron that thing you said you'd never dare tell him." He waves at me spastically.

"Gods." Horace releases a strangled yell. "Are you trying to get me killed?" His voice rises to a high-pitched squeak.

"Speak!" My voice shakes my entire body. A beaker falls from the shelf behind Horace's head and shatters on the floor. No one reaches for a broom.

Horace takes a few tentative steps out of the closet, into the room's bright torchlight, and clears his throat. "I…um… after…when I was first tending to the Omega after you brought her from the woods, I thought she smelled a little…"

"Smelled?"

"Her Omega scent was strange. It was…I could…" He glances at Okayo. "Please don't make me say it…"

"Go on. It's important. It's also something I've never come across before." He's pulled a book of thick parchment paper out of a cabinet, and an ink pen forbidden in the Shadowlands. He should be using ink and a quill. "This is all quite fascinating. I'll be able to write a strong dissertation on this. The Medical Guild of Gatamora will be thrilled with my findings. That is, if we're ever able to reconvene." His indolence makes me want to strangle him as he speaks so insolently about the end of the world, about the end of my sanity. "Go on, Horace. Tell him about the smell."

"She smelled, my Lord...she um...she smelled of pre-heat."

"Pre-heat?" I shake my head. "What the fuck are you on about?"

"It was a good scent. An enticing scent. I thought it was a lingering heat, but I... After speaking with...some of the other Alphas working in the castle...in the days after, they smelled it, too."

Okayo chooses that moment to spare Horace from an early demise. "We have discussed it at great length with some of the keep staff as well as some of the Crimson Riders who knew Ugaros. You know, the one who tried to rape Kiandah?"

"Do not speak of the incident and do not speak his name," I shout, wishing I hadn't broken the chair because my fists long for something else to break.

Okayo simply scratches away in his book. I'm going to tear his arms off. "They said that while his behavior wasn't *entirely* out of character for him, it was still bolder a move than any suspected he'd make. He is a Crimson Rider, after all, and even before you were aware of your reactions towards the Omega, many could see where you were headed and no one with an ounce of intelligence would have dared stand in your way...my Lord," he tacks on absently. "However, given Kiandah's state, it could trip even the marginally clueless into attempting an assault..."

"Her state. What state?"

"I have come to term it a heat stroke." He looks triumphant. I've never hated him more.

"Kiandah is sick? She has heat stroke?"

"Well, more accurately, my Lord, *you* do. I found it rather suspicious that her heat only lasted two days. Two days is very short for an Omega, my Lord. The shortest known Omega heat previously recorded in the Shadowlands was four decades ago and that lasted three days. Two days is the shortest recorded heat in history. I recorded it myself and submitted such findings to the Medical Guild of Gatamora. My counterparts in the other cities were very surprised and searched their own records. None were able to find a heat shorter.

"I suspect that, given the circumstances surrounding her heat and the brutality her body endured..." I flinch as if struck, not by a hand, but by an anvil. "In order to protect herself and stay alive, her survival instinct repressed her heat. Repressed, my Lord, not killed. It is a very important distinction." He waggles his pointer finger at me like a schoolteacher correcting a child. "It is my present theory that she has been in a constant, but very mild state of heat ever since you took her in Paradise Hole. Unsated, that energy has had nowhere to go. It seems that it is mild enough that she has been able to overlook it — or perhaps, the events of the days between have been high-stress enough for her self-preservation instincts to repress it entirely — but the Alphas in her vicinity do not seem to be able to."

I growl. Okayo continues glibly, unconcerned for Horace's life, apparently, or his own. "I theorize that her heat, subdued as it is, will need release. Perhaps, the draw it presents to other Alphas is an attempt to provoke a rut so as to draw a full heat from her in response." He shrugs, slams his book shut and tucks it under his arm. "In either case, it would seem that your rut is imminent. I'd suggest being very careful around her, in the case that I'm wrong."

"Wrong?"

"If you fall into rut and it doesn't trigger her heat and she is unwilling, then you could kill her."

"Unwilling," I snarl, hating that I'm repeating his words like an imbecile. "She wouldn't be unwilling."

Okayo blinks at me like I'm every bit the imbecile I just supposed I was. *How could I have so badly failed her in her first heat?* Shame cuts through me.

"I didn't mean sex, my Lord. I meant the bond. She didn't complete her heat the first time because you didn't bond her — she couldn't. Her body couldn't heal itself and was too weak to survive without a bond, should you have continued. Given your state and the behavior I've seen you exhibit towards her — not to mention the fact that you've *said* plainly that you plan to bond her — the resistance isn't on your part. If she won't accept your bond, then that's another story. I don't know of any unbonded Omega who's ever survived a Berserker's full rut. Will she?"

"Will she what?"

"Accept your bond, of course."

"I…" I don't answer. I don't like the answers I come up with. Because there were rules for this. Rules like, Shadow Lords don't take Omegas. Rules like, Omegas submit. But the rules of these Fallen Omegas are different. Kiandah. Echo, the Fallen Earth Omega… They aren't saying yes like the other Omegas I've been introduced to. They're saying *no*, writing conditions, drawing lines in the sand that we sad and sorry Berserkers cannot cross and do not want to. Not without permission.

I wish for the first time in my entire life that I'd been born the Berserker of a North Island city for no other reason than then, I could pick up a disgusting piece of technology — *a phone* — and call the Berserker of Dark City. We cannot place calls across Zaoul, even on the contraband satellite phones I'm certain I could source on the black markets. And there is no precedent for this situation with my Omega, except in the case of young Lord Dragnovic and his. The youngest Berserker among us, the little whelp, successfully bonded a Fallen Omega. He almost lost her, but he managed to gain her trust, her heart, her bond. I wish desperately that I could ask him what to do.

"I…" I falter. I feel a sudden surge of heat overwhelm my face. I start to sweat and rapidly rub at my hairline, fighting back feelings of longing and regret — along with the desire to rip off Horace's face. "Yes. She will." But only because I will explain to her the risks and she will feel sorry for me. That's not what I wanted. I wanted to honor her. I think of the item I procured for her at the Night Market. I envision what it would be like to use it…

"Then your first problem is solved. Run to her now, beg for her bond, fall into rut and hope that she falls into heat."

"If she doesn't?"

"Pray that your bond is strong enough."

"You are courting death."

I notice Horace edge backwards into the closet, trying to push himself behind the parted curtain. Okayo meanwhile shrugs. "Then you won't want to hear my greater concern."

"Say it anyway. Gamble with your life."

"My larger concern is that none of this matters. That you'll fall into rut and regardless of whether she accepts your bond and whether it is enough, the Fates will take advantage of your distraction and while you're in the middle of your rut, the city will fall to a zombie invasion."

I turn my back on him and slam the door shut as I depart. He's right, of course, but I don't know what I can do about it except for vanquish the Fates, vanquish the undead, vanquish Trash City and do all of this quickly so that I can have Kiandah all to myself.

Until then, I have to stay away from her.

I think back to the dungeons I once placed Kiandah's family in and laugh miserably, because my plans to stay away from her are not so dissimilar to spending my days in those dungeons. Either way, I die a slow, torturous death.

KIANDAH
SHADOW KEEP

"WHERE'S YARON?" I ASK LADY RADMILLA FOR THE third time that day.

She gives me a face, lots of lines twisting down, as if she's not happy with what she's said to me already and what she's going to say to me now. "He's elected to sleep in his chambers off of the throne room. He wanted me to relay a message."

She clears her throat, looking decidedly uncomfortable as she stands at the foot of the bed after having turned it down — a thing I didn't even know servants did for Lords and Ladies and still don't understand why. My hands aren't broken. It's not like I can't fold a sheet. If I'm going to be living here in the long term, I'm going to need to talk to Yaron about making some changes to the scope of work of the...

...staff.

I realize I'm staring when Radmilla's expression changes. Her mouth is open, prepared to tell me whatever it was she was going to tell me, but at the last moment, she cocks her head to the side. "Are you alright, my Lady?"

I shake my head and grip the back of the low-profile armchair before me. I'd been standing behind it, folding some of my new clothes and debating where to put them. Yaron has a closet the size of a shoe box on the other side of the room, behind and to the right of the bed. His armoire is massive, don't get me wrong, but it's entirely filled with cloaks, armor and weapons. The smallest shelf has a few pairs of thick boot socks, trousers and tunics scattered across it in a way that surprises me for a male who does everything else with precision. *Except fuck me.* I blush at the thought of how… crazed he was at the inn. It was nice. Fun.

Returning my thoughts to the closet, I find myself struggling not to smile. Hanging my pretty dresses in the mix of leather and steel didn't seem quite right, though I will need a place to put them in the short to medium term. And now I realize I've done it again.

Just by folding my clothes and inspecting Yaron's closet, I've already made a decision, haven't I? But maybe, now that Yaron's had me again, he's changed his mind. He didn't seem quite right after the Sea Witch. Perhaps, he really is much angrier with me than I thought he was for leaving his bed in the night. Or worse, maybe I really did overstep and what I wrote to some of the Berserkers of other cities was wrong.

"My Lady?"

"Kiandah," I say, almost at a bark, instinctively.

"Of course," Radmilla responds.

"Sorry, I'm just a little confused. I thought that Yaron would be coming back."

Radmilla shakes her head again, her gaze flitting to the side. "He has requested you remain in your chambers. He will be remaining in the throne room until the threat of Trash City has passed."

I almost choke. "What? That could be months." That could be never.

"I um...my Lady — Kiandah. I...I think once we hold the Red Moon Festival and he has bonded you, he will feel differently."

"Does he even still want that?" I balk. "After we left the inn and returned to the keep, he's been nothing but distant. I know that he's stressed about the crisis on the North Island, but I can help. He wouldn't have even known so soon that Ruby City fell if I hadn't told him." Anger ticks at my temples and I struggle to keep it from infecting my tone.

"And he knows that. He doesn't value you any less now that you've returned to the keep..."

"Then what is it, Radmilla? I'm tired of him treating me like a prisoner..."

"He doesn't view you as a prisoner. You are precious to him..."

"Yes. A thing too precious to release from its cage."

Radmilla swallows her next words. She swipes her fingers across her grey hair, tucking its thick mass behind her ear. Outside the door is a slight commotion. Though the sound is perfectly ignorable, she sighs, as if relieved for the interruption. She goes to the door to peek outside and then opens it fully.

"Come in." She gestures for Zelie and a girl I don't know to enter — wait...I do know her, I realize on closer inspection. She's the young girl that arrived from Ruby City with her grandparents. I'm surprised at the sight of her and don't immediately respond when Radmilla tells me to eat and that she'll request a more satisfactory response from Lord Yaron.

I nod noncommittally, too distracted by the sight of my sister with this little girl. Radmilla shuts the door and I can see Cyprus standing outside, a curious expression on his face as the door clicks shut between us.

"Hey, Kia, are you alright?" Zelie sets her tray down on the low table in front of the armchair I'm standing behind. I round it and am only partially distracted by the thick, spongy rolls of n'jorra bread beneath piles of n'sheer and gora — decadent delicacies more often cooked by our relatives further east in Undoline and beyond. N'jorra bread is the staple base diet of Gold City.

"Yeah," I sigh. "It's just tense with this...news." I give Zelie a quick hug before gesturing for the two women to sit with me and enjoy the food — most of our foods, though they're served on one tray, are meant to be shared. "Please. I can't eat it all by myself."

The two females don't hesitate more than a second — Zelie less than that. Together, we dive in with our hands, the young girl eyeing us both skeptically at first before diving in with zeal. My heart clenches at the sight of her tattered black hair hanging by her knees as she bends over them to reach the table.

I stand up and push her chair further in. She thanks me, wiping her brown hand across her mouth. She's still a bit dirty, even though I can see that someone tried to clean her up the best they could. I take another few bites before going to the door and opening it. I tell Cyprus to find whoever he needs to find to bring fresh clothes for her. I plan to let her bathe in our quarters and she needs fresh clothes afterwards.

"Everything okay?" he asks.

I nod. "The girl needs some care."

"She's from Ruby City?"

"Yeah."

"What's she doing here with Zelie?"

"I don't know yet, but I'm about to find out. I'll tell you when you're back. Just knock."

Cyprus looks like he's going to say something, then doesn't. He nods, and I step out of the room and grab the edge of his cloak. He jerks away from me like my hands have been covered in acid then dipped in shards of glass. "What?" I say, feeling my frustration mount with Yaron, with the day, with the refugees and the troubling news that they bring.

"Fuck. Did you just touch me?"

"Yeah." I glance to the left and to the right, feeling dumb — feeling like *he's* dumb. "You're my brother."

He's not listening to my reply, but rubbing at his shoulder roughly. "Fuck. Kiandah, you can't touch me. Or any Alpha. Or anyone at all, really. Yaron's fucking losing it." He drops his tone so he can't be overheard, though there isn't anyone in the small stone alcove, anyway. "He's given a castle-wide edict that anyone that touches you will lose a hand."

I blink at him, stupefied, wondering if this isn't some kind of joke. "Is this a joke?"

"Do I look like I'm joking? I'm going to have to burn this fucking cloak. He's already pissed at me for taking you out of his room at that inn. He told me personally that if he didn't need me here while he's out, he'd string me up in the dungeons by my heels."

"Wait. What? He's out?"

"Yes. He left as soon as we returned. He and a small war party are in Paradise Hole, trying to root out where the undead are being stored. Apparently he scented the undead on some of the refugees and a few more of the port workers came forward, admitting to having seen some of the undead loitering in the woods of Paradise Hole. I think that people are actually starting to panic about the undead now that the news of Ruby City's fall has spread and the threat feels more real. When it was just a matter for those northern idiots to take care of, people were fine staying quiet about the undead and the Fates. But now that they've taken Ruby City? Our closest ally to the north? It must have people spooked."

I nod, but I'm still too shocked to properly digest his words. "Yaron…Radmilla told me he was in his chambers in the throne room."

"He was. He left them a short time ago."

I feel a little unseated, like the floor beneath my feet is sloped and I'm falling towards something. *A trap.* The thought blitzes me and I shake my head, unsure of what I'm feeling and why I'm feeling it. It's just Yaron being erratic, I conclude as I softly shut the door behind me. I'm feeling betrayed by him. We shared…what we shared…after he took lashes for my family and asked me to be his bride and I confessed that I was falling…*am* falling…*fell months ago…years…*

Then poof. Gone in the light of day. Like a dream. Or a nightmare. Only because the feelings he made me feel were so very real and now they feel like they're no longer reciprocated.

"Kandia? You all good?" Cyprus says. He puts his hand on my shoulder then cringes and curses at his palm as he lifts it. The whole episode makes me snort-laugh.

Cyprus glares at me. "Laugh all you want. It's only *my* hand we're dealing with."

"Get out of here, crazy." I kick him in the butt.

He points at me sternly from the top of the stairs. "You never used to talk to me like this before you became the Lady of the Shadowlands. Don't forget, you're still the same girl who laughed so hard when that bag of flour burst all over me, she peed herself!"

"I'm not Lady of anything yet! Now, get out of here!" I say, turning my back on him as he slips down the staircase and returning to my sister and new friend.

"Kiandah? Are you okay? Come eat," Zelie says, gesturing me back over to them. I see they've finished off about half of the tray in my absence and I quickly dive in before it's no longer warm.

I glance at the little girl who now lies back in her chair, looking like she's going to fall asleep right there. I smirk.

"Hi there," I say to her.

"Kiandah, this is Margarite," Zelie offers.

I give the girl a gentle smile, trying to ignore the strange feeling I get while watching her. It's like...I know her — not just from the inn, but from somewhere else. "Hi there."

The girl's eyes get big and then she sits up. "Hi. I'm Margarite," she says in her Ruby City drawl. It's such a cute accent, cuter in her voice, which I'm starting to think may be even younger than I initially thought.

"What do you think about the food?"

"It's so yummy. I wish my people could cook like this."

Huh. A strange phrasing, I prompt her on it. "You mean your parents?"

"That's right." She nods, eyes lighting up as she smiles.

But I tilt my head. "Did your parents come with you across the sea?"

"Yes, they did. We were very lucky to stay together."

"But…" I don't know how to phrase this politely. "Sorry, it was late and I might have been mistaken. Didn't you arrive with your grandparents?"

"Oh yes," she says again, just as adamantly. Then, as if realizing that I'm looking at her funny, she shrinks down in her seat. "Well, they are my parents now. My real parents died."

I feel like immediate shit. "I am so sorry. Did they…" I was going to ask her if they died in the battle of Ruby City — if they were killed by the undead — but then I remember this girl must be somewhere between six and ten and I don't have the heart to make her relive it. Changing topics, I say between bites of savory bean curry and sour sponge bread, "I saw you at the inn, didn't I?"

She nods vigorously.

"You were very brave, crossing Zaoul like you did."

She frowns abruptly then, looking very small and making me feel even worse. I scoot forward and place my food-free hand on her knee. She doesn't flinch away from me like I thought she might and I take that as a win. I smile at her and she holds my gaze a little easier.

"Very brave," I repeat. "How did you meet my sister?"

"Which one?"

She glances at Zelie then, who smiles and says, "Her quarters are close to ours. Much nicer, though." She sticks out her tongue and pushes her voluminous twists over her shoulder. "You get to stay in the room right next to that cool suit of armor. I call him Harold. He's pretty nice, don't you think?"

She giggles and shakes her head. "He can't talk."

"Oh yes he can. Harold and I chat every day. I'll introduce you when we go back."

She giggles again and I smile, feeling a little more relaxed. "Were you helping Zelie in the kitchens?"

Margarite shakes her head. "I just saw her when she was leaving. She looked like the other one who helped us before we got here. So do you."

"The other one?" Zelie says, sounding as confused as I feel. My pulse has started to increase...

"Your other sister. She said she was the sister of the Lady of the Shadowlands and that the Lady of the Shadowlands would keep me safe. That's you, isn't it?" She points at me, but my throat is dry.

I stare at Zelie and shake my head. Zelie's eyes are equally wide. "You don't think..." she starts, then swallows hard. "Do you think she met Owenna?"

"What? Where's Owenna?"

"Remember, after the whipping, she left?"

"That was days ago!" I would have shot up to my feet if I didn't simultaneously feel like fainting. "Ancestors help her, where is she?"

"I…I don't really know," Zelie stutters, waving her hands. "She said she was going shopping and then never came back. One of the Riders reported that Sipho escorted her to Undoline to visit relatives…"

"Why would she go visit relatives?"

Zelie shrugs.

We glance back to the girl in unison. I speak first, trying to keep my voice light, pleasant and calm so I can keep her talking. "Margarite, the woman you saw who said she was my sister…where did you see her? At the ports?"

"No. We didn't land at the ports. We crashed on a beach beside these big cliffs in the morning. There were caves in the sides of the cliffs. That's where your sister was."

"Oblivion?" Zelie says, startled. She looks at me and shakes her head and I know that she's just as shocked as I am.

"Yes." Margarite nods enthusiastically, her drawl growing drawlier as she becomes more and more absorbed by the food. "This is very tasty, by the way. I've never had anything like it."

I smile at her when she looks at me, but it's delayed. It's hard to keep the worry from my voice as I prod her again, "Was there anyone else with them?"

She looks at me, her mouth full, her eyes bugging out. She smiles. "Oh yes." The girl nods vigorously. "Lots of people. They wore rags and had big guns and brought us up a path through the cliffs. It was really narrow and steep and it came all the way out onto the top and that's where I saw your sister and she told the lady with the goggles that she'd take us to the ports, but she lied."

The girl frowns. "She said I'd get to see my mommy and daddy again, but instead she brought me and my grandparents to that inn. We had to walk so far. It took us until the sun got dark. The woman who owned it didn't want us there — she wanted us to go to the ports, too — but your sister lied again. She said that she didn't want us to go to the ports, so she should make us the Lady's problem. That's you, isn't it? The Lady she was talking about?"

I'm so frazzled I don't answer except with a dull nod. The girl grins up at me. "Your sister wasn't very nice but she said you would be. And she also gave me a message for you. Just for you. She said I wasn't allowed to tell anybody else."

"Can my sister hear it, too?"

The girl glances at Zelie and then, in true little girl fashion, shrugs and smiles and says, "Sure."

"What did she tell you?"

"She said to tell you not to try to find her. She said she'd be fine, but I don't know, she sounded very scared, too."

"What?" I say, voice sounding very far away. I feel my sweaty fingers curl into the nice fabric of my new dress. This one doesn't have a corset, but built in boning that stabs into my ribs when I jerk abruptly forward. I almost topple the tray as I reach for my glass of wine and down half of it in one swallow.

The young girl stares me in the eyes unflinchingly in a way that unnerves me as she repeats what she said before, word for word. She cocks her head as she finishes. "But if it were my sister, I think I'd want to help her."

"And you'd be right," Zelie says, rising to her feet at once. "We have to go."

"We should tell the Riders," I say.

"Yes," the little girl nods. "That would be good. The Riders are friends with the people in the rags, right? They were dressed like refugees, too. And you were so nice to us, maybe you and the Riders will be nice to them, too. Since your sister was with them, they'll give her a nice room and some good food." She smiles. Her teeth are so clean compared to the rest of her body. I feel...sick. The girl is nodding along enthusiastically, but I know better than she does. I know the truth of it.

Zelie and I exchange a look. I'm sitting. She's standing. I drink the rest of my wine and set down my glass, then I stand, too. We don't need to speak for me to know what she's thinking. "We can't. Owenna is a grown woman. She needs to own her decisions." I try to remain cryptic — the little girl doesn't need to overhear talks of war and torture.

Zelie doesn't have such qualms and spits, "If Lord Yaron finds out she's working with Trash City again, what do you think he'll do?"

I wince. My heart sinks, shattering into pieces. I can't picture it, but I know I won't survive whatever it is...not only because I'll lose Owenna... I'll lose Yaron, too. "It's too dangerous, Zelie."

"We have to try for her. You know she'd try for you."

I don't know that, but Zelie must know as well as I do that my decision is already made. I will have to beg forgiveness from Yaron later, if he finds out, and I have no doubt he will find out. If he was on the fence about me before...then he will certainly forsake me after this. My heart will be broken no matter what. But…Owenna has left me with no choice.

Again.

I look into Zelie's pretty, familiar eyes and clench my hands into fists, feeling how they heat at the center of each palm. She says, "If we find her, how will we get her out of there?" She scratches the back of her arm, looking so beautiful in her new dress.

"I don't know. But we need to go to the Cliffs of Oblivion. Now. I just…I don't think I'm allowed to leave the castle… After what happened last time, the guards will stop me, I'm sure of it."

"I know a way." The little girl stands up, her head tilted to the side. "One of the boys who works in the stables showed me when those nice ladies brought us to the castle and gave us our rooms. I got to go play for a little while. That's how I got all this dirt on me." She smiles as she shows off her skirts, covered in dirt — or possibly, horse manure. "My grandparents weren't happy."

I smile hesitantly. "I couldn't ask you to risk yourself…"

"No, no, no risk. I will just go right back to my grandparents after this. They don't even know I'm gone, really." She gets up and, with the confidence of a much older girl — or perhaps, a much younger infant who doesn't understand rules or the consequences breaking them can bring — she comes to me and takes my hand. She leads me to the door and then opens it. Cyprus isn't back yet, which is our first bit of fortune, but what makes me instantly suspicious is that the guards that were at the bottom of the stairs earlier en masse are no longer there, either.

"See here, this way," she says, taking a servant's passage hidden behind a pretty tapestry, instead of the central corridor that tapestry hangs in. She walks like she knows her way, like she's done this a thousand times before, taking twists and turns, leading Zelie and I down suspiciously empty servants' passages, through a suspiciously empty castle, out of a conveniently placed side door that deposits us right near the stables. "You can just follow that dirt lane to the main highway line there, I think. That's what the little boy said. Good luck saving your sister! Tell her Margarite said hi when you find her!"

The little girl leaves us, returning the way she came, and Zelie and I stare at one another in her absence. It isn't cold, but I feel cold as I stand there, prepared to defy Yaron yet again.

"This isn't a good idea, Zelie."

She nods. "You're right. It isn't."

"But if we don't, Owenna's as good as dead — either killed by Trash City, or by Yaron when he discovers her. Right?"

Zelie nods, glancing back at the castle, grim determination etched into the lines of her expression. "Trash City has guns." She hugs her elbows, her dress a pretty pattern of bright oranges and purples. Not armor. Not even camouflage.

I scratch the back of my neck. "I'm a Fire Omega. I can protect Owenna." I think. I hope.

"You know what they say about fighting fire with fire."

I smile, though it feels shaky. I don't think my fire can melt bullets, but I don't dare tell Zelie that. Instead, I lie again, "I can do this." She nods her head just once, looking longingly back at the castle, towards the small servants' exit, but we take the other path.

KIANDAH
ORIAS HIGHWAY LINE

ESCAPING THE CITY IS EASY WITH THE HELP OF OUR industrious little friend and aided by the fact that most of the Crimson Riders seem to be gone — likely with Yaron scouring Paradise Hole and securing our northern border. It's finding a horse once we're in the village that's difficult.

I didn't think about money when we left and even though we aren't tossed out on our asses when we approach several vendors — not like I was a fortnight ago — no one readily offers up their horse for our clandestine use. Instead, we manage to secure passage with a pair of merchants heading west along the highway line that splits from the Orias highway line and leads to Shadow Ridge.

They're headed to the mining town just south of the Cliffs of Oblivion, Heatherlen, but have agreed to take us as far as they can. I anticipate that we'll have to walk a good bit of the way to reach the cliffs, which means we'll only arrive by nightfall. *Yaron will have discovered my absence by then.* I try not to outwardly wince every time the thought crosses my mind, but it's difficult. It crosses my mind often as the cart, dragged by two horses, makes its towards Owenna and whatever else awaits. Whoever else.

Instead of dreaming up horror scenarios about what might happen when we arrive and what will happen if we have to confront Trash City, I try to focus on our surroundings. I've never been down the Shadow Ridge highway line before and, if this were any other journey for any other purpose, I'd have found it thrilling. The South Island has such beautiful topography. Microclimates separate regions that are pressed up against each other so tightly, it feels like walking through doorways to new worlds when they change. Today, the sky is even clearer than usual, helping me to see what lies before our *doomed* westwardly way.

Unlike the Undoline highway line, which leads to more rolling fields and grasslands, or the Gold City highway line that leads south from Undoline through dry, arid deserts studded by high sandstone mountains or the Hjiel highway line that leads south from the keep through increasingly cold and harsh temperatures, the Shadow Ridge highway line will take us to stark, rocky hills and eventually, a harsh sea and winds that clash over jagged cliffs.

Already, I can see the rising of Shadow Ridge on the horizon as the road cutting to it veers ever closer to the forests of Paradise Hole to the north. The trees once sat well back from the highway line have started to encroach, especially with no heart trees left to contend with them.

In some places, dark roots looking like the limbs of an ancient god claw their way out of Gatamora's black heart to cause massive bumps in the road. I watch them now with concern and suspicion. I worry that Yaron's forces will have headed this way. I don't know where they went within the dark woods, but they could be close. I stare into the trees, searching for any sign of a red cloak, but see nothing. Only shadows.

Shivering, I sit up straight and look at Zelie. We should probably come up with some scenarios around which we can form some loose tendrils of plans, but the wagon we're on is small and I worry about our drivers overhearing us — they might not want to abet our insurrection if they know where we're truly headed and who we're planning to meet.

The two men driving the horse cart are father and son. The younger of the two appears my age, and when I try to get Zelie's attention, I realize it's on him, not me. He's pointing up the road to a tall tree on our lefthand side. Its thick red trunk and vibrant dark blue leaves are a distinct contrast to the trees on the other side of the highway line, which are grey and darker grey.

"Do you see the tang bird's nest? They migrate here and roost every year, coming all the way down from the North Island. They aren't water birds and it's incredible they make it, taking rests only on the boughs of crossing ships."

I'm so caught up in wondering if the birds will have a way to make it back home or if they'll all drown in the sea now that the port of Ruby City has been destroyed that I don't immediately notice Zelie smiling and blushing and tucking her twists behind her ear.

"The birds are very beautiful, Desmond," she offers coyly. *Coyly.* As if Zelie has ever once in her life been known to be coy.

Wait a second… This whole time that I've been sitting here panicking, has Zelie been *flirting?* I guffaw loudly and unattractively. Zelie shoots me a dirty look, but the younger of the two men — Desmond, apparently — doesn't notice.

He prattles on about the birds and other interesting facts about the landscape while his father gives a chuckle every once in a while and Zelie's skin darkens and flushes. At one point, he makes a pretty poor joke about the state of the Paradise Hole trees and she giggles. *Giggles.* It fills me with both irritation and glee.

"It's very kind of you to deliver us all the way to the western ridge crossroads. No one else was willing to take us so far."

"It's no problem," Desmond answers with a wink that borders on the salacious. It makes me concerned that he's just a flirt and that Lord Yaron is right — we Ubutu sisters don't get out much.

"My boy is wrong," his father says.

Zelie's head sinks into her shoulders. His son gives him a stern look. Flustered, I prattle, "I'm — we're — so sorry…"

"I wasn't finished, m'Lady. I was going to say, we're honored." The boy's father looks over his shoulder at me and smiles, his teeth glowing bright in his wind-chapped white face. "It isn't every day that humble steel workers like us get to drive the Shadow Lady and her kinfolk to their destination. And we'll take you all the way, m'Lady, if the cliffs are where y'all are headed. Don't you worry about that."

"Oh…I…" I hadn't realized he knew who I was. I hadn't realized anyone would know who I am. And I'm also not who he says…*yet.* Yaron may have made me an offer, but that was before I ran away. *Again. He's going to be angry. He's not going to accept me on my return* — I refuse to think about that, lest I puke. I forcefully return the father's gaze with a smile of my own, no matter how brittle. "Thank you so much, sir, but we couldn't ask that of you." *It's too dangerous.*

"Lucky for you, then, that you didn't ask, m'Lady." He winks and I feel a warmth in my chest astride the uncertainty that's plagued me ever since we left the keep. Leaving was so easy. So impossibly easy. *Maybe, we should turn back.*

"I…" I don't want them to come. I can't be responsible for their lives. But I can't think of any words to say that will make him change his mind. "Thank you," I tell him.

"It's what anyone should do for their Lady."

I wipe my brow. He's doing nothing for my pulse, which has lost its mind. I lean forward over my knees. "Zelie, we should turn back. We're going to get these people killed. And ourselves along with them."

"What? I can't hear you when you're mumbling."

The cart is empty between Zelie and I save for a few canvas tarps, so there's nothing to stop me from getting up and sitting beside her. I do just that, wobbling as we go over another rut in the road. I bounce down onto the seat beside her.

Zelie chuckles as she catches my arms and helps me untangle my skirts. "What are you saying, Kandia?"

"I'm just thinking," I say, lowering my voice even further and speaking directly into her ear. "What if…maybe this is a bad idea."

Zelie gives me an incredulous look. She looks so much like our father in that moment, I'd have laughed if I weren't feeling so appropriately scolded. "Are you for real?" she hisses, grabbing my wrist and yanking me towards her even though there isn't anywhere left for me to go. When I don't answer, her voice shoots up an octave. "We're more than halfway there now! And Owenna — "

"It's about Owenna," I whisper-hiss loudly enough to cut her off. I pull back just enough to be able to look into her eyes, but still smell the scent of clean shea butter on her skin and Mama's signature hair grease in her curls. "What if Owenna doesn't want to be found? What if Owenna issued those warnings to us through that girl as just that — warnings? Maybe of what's to come. What if Trash City is planning something? What if Owenna is in on it?"

Zelie's eyes are wide. She hadn't even considered it. I feel like an ass for daring to have such a low opinion of my own sister, but I can't help it. She already betrayed us once. "You think she left to rejoin them? After everything we went through? After what Lord Yaron did for us?"

I wince, hating that I don't...that I no longer have trust. "I mean..." I glance away, then back again and shrug.

Zelie quiets, expression growing distant and more thoughtful. She's staring down at our linked hands, dark brown skin against dark brown skin. Little scars on her wrists. I know the provenance of most of them, but not all. Because I am not her. I am not my family.

But I do love them, though.

My mind flashes with Yaron's face, a yearning I can't suppress accompanying it. My whole body floods with the sudden urge to return to him and I open my mouth to tell

Zelie as much, but she's already talking. "I think we should…"

"What's this now?" the older man says and suddenly the cart rolls to a jerky stop.

"Hey! Get out the way!" Desmond shouts.

But whoever it is does not get out of the way. The road has been almost completely empty, save for three other wagons that rolled silently by since we branched from the Orias highway line. That's no surprise. Trips from Orias north are common, east less, and west even less than that. South beyond the keep, least of all.

When the cart comes to a complete stop, I use Zelie's shoulder to stabilize myself as I stand up. And what I see standing in the center of the highway line couldn't have shocked me more than the sight of a sunny, cloudless sky. No, not what. *Who.*

A woman with a shock of blonde hair stands directly in the middle of the road. She doesn't have a horse or a wagon. She's completely alone. She's wearing rags and has goggles pushed up onto the top of her head now, but as she turns to face our horse cart fully, she lowers them.

I lurch forward, stumbling over the uneven slats of the cart beneath my feet, and practically fall onto the father in my haste to move forward. "Sir — sirs, we need to turn back. With great haste. This woman is not a friend to us."

The father, much to his credit, immediately snaps his horses' reins and starts to turn the cart around, bringing Zelie and me closer to Merlin. Merlin, who I remember clearly from the dungeons and who I've heard much more about since. She looks better than she did then, dripping in rags and blood, and no less spirited. Her rags have been replaced, her wounds evidently healed enough for her to be able to walk upright and without difficulty — I shouldn't have let her go, I know that now, but back then I feared Yaron. I *still* fear Yaron and what horrors he's capable of inflicting on his enemies. I don't want him to be capable of such violence. Of such... inhumanity...but...

I know now, meeting her gaze through her murky goggles, that if granted the opportunity, I would not make the same mistake I once did. She is *dangerous,* this woman.

"Can we move any faster?" Zelie says, voice trembling.

Desmond encourages the horses along with light swats to their behinds with the prod. "She stands alone. She can't be such a threat. You can calm yourselves. We'll be out of her vicinity soon," he says to Zelie and me, but I'm not listening. My focus is on Merlin.

She smiles and winks and waves at me. "My Lady, don't be discouraged. You're just the woman I wanted to see," she shouts over the sound of the horses stamping their feet.

I shudder while my heart slams against my chest. I'm feeling nauseous on my regret. The cart turns all the way around, but I continue to pivot so that I can keep Merlin in my sights. I scarcely dare to blink. *What is she doing here?* I glance worriedly towards the woods, wondering — knowing — that she must have more members of her tribe hiding somewhere close, ready and waiting... Is this an ambush?

I glance around, suddenly horrified that these two men are being dragged into this alongside us. I'm petrified for them. They did us a favor and how do we repay it? By getting them killed? *No. No, I won't let that happen.* I clench my hands into fists and try to give Merlin my best, most courageous gaze. She smiles wider, to show all of her teeth. Some are black or missing. She tongues the gaps as Zelie tugs on my wrist.

And then Merlin mouths words I can hear as if she'd shouted them, *"You should have killed me when you had the chance."*

"What the…" Desmond's voice murmurs, followed by his father's lower baritone, "Is that…a relation, m'Lady?"

"Kiandah!" Zelie shouts, yanking hard enough on my wrist to break the spell Merlin had me under.

I flinch and look back over my shoulder, meeting Zelie's gaze. She points forward and I look over the top of Desmond's and his father's heads, but my mind blanks as I take in the strange sight. The strangest I've ever seen in my entire life. Stranger than seeing the leader of Trash City alive and not dead and just standing in the middle of the Orias highway line like she owns it.

There's another female standing in the road. Unlike Merlin, she wears no rags, but a dress in dark crimson. It swirls around her ankles. Its corseted middle accentuates curves just as subtle as the ones visible through my own dress — a dress that is the exact same color and nearly the exact same style, minus the lower cut of mine and the higher cut of hers, which has a collar that cinches tight around her throat.

The woman has medium brown skin, the exact same color as mine and Zelie's, thin box braids that fall to her waist, just like the ones I used to wear, and one brown eye that's shaped so eerily like my own it almost feels like I'm staring into a mirror. It almost does, except for her one blue eye. That blue eye and that brown eye are fully focused on me as her pale brown lips curve in an expression that could only bracingly be considered a smile. It's carnivorous, whatever that expression is, flashing white teeth that could be fangs for what they do to me.

Fear swells in my chest and the woman lifts her hands, both of them, palms up to the sky. Flames dance at her fingertips. "Get down!" Zelie shouts, yanking on my arm at the same time that Desmond curses and his father shouts, "Fates!" Whether he means it as a curse or as an identification, I'm not sure, but he's right either way.

I'm not given long enough to dwell on the fact that the Fated Fire Omega is here, standing before me, wearing my face.

The flames between her hands swell in a brilliant wall of red before crashing down on me and my sister and our two unsuspecting travel companions in a wave of terrible vengeance.

Zelie screams. My body takes flight. One of the men shouts and the other is eerily silent. I feel energy pulsing through my arms, but they're shaking and the breath is knocked clean out of me as I hit the packed earth. Our horse cart. My head. The explosion. I glance around, disoriented.

"No, wait! Please!" a male voice says. I look up to see the splintered remains of the cart and the horses struggling to free themselves from flaming debris. The Fate lords above the two men who are further down the road, closer to her than Zelie and I are. Zelie is trying to get to her feet, struggling. I don't have time to move at all before another wave of fire pummels the men, attempting to engulf them.

I don't have to move at all, but I can feel...not an energy, so much, but a desire, a *will — my will* — beating through the fire, pressing it back with such ferocity, it causes the Fate to stumble. Her red fire disappears.

"Run!" I tell the men.

They don't hesitate, but head straight for their horses. The father cuts the animals free and grabs the first horse by the reins. He vaults onto its back in a surprisingly agile movement for someone his size and looks back to his son. "Come on, Desi!"

But Desi is rooted, his hand on his horse's back, looking at Zelie and me. "Come on!" he roars, his white cheeks splotchy with pink, his brown hair tousled in the wind that I created.

"Go, Zelie!" I shout and another breath of violent wind pulses from me, pushing Zelie in the boy's direction.

She launches herself towards Desmond and a blast of fire chases her that I beat back, pushing up onto my knees. The flaming bits of horse cart are hot, but I suspect that isn't the reason for the sweat pebbling on my hairline and the back of my neck.

Zelie sways, unsure on her feet. She trips over a piece of burning wood and goes down hard among the embers. I'd have called her name if I could find my voice, but as it is, all of my concentration goes into keeping her from being burned alive right in front of me.

Another wave of fire.

Another burst of air that redirects it.

Another clash of vibrant red and orange flame against the wind that I create only this time, the flames just die. I manage to will the air to swallow them up.

Zelie makes it to Desmond, who grabs her and tosses her up onto the horse before climbing up himself. He looks at me but I shake my head and he takes no more direction than that before charging after his father, who takes off after him down the rocky hill covered in dark grey grasses and rich green mosses. It'll be a hard ride to Orias Village from here across the wilds, but they'll make it. They'll make it to the keep.

I can hear Zelie shouting, screaming, likely wanting to go back for me, but I know that I'm not getting out of this now. This woman, this Fate, this doppelganger of mine, came here for me. She's looking at me now, her hands down at her sides, a considerate expression strung between her mismatched eyes.

"So you're my counter," she says, and I'm shocked by the sound of her voice. Ancestors help us all, she sounds *exactly* like me. She smiles and laughs wickedly, her skirts swishing through the flames, dousing them, as she takes a few steps towards me over flaming chunks of wood. The acrid scent of smoke fills my lungs, but I inhale it without feeling faint from it. It feels as familiar as she.

"You seem so surprised. Did your sweet Lord Yaron not think to warn you about me? He must have known who you were the first time he saw you."

Stunned, I don't need to answer. She can read everything I don't want her to in my expression alone.

She laughs louder, her hand on her belly. It's flatter than mine. A lifetime spent enjoying food clearly treated me well. Much better than whatever hate she was up to. "Oh my. He doesn't trust or respect you at all, does he? He must know already what we all do, all of us that matter, anyway." She pauses, as if giving me time to answer. I don't have anything to say. "You are no match for me, my sweet little Fallen Fire

Omega. Can you even produce flames on your own, or do you require a catalyst?" She waits again and then shakes her head, her smile falling. "You don't even know, do you? Have you even been given a chance to explore your powers at all?"

I find her sentences funny, strung together in an order I don't understand. She speaks to me as if power is all that there is. I worry now for her, that power is something *she* does not understand.

"He uses you," she snarls, expression becoming vicious as I continue not to respond. "Controlling you like a puppet."

What?

"Oh, don't even attempt to convince me otherwise. Alphas are all the same. He probably orders you to repress your powers, fearing the damage you could wreak if you were truly untamed, truly unleashed. This is why you wield fire like a frightened little girl. Like a frightened little Beta. Or do you even wield it at all? Do you only use your gifts over air?" She waits for me to answer like I'd have one, but even if I did — which I don't — I wouldn't know where to start. She's gotten me so, so, so wrong. And Yaron?

I can't help the small twitch of my lips, begging a smirk as she speaks of domination from the Berserker beast who wants only to be dominated by *me*.

The Fate stills, the corners of her lips twisting downward, her brow knitting together so that her thin black eyebrows bunch together over her nose. "You mock me?"

"No. No, not at all." I have to clear my throat. It's full of hesitation and fear, the sensation like choking on wet cotton balls. But I also feel strangely…sorry for her. My lips quirk up where hers went down and I say as loudly as I must, "I think

Yaron would actually like me a lot better if I were more like you."

She frowns and swishes her skirts, coming even closer. We're only ten feet apart. It feels like so little. It feels like I'm staring into a dark mirror where I can see how my life might have looked if I'd been born without the love of a family...or a Berserker who would and does and *loves* to drop to his knees at my feet. It is hard not to pity her. She must have had a hard, long and miserable life, one full of fire and the scent of burning things, instead of the rich smell of Orias rice and charred chicken wings...

She must see something on my face because she stills. Fire flicks up her fingertips to her wrists, but carefully avoids her sleeves. "The fact that you care what he thinks of you disgusts me. You know the beasts cannot be trusted."

This woman looks just like me, more like me than any of my true sisters. I just didn't...couldn't have fathomed that the Fire Fate would be my twin in likeness, and my opposite in everything else. Her heart is made from something that mine isn't. Her heart is barbed wire wrapped around pulsing hate. Mine is just a heart. Nothing different from any other heart, soft and squishy and happy to simply beat.

"What do you intend for him?" I muster the courage to ask.

"What we intend to do to all Berserkers. Use them to rewrite the world. Betas on the bottom, Omegas on top and Alphas erased."

I frown, uncertain. How can she mean that? "I...we'll stop you," I correct. And something about that correction sparks something inside of me. *We, I said we.*

Before I can lift my hand to stop her, she's already pummeled me with a fiery blast. I feel it against my skin, a sublime heat that hurts, but doesn't burn anything except my clothing. The force of her strike has taken me off of my feet and I tumble over the ground, the dirt on the highway line luckily putting out the flames before they can render me completely naked. When I come to, I'm lying on my back and a white face shielded by goggles is staring down at me with a smirk.

"Well, come on then, killer," she says with a laugh. "Let's get you to the cliffs."

"Cliffs?" I croak, trying to sit up. But Merlin steps on the center of my chest, her boot heavy and caked with dirt. She leans her weight onto that foot, squeezing the breath out of me.

"'Course," she replies. "Cliffs of Oblivion. We need your beastly friend to meet us there so he'll be nice and out of the way when we take the city. And you're the bait." She grabs me under the armpits and hauls me upright. She drags me so that I can't catch my footing and when I try to fight back, try to bring fire and flame and strike them both down, I can't. I wasn't built to kill anybody. All I can do is struggle feebly when she drags me to a wagon that's pulled out of the woods by horses with rotten pelts and matted manes, driven by riders that have bones sticking through leathery skin in places and guarded by more of the undead.

The undead, wearing tattered crimson cloaks, drag me away.

YARON
THE PORTS

THE WIND IS WARM AGAINST MY SKIN, WHICH IS ON fucking fire. My rut is raging in my bones, exacerbated by the fact that my beast and I feel eerily apart in our wants but in sync in our sense that something is very wrong.

The ports are typically a hive of activity, but not today. Today, there is no laughter, bartering, buying or selling. Today, there are only murmurs and whispers and fearful gazes and retreating backs seeking shelter. The mood is that of a city right before an impending storm. I glance up at the sky again and feel my lips curl back, as if I might fight the shadows. A low-hanging cloud casts more than a shadowy pall over the harbor, because beneath it, there is a terrible gloom.

Something is coming.

But from where? I've already stationed every guard that I could spare on the northern border, I've sent out patrol ships, I've had black cloaks inspecting every crevice — the black markets, the illegal fishing villages, the beaches, and even further south than that in case the undead come up from our disputed borders with Hjiel or on the Gold City side of the island. Even Owenna, for all of her promises and desire of a black cloak, too, has yet to deliver. I have yet to even hear from her and Sipho.

Nothing.

It has left my nerves frazzled and shot. My guards don't speak to me. They cannot. I am surrounded by Betas, having sent the Alphas among my Riders in separate platoons so as not to further agitate me, but it doesn't help. I am agitated. I am *obsessed*. I cannot even use my beastly senses to root out the undead because if I draw my beast forward, all he wants is to sprint back to the keep as fast as he can. She's pulling me that way. She's pulling me. She's *torturing* me. And I do not have time for this.

I should never have broken the mandate. I should never have bedded an Omega. I should never have presumed to take a Lady.

The thought screeches to a stop, the wrongness of it assaulting me like ten thousand undead. My beast surges against my breast, my heart throwing itself against my rib cage, desperate to fight the thought that's taken root. Thoughts of forsaking her beneath the blood of the red moon.

I would rather fall on my own axe than break that oath to her. I would rather offer up my crown.

"Is there, um…something wrong…uhh…my Lord?" Jesús pulls his horse next to mine as my contingent begins to convene at the mouth of the highway line.

I am defeated. I am horrified. I am *needy*.

"We will need to source wood from Glass Flats," I mumble, turning Brega around.

"My Lord?"

"The highway line," I say, pointing behind us to the dark fucking woods and the swampy highway line attempting to be made visible through it.

"The builders added gravel, sand and stones at your request," Jesùs offers. "It is an improvement."

"Now the mud has become so thick we will need to build bridges — gangplanks and a raised walkway," I snarl. "It will be an effort, especially now that wood is so scarce on the South Island. We will need to import it and that is impossible with Mirage City holding both ports. Dark City will be no help until they erect the new port — if they are even able. It will be difficult to hold both Dark City and a new satellite port so far away. But if they are successful, Paradise Hole is too thick surrounding Dark City. I'll have to go further north than that even to source wood enough to rebuild the highway line through Paradise Hole."

"Ah. To Glass Flats?"

"Yes," I reply gruffly, welcoming the distraction of tallying costs and coin to avoid thinking about Kiandah. *Kiandah would enjoy traveling to Glass Flats. The castle is magnificent.* And suddenly I'm spiraling. Picturing her expressions in my mind as she saw the Night Market... She is magnificent.

She is mine.

I am no coward. I will rule the Shadowlands, defeat the undead, kill the Fates and then I will sate myself like no Berserker has ever been sated. *Fangs sunk deep into her neck. Knot fisted high in her sex.*

My mind thrashes with unease and insecurity while Jesùs continues to blather on, engaging me in this mindless prattle about wood when it is likely the least of our concerns at the moment. "Rebuilding the highway lines through Paradise Hole seems prudent. Especially now. We could clear out more of the forest. It might make…occurrences like these less common. And of course, the merchants will be pleased. Well, once northbound trade resumes, of course."

"Yes," I grunt. My mind races, my toes curl. I want to be back with her. I never want to see her again. I want to ship her far, far away from me until the night of the red moon so I am not tortured like this. I want to keep her close, sear her to my skin. Brega stirs beneath me, neighing and stamping his feet. I correct him with a hypocritical huff, feeling restless and unsettled myself.

And it's in the midst of my and Brega's shared stamping and huffing that I happen to glance west. In the distance, somewhere shining over the cliffs, an errant burst of sunlight filters down through the dense cloud cover. I saw the sun too few times as a boy.

Looking at Paradise Hole, I've thought so often that ruin has come beneath my rule. That that is all I will leave behind. A legacy lost when the last Shadow Lord gave up his crown. I have worried often that I am not the Lord I thought I was — that he saw in me.

But looking at the sun? I have seen it shine in the presence of Fallen Omegas more than I have ever seen it in my life. I have seen it shine on Kiandah. I have seen it shine through her and it brings me the belief that perhaps, I am not a fallen Lord. Perhaps, it is a Fallen Omega who will help me shape a new legacy. I exhale, feeling calmer. I pat Brega's mane as he too calms beneath me.

Jesùs clears his throat. "My Lord?"

"A moment."

"I am not in a rush."

"Then what is it?"

"I wondered merely if the Red Moon Festival would still be taking place in light of recent events?"

"The red moon will rise in a little over a week. That is enough time," I say, but time enough for what? For me to raze Trash City and send the Fates and their dead army back to the underworld where they belong? Or for me to fuck it all, ignore her honor and simply throw her down and bond her? *It isn't enough time for any of that.* And I wanted to honor her. *Fuck honor. Throw her down and bond her...*

"That's good, my Lord. Very good. Dorsten's and Hector's packs were right then."

"What?" Three more of my guard are visible now at the mouth of the Night Market. They are the last to return. We will be off, then.

He gives me a hesitant glance from the corner of his eye. "Uh...I only meant, for the packs that will vie for her. I heard rumors, rumblings that there were a few...preparing...in case it did happen at the next red moon."

I cannot control my reaction, which is a problem for me. This whole thing is a fucking problem. I should have just fucking bonded her. Fuck her honor. Fuck the Fates. Fuck everything.

I snap Brega's reins and steer him towards the docks where six large ships and many smaller ones remain tied up. There is a larger marina on the eastern side of the ports, but these ships are meant for the North Island. Now, they are simply idling, their wares being offloaded lest they spoil.

I frown as I look across Zaoul. His dark and murky waters hide many secrets, none greater than the question of how the undead are creeping onto our borders. We have yet to source the ships that brought them here. Perhaps, they were destroyed or burned and lie now on the bottom of the sea floor. It would be little effort for the Fire Fate to dismantle them. I have seen her in action. Her face so similar to Kiandah's, her power so much more visible. But not greater. Oh no, her power is not greater.

I tilt my head to the side, my eyes unfocusing as Brega shuffles to the very end of an empty dock, his hooves clattering over the sea-salt-encrusted wooden planks. I think of the fire I saw from the Fate. It always came in bursts of red and orange. But everyone knows that the flame is hottest at its center where it shines the color of the clearest sky.

A bird caws overhead. Nothing new, but the sound becomes annoyingly persistent.

"Lord Yaron, we are ready to depart!" Leonard, a Beta and one of my Crimson Riders, shouts at me from the foot of the dock. His horse is braying almost uncontrollably and I can feel the trembling of Brega's muscles beneath my legs. I frown.

"Calm that horse, Leonard."

"Apologies, my Lord. All of the horses are agitated." He points back towards where my guard remains clustered, about fifteen Beta men and women wearing cloaks that, at this moment, appear rather silly. They look like children attempting to control unruly horses on their very first rides.

I frown and open my mouth, but the bird caws once again. And then again and again, swooping lower before flying higher once again. "Fucking…" I turn and look up at the dark sky, which silhouettes this bird in sharp relief. Only, it isn't one bird, it's a dozen, and they're *huge*. Larger birds than any I've ever seen. They have faces like owls and shine all in white. Bright white.

And when they dive, they dive as one.

A dawning realization only catches up to my reality when the birds crash in the center of the dock between Leonard and me. The pile of feathers congeals, bone and beak fusing together until a female form rises up from the mass that once was. Leonard has not met this female before and draws his sword while Jesús charges forward, calling for him to stand down. He and I have fought alongside this Omega before.

While Jesús explains to my other Riders who she is, she looks only to me. The female with the white skin and the white hair and the painfully light eyes has blood on her mouth that drips down her chin and jaw and neck. She lifts a thin arm and points to the sea. "Call your army. They have come."

I turn as the world hangs on a pronounced and pregnant silence. The sea continues to lap and froth, charging in the directions Zaoul directs it. The boats continue to rock. I stare out at the horizon, against which I can only see the faintest outline of land far, far off in the distance, and only through the eyes of my beast.

"Freya, speak plainly." Panic-fueled rage laces my words.

Freya's frustration with me is clear in her tone, which rises to an inhuman screech. She advances on me, coming to tower over the top of my head on the knobby legs of a giraffe with a white pelt. Her bloody mouth distends and I am left looking into her black maw as she grabs me by the collar of my shirt and shakes me with the arms of a gorilla.

"They are here!"

Brega is calm. He responds to her dominance with a submission I have not seen him show anyone before. Freya and I stare one another down as I seek out the answers to my questions in her nightmarish eyes. Her face reforms to that of a human — in her case, a Fallen Omega's — and she hisses out a final whisper, "The water."

My lungs inflate, the air tasting of salt from the sea. I haul back on Brega's reins and wheel him around to charge down the dock. Halfway there, I hear the boards of the dock explode apart. Brega lifts his front hooves and when he falls back to the rickety floorboards, I watch as an undead male soaked in sea water drags himself up onto the dock. He reaches for me, bones protruding from his arm.

Behind me, Freya releases a screech as she takes to the skies. She drops down again on the boardwalk of the port, right where it meets with the dock. I follow her, releasing my axe and, as Brega leaps, I lean over low enough that I'm able to reach the undead creature and cleave off its head.

"Everlyn, Gareth, Preena, Charles, Leonard, Natalya — disperse! Call the patrols dispersed east back to the docks. Call the patrols dispersed west to the keep. Clear the port town, clear the Night Market, and clear Orias! Take all civilians back to the keep!"

My Riders have not yet caught on to what is happening. It takes them several moments to react and drive their horses down the sodden highway line to do my bidding. In this time, I have rejoined the rest of my Riders at the edge of the water, which had begun to froth in earnest. This is not Zaoul's doing. This is something else.

From the shallows rises a woman. A female. An undead female with black hair knotted with algae and sticks, skin slicked with water and grey-brown beneath, eyes murky and green, fangs for teeth. Her clothing is all but disintegrated, black with rot and dripping with sea life. She releases a screech and claws her way from the waves, finding the short stairs built into the stone that will bring her to land.

"My gods!" Jesús shouts, his horse threatening to free itself from his control and run. "How long have they been here, lying in wait like this?"

I do not know. I lift my axe and snap my reins to drive Brega forward, but Freya beats me to it, slicing forward as a white tiger and taking the undead's head off with her teeth. She spits on the stone boardwalk and looks up at me, but my gaze is focused on the sight of the undead rising from the water one-by-one.

"How did they get here?" another voice shouts. I should have thought the answer obvious enough by now, looking at the state of these beings. They may not be swollen with saltwater, dead as they are, but their clothes and hair are a testament to where they've been.

I don't answer, but Freya does, in an indolent tone. She says, "They walked."

Heads pop up all over the place, as far out as the farthest boat. There must be hundreds of them — no, not hundreds. *Thousands.*

I feel the burn of bloodlust ricochet through my bones. We are but fifteen warriors here, and a Fallen Omega. We will not hold. "We will not hold…"

"My Lord, what would you have us do?" Jesús shouts. He must have arrived at the same conclusion.

I roar over the sound of the undead screeching as they rise up from the depths. "Once the port city is cleared of civilians, fall back to the keep. On our way out, we will barricade the highway line leading to Orias with whatever we can to slow them down. We will need to use the extra time to clear Orias. At this point, call all forces back to the keep. Mirage City has come for us and we will need to make our stand at the castle where Kiandah is."

I had not meant to voice those final words aloud as an undead male draws himself from the water and comes towards me at a run. He is a fast fuck. Brega rears back and, before I can swing my axe, has trampled him. Two more undead follow on the heels of the male and as I feel my Riders move into line beside me — fifteen of us against an army — Freya comes to stand very close to me. She is scanning the skies, as if unconcerned with the bloodthirsty, venom-laced abominations.

Her lips move almost absently. "She is not at the castle."

I freeze. Everything in my body freezes. "What?"

"They took her."

There is only one *they* that Freya can mean. My blood runs cold, my face tightens. "Freya," I bark savagely. "Speak plainly, girl!"

"There!" Her voice rises in an ear-splitting shriek. She points at a black and white falcon circling the bay. "The Beast Fate has unleashed their army. Your army will fall. They will kill your Omega at the cliffs. That is where they intend to draw you. But if you move now and fast, perhaps I can kill the Beast Fate and the Death Fate before they kill the Fallen Omega you have enchained." She guts me a glare. "I will not stop them from killing you."

I feel the threat of rut come over me at the thought of Kiandah in the grip of the Fates...

...and I am only just successful in battering it back.

"I cannot leave my Riders to die."

Freya does not reply, but takes off into the sky as a bird, chasing the black and white falcon west, towards the Cliffs of Oblivion where my heart currently is. To where it has been stolen. Wrath is a difficult emotion for my beast to chew through, but I know that defeating the undead and the Fates and saving my female as well as my city requires calm. I choke on it as I turn to my Riders, who are all engaged with undead, cutting them down as they rise from the water...but there are too many.

"Jesús, I must confront the Fates at the Cliffs of Oblivion. You are in charge in my absence. Stick to the plan and hold for as long as you are able. Do not lay down your lives here when they will be needed to defend the castle. Triage where you must."

Jesús raises his longsword and brings it down onto the skull of an undead male, who falls like a brick, just as dead as he should have remained. "My Lord, you cannot go alone!"

I cut down another undead, which claws at Brega's hide. Already, my Riders here are so badly outnumbered. Natalya releases a scream as her horse is taken down. She defends its life with her own, slashing and cutting at the undead that rise up around her. It has been bitten. I charge over to it, Brega clearing the path before me.

I slash at the undead that cover her horse like ants over a crust of bread. The horse makes it to its feet, but it is no use to us now. I slap its hind and send it towards the highway line. Perhaps, it can carry a child or two to the keep. Natalya turns and continues to fight. I weigh the cost of my Riders' lives against Kiandah's…and know that I must sacrifice.

"Hold for as long as you can and then retreat as fast as you can. Barricade the way. Buy us as much time as you can afford."

I snap the reins of my horse and take off down the highway line to Shadow Ridge, unsure of what I will find there, and equal parts furious and terrified.

My heart pounds louder than the thrashing of Brega's hooves as we clear Paradise Hole and take the crossroads west, towards Shadow Ridge. We move at speed. Ordinarily the journey to the cliffs would take the better part of an afternoon, but Brega makes the journey within a quarter of that time.

On the way, we cross smoldering piles of burning wood. Oh yes, there was a battle here. My beast is ravenous and I feel my mind growing hazy with bloodlust as we crest the ridge and the murky outline of the Cliffs of Oblivion come into view as far west as the island allows and I know Kiandah is there. Because despite the fact that shadows have chased us all the way here, there is but a single errant ray of sunshine spearing down directly atop the largest finger of the cliffs. I know she's there and that she's still alive. I also know that she cannot have been taken by anyone other than the Fire Fate. And I cannot wait to bring justice down upon her in a rain of fiery vengeance.

The wind has picked up, as it is known to near the cliffs, though it carries the scent of something else. Something sweet and sickly that I recognize distantly. Something dead. They intend to attack from both sides, swarming south from the ports and east from the cliffs. They would not have drawn me out to the edge of the world without intending to throw me off of it.

And I'm walking willingly right into their trap.

The cliffs jut off of the mainland like fingers, each one no more than a kilometer wide at its thickest. They stand proudly several hundred feet above the thrashing sea waters below. Small beaches form inlets between them, like the skin between fingers when stretched, but the waters claim them often. The peaks are known for violent winds and rains, their grounds mostly rocky and covered in mosses and the occasional muddy patches of grass. They remain uninhabited — for good reason. Blocked by the highest peak of Shadow Ridge that separates them from the mainland, they are like little violent isles.

The road is clear. There are no travelers out today. I think back to the overturned cart and wonder who was among the wreckage. There were no bodies. Did they escape? Or were they killed and repurposed for the simple sin of having been out on a day that the Fates decided to come for me? It does not matter. Either way, they will be avenged. I do not intend to lose my life or Kiandah's on this day. The Shadowlands will stand.

I descend the ridge and my heart and beast are intertwined in a violent dance as I take in the supremely unexpected and yet wholly expected sight.

Expected, because I know that Kiandah is here and that the Fates have her.

Unexpected, because the *how* is what I have yet to uncover.

Positioned in the center of the widest cliff are two Fates, an additional Fate enchained, and a little girl perched on the edge of a large boulder, kicking her feet. A whole host of accomplices continue working along diligently behind them, many from Trash City, but several from the Shadowlands — I can tell by their wardrobes. Owenna is among them.

She glances up at me as I approach, but looks away quickly and continues her discussion with a female I recognize as the Sea Witch innkeep and I am hit with a renewed rush of rage that Kiandah slipped away from me in the night to speak with this traitor. Then I dismiss it. It matters little now, but I do vow that, before this is over, that innkeeper will be dealt with.

I quickly calculate approximately twenty helpers plus the Fates, but no undead, which surprises me a little. The odds would be in my favor, except for the fact that my Kiandah sits in a vulnerable position in their midst. A lamb among two dozen lions. *And this is why Shadow Lords do not take Ladies.* Any other Shadow Lord would not have lost his most important possession to the cruel hands of another. His heart. My mouth twitches, as if to smile. Though it is a sad smile. The odds are in my favor, but it does not matter. I will likely die here, I realize. And I still do not regret any of it.

Our time was short but it was the best use of time I could have never dreamed up, because to dream it would have been to know that it even existed — that *she* even existed. I did not. And I know that, when the Death Omega switches from her task of creating undead, to taking my life so that I may join her foul creations, it is not my life that will flash before my eyes. It will be these past four weeks.

I come to a stop about twenty long paces from the clustered Fates, the wind whipping at my cloak and hair. Sipho, in chains of his own, kneels next to the Fate who is also wrapped head to toe in thick metal chains. She's on her knees as well, her eyes flitting between me and Kiandah desperately. I recognize her and am aware that she must also recognize me. It is a far departure from the glassy-eyed female who sloughed off Berserker Maengor's dead skin as if it were water.

And then a moment later, tried to kill her brother.

Now, her eyes are bloodshot and full of fire. She struggles against her bindings, her long brown hair tattered and unkempt. She has on a thick wool dress that appears mostly wet. Her face is drawn and her cheeks sunken. Her eyes are dark and miserable. A dagger of pity stabs me in the chest as I look upon Berserker Dragnovic's sister, a powerful Omega who has only known captivity her entire life.

And yet…she is dangerous. Do I believe I would let her roam freely if I were given the chance? I do not know. It is a question I do not wish to answer.

My gaze switches across the Omegas and Sipho to my Kiandah. My sweet Kiandah. The only unchained ally I have here, and yet I know she has been left unchained for a reason. It is a slight. They do not know her at all and yet they know she is not a threat. Because she isn't. They brought her here to kill her, and in all likelihood, she will let them.

But will she let them take any other lives?

I do not know how to answer that question, but I know I cannot rely on her to get us out of this. My beast beats out a rhythm beneath my sternum, thrashing and struggling, wanting to escape. I will let him do his best, but first, we must wait.

I gather strength and return my gaze to the Fates and the little girl. I hadn't bothered to assess her face earlier, but I do when she smiles and waves at me.

"Ah. So that is how it was done. That is how you separated us." I nod. "I am impressed, truly. You are a formidable group."

"Thank you." Odette steps forward and places her hand on Kiandah's shoulder, tightening her grip. Kiandah winces and flattens her lips.

There is wetness to her eyes that makes me sad. I tell her softly, "It's alright, Kiandah."

She looks up at me, blinking quickly. "I'm sorry, Yaron. I should have stayed in the castle."

"It is not your fault. You were deceived by the Fate of Mind and Madness. It would have taken a strong resolve not to fall to her," I say, tipping my head towards the little girl who pretended to be a refugee from Ruby City — and I believed it — as she claps her hands. "And I should have killed Odette the first moment I saw her at the Dark City Omega's ball..."

"Are you finished? Your parting words can wait. We plan on taking you alive."

Interesting. I nod, my hands clasped behind my back as I continue to struggle through my beast's reaction. He will get us killed quickly. And I am alright with that. Just...not yet. "What do you intend to do with me?"

"Something fun," Omora, the Beast Fate, answers, a flash of teeth that look suspiciously fanglike peeking from between her pale lips. She is so pale. She looks so eerily like the Fallen Beast Omega in all but expression, it makes me wonder what happened to the female. She would not have fallen so quickly. Not without a savage fight. I fight not to scan the skies, wondering...would Freya truly wait for them to kill me before attacking herself? I nearly snort out a laugh. *Of course she would.* Her hatred of me only just falls short of her hatred of them.

Omora claps her hands twice. "Alright, I suppose we should get on with it then."

"You're handling this very well, my Lord." Odette's voice creeps me out. I've heard it before, but that was before I knew Kiandah existed. The voice, the one they share, is Kiandah's now. Odette has no right to it. "If you wouldn't mind coming right this way, you'll see we have a ship waiting at the base of the staircase. Unless you prefer to use the cage. We had it created from the finest iron, one that cannot be broken by a Berserker's strength — and we should know, we tested it."

"With N'dogo?"

"Who else?"

I drift lackadaisically in the direction she's pointing, to the nearest edge of the cliff, my hands still clasped behind my back. Once there, I look down. It takes me a few moments to see the stairs built into the sheer black cliff face and when I do, I'm surprised and can no longer unsee them. Jagged and dangerous, anyone who attempted the climb would be risking death. Each stair is a different shape than the next, some steps simply gaps in the rock, little more than foot holds. As I gaze down, a small white lizard passes from one nook upward to the next. I cock my head, then turn from it with a nod.

"Does Adoqhina wait for me on the ship?"

"No. She's holding Ruby City. It doesn't take much to hold it. The Betas there were so eager for our arrival, they turned their bellies up to us right away." Omora smiles, flipping her white hair, streaked with black that Freya does not share even though they are counters to one another. The doppelgängers have so much in common…and so little.

I nod. This makes sense. I tip my head at the young girl. "Very clever to have disguised yourselves among the refugees. An impressive display of your gifts, Sy."

The little girl giggles and, as she rises to standing, a tall, spindly female with black hair and eyes and menacing grin rises up and out of her skin. "I am assuming the ones who posed as your grandparents were your other Fated sisters?"

She bats her eyelashes coyly but, on her, the expression appears violent.

"How long could you have kept that up?" I ask, genuinely curious.

"Long enough for its purpose."

"But not long enough to pose as Berserker Maengor for all those years. Which is why you had the Death Omega do it?"

Sy's gaze sharpens and shifts to the Omega in chains. She doesn't answer, but returns her gaze to me and presses her lips together into a tight, thin line.

I snicker, causing all three Omegas to stir. "But you failed, didn't you? Your control over her mind has weakened since we last had the pleasure of meeting one another. She does not appear as Berserker Maengor anymore. She appears to be quite her own."

The Death Fate, Noon, shifts in her chains, her expression burning furiously at the other Fates. Tears track down her cheeks. Sy hisses and lunges at Noon and Noon falls to her side in a clear display of pain. I regret my words and untangle my hands from behind my back.

"Alright. You are here for me. As you said, let us get on with it."

Odette leaves Kiandah's side and swishes towards me in a dress just like Kiandah's, all but the scorch marks. Kiandah's dress hangs from her skin loosely, riddled with charred bits and holes that expose her unblemished skin. *She is stronger than she thinks she is.* I know her strength. My beast and I submit to it gladly.

She must see something in my gaze that causes her to thrash. Sy goes to her and places her hand on the top of her head, causing her to wince. But she doesn't cry out.

"Sy. Enough," Omora hisses. "We've wasted enough time. Let's go." She gestures to the lethally narrow staircase, as if expecting me to simply walk down to my doom. As if they truly think I'd leave Kiandah with them without first offering up my own life.

I cock my head at Sy and she must read my expression because she withdraws a short, stubby knife from her robes and presses its tip to Kiandah's throat. "I don't need my gifts to kill her."

I don't react, though my pulse is pounding. On the outside, I appear calm. Calm.

Right.

"You really think I will go with you willingly?"

Odette, wearing Kiandah's face, snarls, "I think you are bonded to this female. I don't think you have a choice. Now *go*. And when you go, you can control Kiandah through your bond and force her to obey our will. She will anyways because it's clear this pathetic excuse for an Omega is in love with you."

I smile, feeling the heat of her words warm me. Both because they are true, and also because they are so, so wrong. "You are wrong." I am not bonded to her, though I ought to be.

"Oh? You think I'm bluffing." I. Always I. Never *we*.

I nod. "I do."

Odette turns from me and makes it to Sy's side. She pushes the female out of the way, malice in her gaze and in her arm as she takes Sy's dagger and presses it to Kiandah's neck…

And slides it in cleanly.

I have miscalculated.

The Fates have miscalculated. "Odette, what have you done! We needed her!" the other Fates scream.

But I hear them as if standing at the end of a tunnel. All I can feel are Kiandah's breaths shortening as she chokes on her own blood. All I can taste is her life as it fades.

Her eyes roll back into her skull and my beast claws its way to the fore as I attack, panic fraying my conscious and unconscious thoughts. I surge forward, claws extended, intending to what — save her? I can't. I know she's already gone, lost to me, to the ashes...

And then comes the fire. Bright reds and oranges. They engulf me, but I don't feel the pain on my skin as I fall, defeated. I feel only the horror of having lost what no other Shadow Lord ever has.

His heart.

His Lady.

Did you just call your Shadow Lord a liar?

You'd have been correct.

But you believed your Shadow Lord there for a moment, didn't you?

I am not an accomplished liar, but there are some *extenuating* circumstances I have discovered in my forty-two years in which I deem lying not only permissible, but necessary. Actually, I have found only one excuse for these... untruths.

Embarrassment. Mine, no one else's.

And to divulge the truth about what happened on the cliffs would be an affront to my own dignity, so it shall not go down in the record.

Fine. If you insist. The truth is that I never made it to the cliffs. *I* never made it to the cliffs. The thing that made it there in my stead was a wild animal, devoid of rational thought.

My beast.

THE BEAST
TOO FAR FROM KIANDAH

"**MY LORD, WHAT WOULD YOU HAVE US DO?**" ONE OF the Betas shouts.

I don't care about him. Or Yaron's response.

I roar at the encroaching threat to Kiandah as the things that reek of tainted Berserker venom rise up from the salty sea. I am not in my true shape. I'm still riding a fucking horse. Yaron is still fucking talking.

"Once the port city is cleared of civilians, fall back to the keep. On our way out, we will barricade the highway line leading to Orias with whatever we can to slow them down. We will need to use the extra time to clear Orias. At this point, call all forces back to the keep. Mirage City has come for us and we will need to make our stand at the castle *where Kiandah is*."

I force his lips to form the words that matter. I can tell he is angry with me but I don't give a fuck about him or anything besides returning to Kiandah. I don't care what would happen if we left these Crimson Riders here. I don't care about the Omega who smells like blood and dirt. I don't care about the presence of another Omega somewhere in the clouds above us, waiting to strike. Kill them all so we don't have to worry about them anymore. That sounds just fine.

"She is not at the castle." I hear the words through Yaron's ears, but cannot make sense of them. Is she saying…

"What?"

"They took her."

"Freya, speak plainly, girl!"

"There!" She isn't listening to us. She is pointing up at the Omega in the air. "The Beast Fate has unleashed their army. Your army will fall. They will kill your Omega at the cliffs…" She speaks more, but I am not listening. Because she has told me what I need to know, where they have taken my mate, and I am not willing to let Yaron wait any longer to do what we should have done days ago. Years.

Follow her scent.

Fall into rut.

Kill everyone.

I feel the threat of rut come over me…

…and I feel Yaron try to batter it back.

But I do not let him this time. I cut through his chest with both of my arms, force them free, and listen to the sounds of pain he makes as we jump from his horse and take control of him limb by limb.

I leave the Riders to die. I am nothing but loose marbles rattling within a glass cage. I am shattered. I am rage.

I kill a dozen undead on my way out, release a horse and chase it down the highway line with my own horse neighing at my heels, a flock of white birds clawing at the skies above me. I don't care for them. I care for nothing but the one thing.

Kiandah, I am coming.

KIANDAH
CLIFFS OF OBLIVION
WHAT REALLY HAPPENED

THE WINDS ARE ICE-COLD AND FILTER IN THROUGH THE burn holes in my dress, my hair and eyelashes freshly charred. Not that that matters. I'm probably going to die here.

Definitely going to die here.

All because I did something else stupid.

I glance at the little girl standing above me as I kneel in the center of the cluster of Omegas. There are three on my right-hand side, the little girl I once knew as and believed to be Margarite, included. When I was brought here, she gave me a wink and a wave before shivering into a different woman's body. It was alarming and disorienting to watch, and ultimately disappointing, because it made me realize how easily I'd been played. I should have waited. I shouldn't have panicked. I should have known that my sisters can handle themselves. Owenna, for example, seems right at home here. *I was right about her, too. Once a traitor, always a traitor.*

My oldest sister is among the two dozen people here working under Merlin's direction, moving objects back and forth, clearing a space and setting rigging to presumably pull something up from the thrashing waters below. A boat? A getaway vessel? I'm not sure why they would need to bring it up, given the treacherous staircase carved into the side of the mountain that they could take down to it.

It's no wonder Yaron's people weren't able to find Trash City — they were hiding, not below the Cliffs of Oblivion, not on them, but *inside* of them, in caves that no one in their right mind would have dared explore, connected to sea and surface by a staircase that no one in their right mind should take. But I suppose they aren't in their right minds, are they? Owenna. Madame Zenobia. Merlin. The Fates.

Bastards.

I glare at Merlin, who sits atop a rock to my left eating an apple like she hasn't got a care in the world. On her other side, Sipho hangs from a pole they've erected, covered in what look disturbingly like bite marks dripping in black venom rather than blood. He's not fully conscious, though occasionally his face flashes with pain.

Between Merlin and me, a woman kneels in chains. She's got her eyes closed, though she doesn't seem quite like she's sleeping. It's almost like she's meditating. If she is, I don't blame her. It can't be fun to be that viciously restrained. If she's at all claustrophobic, it would have to be unbearable. I feel sorry for the woman and wonder what twisted turn of events brought her to this miserable state among these wretched people on this windy hill.

Merlin must be a mind reader because at that moment, she says, "Don't feel bad for the little lady. She's the single most dangerous person in Gatamora. Creates all the undead

Alphas your family got in so much trouble for helping her out with and could kill *you* with the brush of her fingertips." She waggles hers and a puff of orange fire blasts in her direction, knocking the apple from her other hand and her whole body from its wobbly perch.

"Silence," Odette barks. She is the Fire Fate. Sy is the Mind Fate. Omora is the Beast Fate — names that I've only heard in whispers before today. Now, I hear these females responsible for so much death solidifying all that gossip into truth as they plot the destruction of my home and everyone I've ever known. "Ready the cage."

Merlin dusts herself off, running her fingers through her blonde bangs, which are singed at the tips. She tosses Odette a dirty look but trudges off, past the Omega lying on the ground, who she kicks a tuft of moss at. I hate her a little more than I did for that.

As Merlin starts barking orders, the Fates chatter among themselves. They aren't trying to whisper. I don't suppose my overhearing their plans matters. "So you did find her, Omora?" Odette says to the Beast Fate, a very pale white woman with black hair that has streaks of white interspersed through it. She looks like she's been through hell. She has bright red abrasions and scratches all over her arms, neck, chest and the two feet of her long legs that are visible beneath the hem of her simple black dress.

She looks nervous as she says, "I had her at the ports. She attacked me on my way here, and I...I lost her."

Odette hisses, "You are a fucking disgrace. Adoqhina is stronger than that bonded bitch in Dark City. I am *infinitely* stronger than the Fallen imbecile who walked right into our trap," she gestures dismissively at me. "And Sy's Fallen Omega has yet to be discovered and may already be dead. But you...you are *nothing* compared to Freya and if you don't figure out how to best her, then I will not stop Adoqhina the next time we suggest replacing..."

Omora slaps Odette across the face in retaliation. "Do not threaten me. The venom and the claws and the reason our undead army is so deadly, even to Berserkers, is thanks to me..."

"Enough. We don't have time for your petty squabbles," Sy says, her voice hard, her smile grim as it falls to me, looking absolutely nothing like the little girl she once did. Now, her pin-straight black hair hangs long and clean and untangled to her waist. Her monolid eyes shimmer when I look into them, making it impossible for me to tell their color. Her skin is pale, though not as pale as Omora's. Her soul is just as dark though, her smile just as chilling.

Sy's gaze snaps back to her sisters. "If Freya is gone, then good. We should act now before she returns. It was enough of an inconvenience having her harass us all the way across Zaoul."

"Good thing she cares little for Betas and even less for Alphas, otherwise she might have made toppling Ruby City more difficult," Odette suggests.

"She cares only for her precious little pets. Hopefully that means she won't care what we do with this one." Omora points offhandedly at me.

"If we hadn't turned so many in the beginning," Sy says, approaching the bound woman while pulling on a pair of black leather gloves. She pulls at the heavy chain dragging over the ground and the woman stirs. "Maybe we'd have been able to convince her to our side."

"We'd have been even more powerful, then," Odette mumbles, eyes growing distant. I wonder what fantasy she has conjured up in her mind. A world of undead. A Gatamora newly forged as a realm of witches and monsters.

With a single flick of Sy's wrist, the chains fall to the ground with a loud clang and the once bound woman rises to stand. Sy holds up her hands, then winces. She approaches the female very carefully and rattles the thick length of chain. No longer draped in it, I see that the shackle is actually around the woman's ankle. She's not free, only unbound and capable of moving her arms and legs now.

"Are you alright, sister?" Odette says to Sy. The Fates are quite still as they watch the sleepwalking woman.

"Yes. She's still fighting. It takes much more energy to keep her down than it did before."

"It was easy when she was a girl. You hardly needed to influence Noon at all. She simply trusted us."

Noon. The female's name is Noon.

"I suppose we have Dark City to thank for that," Omora snarls, massaging her injured shoulder. "No matter. It'll be over soon."

They all look to me then and the mood lifts between them, which for me can mean nothing good. "Lord Yaron will be here shortly," Odette says, making me tense. "We will release the beast and he will walk willingly into our cage once he sees his precious little bondslave under our control."

"And if he fights?" Omora says.

"He won't fight," Odette replies with a certainty I feel in my bones and hate that I feel it. *I cannot be his downfall.* "You saw how the Dark City Berserker was towards his Omega, and he is young and stupid. This Berserker is calculated and rational. He will walk willingly into a cage."

They're right. I know that. And I hate them for it. *I'll have to stop them.* As if hearing my thoughts and knowing their futility — me, against three Fates, alone? — Odette gives me a knowing, evil look. I look away from her, over my shoulder, and happen to catch Owenna's gaze. She shakes her head no once, swiftly, but for once I can't read her and as quickly as she caught my eye, she looks away.

But Merlin sees.

The blonde is talking to a man with similar goggles to hers pushed up on his forehead. Through goggles of her own, she glances between my sister and me with her signature, trademark leer. The feeling of foreboding in my gut becomes nauseating. What's she going to do? What are any of them planning? It somehow feels like they each have their own agenda here. Even the Fates...between them there is misalignment that, if I were a cleverer, angrier female, I might be able to figure out how to exploit...

Odette glances towards Shadow Ridge looming above us, separating us from the main island. "Where is he, anyway? I hate this fucking place. I'm ready to negotiate."

"Negotiate," Omora chuckles and the Fates all start to chuckle, and then that chuckle rolls into a loud laughter that fills me with ice, cold enough to douse my fire. I start to edge back, away from the Fates and the sleepwalking female and poor Sipho hanging in agony, but a boot to the spine keeps me from going far.

Merlin crouches down at my shoulder. "Whatever your plan is, you better get to it." She chuckles when I don't answer. "You just gonna let them kill you? Sheesh. Even Echo was made of tougher stuff. Had to shoot that woman a couple times and she kept crawling back. But you? You even got gifts?"

I purse my lips together and she shakes her head. She opens her mouth to say something else, but the caw of birds cuts between us like a strike of lightning. I flinch and follow Merlin's goggled gaze up, up, up...and I gasp. Because the sky is filled with birds. Not one. Not a dozen — but thousands of them.

"She's on us. Omora, handle it," Odette hisses.

Sy says, "I won't be much use to you until the Fallen Fire Omega is dead and I can wrap Noon back in her chains. As it is, she takes too much energy for me to concentrate on other illusions."

"That's fine. I have the Omega. Odette, you handle the Berserker." Omora takes to the sky as a flock of vultures, all black with flecks of white among their feathers, and the two groups of warring birds meet in the sky like competing clashes of thunder.

"Well, things just got exciting," Merlin says, giving my shoulder a squeeze that, from anyone else, I might have called reassuring.

"I..." I don't speak — I'm not given a chance because a roar drags our attention back to the ground, back to the rocks that cascade down the ridge and the Berserker beast bounding down them looking...

Ancestors be...is that Yaron?

...he looks completely unhinged.

"Wow. Things have gotten very exciting. That's my cue." Merlin starts to walk away from me, and is she...is the bitch *whistling?* She glances over her shoulder with a grin and adjusts her goggles as she heads for the end of the cliff where the traitors are working feverishly at the ropes, positioning themselves into twin lines on either side of them. They start to pull at Merlin's command.

The Berserker beast roars again. I switch my gaze back to the Berserker that I suppose must be Yaron, only I've never seen Yaron like this. The beast is frothing at the jowls, its strong jaws closed around the handle of an enormous axe, its eyes no longer storm cloud grey but black and ringed in red, the pupils glowing like embers.

Constant rumbling roars fill the air, emanating from his chest, and are even louder than the cries of the birds fighting each other overhead. I hold my arm up, terrified that I might get knocked out as birds drop all around us, falling like rain in blacks and whites but mostly blacks, but as soon as they hit the ground, they vanish in clouds like smoke, but even more effervescent.

"Mother's bastards!" Odette shouts. "The Berserker is in fucking rut! Sy!"

"I can't release Noon! We *need* him."

"Then kill the Omega quickly and wrap Noon back in her chains! I need your help with this!"

"Can't you do anything yourself?" Sy snarls, then curses, one of her knees buckling when the sleepwalking woman subtly sways. "Bring forth the creature, then!"

"Merlin," Odette shouts, "open the cage!"

The traitors begin to pull the massive ropes on Merlin's direction. Everyone but Owenna. She's staring at me, an expression on her face I've seen many times before that makes my heart pound. She's determined. And even though she turns towards me, the Fates don't seem to notice. And shouldn't they know better? Isn't that how we all got into this mess? Underestimating a woman?

"Merlin! Now!"

An enormous clanging sound like metal hitting metal is followed by a roar. Owenna does not turn towards it, starting to come towards me instead, but I'm distracted. Everyone is distracted. How could they not be? Because the peek of a metal contraption appears above the edge of the cliff, one built strangely, in a sphere, without any bolts or seams that I can see. Just smooth metal disrupted by one great black opening, through which massive paws reach. The paws, each the size of my chest, are tipped in claws, black and dripping with what looks like ink. They sink into the soil and cut into the stone cliffs and haul forth the body of an undead Berserker beast.

My blood runs cold as the creature makes it onto land. The rotten head swivels back and forth, sniffing, though the nose is crusted in dirt and rot like the torso, which also boasts fur that might have, at one point, been light brown, but that's now slimy green and blackened in patches, clearly burned. The jowls are massive and dripping globs of inky venom —

but it's black, not silver like Berserker venom ought to be. The eyes are black orbs shadowed in murky like the scum from a pond. One ear has been torn clean off and its back leg is half exposed bone, but its injuries don't slow it down any. Instead, it prowls forward and tips its snout up towards Shadow Ridge. It releases a roar that sounds *wrong*, a burst of clicks that has me clutching my hands to my ears because it's a horrible, grating sound. Yaron returns it with a roar of his own.

A battle cry.

The undead monster takes off at a sprint, running past me in a thunder that shakes the very foundation of the mountain. It meets Yaron at the base of the ridge, Yaron holding higher ground as their bodies collide. I lift up onto my knees and lift my hands, looking for my opening to burn the undead thing where it stands, but their bodies are too intertwined. Long limbs wrap around one another, and though Yaron fights with his axe in his mouth, he's not able to keep enough distance between himself and the creature. I don't want to hit him.

"Omora," Sy shouts up at the sky, "call forth the other undead. Direct them towards the Berserker. Corral him towards the cage."

A bird hits the ground feet away from me. I flinch, struggling up to my feet. Sy sees me moving and hisses to Noon, "Kill the Omega."

I canter back, distracted by the sound of feet crunching over rock, scrabbling hands, rocks sliding and then crashing on more rock, and water thrashing below that. Bodies of the undead emerge from the treacherous staircase and start to sprint directly towards my Berserker. I hold up my hands and fire flows freely from them in a gigantic bright blue burst the size of our kitchen oven, taking out the entire line of them. Three fall over the edge of the cliff and four more stagger forward wrapped in flames. They don't scream as they fall and somehow I find their apathy about the brutal nature of their deaths…their second deaths…their *final* deaths…even more sickening.

A blast of wind hits me, followed by orange and yellow flames this time. They wash over me, a cool balm that incinerates my clothes and my hair but not my skin and keeps Noon from coming any closer. I can hear the Berserker that is mine roaring terribly and Owenna screaming my name, terrified, though she shouldn't be. This fire and I know one another well. It's my counter, the red flames to my blue, but I run hotter and this fire does nothing to truly hurt me. All it does is slow me down and it will keep slowing me down, giving the Fates time enough to truly hurt the people closest to me. That is, unless I come to terms with the fact that I was wrong in what I told Zelie earlier. I can't fight fire with fire. No, I can fight fire with something else that the Fate doesn't have…I can fight her fire with my love.

I open my arms wide, my fire dying, and I pull all of the red flames towards me and then towards me further. Air and wind pick up the red flames, tossing them in the sky, bringing them to me in a cocoon that surrounds me, and then I kill it, cutting off the air around me, sucking it in like smoke. It dies like a candle flame under a snuffer when I wave my hand casually through it. The Fates are stunned and stare at me like they've never seen me before in their lives, Odette looking particularly stricken. I drop my arms, woozy now in the fire's absence.

"Noon," Odette says, sounding none too certain. Her bottom jaw trembles. "Now! Kill the Omega — " But before she can finish her sentence, a dark shadow moves past me in a blur. Feet in brand-new leather shoes thump down onto the ground as Owenna charges the Fate of Mind and Madness. She reaches her in the blink of an eye and thrusts her fist forward, wielding a paring knife, which she manages to sink directly into the woman's stomach.

Sy screams as she falls back, staggering away from the shackled Omega. She lands hard on her back beneath Owenna, who raises up, lifts her blade…and then screams. Owenna releases her blade and clutches her head as she rolls off of Sy. She sounds like she's in agony. Behind her, still chained to the pole, Sipho seems to have woken up and starts thrashing.

I don't understand what's going on, but I turn towards Owenna, wanting to go to her, except Noon stands between us, blocking my path. I rear back, terrified after what Merlin said about Noon's abilities, and hold up my hands. She's blinking quickly now and glances down and around, looking so small. She looks so lost.

My desire to comfort her is strong, but I need to get to Owenna first. There's too much happening. "It's okay…" I start, but Noon shakes her head, her expression shuttering.

"It's not…"

"Noon! Kill the Fallen Omega!" Odette screams. A screech shatters the sky followed by the rumble of a mad Berserker roar as Yaron swipes at the undead Berserker with axe and claws. He cuts into it every time, black blood spewing and matting his fur. The whole world shakes and I gasp as Noon starts running towards me. I hold up my hands instinctively, even though I know that, if she were to touch me, it would do me no good, but at the last second, she veers away.

I stagger back, stumbling over stones and my own two feet. I'm about to fall, but arms come around me and I know whose they are only by the smell they carry. She smells of gunpowder and body odor. Death and decay. She wrenches me back against her chest and starts to walk us towards the edge of the island, following Noon at the same leisurely pace she always has — the pace of a woman who has discovered everything there is to know about death and knows how to cheat it. Over my shoulder, I catch a glimpse of Merlin's face. Her mouth opens and I catch a flash of her pink tongue as she licks her lips and grins.

"This is even more exciting than I thought it would be," she cackles at the same time that my body starts to heat. "You think you're gonna muster up a few flames for me, Kiandah?" I didn't even know she knew my name and I hate the way she says it. Like I'm a child — no, not even that. Like I'm nothing. "You can try, but be warned — I'm fast. You better hope you're faster." Merlin's warning makes sense then when it coincides with the press of the cold edge of a thick knife to my throat.

I hiss out a breath as Merlin turns us around, pushing me out in front of her, following Noon and the erratic path she takes to the edge of the cliff. It's like she doesn't see the edge, only a few paces away…

"Noon!" I shout, reaching for her. She may be a Fate, she may be able to kill with a touch, she may even be somehow responsible for the army of the undead, but I *feel* something towards her. Like...we've already met. And I don't want to watch her die.

"Merlin, what are you doing? Kill the Omega and stop Noon! We need her!"

But Merlin doesn't answer. She doesn't let me go, either. She pushes me towards Noon, who stands on the edge of the cliff. With her heels practically hanging off of the rocks, she starts gathering up her chain, looping it around her neck and shoulders many, many times. She's looking frantic, glancing over her shoulder every few seconds, looking down at the thrashing waters of Zaoul as if they hold all the answers before returning her gaze to Merlin and me.

Merlin just laughs and gestures at Noon with her knife. "Don't worry, I'm not gonna stop you."

"Merlin!" Fire charges towards us, but I shield myself, shielding Merlin in the process.

She laughs, "That's pretty nifty, there, Kiandah."

"Let go of me," I hiss.

She chuckles louder. "I don't think I will. Your boy's making good work a' that thing though."

"Forget the Omega, Odette! Help Omora! The cage will hold Freya, too!"

I look away from Noon to the birds overhead as fire lifts up from the cliffs to overwhelm them. I look away from the burning birds to Yaron, roaring his way towards us. I look away from Yaron to my sister who writhes on the ground, screaming next to Sy, Sipho raging down at the Fate. I look away from Owenna to Sy, from Sy to Odette running towards her, from Odette back to Noon, from Noon to Zaoul —

"Don't!" I shout. Grief opens up in my chest like a mouth as I watch Noon take another half step back. "Let me help you," I say to her, meeting her shattered gaze with determination that I'm not sure I have a right to, given the knife at my neck. I have to get to her. I have to save her.

"You really are a goodie two shoes," Merlin says on a laugh. "Don't let Echo find out you let me go, or she'll kill you herself." She kisses the side of my temple and I bang my head back into her nose, hearing the satisfying crunch of bone and Merlin's responding curse. I decide then that I like bad things happening to Merlin.

"Fuck you, Omega," Merlin shouts, but she's also loosened her grip. I fall, rather than fight, and Merlin curses again when I hit the ground, shooting right out of her reach. I scramble over the stones, scraping up my hands and knees.

"Noon!" I lock eyes with her. Someone is screaming her name, one of the Fates. I say it again, too. "Noon, wait…"

But she only looks at me and whispers, "It's better like this…" She takes a step over the edge of the cliff.

Not a leap, not a dive, no twist, no finesse. A simple step that could have looked accidental if I hadn't seen the end written in eyes filled with such sadness. She disappears into Oblivion, into Zaoul's greedy embrace, and I…I push at her with my wind, but it's not enough to keep her here.

"No…" I gasp, scrambling to my feet — or trying to — but a hand that can only be Merlin's grabs me by the back of my tattered dress and yanks me backwards. Something hot hits me. I can hear Owenna screaming. I can hear Yaron roaring. I can feel wetness on my back, dripping down my dress, but I don't feel the pain from where Merlin just stabbed me until she withdraws her blade.

"Hawh," comes my surprised gasp. I look down as Merlin pulls me back into her chest. She turns me around to face the cliff and all of its occupants, to face Yaron, who is thirty long paces away now, blocked by a Berserker that has taken tags out of his flesh. He's too deep in his rut. He isn't protecting himself. I should...I have to stop...have to...have to save... My thoughts are flickering and have begun to fade...

"Gatamora doesn't need Alphas or Berserkers or fucking Omegas," Merlin whispers in my ear. "Gatamora is mine, meant only for Betas." Merlin pushes me away from her and slides her blade across my throat, slitting it. Blood spurts — my blood — and I gasp, choking on it.

I'm cold when she shoves me away from her body and I fall to my knees. "Kiandah!" comes the roar, this time, a man's.

I blink and see Yaron caught in a transformation — half man, half creature. He jumps from the undead Berserker's back, landing on two legs instead of four limbs. His distended jaw snaps shut, the axe falling from it into one of his hands. He cocks it back. Yaron bellows out a roar as the axe flies from his fingertips, inches away from my face. *THUNK.* The sound it makes when it connects with flesh.

Screams rise up. I can hear the voices of Trash City Betas screaming Merlin's name. Running. So much running. A wall of crimson runs down from Shadow Ridge, meeting the dozens of undead and disposing of them. The Fates are sprinting towards the edge of the cliff. Their faces are elated, despite the loss of the chained Omega and of Merlin. They seem victorious and that's when I realize that I can no longer hear the birds battling.

Yaron is rushing towards me, his limbs all distending and contracting uncontrollably, but the undead Berserker still has him in its sights. It tackles him to the ground. I choke on my own blood, but Yaron — as a man — manages to grab the creature by its back fur, toss it over his head and slam it on the ground between us. He charges it, *diving* into its deteriorating flesh and entering it as a man, but emerging from it as a beast.

Yaron...

Yaron explodes from its belly as a Berserker, drenched in black venom and reeking of blood. The lower half of his head shimmers in transformation, never fully forming into that of a man, even as he opens his jowls and says, *"Do you accept my bond, Kiandah?"* The raspy hiss hardly sounds like him and I know I'm not talking to Yaron at all. This is his monster. And it is mine. And it wants me to keep. And I am its. Because I was even before he knew I existed.

I nod as darkness comes for me. Pain comes next, stemming from my throat and my side, and then moving everywhere else. Heat and warmth radiate through my body. I don't want to die.

THE BEAST
CLOSER TO KIANDAH

KIANDAH LIVES. SHE IS SHAKING. MY HANDS — MY Alpha's hands — cover the wound on her throat while I bend over her and drip thick ropes of venom directly into the wounds. It was not as deep as it looked. The wound on her back is, but it did not hit her most vital organs. She will live.

Kiandah lives.

And my rut has retreated enough for me to be able to relinquish control of this body back to Yaron. Just long enough for him to get her to safety.

Then I will return.

YARON

ORIAS HIGHWAY LINE

MY MIND IS CLEARER THAN IT WAS, EVEN IF MY BODY remains that of my beast. I need him and he allows me to manipulate him as *she* needs.

I carry her cradled in one of my beastly arms, the other three limbs pounding even louder against the hard-packed earth of the highway line. I've done this before and I *hate* it. Brega's hooves beat beside me, carrying Sipho who sits stiffly, covered in wounds, Owenna's unconscious body draped across his lap.

Kiandah's heartbeat returned to normal with my venom flooding her veins, aided by the copious quantities my body in rut was able to produce. And now her beautiful, wondrous heart pounds as she wakes. She struggles in my arm. She wants to walk, to ride, to see her sister, to check my wounds. She's been speaking to me the entire time, but I cannot speak to her and not only because I use my beast's throat.

I could not speak to her in any other form, in any other state. My heart is in my mouth, sitting in the back of my throat.

Biting her, injecting my venom into her system, bonding her but only because she said I could…

Everything about the moment was bliss.

Everything about the moment was torture.

Because I had plans…oh the plans I had for her. Plans to lay her across my bed, to worship and be worshipped, to dominate and be dominated, to beg and plead and please her. To take her beneath a cloudless sky underneath a moon that rose red. Instead, my moment was stolen from me by a weak pulse, gushing red blood, a simple, fluttering nod, and fucking Merlin.

I had plans for Merlin, too, all of them intended to last years in the lowest rung of my dungeons. And she spoiled those, too, when she forced my hand. My axe all but cut her in half. She died instantly in rivers of blood that left a bitter taste in my mouth as acrid as the smell of burning garbage. I wanted more. Worse. For her to suffer. But I was even required to abandon the body, which will now never to hang from my gates, in favor of securing Kiandah and getting her back to the keep, just as I had to abandon Freya to the Fates.

Guilt clenches in my gut and I release a low roar. The fucking Fates took fucking Freya, all three of them working together to contain her in the cage that the undead Berserker once occupied. I was powerless to stop them.

They are gone now, fled far if they are smart, and I do believe they are. Things did not work out in their favor entirely, but as I cross Orias Village, finding it successfully cleared, and rise up the hill so that the keep comes into view atop the next hill over, I know that the Fates are smart enough.

The keep is under attack and the undead — thousands of undead — are fighting to gobble it up.

KIANDAH
SHADOW KEEP
THE LAST STAND

I EXPECTED TO WAKE UP BACK IN YARON AND MY chambers in Okayo's care after having had my throat slit and being stabbed in the back by fucking Merlin. Instead, I woke up to the feeling of Yaron's furry body wrapped around me, a deep, stabbing pressure in my back and in my throat — and shortly thereafter, to the sight of zombies attacking the castle.

Yaron's beastly body charges to a stop in the center of the highway line and, if given the chance, I know what he'll say, so I speak first, "You can't leave me here." My family's in there. The town is in there. All of Shadowlands is in there. But I know those arguments won't sway him, so I try another. "There's nowhere for me to go."

He glances towards Owenna, his fur matted with venom. He has scratches all over him, deep and appearing infected. Owenna's still asleep — ancestors, I hope. Yaron glances up at Sipho, who is barely conscious as he holds her against against his lap to the best of his ability.

"I can watch them, my Lord," he says, each word laced with pain as he pulls Owenna up and against his chest. Her body is slumped, but she moans when Sipho moves her, a pained sound that fills me with relief. "I'd give my life before I let anyone harm them."

"Sipho," I command, speaking without giving Yaron a chance to. "Take Owenna and find cover. We will come back for you when the battle is won." And then to Yaron, "Sipho and Owenna are too injured to fight. But *I* can."

He doesn't speak. I don't even know if he can. I gently tangle my fingers in his fur and tug. "I couldn't fight before because there was too great a risk of hurting the living, but not now, not against them. You have been my shield before, for all of this time. Now let me do this. Let me be this for you. Let me do what I do best — the only thing I know how. Let me save them. I can do this." *Let me save you.*

He still doesn't move, he barely even acknowledges me, but keeps his snout swiveling between Sipho and the undead on the hill, so I do the only thing I can think of — I punch him as hard as I possibly can. "That, my little Berserker, is my command, now *move* before you anger your Lady."

He releases a roar and doesn't hesitate a second more. He plunges ahead, leaving Sipo and Owenna behind, fighting on despite the wounds he's sustained. I can feel him flagging, though, and it worries me. He can't even help me fight an entire army of undead…

…I'm going to have to do this all by myself.

Nervous flutters pick up in my belly as we approach the undead masses swarming the gates of the keep. There are so many of them. Maybe more than hundreds, even. They face away from us, trying to get into the castle. High walls keep them out, but some are climbing and climbing successfully. They haven't gained entry yet and it's because of the mounted resistance — not just Crimson Riders, either. The people have come out in defense of their town, their city, their Berserker Lord and his Lady.

They are defending the keep.

Townspeople fight arm in arm with Crimson Riders using swords and battle axes, sure, but also torches and pitchforks to try to hold back the horde. I can't make out faces from here, but I can see up the hill how savage the fight is and I can see that the dead are gaining ground. They're winning.

My heart is a drum and I taste ash in my mouth. I can feel Yaron's indecision, sense his hesitation. He would abandon his castle and his keep to protect me, I'm sure of it. And I both love and hate that I could be the downfall of the Shadowlands.

I won't be its downfall. And I won't be his, either.

I've had enough of other people saving me.

I use his fur to pull myself higher on his body so I can speak over the sounds of battle, battling for his attention. "Charge ahead. Get me past the horde. Get me on the side of our fighters." He lunges ahead, but rears back up the moment the first undead — a male with one eye missing and a broken left arm — turns towards us. He opens a mouth full of fangs, dripping with venom that's black, not silver like the venom that now swims through my veins, bonding my lovely beast to me forever.

I grip his fur harder and shift, pulling myself up onto his back with shaking arms. I'm strong enough from my time in the kitchens, but injury and inactivity have taken their toll. I'm panting by the time I'm upright. He lurches forward and decapitates the zombie, but he's not moving forward with any sort of zeal as eight or nine undead Alphas turn towards us.

He releases a low growl and begins a slow retreat. I bend forward over his back, my fingers tangled in the black fur of his neck, streaked with silver. Those silver streaks *do* things to me. I brush my lips behind his ear. It twitches wildly, this massive thing as large as my face is, as I say, "Move forward, beast. I am your Omega. Do not disobey."

He starts forward, rattling loudly and swiping creatures out of the way with his massive paws. He's attacked by several at once but he's quick to dislodge them, and the ones he doesn't, I am able to douse in fire. Bright blue flames spiral from my fingertips in gusts and bursts, incinerating zombies to dust the moment they make contact.

We move forward like this, the swarm getting thicker and thicker, my flames getting hotter and hotter, my hands shaking with need — a need to do something even greater. We reach the line of our fighters, who part before us, trying to create a path for their Lord and his Riders to reach the keep, but I shout, "Stop, Yaron. Turn. Let me dismount."

As my feet hit the sodden ground, I see Renard fighting close to where I stand and shout up at him. "Order your soldiers to fall back behind the line of fire."

He swings his sword and it lodges into the shoulder of an undead female who lunged at him and grabbed hold of his forearm. His vambrace is covered in black bite marks. He's sustained many bites and scratches so far, but his determination is clear. I can see it in his eyes, in the lines of his face. He looks at me and at his Lord standing at my side, fighting off any undead who come too close to me.

"You should get inside, my Lady!"

I grab his shoulder as he finally tugs his blade free of the corpse. She comes at him again, but I lift a hand and her head all but disappears in the blink of an eye, leaving behind only ash and a flickering blue. More of the undead turn towards us then and Yaron's battle cry gains in volume. He starts forward, but I grab his fur and tug as hard as I can. It doesn't have any effect — wouldn't if he didn't let it. He obeys instantly, returning to my side. To heel.

"I said fall fucking back, soldier! Do not question me again!" I shout at the top of my lungs, my voice all but a shriek. "Behind the blue flames!"

"What flames?" he grunts in reply.

I step forward, nearly getting myself buried beneath two undead that loom much taller than I do and seem to have me in their sights. Renard manages to swing his sword across one of their throats while Yaron bites off the arm of the other. I use the small space they've afforded me to step forward into the undead horde while Yaron roars his displeasure at my back. I lift both arms and I recall words once said to me by Yaron as a compliment. Little did we know then that they were really a premonition.

You have the heart of a warrior, standing alone on the plane of battle against an army of the undead. You carry the conviction that you can and will vanquish them all because you have the lives of those you love to protect.

I gasp, breathing in a lung full of sickly, spoiled air and I see what I want, visualizing it, feeling it in my whole body, the desire not to hurt, but to save. I gather that deep breath, I gather my nerves, I gather all the love I have within and around me…and I exhale.

Blue and purple fire zips across the ground, a clean line that holds despite those who attempt to trample it. Shouts of confusion rise up from our people. Renard chokes once, but recovers in the next instant. "Fall back! Behind the flames! Cyprus, Dorsten, relay the order!" He shouts to his right and then to his left, somewhere behind us so that his voice can be heard over Yaron's immense breadth. Even though I can't see him over many taller bodies, my heart beats brilliantly, knowing that at least my brother is still here, fighting among the living against the dead.

The undead fall into the flames, undeterred, but our people are quick to burn, to hurt. I can feel their pain as the fire dances up their pantlegs, but eventually shouted orders are relayed back to us. Renard looks down at me and nods once. "It is done, but the undead are advancing…"

"Are you sure? Anyone caught on the other side of the flames will *die*." And I can't have that. I can't stomach it.

Renard blinks at me again, looking confused. An undead attacks, but he shoves them back with all of his might. He relays my order again and after a tense moment that lasts an eternity, in which time an entire line of undead are able to cross the fire, moving around and past me and Yaron, who works hard to dispose of them but is *flagging*, Renard shouts — half in fury, half in pain with a female hanging from his arm, her teeth sunk deep into his wrist — "It is done, my Lady. But you better act fast or we'll be over…"

I duck beneath the swinging arms of an undead male and step forward, directly into the fire. Yaron roars at my back, but by now, two undead separate us and more are coming, closing in, crawling closer. I can feel the fire on the soles of my feet, soothing and warm in my wounds, and I can feel the heartbeat of the earth begging me to rid it of this abomination.

An abomination my family helped cause and whose sins I will now undo.

I suck in another breath that tastes of sour fruit and rotten flesh and close my eyes just as grizzly, skeletal hands close around my once severed neck. And when I open my eyes a heartbeat later, blue appears everywhere, as a wall, as the wind. It moves forward, rolling silently like a beautiful sapphire veil dancing in the lightest summer wind.

Lightness fills the world and it's almost like a summer day, back in a world that once existed before the Fates and the rotten woods of Paradise Hole and inequity and cruelty stole everything. Every rose, every bloom, every dry grass, every full moon. The sun and the stars, it took those, too, but they can come again, I know it. I know it…

The blue rolls beautifully down the hill, away from the keep. The undead fall beneath it, but because they are dead, they don't scream. They do not try to retreat. When the blue light reaches their reanimated bodies, the undead falls in its first step, turns to ash in its second, and then to nothing at all.

The fire burns so hot, it doesn't matter if there is metal studding the moldy rags of their clothing, it doesn't matter if they're wet or dripping in undead venom or the blood of the living. It doesn't matter, because the fire isn't cleansing, it's reductive, returning the undead to what they should have been the moment the souls left their bodies.

Nothing.

Nothing but memories of the lives that were before. Beautiful lives, I'm sure. Just like the lives of those behind me, still fighting the final undead my flames couldn't reach without hurting someone breathing.

The blue makes its way all the way down the highway line, rolling over the ground and turning the tan, packed earth to a patchy dark brown and black. The grass is gone, blackened to dust, the mud is dried beneath it and its flakes spiral into the air in the second wind my body makes. The wind blows down the hill, chasing the blue and then billowing through it, dispersing it as the hill reaches its valley and then scattering it finally as it climbs up towards the next peak that leads to Orias.

There are no undead between me and Orias now. No undead in sight. There were also oxcarts and horse-drawn wagons left in the middle of the road, undoubtedly abandoned when the undead first attacked. They're gone now, too.

The quiet fades as the last of the blue is washed away, like sandcastles fighting high tide. The cerulean fire licks and flicks at the air and it's almost as if it succeeds in transferring its beauty, because without warning, the sky opens up. Right over the hill that leads down to the village, a patch of blue sky appears bright and holy. I know that the ancestors are watching now and I know that I've done them proud and brought them glory.

I turn as the clanging sounds of armor and shouts from the battle blink back into my awareness. I see the last of the undead fighting for nothing, because they don't know they've already lost. They don't know anything.

I turn to see my brother, Cyprus, striking one down a second before another turns to face off against him. His gaze meets mine and he tells me to look out. I turn and stagger a step back, feeling woozy and wobbly on my feet as I make eyes at the undead female who leaps towards me. I throw up my hands, but my magic is finished and also…unnecessary. A blurry shadow slams down between us as Yaron's massive jaws crunch through her torso, tearing her to shreds. The pieces of the creature scatter around my feet and I slowly lower my hands when I sense the danger is over.

I blink to see Yaron kneeling before me in the dirt as a man, his naked body covered in black slashes and bite marks that make the scars on his back look like child's play. I gasp, "Yaron…"

His chin tips up, his hair slashing through the air and away from his face, the grey at his temples revealed. He rises in one sinuous movement and grabs me around the ass, lifting me up high on his shoulder so that I tower over him and everyone else as he steps out onto the blackened field where undead once fought, where his people made their stand.

He moves out far enough that I can see to the left and to the right, all the way down the line of our fighters, all of whom risked their lives to fight with all they had. The undead are vanquished. I can't see any more of them among the living, bruised, and very injured faces that shine back at me. All eyes are on us, on me.

Yaron transfers my weight to one arm and lifts his other fist. He bellows, "To the Lady of the Shadowlands! To our Fallen Fire Omega!"

A roar slams into me with more force than the fire had as our people scream and shout and applaud for *me*. Tears fill my eyes as I brace against the force of their cries of adulation, and against the force of the pride that batters me. Overwhelmed by emotions, by what I've just done, by my body's spent energy, by the dust swirling around us, I cry and laugh at the same time and wave to the people.

Yaron lowers me to the ground a moment later and as soon as my feet touch down on packed, scorched earth, he staggers. I lunge to catch him, but he's too heavy and we hit the ground together, me on top of him, both of us near naked except for the scraps I'm still wearing.

"Yaron," I whisper down into his face.

He grins up at me and says, "I knew you were capable of taking a life when it truly counted. Thank you for saving us." His eyes are fluttering. He needs medical attention. I can hear people approaching us, voices shouting orders. I know he'll be okay. He'll have to be. Because I didn't do what I did to kill anybody. Only to save. Always to save him.

"Saving you," I whisper. I lean down and kiss him gently, tasting the venom on his silver-coated mouth. "Besides, it's not taking a life if they're already dead."

YARON
SHADOW KEEP

I REPEAT THE SAME MESSAGE TO THE SCRIBE FOR THE hundredth time since the attack eight days ago. My irritation must show, because the scribe responsible for sending messages to the other cities — in duplicate, because I do not trust anything anymore and cannot ensure their reliability — scribbles faster.

"Owenna, sister to the Shadow Lady, stabbed Sy, the Fate of Mind and Madness, but I know the Beast Fate, Omora, capable of healing her. Merlin, who ran Trash City, will not be so fortunate. My axe embedded deep in her chest, all but halving her."

"Was the body recovered, my Lord?"

"What?" I all but snarl, irritation flaring. It's been eight days since the battle, and six days since I've seen my Omega. They are keeping her from me because my rut is flaring and her heat is still dormant. I still have fucking heat stroke, according to Okayo, and in my attempt to honor her *despite* having already bonded her, it's been suggested that I wait to bed her until after the Red Moon Festival — tomorrow. One. More. Day.

I might have ignored their wishes were I not also injured. Kiandah is also still recovering, even as she tends to her sister, Owenna, who only just woke up this morning. Weak and suffering from severe migraines, it appears that Sy did a number on her. She's had Sipho very willing and content to keep her company, though. It is, apparently, because of her that he survived his imprisonment by the Fates at all.

Operating as a true black cloak and in the most clandestine fashion, she managed to keep him fed and tended his wounds without the Fates' or Trash City's detection. There were chances for her to escape, but she stayed and continued to pretend to work with Trash City and ally herself with the Fates once again because of him.

"My…uhm…Lord?" the squeaky male asks.

I glare at him and snarl, "You mean the undead Berserker or Merlin?"

"Horace, Finn and Okayo have preserved the undead Berserker for study. I was speaking of Merlin, my Lord?"

"Picked apart by crows, undoubtedly. Nothing but blood and intestines left. My axe was undoubtedly also stolen, but that is irrelevant. The threat of Trash City has been neutralized, though I still want it communicated that Trash City allies are enemies of the Shadowlands and any found to be aiding or abetting any of Merlin's former partners should be imprisoned or killed. Killed is probably most effective." I reach across the thick slab of my desk and stab my finger down on his paper, making him jump. "Write killed."

He nods, scribbling fiercely.

"And burned."

He scribbles some more, then says, "And so the Fates did manage to escape?"

I hate his tone and glare hard enough that I will him to explode into blue flame. I, unfortunately — or perhaps, fortunately — lack the self-control and desire to preserve life that my Lady has. Also, the skills to make that blue flame happen. Reluctantly, I consider that Kiandah may be better equipped to manage such an extraordinary gift.

I sigh quite abruptly, startling the male, though he seems to exist in a perpetual state of surprise around me, as I think to myself... *My female is extraordinary.*

"The uh...Fates, my Lord?"

"Yes, they managed to escape," I grunt. "Three only. The fourth...the Fate of Death, Noon Dragnovic, did not survive. She died, but by her own will. We had ships comb the beaches and shallow waters of Zaoul, but no bodies were found. My Omega says that she used her own chains of captivity to weigh herself down." Berserker Dragnovic will not be pleased that his sister took her own life. I feel a brief sorrow grip me that I could not save her, either. Though I'm not sure...would I have, if given the chance? With one touch, Noon had the ability to kill everything I hold dear to me.

"Zaoul is not a kind master." The man mutters, sticking his tongue out of the side of his mouth in a way Kiandah does when she's thinking very hard while simultaneously stirring or chopping or otherwise making whatever food concoction she's dreaming up. I watch her in the kitchens sometimes, though I'm not supposed to. I like stalking her very much, seeing the way she is with people when she doesn't know I'm there, watching her.

"No, he is not."

"Was it ever determined how so many undead made it onto our shores, my Lord?"

I grit my teeth, feeling appropriately foolish. "The ports."

"By ship, my Lord?"

"No."

"Then how?"

"The answer was always right in front of my eyes, young scribe. They were undead." Slouching into my seat, I lean forward onto my elbows and roughly rub my face. I've already removed my cloak and unbuttoned the buttons of my tunic as well as the ties to my pants. I am itchy and uncomfortable, hot periodically and overwhelmed by waves of desire that I am not to act on until tomorrow when I can take Kiandah beneath the red moon's fiery light. I want to do this. I want to honor her. I have to tell myself this again and again so that, through sheer repetition, I may believe the lie. Because the truth is that I want to tear my castle down stone by stone until I find her and then fuck her mercilessly among the rubble.

"What...do you mean, my Lord?"

"They don't need air to breathe so they fucking..." I growl, gripping the edges of my desk. "They *walked* from the North Island. They must have weighted themselves down by some means and walked on the sea floor where Zaoul's foulest creatures cannot reach, and they simply walked ashore. Many others were buried in Paradise Hole, but the majority came from the sea.

"They overwhelmed the docks, destroying many in the process, killing two Riders who fought them there and ensured the safety of the citizens through Paradise Hole." I sigh, furious that I had to leave them. No, not that I chose to leave them, but that it was required at all. Two Riders' lives were lost in their battle to save their people. They honored themselves and their sacrifice was a worthy one.

I clear my throat. "We have rebuilt the majority of the docks now, though," I say, nodding. "Our people have truly come together in ways we haven't seen in years. I credit our Lady. She has rallied them with her strength and determination. I believe she is the Lady that the Shadowlands need — have needed for some time — she is the fire in the darkness that will lead our people to safety, to hope, when all other lights are out."

"You're making me blush, my Lord," comes a voice I have no right to hear — until tomorrow. I look up, my attention homing in on her, the scribe immediately forgotten as my gaze snags on the vision of perfection standing in the doorway to my throne room.

Her hair is freshly razed down to the scalp, and I fucking love the way it accentuates the stunning features of her face. I do not understand how she could think herself ugly, though I know her youngest "pretty" sister many times made her feel that way. I have vowed to help her see herself as I see her — as anyone would see her — for the rest of my days.

But not today.

Today, I clamp my lips shut. I ignore the pulse of cum that spurts — not leaks, not drips, not dribbles, but fucking *spurts* — from the tip of my erection. My penis is on fire and my knot is pulsing at the mere sight of her. I lift my nose to the air, hoping to catch her scent, but she's too far. When that smell remains elusive, I make the dangerous and altogether unwise decision to transform my nose and mouth into a snout so I can smell her better. As I do, I can only hope that my beast remains caged and does not lose his ever-loving mind, as he's done already many times since I first met Kiandah.

The scent of her carries and it's a lovely thing. Not fire or flame but almost like rain. It reminds me of the first time I ever rutted her in the woods. This time will be different, though. I stopped taking the herb eight days ago and I will not give her the elixir tomorrow unless she commands me to. I want to breed her too badly to stomach anything less. It's dangerous, I know, but she has something I want. A big family that's also *hers*. I want to add to what she already has, building on it, protecting it with everything that I am.

I inhale a little more deeply and frown and grip my desk even harder, with all my might. Kiandah giggles and drifts further into the room.

"Uhmm, should I depart? Come back later, my Lord?" the scribe asks.

Kiandah shakes her head, her skirts swishing over the floor — cream, with white embroidery…fuck, she looks lovely, the colors bring out the vibrancy of her brown skin. "No, no don't worry. I'll go. I didn't mean to intrude."

I keep my eyes shut tight, my grip slipping on the table, on control too. "Why are you here?" I say between clenched teeth.

She's on the other side of the table, her fingers on the corner. I can *feel* her through the massive slab of wood. "I missed you."

"Scribe, out!" I roar.

The male all but sprints out of the room. Meanwhile, Kiandah makes the unfortunate misstep of backing away, too. "Not you, my Lady," I hiss, the smell of her even stronger now, and I'm more certain she is nearing heat, that I could trigger one with my pheromones alone. Now that she's been bonded, she'd survive it...or is it too risky? I don't know and hate that I do not know.

What I *do* know, however, is that Kiandah should have come to me days ago if she was in need. I frown at the thought.

"Yaron?"

My hallucinations fade, leaving me restless and needy. My cock is misbehaving, as is the beast within me. I keep both hands visible, because if I touch my cock, even to reposition it within my trousers, it'll all be over. I try to remember honor and decorum or the fact that her entire family is busy preparing tomorrow's feast, including Zelie, after having been safely returned to the castle by passing steel workers, as well as the new staff of ten they have hired. The menu will be based on old Orias cooking methods passed down from their ancestors so as to honor her, and by honoring her, honor me.

"Yes, Omega? What do you need?"

Her breathing changes, becoming more shallow. She licks her lips and I inhale deeply, frustration tickling my nostrils as I breathe her in.

"I was asking about the stock?"

What? My mind skips, imagining her in stocks. Ah. Perhaps, this is what she means. "You'd like the stocks?" Chain her head and her hands so that her ass is presented for me at all times. Yes, I could see that as an acceptable alterna…

"Yes, the stocks for the kitchens?" She smiles, licking her lips again. Her chest is rising and falling in small waves.

I shake my head. What is she on about? Stocks for the kitchens? There are no stocks in the kitchens. I frown. "Speak plainly, my Lady."

She bites her bottom lip. "My family is low on flour for the festival tomorrow. We need a few other last-minute supplies as well. The spice selection from the Night Market was amazing. I found a rare northern spice that tastes incredible in the cake I've prepared. I was hoping to get some more. Cyprus can take me."

"You're joking."

"No," she pouts.

Even though Cyprus has proved himself capable in battle, he is not capable of standing up to his sister and neither am I. We make a poor protection detail, but I won't allow any other. And even though the docks have been fortified, reinforced by hideous, yet necessary walls and gates to prevent any off-shore entry except through a single well-guarded point, a zombie horde just passed through. If she thinks I'm letting her leave to go fucking shopping a day before our bonding ceremony, she's lost her goddamn mind.

"Have you lost your senses?"

"No," she says again, slightly more breathlessly this time. I can't believe this. This is actually unbelievable. She truly came here for this?

"You truly came here for this?" I have to ask.

She smiles at me, taunting me, and produces a long scroll from between folds in her dress. She slips it onto the edge of my desk. Her scent hits me like a wave when she leans forward and I'm momentarily lost in the mire. Delusions and hallucinations involving chains and stocks, dripping cunts and my own body arching and pumping and stiffening and knotting cloud my mind.

I hear her lovely voice through the haze of stupid things she says. "I missed you, wanted to see you, and needed to deliver the list anyways."

Present for me. The words are on the tip of my tongue. I drop my ear to my shoulder and roll out my neck. "You came to torture me."

"Only a little, my Lord."

"You have succumbed to madness then, if you truly think I will let my bonded, yet unclaimed, Omega wander recently ransacked streets where a few stray undead still roam, while also approaching her heat? I can only deduce that you are not aware of how close to your heat you are, that you are trying to get an unsuspecting Alpha killed, or that you have been sating yourself in some other way in my absence."

Her eyes widen. She bites her bottom lip. Oh no. Oh no no no.

I rise up to stand slowly. Very slowly. I pin her down with my gaze.

"How have you been sating your urges these long, long days while we have both been suffering through the recovery of our injuries?"

"I…" She clears her throat and looks down. "I don't think that's an appropriate question to ask a Lady, my Lord." Her downcast gaze flicks up to me.

"You have not come to me with a request for relief."

"Of course not." I growl as she speaks. "I was told we had to wait for the Red Moon Festival. I…they showed me the dress I'll be wearing for you…the robe you had Zanele commission…" Her breath catches. Her tone becomes breathy and lustful. "That you would be…dressing me in other ways during the festival. And that the paint you bought at the Night Market is edible…"

"Do not speak of it. Tell me now. Have you gone to another Alpha with a request for assistance, then?" The knot at the nape of my neck tightens. I close my eyes and shiver with restraint.

"Don't make me angry, Yaron. You won't like your punishment."

"*My* punishment?" I snarl. I cannot stop myself from rounding the desk even though it is my last barrier. "You come in here with the express intention of taunting me, *baiting* me, knowing the state that I'm in, and you expect to be able to punish me? Oh no. It is time, my little Lady, for your punishment." My gaze devours her chest. Through her dress, I can see her tight brown nipples perking the fabric. I can't help myself. I reach forward and cup her right breast simply because I'm a crude, naughty boy and want to cop a feel.

Her neck muscles work as she swallows. Her pupils are blown, but she still tries to maintain the upper hand. "You're right, my Lord." She gasps, wilting towards me like a flower. She's anything but. But everything is topsy turvy between us, between her heat and my rut. "Punish me," she breathes.

My back arches and I grab her by the neck, my palm molding to her throat just below the thin scar only visible to my beast, still etched there in memories of a moment I thought I would want to forget. I thought I would hate the sight of it, that it would bring me shame, but it does not. Her scars only further prove that she is a beautiful, violent, extraordinary thing.

I toss her face-down onto my desk, which stands so high her toes barely reach the ground. I fight the urge to throw her dress over her head, and instead, slap my palm against her ass. She bucks and moans and I almost perish on the spot. My burning wounds from the venom of the undead Berserker feel like they're all opening back up again and bleeding for her.

"Now tell me, did you touch yourself to relieve your desire for me?" I say, arching over her body.

She says nothing, so I spank her again, hand falling even harder than it did the first time. "Yes!" she finally screams.

"When?"

No answer results in another three slaps. The scent of her...she's releasing slick moisture that has as powerful a smell as any of her spices. A rich bergamot, a powerful cayenne, rosemary, thyme.

"Kiandah..." I growl. The globes of her ass are staring up at me, so inviting. Her soft waist, thick enough for me to fit two hands around or one massive paw. To hold her down while I fuck her into the floorboards. "Answer me." I slap her again, a sharp pain radiating through my palm, almost as if I can feel each strike someplace else on my body through our bond.

She's clutching the papers beneath her cheek, her eyelashes fluttering. I gently curl my claws over the back of her head, stroking them down over her skull. "I like your hair," I whisper.

She makes a soft sound, a subtle moan. "Every day, my Lord."

"Hm?"

"I stroke myself every day to thoughts of you."

I grab the bottom half of her face and force her to look up at me from her position, immobilized across my desk. "You touched yourself?"

Her eyes are wide and dilated, those thick lashes blinking at me seductively. She nods.

I squeeze her face harder. "Did you forget?"

Her lips part in question.

"You may own me, body and soul, but I own you, too. That pussy is mine and you have no fucking right to touch it unless within my presence. Understood?"

But Kiandah. Oh dear, sweet fucking Kiandah. She is constantly surprising me, because she says, voice barely above a whisper, "No, Yaron. I think I'm going to need a *harder* lesson."

Fuck it. Fuck everything. Fuck the red moon.

I reach down to throw her skirts up when the most horrible sound imaginable rings in my ears. "Ancestors help me! What the fuck are the two of you doing?" Cyprus's disorderly and disobedient shout should get him cast into the dungeons, but that would displease my Omega, and I can't suffer through another long wait.

"Go away, Cyprus," Kiandah shouts.

"You tricked me," he shouts from the doorway to the throne room. I look up and see him standing there holding a messy bundle of scrolls in one hand, covering his eyes with his other. If I weren't so sexually frustrated and needy, I'd have found his stance and his words comical. I'd also have been more...touched? Impressed? — that he was willing to say them in front of me. Almost like we're already family.

"You sent me off on this wild goose chase to find these stupid scrolls all so you could do exactly what you told me you wouldn't do and track down Lord Yaron even though Okayo said..."

But Kiandah has stopped listening and jerks upright, practically vaulting off of the top of the table. She shoves me away from her.

"But..." I start, sounding like a whiny child.

Waving me away, she beelines it to her brother. She immediately rips the scrolls from his hands. "You actually *found* them?" Her voice is so high-pitched, it's nearing a decibel only beasts can understand. It's a tone I've never heard from her before and my curiosity is swiftly and successfully piqued.

"You didn't even expect me to find them?" He makes a choking sound that again, might have caused me to laugh, if I weren't simultaneously annoyed and intrigued. I take a step forward that causes Kiandah to spin around. She quickly slips the scrolls behind her back, as if expecting me to think they've suddenly disappeared — or that her body will present an actual barrier against my getting to them.

"Let me see those scrolls, my love," I coo.

Her pupils dilate slightly, then she shakes her head. "What scrolls, my Lord?" She gives me a little curtsey that makes me want to put her in those stocks we were talking about and finish tanning her hide.

"Kiandah," I say in warning.

"It's nothing. Some old doodles. Don't concern yourself with them, Yaron." And I've abruptly become Yaron again. Hmm... "I'll put them someplace safe and return right away so we can finish what we started." Panicked, she whirls around on the ball of her foot and pushes Cyprus towards the door. Before leaving, she turns to me and says, "Stay right here. I promise, I'll be right back." She departs in a rush, slamming the door shut, but she made a mistake. She may have told me to stay, but she didn't command me to.

I wait a moment before leaving after her. Whatever papers litter my desk can wait. I follow her, at a distance of course, down the hallway. I notice Alphas out and about coming to a stop or staring in her direction as they pass. I growl or snap my jaws in their direction as a warning, though I already know none would be so stupid as to attempt to address their Lady while she's weeping a slick that I caused.

My clothes are in disarray and my cloak hangs askew off of my shoulders. I realize as I round the corner and the stairs leading up to our private chambers come into view that my staff is staring at me just as much as they are staring at her, regardless if they are Alpha or Beta.

Some of them giggle as I pass and it occurs to me that they seem…happy. We were just set upon by zombies and yet, they're smiling like they're pleased. Perhaps, because my Omega and I saved them. My Omega, mostly. I am not sure, but I make a note to ask Kiandah if she has any theories later — after I've seen those scrolls.

I open the door to my chambers and see Kiandah attempting to stuff them behind the books in a bookcase in the back of the room while Cyprus watches her.

She squeaks when she looks up and sees me. "What are you doing here? I told you to wait."

The insolence. The punishment she's owed. The beginnings of a purr strike up deep within my chest. I force myself to calm and remain calm when I tell her, "My cloak is wrinkled. It needs replacing."

"Along with the rest of your clothes, too, my Lord?" Cyprus grunts.

I finally do break and laugh then. "You truly are gluttonous for punishment, brother."

He seems to stall over the term of affection, but he gives me a dry look and smiles as he finally says, "Lucky for me the dungeons are all full."

I snort and turn to my cloak rack, remove the one I'm wearing, hang it back up and then begin listlessly pawing through the others. He's right, of course. The dungeons are overcrowded with individuals Owenna identified as having worked with Trash City and the Fates to either kill, embalm or transport the dead Alpha bodies.

Those responsible for the deaths directly number only six and exist in the dungeons' lowest rung where the rest of the world no longer exists for them. The rest — another thirty civilians — occupy the next two levels, including the daylight cell where the Ubutu family once hung. Where Kiandah first attacked — not to kill, never that — but to save her family from me. I can still remember the suddenness of the feeling of her fire washing over me.

Owenna identified more than that, forty-eight to be exact — the female was organized and, even before donning a black cloak that none will ever see, she kept lists, amassing her power through information that she carefully documented.

However, twelve of those identified changed sides and were spotted fighting the undead at the keep. They were punished — sent to work rebuilding the docks — but spared from the dungeons as a recompense for their wrongs and an acknowledgement of their renewed loyalty.

I turn back to my closet while Cyprus turns back to his sister. He drops his tone to a whisper. "Are those the…"

"Don't!" She slaps a hand over his mouth.

"You can't be serious," he whispers again, pulling away. "You really fancy him that much?"

"Fancy him? What are we, five years old? And shhh! Keep your voice down."

"What arc you talking about? He can't hear us."

"If you keep talking about my drawings, I will light your hair on fire."

"If you try, I'll slap you upside the head."

"You do, and you will lose yours." I don't look up from my wardrobe, where I'm putting on the pretense of sorting through identical cloaks.

"Ancestors, he can hear us." Cyprus continues to whisper.

I can't help the twitch of my lips. I know her brother would never hurt her and that he's joking, but I don't much like the threat. I turn to face them and he turns to face me, his shoulders slightly sagged in his defeat. It's my triumph and I can feel my own shoulders roll back, but that's not the only reason. I abandon my fake cloak project and prowl forward. Couches and divans litter the space like unwanted clutter. I've never liked them and the only reason I don't get rid of them all now is because I can imagine fucking Kiandah on each of them.

Kiandah hasn't smiled. She doesn't laugh. There is no levity in her movements, only panic. She's got her hands in the bookcase and is feverishly trying to smash books over the scrolls to cover them.

"I can hear you just fine. Your words. Your breath. The shifting of your feet on the floor. Your pulse, how it races."

I inhale deeply and the skin across my many wounds stretches, even though I'm on my way to being fully healed — as fully healed as scratches and bites delivered by the undead ever will be. Scars still decorate my sides from my first confrontation with them on the North Island. And I still bear scars on my back from the whip. But I have no feelings about my scars, those from the whip especially. I do not worry if they are revolting or beautiful. They are as they are. And Kiandah holds them in reverence.

I pull my arms behind my back and clasp my hands together, letting my unbuttoned shirt fan open across my chest. The blood is surging through my body. I feel like a beast on the hunt. "What did you draw, Kiandah?"

Kiandah curses. Her brother starts. He tries to whisper to her again, a fact I find amusing. "Just show him. What's the big deal? You drew them long before you ever started to… fancy him," her brother spits, looking even more defeated at the prospect of his sister fancying anyone, let alone prepared to marry…

I chuckle darkly. "Kiandah, I will not be upset. Show me. What evil things did you draw and write about me? What hateful images did you use?"

She hesitates, then looks at me and I can see the very faint traces of a blush in her dark brown cheeks. She shakes her head no.

I feel sorry that she is so worried, but there is nothing she could have in there that would deter me from loving her with every ounce of my beastly heart. Whatever she drew and once thought of me, I will change her mind if I have not already.

"Kiandah, my love…" She melts a little more. "Why don't you just make this easier on everyone and hand them over? I'd hate to have to wait until you were asleep. I'm sure your lovely drawings would be better revealed in the daylight."

She pulls them from the bookcase slowly and clutches them to her chest. When I snatch at them, she twists away, like she might use her body to keep them from me. "A human shield is not an effective shield. Arrows, like bullets, pass through easily."

"You going to shoot me, Yaron?" she bites. There is defeat in her tone. Fire there, too. I am a reach away from grabbing and punishing her properly, as is her due.

"I would rather shoot myself, Kiandah. But I will see those sketches."

She groans, her head falling back on her neck. She drops her scroll and lifts her head up, shoulders back. She slaps Cyprus in the chest with her artwork and snaps, "Cyprus, could you not have been a little more careful?"

He guffaws, truly sounding like a younger brother, and throws out his arms. "What is the big deal, Kia? They're just drawings. You did most of them a million years ago, anyway."

"Hand them over, Kiandah." I lift my hand towards her. "Do not fear. I won't be angry. No matter the contents."

Her lower lip juts like she'll say something, but eventually she sighs and slaps the scroll into my palm. I take the crumpled papers, my heart beating with surprising urgency in my chest as I retreat to the closest ceiling-to-floor window, through which the entirety of Orias is visible. I unfurl the scroll and stare down at the first drawing.

I frown. The drawing is of a man. Not me, but an older male. He's mid-draught of a pint of ale and the depiction is so realistic, I can feel the condensation of the cool beverage on the side of the flagon and I can smell the sweat wafting from his skin. I can read his exhaustion in the lifelines running across his palms. I set the page aside on the wide window ledge and paw through the next pages, finding various depictions of townspeople mid-activity in various sizes and shapes but all impeccably drawn.

"These are impressive, Kiandah. You have incredible talent..." My voice trails off.

"What are you looking at him like that for?" her brother grumbles, but Kiandah says nothing to me or to him. She's been waiting for me to arrive at this page.

I flip to the next and the next…and the next and the next. I move them aside, setting them down one by one, but the sheets are stacking up. Some slip onto the floor and I let them scatter. They're all the same. No, they're all different, but the subject matter isn't. They're all me. Over years. Years and years of drawings of me. Some are scenes that are plausible. Me, speaking to the shadow people. Me, in the village. Me, once as she saw me in the halls of the castle.

But many are clearly visions found only in her thoughts. Me, shirtless in the bath. Me, spinning her close to my chest on an empty dance floor. Me, staring down at her face, the grey at my temples accentuated in lighter shades of charcoal so that it matches the color of my eyes. Me, me, me, me, me, me me mememememememe.

And each image, no matter how small or badly smeared, is spattered in love. Like blood from a corpse after a swift beheading. It stains the pages. It's inescapable.

I arrive at the final image and stare. I stare and stare and stare at it, then I spin, whirling away from Kiandah and her brother. I slam my fists down on the window ledge, the image trapped between shaking fists. I hold onto it, like a lifeline, and don't move. I don't dare. I need my concentration now more than ever, because the feeling is setting over me with the same urgency it did at the ports.

"Is he losing his mind?" Cyprus asks. "*Is* he angry? Maybe, we should just go." He grabs her arm. I don't see it, I can *feel* it, like I can feel the pressure of her hand on the pages as she drew this image of what was to come. *Her body presented before a beast — not my beast, to be sure, because she had not seen him before and could not envision him properly... But that doesn't matter. She thought it was him.* It rips through me, the pressure, and when it takes my hands, I know that I've already lost.

Over my shoulder I shout, "Cyprus, get out of here immediately. Run!"

Cyprus's eyes widen, but he doesn't quip. Instead he takes a step and gestures towards his sister. "Kiandah, come on!"

"Don't..." I roar as pain fires through my bones. Fighting this...fighting this is not done. I tried once before, and was only able to use the blood leaking from Kiandah's injured body to stop myself from falling further, the need she had for me to save her. Now, here in our chambers, the palest light filtering in through the windows...the circumstances are perfect. Nothing will stop me. Especially not Cyprus. "You touch her and I will kill you. I won't want to, but I won't have a choice. You need to be gone, Cyprus. Gone in the next ten seconds. Leave. Kiandah..."

I turn to see that she's moved to stand in the middle of all my stupid fucking furniture with pupils that are fully fucking blown. Her lips are parted. She's looking at me like she's only half conscious. Like the other half of her is unconscious and already sinking into the place where I'm about to be. Oh fuck. Oh yes. Oh gods. Help me.

"Kiandah, do not run. Whatever happens, do not run." I swivel my neck, fighting back the surges of transformation as they come on. "Make it easier...present for him...for me... whatever he wants...I don't want to hurt you, Kiandah... Don't let me hurt you..."

"You won't, Yaron. You've seen already what I want and that I'm not afraid of you. In any form…"

I roar and surge away from the window just as the door to my chambers slams shut, locking Cyprus and the world out and Kiandah and me in. I turn and the world appears so much smaller beneath me. A hazy warmth prickles my skin and I know that whatever happens next, I will only be partially present for it. I give in…

I fall fully into rut.

And I am stunned when I gaze upon Kiandah, standing there patiently waiting… because I register her eyes and I realize, her heat is upon her.

And all I can think is…

Thank. Fuck.

KIANDAH
SHADOW KEEP

THE BEAST APPROACHES ME AS MY LUST TURNS INTO something untamed and wholly primal. I remember the feeling before, from the cabin. I'd been hurting then, so scared, so embarrassed. I don't feel any of those things now.

I feel powerful and I feel restless.

The beast is massive, towering over me by the length of two Alpha bodies. Its lips are curled away from its massive fangs that gleam silver. It comes towards me, its pants torn over its legs and its erection pushing free of the silver and black fur that surrounds it. Semen leaks from its tip.

He swipes the furniture out of his way like they're the discarded toys of children, but I don't back away. My pulse is pounding. I surge forward to meet him. I grab his massive, wet snout in both of my hands and I use all of my might — and some of my gifts — to force his snout down to my feet.

"Heel," I command. The words are rippling, like the air. I feel everything vibrating.

The beast snaps and snarls, but I force it down, force him to obey my commands until he eventually settles on a whimper. I hold him there a few more moments and then slowly back away.

"You will wait until I give the command, beast," I hiss as I feel my concentration start to slip.

My legs are wobbling. I don't have much time. I quickly turn, when I'm sure the beast is settled, and survey my surroundings. Yaron has cleared out all of the furniture. It sits upturned against the walls.

Perfect.

I cross the room and grab the blankets from the bed in shaking arms. I throw them on the floor on top of pillows. I take my time arranging them — as much of it as I can spare — while sweat beads on my hairline and glistens across my scalp. Yaron whimpers behind me and I turn to see the beast standing so still, its claws extended into the carpets below, shredding them. He's so big he nearly blocks out all of the light from the windows. Almost, but not quite. Because scattered between his massive feet are errant rays of sunlight.

I step back into the center of my makeshift nest and cast my hand towards the fireplace. Fire erupts within it. I bring my hands to the front of my dress and undo the ties, then let it pool to the ground at my feet. I turn around, lower onto my knees and then stretch, like a lazy cat, out before the Berserker who loves me.

"Wait," I whimper when I hear claws scrape. My core is contracting, the sensation painful. "Not yet. One more moment." My chest heaves as I reach around my body, my cheek and chest pressed to the ground as I use my hands to spread my pussy lips from behind. A gush of slick releases.

"Now come, Yaron. Come fuck me."

The beast roars and rushes to cover my body, trapping me against the ground between two walls of fur. His cock spears me and it's huge — bigger than Yaron's, and feels different, too, slicker somehow, softer, more ribbed and fucking incredible. It pounds in and out of me, fur meeting the back of my thighs in a way that I should find disturbing, but don't. He's seen my darkest fantasies now, and responded to them in kind, rather than ridicule them. And for that, we are both rewarded.

His rut tips my heat out of this world and into another reality. We end up fucking for hours, until the sunlight disappears and moonlight rises. He fucks me as his beast for a while, and then in his Alpha form. The haze is difficult to make memories out of, but the sensations are everything. His beast's knot filling me, like a series of massive marbles. His cum spilling out of my body when he's ready to go again. We don't speak — there's no time for that — there's only the occasional kiss, bite, bond.

He bonds me over and over again and I welcome it, displaying my neck, presenting my inner thighs, letting him bite me and fuck me wherever he likes. He spurts cum across my chest and I smear it over my body. I slam him down onto my nest and straddle his face, releasing slick all over him.

He whimpers every time I offer him praise. He moans every time I tell him how he feels inside of me. He purrs each time I come and purrs even louder each time his knot fills me, making it possible for me to overcome any pain resulting from his knot's expansion or his erection leaving my heat in preparation for the next round.

The hours span into night, until the sun rises again. And again. And again.

Seven more times.

By the seventh night, my heat is spent and I finally collapse in Yaron's arms. He's kissing my face, telling me how good of a girl I am and how well I did. I love the praise and I love giving it back to him.

Yaron leaves me sleeping alone in our bed, covered in heavy blankets. I want to know why he's leaving and where he's going, but a few moments later, he returns with water and a lavish food plate. I gorge myself, only to pass out, wake up when Yaron urges me to, gorge myself and sleep all over again. I do this in several rounds and each time I wake, Yaron is there, touching me softly, urging me to eat, to get up, helping me to the bathroom, carrying me there…and only occasionally fucking me in between each cycle.

He's back to his skin and I'm out of my heat, so this is just for fun, for the sheer beauty of it, for the memories made and shared. At some point, I'm sated and lucid enough to open my eyes and see Yaron staring down at me. The look in his eyes — it hits me like an eclipse, so hard to watch, but I can't look away and so I'm blinded by it.

It brings tears to my eyes, so I tell him a truth I've held for some time. "I love you, Yaron."

He smiles. "You know, I thought for a while that you were half in love with me already, but didn't know it."

I roll onto my side and slip my arm beneath my head to use as a pillow, just so I can watch him better. The dusting of hair on his chest. The scratches. The healing wounds. "Maybe, I was."

"Kiandah," he groans, rubbing his face. He reaches behind him and picks up something on the bed — pages of my artwork — and tosses them down onto me. I let him without picking up any of the pages. "You are not and never have been half in love with me. I have been fighting for your heart this entire time and you've only pretended to deny me. Your heart has been mine this entire time. It's always been mine. Even before I saw you, you saw me."

"Yes." I cannot lie. Wouldn't dare it. "You're right, my Lord."

"You are wicked." He growls and plants his fists on either side of me. "And I love you."

He begins kissing a line from my chin down my chest, over my clavicle to my right arm. He lavishes it with love and a tenderness most unbecoming of the severe Shadow Lord, eventually reaching my fingers. They feel kind of funny. I lift my arm and find thin gold rings adorning each of my fingers, but not the thumb. The ring on my pinky is studded with small, light blue stones, the stones on my ring finger are purple, on my longest finger the stones are red, and on my pointer finger, the stones are black.

His hips come to rest in the cradle of mine and he props himself up on his elbows. There is no sunlight today, but today I don't need it. He kisses my ringed fingers one at a time. "Blue for your flames. Purple for the color of your fire above it. Red for the embers they create. Black for the ash they leave behind. I had them made for you. I hope you like them."

I grin so giddily that Yaron smiles, too. "I..." I feel embarrassed at what I was about to say and shake my head, then nod, realizing he'll misinterpret. "I love them."

"What?"

"Nothing. They're perfect."

"If something's the matter or they don't fit right — though I did bring different sized rings in here to test while you were sleeping," he teases, "then tell me. I'll have them changed. And if you don't like wearing them, that's fine, too. I'm still learning with you."

He's got such an easy way about him, I feel like crying all over again. He's so, so...happy. I've never seen him like this. Like there aren't Fates out there. Like Ruby City hasn't fallen and the ports with them. Right now, he's like this and he's fully here, present, with me.

Overcome, I blurt, "I love them, Yaron. I've just never... gotten to wear jewelry before. Never owned any. No one in my family has."

He blinks at me and a range of emotions crosses his face too quickly for me to interpret all of them. What settles, when it's finished, is frustration. He smooths his hands over my head, cradling me like I'm something very precious and not capable of vanquishing an undead army almost entirely by myself. He kisses each of my cheeks, the tip of my nose, the space between my eyes and then my neck. It tickles, the scar there, but I don't fear it or flinch away. I trust him with everything that I am and let him kiss and bite and lick before pulling back.

"I will do better for the females of the Shadowlands, Kiandah, I swear this to you. I will give no other family reason to despair. And you will help me." He kisses my neck where Merlin sliced it.

I shiver and nod and then settle into the warmth of his words. "Of course I will."

"We will change things together, Kiandah. Things that Shadow Lords have failed to. The Shadowlands deserve a better Alpha, which they will have, but only because they have their first Lady, too."

"Thank you."

He snarls, "And I will have you dripping in jewels, my Lady."

I laugh again, admiring my new rings as my fingers card through his hair. "You know I don't want that."

"What do you want?"

"To live happily with you forever."

"I accept your proposal, Lady Kiandah. It is done."

I laugh. "What do you mean, it's done? I thought we had a whole ceremony to get to."

Lord Yaron lifts up onto his forearms and gawks at me, then grins. "My Lady, do you speak of the Red Moon Festival?"

I nod. Laughter bursts out of him that makes me laugh, too. "What is it? What's so funny?"

Lord Yaron collapses on top of me in a pile of lovely kisses. He kisses my cheek and rolls to the side, pulling my body onto his. Looking up into my eyes with crows' feet surrounding his, he palms the side of my head and says, "Lady Kiandah of the Shadowlands, the red moon passed nearly a week ago."

"What? Are you…are you saying…"

Laughter bursts out of him louder and more boyish than I've ever heard it before. "We missed it, my Lady. My sweet, insatiable queen."

YARON
THE NOT-SO-RED MOON FESTIVAL

THREE DAYS LATER, WE ARE ABLE TO CELEBRATE OUR union out beneath the light of a moon that shines silver, not red. I refuse to wait the twelve weeks it will take for the red moon to shine again.

I shake off the adrenaline in my blood and the energy in my bones. The fights for Kiandah's hand were swift and all for show. I'm left to approach my female now, standing at the end of the arena. She drips, not in jewels, but in robes that are parted, revealing stretches of the perfect skin that awaits me.

I lift the small golden jar in my shaking hand that I purchased at the Night Market on our first date. The air is warm tonight, even though the cold winds of winter are soon to creep up from Hjiel. It is either because her ancestors favor us, or because of the fires that decorate the wide field before the castle, still stained and blackened from her flames, but prepared to grow again with the right nourishment.

I wear trousers and no shirt and dip my pointer finger into the small golden jar. I part Kiandah's robes with the back of my hand and paint her precious skin in even strokes, designs varying but coming to me organically. I paint her until she is a vision. I paint her while the town cheers on, drunk on the good food she and her family prepared — and of course, copious amounts of wine.

I do not think in this moment of the coming war, of the Fates, of the rescue mission we have begun to prepare to free Freya. We have called on the Berserker of Hjiel to join us in convening with the Berserker of Gold City to mount a coordinated attack on Mirage City from the South Island, but he has thus far remained resistant, preferring instead to keep to his brutish ways in the cold, apart from the rest of Gatamora.

I do not think of Dragnovic and the sorrow he expressed in his last letter after I told him what befell his sister. I let those thoughts lie and linger in another part of my mind that belongs to the Shadow Lord, but not to Yaron.

Yaron is here now with his Kiandah, his fingers moving with surety over every inch of her flesh, which pebbles and shivers under my touch. She stands so strong. So beautiful. Shining like a flame. And finally, when all of the paint glitters gold on her skin, the small tin in my hand now empty, I step back and toss the tin aside.

The crowds roar out their drunken cries and Kiandah smiles at me like she does not even see the drunken fools her people are making of themselves in her honor as they laugh and dance and sing up into the surprisingly clear night sky. She looks at me like I am the only other person in the world and it makes me feel like something greater than a Lord for the very first time. A king? No. Not that. A man. *Her* man. A husband with a wife who loves him and is content with him, because she chose him and is content with everything she has.

"What now, my Lord?"

"Whatever you like, my wife, but I may be partial to returning to the keep."

"Your wife," she repeats dreamily. "My husband, you're ready to go home so soon?" she teases.

I smirk. "I did not buy edible paint for nothing, Kiandah."

She steps towards me and I sway when she places her palms flat on my chest, marked with scars for her that I know will not be the last. "Are you going to be a good boy, Yaron?"

"I'm going to be whatever you need me to be."

She laughs and I drown in it. "Then take me away, my husband."

"I will bond you and then rut you savagely, wife." I lift her up and let her smooth, bare legs wrap around me as I tease, "Under the light of this moon, as I will under the light of every moon henceforth."

A THANKS FROM THE AUTHOR

Thank you for joining Kiandah and Yaron in the Shadowlands!

For early access to ARCs, artwork, teasers and trailers of the next books in the Beasts of Gatamora series, as well as my other exciting projects, sign up to my reader list at www.booksbyelizabeth.com.

You can also follow me on social media :
TikTok @elizabethstephensauthor
Instagram @estephensauthor

Book 3 of 5 in Beasts of Gatamora is aiming for an early 2025 release. Can you guess whose book it will be?

Turn the page to find out…

FALLEN
OMEGA

NOON
SHORES OF HJIEL

Coming soon…

SERIES STARTERS

LORD OF POPULATION (BOOK 1)

Looting the dead alien's corpse seemed like a good idea at the time, until he comes after her — very much alive. When he catches her, Abel's got a choice to make: accept Kane's help or die. But as they cross the hostile post-apocalyptic landscape together, Abel begins to realize that Kane may want more than a temporary alliance, but her body, her blood, and her heart — to keep.

TAKEN TO VORAXIA (BOOK 1)

Every three years, aliens come to hunt the most beautiful women of their small, derelict human colony. Miari's managed to escape notice to now, but this year, the alien king has her in his sight. Raku wants her, and not just once, but for life.

THE HUNTING TOWN (BOOK 1)

Mer is new to town and on a mission — one that does not involve getting involved with local small town boxer, Knox. Knox has never been known to back down from a fight. But getting involved with Mer turns out to be more challenging than saving her battered heart. The nefarious underworld of the city they live in has Mer shackled, and she might also need him to save her life.

ALL BOOKS BY ELIZABETH

Beasts of Gatamora - Knots and Nests. Villains who get the girl. Magic.

Dark City Omega, Book 1 (Echo and Adam)

Shadowlands Omega, Book 2 (Kiandah and Yaron)

more to come!

also available as audiobooks

Population - Dystopian Romantasy. Heroines with swords. Heroes that Bite.

Lord of Population, Book 1 (Abel and Kane)

Monster in the Oasis, Book 2 (Diego and Pia)

Immortal with Scars, Book 3 (Lahve and Candy)

more to come!

also available as audiobooks

Twisted Fates - Mafia. Murder. Spice.

The Hunting Town, Book 1 (Knox and Mer, Dixon and Sara)

The Hunted Rise, Book 2 (Aiden and Alina, Gavriil and Ify)

more to come!

Xiveri Mates - Horns, Fangs, Tails, and heat.

Taken to Voraxia, Book 1 (Miari and Raku)

Taken to Nobu, Book 2 (Kiki and Va'Raku)

Exiled from Nobu, Book 2.5, a Novella (Lisbel and Jaxal)

Taken to Sasor, Book 3 (Mian and Neheyuu) *standalone

Taken to Heimo, Book 4 (Svera and Krisxox)

Taken to Kor, Book 5 (Deena and Rhork)

Taken to Lemora, Book 6 (Essmira and Raingar)

Taken by the Pikosa Warlord, Book 7 (Halima and Ero) *standalone

Taken to Evernor, Book 8 (Nalia and Herannathon)

Taken to Sky, Book 9 (Ashmara and Jerrock)

Taken to Revatu, Book 10, A Novella (Latanya and Grizz) *standalone

series complete!

also available as audiobooks

also available as three e-book collections